Slough Library Services

TO urn this book on
THE on your

After the disastrous end to its last case, the Intercrime team — a specialist unit created to investigate violent, international crime — has been disbanded, their leader forced into early retirement.

The six detectives have been scattered throughout the country. Detectives Paul Hjelm and Kerstin Holm are investigating the senseless murder of a young football supporter in a pub in Stockholm, Arto Söderstedt and Viggo Norlander are working on mundane cases, Gunnar Nyberg is tackling child pornography while Jorge Chavez is immersed in research.

But when a man is blown up in a high-security prison, a major drugs baron comes under attack and a massacre takes place in a dark suburb, the Intercrime team are urgently reconvened. There is something dangerous approaching Sweden, and they are the only people who can do anything to stop it.

30130503648652

SPECIAL MESSAGE TO READERS

THE ULVERSCROFT FOUNDATION
(registered UK charity number 264873)
was established in 1972 to provide funds for
research, diagnosis and treatment of eye diseases.
Examples of major projects funded by
the Ulverscroft Foundation are:-

- The Children's Eye Unit at Moorfields Eye Hospital, London
- The Ulverscroft Children's Eye Unit at Great Ormond Street Hospital for Sick Children
- Funding research into eye diseases and treatment at the Department of Ophthalmology, University of Leicester
- The Ulverscroft Vision Research Group, Institute of Child Health
- Twin operating theatres at the Western Ophthalmic Hospital, London
- The Chair of Ophthalmology at the Royal Australian College of Ophthalmologists

You can help further the work of the Foundation
by making a donation or leaving a legacy.
Every contribution is gratefully received. If you
would like to help support the Foundation or
require further information, please contact:

THE ULVERSCROFT FOUNDATION
The Green, Bradgate Road, Anstey
Leicester LE7 7FU, England
Tel: (0116) 236 4325

website: www.foundation.ulverscroft.com

TO THE TOP OF THE MOUNTAIN

TRANSLATED FROM THE SWEDISH BY ALICE MENZIES

ARNE DAHL

ISIS
LARGE PRINT
Oxford

First published in Great Britain 2014
by
Harvill Secker

First Isis Edition
published 2015
by arrangement with
Harvill Secker, one of the publishers in
The Random House Group Ltd.

The moral right of the author has been asserted

Copyright © 2000 by Arne Dahl
English translation copyright © 2014 by Alice Menzies
All rights reserved

A catalogue record for this book is available
from the British Library.

ISBN 978–1–78541–034–5 (hb)
ISBN 978–1–78541–035–2 (pb)

Published by
ISIS Publishing Ltd.
7 Centremead, Osney Mead, Oxford

Set by Words & Graphics Ltd.
Anstey, Leicestershire
Printed and bound in Great Britain by
T. J. International Ltd., Padstow, Cornwall

This book is printed on acid-free paper

CHAPTER
ONE

"I didn't see anything."

Paul Hjelm gave a heartfelt sigh.

"You didn't see anything?"

He tried to catch his eye, but the young man kept looking down, morose.

Morose? When had he last used the word "morose"? Had he ever, at any point in his life, used the word "morose"?

He felt old.

"Let's try again," he said calmly. "Even though a full-on fight broke out behind you, you saw nothing at all. Is that right?"

Silence.

Hjelm sighed again. He lifted his knuckles from the interrogation table, stretched his back, and cast a glance in the direction of his colleague, leaning against the drab concrete wall.

As their eyes met, he felt the contradictions of the moment. On the one hand, his relocation to the violent crimes division of the local police force, working in Stockholm's City district, and the whole range of hopeless, everyday crimes that went with it. On the other, the return of his favourite colleague, Kerstin Holm, to Stockholm.

And the first challenge facing the seasoned duo after their reunion? A pub brawl.

Paul Hjelm sighed once again and returned to his reluctant witness.

"You didn't glance over your shoulder even once?"

The young man smiled faintly. A slight, introspective smile.

"Not even once," he said.

"Why not?"

The young man met his eyes for the first time. Bright blue. There was an unexpected sharpness, as though he were on the verge of saying something completely different, when he said: "Because I was reading."

Paul Hjelm stared at him.

"Hammarby have just played a home game against Kalmar. It's a 2–2 draw, and they finish last in the Allsvenskan league, and you're sitting in the Hammarby fans' favourite haunt, reading? In Kvarnen — a rowdy bar, heaving with frustrated Hammarby fans — twenty-year-old Per Karlsson is sitting alone, with a book? It's a very strange choice of reading place, I must say."

Per Karlsson smiled again, the same soft, introspective smile.

"It was quiet when I got there," was all he said.

Hjelm pulled out the chair and sat down with a thud.

"I'm really curious now," he said. "Which book had caught your attention to such a degree that you not only managed to ignore all the shouting and screaming

2

and chaos, but also a fight that ended in someone getting a beer mug to the head and dying?"

"Dying?"

"Yeah, he died. He bled to death in the bar. On the spot. The blood just gushed out, he lost two litres in twenty seconds. It just poured right out of him. His name was Anders Lundström, he came from Kalmar and, for some unfathomable reason, he made the mistake of going to Kvarnen, which was about as close to Hell as an opposition supporter could get. And, sure enough, the Hammarby fans killed him with a beer mug. But you didn't see any of this, because of which book? I'm very interested."

Per Karlsson looked stricken. He mumbled: "It's nothing you'll have heard of . . ."

"Try me," Paul Hjelm said in English, with a faux New York accent.

Kerstin Holm shifted for the first time since Per Karlsson had entered the interrogation room. She moved silently over to the table and took a seat next to Hjelm.

"My colleague here knows more about literature than you'd think," she said. "The last time we met, almost a year ago, you were reading . . . Kafka, wasn't it?"

"K," said Paul Hjelm ambiguously.

Kerstin Holm gave a short, slightly bitter laugh.

"K," she repeated in the same faux New York accent. "So try him."

The young man looked confused. Almost completely swathed in black, at the height of summer. Limp, unkempt blond hair. A budding intellectual? No, not quite. His cagey, almost wounded gaze, those introspective smiles. Definitely not a university student. Maybe just a young man reading to educate himself.

A rarity.

"Ovid," said the rarity. "Ovid's *Metamorphoses*."

Paul Hjelm laughed. He hadn't meant to; the last thing he wanted was to mock Per Karlsson. Still, it had happened. It was happening more and more often.

The insignia of bitterness.

Morose.

Hjelm felt a short but fleeting wave of self-loathing.

Holm stepped in. "And what a metamorphosis it was. For Anders Lundström from Kalmar. The ultimate metamorphosis. The transformation of all transformations. Which of Ovid's metamorphoses would you say fits Anders Lundström's fate, Paul? Orpheus?"

"Sure," said Hjelm sluggishly. "Orpheus torn to pieces by the Thracian Maenads."

Per Karlsson stared at them, suddenly quite indignant.

"No," he said, "not Orpheus."

Hjelm and Holm looked at one another, surprised.

"Anyway," Hjelm eventually said, "we know that your little 'I didn't see anything' is a lie. It's going to undergo a metamorphosis now, so tell us what you saw, Per, from the beginning. We're going to do this like a proper interrogation. So, your name is Per Karlsson, born in Danderyd on the fourth of December 1979, currently living in Aspudden; you're unemployed and

4

did nine years of compulsory education. Is that correct?"

"Yes," said Per Karlsson faintly.

"Today is the twenty-fourth of June, the time is 08.13. Tell us everything that you saw in the Kvarnen bar on Tjärhovsgatan at 21.42 on the twenty-third of June. Yesterday evening, that is."

Per Karlsson looked pale. He stared down at the table, fiddling with his fingers.

"Are you recording this?" he asked.

"We've been recording everything since you entered the room. Including this."

"OK, well, when I got to Kvarnen there weren't many people there. I had no idea there was a match on that evening, I probably wouldn't have gone there if I had. It was quiet, I read. Then they arrived. The first fans got there just after nine, then it filled up. I tried to keep reading, it went pretty well, I'm good at concentrating. I was sitting a little way off, with my back to the bar, almost right over by the window, so I heard more than I saw. But sure, I turned round now and then."

"Why did you say that you didn't see anything?" Kerstin Holm asked.

Paul Hjelm said: "Is this how it is now? Is the automatic answer 'I saw nothing' when the police ask? Have things gone that far?"

"It's the most common answer we get in any case."

"Should I go on?" Per Karlsson asked, confused.

"Of course," said Hjelm and Holm in unison.

Jalm and Halm, that famous American comedy duo.

"A gang of six or seven Hammarby fans heard another group, four guys, talking with southern accents, Småland accents. Both groups were standing by the bar. The Hammarby fans started arguing with the Smålanders, who said they lived in Stockholm and supported Hammarby. You could hear that they were scared, that they were lying. The Hammarby fans could hear it, too. They got more and more aggressive. Two of the Smålanders managed to get away and cleared off. Two of them were left. The atmosphere got ugly. Some more Hammarby fans turned up and tried to get the gang to move back, away from the Smålanders, I guess they could see what was happening. Eventually, one of the Smålanders made a run for it. He shoved one of the Hammarby fans so hard that he fell over, and then three of the others from the gang pushed him, the Smålander, up against the bar and the one who'd fallen over got up, grabbed a beer mug and smashed it as hard as he could on the man's head."

"Did you see it?"

"No, not really. I saw a little bit now and then, quick glances. But I heard it. I turned round when I heard the crack, a really fucking nasty crack. Not like when glass breaks, really. I think it was his head cracking. Fuck . . . his skull, the blood. I turned around just when the glass had hit him. There was a little empty space around him. He had his hands to his head and the blood was just gushing out, through his fingers and down his arms. Fuck! Then he collapsed, limp, just straight down onto the floor. And the Hammarby gang, they cleared out immediately, they just ran right out the door. The one who'd done it still had the handle of the beer mug in his hand, covered in blood. A whole crowd managed to squeeze out before the doormen woke up and blocked the door. Then the police came pretty quickly. The other Smålander was down on the floor trying to stop the blood with his jumper, there was a Hammarby fan trying to help, I think, but it was hopeless. Christ, there was blood everywhere."

Per Karlsson was white.

Hjelm and Holm tried to make sense of the information.

"You saw a lot for someone who didn't see anything," said Hjelm.

"Don't keep going on about that," Per Karlsson said sullenly.

"A whole crowd managed to get out?" Holm asked. "Hammarby fans?"

"Mostly. Some others, too."

"How many?"

"I was mostly looking at . . . the victim . . ."

The victim.

Hjelm shuddered.

Per Karlsson said: "About ten Hammarby fans cleared out, I'd say. Him first. The perpetrator."

The perpetrator.

Pseudo-terminology finding its way into his language in order to distance himself from reality. The witness. The victim. The perpetrator.

"With the handle of the beer mug in his hand?" asked Holm.

"Yeah," said Per Karlsson.

"This one?" asked Hjelm, holding up a plastic bag containing the handle of a beer mug. The blood was smeared and clotted over the inside of the bag.

Per Karlsson wrinkled his nose and nodded.

"We found it a short distance away on Folkungagatan. That means he must've run round the corner, past the Malmen hotel and past the entrance to Medborgarplatsen metro station. His fingerprints aren't in the database, so it's of the utmost importance that you can help us to identify . . . the perpetrator. You didn't hear them say anything about where he might have gone?"

"No," said Per Karlsson.

"Let's go back a few steps," said Kerstin Holm. "How many sneaked out before the doormen blocked the door? Ten or so Hammarby fans, you said, but also a number of others?"

"I think so. Some of the people who'd been sitting at the table next to the door disappeared, and a few others, too."

"As you can imagine, we're looking for impartial witnesses who disappeared. The people sitting at the table next to the door weren't Hammarby fans?"

"No, they were already there before it happened, when the game was still on. But there were a few tables between the one where I was sitting and theirs, and they filled up pretty quickly. There were five men. Now that I think about it, one of them stayed behind, a guy with a shaved head and light-coloured moustache."

"But the others disappeared after . . . the killing?"

"I think so."

"What did they look like? A group of workmates?"

"Maybe. I didn't look too closely. They weren't exactly talking to one another."

"Weren't talking? What, were they reading Ovid's *Metamorphoses?*"

"Lay off! Look, one of them stayed behind, didn't he? The one with the shaved head. Talk to him."

"OK. Who else? You were sitting at the table second from the window, second from the right-hand wall, as seen from the bar. This group was sitting on the far left, on the other side of the aisle. What about the tables in between?"

"Like I said, they filled up before the Hammarby fans came in. As far as I remember, there weren't any seats left for the Hammarby fans, except next to me. A bunch of them sat down at my table. A few of them managed to leave after it happened."

"And over by the window out onto Tjärhovsgatan? You were facing that way, weren't you?"

"A group of girls. They were taking up both tables over in the corner. A hen party, I think, having a last few drinks. They were pretty drunk — and pretty damn shocked afterwards. None of them left, they could hardly bloody walk."

"Right next to you? Against the right-hand wall?"

"I don't know, I can't remember."

"You can't remember? You seem to remember quite well otherwise."

"I'm sorry, I don't know. There might've been some people sitting there, but I never looked in that direction."

"Fine. Behind you, then? Towards the bar? You said you turned round a few times?"

"At one table there was a man by himself, staring at me. Closest to the bar. Really tall, in his fifties. Gay, I'd guess. But you have his name, he stayed behind. He must've been closest to it. I don't remember the rest of the tables too well. A group of amateur musician types who stayed behind. Two middle-aged couples. I've got no idea about the tables further in."

Per Karlsson fell silent. Hjelm and Holm fell silent. Eventually, Holm said: "Shall we sum up, then? We'll draw a little sketch. The crime scene, the bar, is set back in the room, against the wall on the other side to the door. In a straight line from the bar, there are a number of tables at the rear. You don't know anything about them, you were sitting too far away. The periphery looks like this, as seen from the bar. Straight ahead, the window out onto Tjärhovsgatan. To the left, the door. Next to the door, one table, running longways. Then the aisle, then three rows of three big tables, with you sitting at the right-hand side of the middle one, facing the window. Before the Hammarby fans poured in just after nine, the following people were present. On the row of tables along the window, the hen party group were sitting at the two to the right. Then, at the window table nearest the door . . .?"

"I don't know. There was a group sitting there, but I've got no idea who they were. They were there afterwards, in any case."

"The middle row, then, the row of tables you were sitting at?"

"I don't know about the table on the far right, like I said. Then me, and after a while seven or eight

Hammarby fans. There was a group of students sitting at the table to the left of mine, I think."

"And the row nearest to the bar?"

"Christ, OK. At the first table, furthest to the right, nearest the bar: those two couples and the tall gay guy who was staring at me. Second table: the musician types, four of them. The third table: no idea. Then the single table by the door: the group of five men. Four of them disappeared."

"Well, then," said Hjelm. "Time for the perpetrator."

He felt pleased at being able to say the word without having to pause first.

"It's mostly the Hammarby scarves that I remember, actually," said Per Karlsson. "One of them had a banner, too; rolled up, green and white squares. The perpetrator had medium-long, pretty blond, pretty dirty hair. I almost only saw him from behind. I think he had a little moustache, too. I don't know, he looked like a mechanic or something, if you get what I mean. I was born and raised in Danderyd, and out there, he was one of those people you'd immediately assume was from the southern suburbs. A Farsta type."

Hjelm and Holm stared at him.

"Judgemental, I know," he said. "I live in the south myself now. Unemployed and uneducated, living in the southern suburbs. Judgemental, but it's the best I can do."

"No, one more thing," said Kerstin Holm. "Come with me to the police artist. He does it all on computers now, so it won't take long."

She stood up. Per Karlsson stood up. She was taller than he was, Hjelm noticed irrelevantly.

"You don't have anything else to add, Per?" he asked.

Per Karlsson shook his head and gave him a furtive glance. That peculiar, paradoxical clarity in his eyes.

"Well, thanks for your help."

They disappeared.

Paul Hjelm disappeared, too. Into the vague half-world of daydreams. Per Karlsson. Born twenty years ago in Danderyd. Born in the affluent suburb of Danderyd, but hadn't even stayed on at school. Unemployed, but sat in the most well-known and notorious of Södermalm's pubs, reading the classics. What had happened? It was impossible to guess. An outsider at school? Thrown out of his father's firm? Made to feel small, but on the way up? Rebellion against his father? Generally obstinate? Former addict? Dim-witted?

No.

Maybe the others, but not that. Not dim-witted. That much Paul Hjelm had seen, even though he felt, well . . . dim-witted.

Demoted to the dreary limbo of pub brawls.

Paradise lost.

No, not dim-witted. On the contrary, Per was unusually observant. But now Hjelm had to forget him. Now they had to plough on through more miserable interrogations with hungover witnesses, and Per Karlsson needed to be on someone else's mind. Only his evidence could remain.

12

Hjelm yawned, his thoughts trundling on. The months spent with the local police. The violent crimes division of Stockholm's City district. Police headquarters on Bergsgatan. The utterly temporary office which, equally temporarily, he had been liberated from. The office actually belonged to Gunnarlöv, a policeman on sick leave, whose telephone he always answered with: "Gunnar Löv's telephone, Paul Hjelm speaking." It was only when an old colleague of Gunnarlöv, now stationed in Härnösand, came in and asked after "Nils-Egg" that he understand why there was always a pause on the other end of the line when he answered. People were simply recovering from his strange pronunciation of Gunnarlöv. His jaw dropped when he looked up the name in the internal telephone catalogue and saw it there in black and white: it wasn't "Gunnar Löv" at all, but "Nils-Egil Gunnarlöv". Shortened to Nils-Egg.

Were people really allowed to be called such things? Weren't there laws? Wasn't it the same as naming your child Heroin, like a family in Gnesta had tried to do a while ago, Heroin Lindgren? They had been turned down and written a whole series of letters to the local press where they went on the offensive against the nanny state.

In any case, Gunnarlöv was on sick leave because he had, while on duty, found himself in the Stureplan branch of Föreningssparbank when a hysterical female bank robber aged around fourteen rushed in with a staple gun at the ready, demanding "all your high-yield shares, ready to go". Don't staple guns need to be

13

plugged in? Gunnarlöv had thought to himself, going over to the robber to calmly point out that fact and receiving, to his surprise, no fewer than thirty-four staples peppered across his face. Miraculously enough, none of them hit his eyes. The first thing he said on waking from unconsciousness was: "Don't staple guns run on electricity?" His wife stared at his bandage-covered head, her eyes swollen and red with crying, and answered: "There are ones that run on batteries."

The adventures of Nils-Egil Gunnarlöv.

Nils-Egg in Wonderland.

Still, Paul Hjelm's own story wasn't all that much more entertaining. Quite the opposite, in fact, since the story of Nils-Egg actually had its bizarre moments.

Kerstin Holm came back, leafing through a notepad.

"Welcome to reality," Paul Hjelm said gruffly.

"It's not much different in Gothenburg."

"Sweden's shithole."

"What're you getting at?" exclaimed Kerstin Holm in her good-natured Gothenburg accent.

"Ah, sorry. No, well, it was just something that was being bandied about in the media a few weeks ago. The Black Army, you know, the AIK supporters' club, it was on their answering machine before the team's cup final against IFK Göteborg, in Ullevi Stadium. Stockholm arrogance and tribal football hate in an unhealthy union."

"Yeah, and now we've got it again. Stockholm arrogance and tribal football hate, only a more serious type. Did you see him?"

14

"Anders Lundström from Kalmar? Yeah. Really nasty. His head was a terrible mess. To think a beer mug can do so much damage!"

"Why? How do we explain it?"

Paul Hjelm looked at Kerstin Holm. They had a shared past which meant that no glance was entirely innocent.

"Are you serious?" he asked, half serious himself.

"Yes. Yes, I am, I really am. Why's the violence getting worse?"

He sighed. "Well, at least now we've been able to see it up close. For just over six months. The grey, everyday violence in the city. It doesn't exactly do much to encourage your philanthropic tendencies. Are you back for good now, Kerstin?"

"I was on loan. You know what it's like with footballers who're on loan, there's something wrong with them. Now I'm not on loan any more."

"For good, though? How was being home in Gothenburg?"

"This is home now, that much I've figured out. That's probably all, though."

"But life is OK?"

"Exactly. OK. No more, no less. Under control. Could wish for a little more . . ."

"Sure, same here. I think I'm beginning to have a little midlife crisis. Is this all there is? Isn't there more to it? You know."

"I think so."

"You've just got to make the best of the situation. We're back together again, and now we're going to smoothly wrap up what the media are already calling the Kvarnen Killing. Right?"

Kerstin Holm chuckled slightly and slipped a sachet of snus tobacco under her upper lip.

"What's this, then?" said Hjelm, pointing.

"A fresh start," said Kerstin Holm without batting an eyelid. She changed to another subject, one from the past. "How are the others? I've kept in touch with Gunnar the whole time, things are going well for him."

"Yeah. Ah yes, our friend Gunnar Nyberg . . . He was the only one who stayed with national CID, actually. A reward for refusing to take part in the final phase of the hunt for the Kentucky Killer. He ended up in the middle of the paedophile busts. The so-called Paedo University."

"I can just see him," Kerstin Holm smiled, leafing through her little notepad. "He's just re-established contact with his kids and his one-year-old grandchild, and then he finds himself thrown head first into the world of Internet paedophiles. Like a steamroller."

"You're right there."

An image emerged in both their minds, doubtless almost identical. A snorting giant with a bandage around his head, hunting paedophiles with a blowtorch.

"Yep," said Hjelm gloomily, "the rest of us got our little punishments. Bad blood always comes back round."

"We should never say that again."

"You're right, never again."

"And the others?"

"I haven't had that much contact with them since the A-Unit split. I ended up on that God-awful loan to the local police. 'Gunnar Löv's telephone.' Punishment. Deep down, I think they held me responsible for the cock-up with the Kentucky Killer, but Jan-Olov was the scapegoat."

"Have you heard from him?"

"No, he just disappeared. Involuntary retirement. Retired Detective Superintendent Jan-Olov Hultin. I think he even stopped playing football. That's the end of the saga of Wooden Leg Hultin. Söderstedt and Norlander ended up with local CID's violent crimes squad, and Chavez has been doing more training."

"At the Police College?"

"Yep. Career plans rumbling on. Are there still superintendent courses? It's something like that he's doing if there are."

"There you go. And our room? The 'Supreme Command Centre'?"

"I think they've got admin staff in there now."

They sat in silence for a while, observing one another. All they had experienced together . . . For a short moment, their hands met, pressing together. That was enough. A lot of work lay ahead of them. Kerstin Holm glanced through her notepad, Paul Hjelm leafed through the mediocre notes from the brief interrogations carried out by the night staff. Together, they looked at the little sketch of the Kvarnen bar.

"They're waiting out there," Kerstin said, sighing.

"Yeah, yeah. The next man to be held to account," said Paul, also sighing.

CHAPTER
TWO

Sky.

How long had it been since he had seen it?

In Sweden, there are fifty-seven prisons with over four thousand places. They are divided into six security classes, of which class F prisons are open institutions and classes A to E are closed. Of these, class A prisons are the most secure, with the most dangerous inmates, and in Sweden there are two: Hall and Kumla.

Now he was looking directly at the sky, actually looking, not from behind bars. He glanced back to the gates which had closed behind him, and for a moment it felt as though he had left his body and become one with the sky; he saw the flat landscape below him, the whole of southern Närke county with its square green, brown and golden fields. The prison looked like nothing more than two square fields among all the others.

He couldn't see the walls.

Dissolved by perspective.

Then he was down again.

Back to earth.

His feet on the ground.

He turned round once more. The walls were completely bare. Nothing behind them, nothing sticking up. Only walls. Grey. Grey walls.

He moved off. A smile playing at the corners of his mouth.

He walked towards the van that stood waiting. Ticking over. The sound of freedom. Freedom was a metallic-green van.

He stopped. Stood for a moment. Gentle, warm summer wind against his newly shaved cheeks. The sun. Morning heat. Asphalt quivering in the distance.

He glanced towards the van. Hands protruding from it. Waving. No sound yet. The sound didn't reach him. The movements within. Like a foetus. An egg about to hatch. Preserved movements. Future events. Many quick steps coming together at one point.

Step one. Wallet out. Pitiful banknotes. Three forty an hour basic pay. Also a small device which looked like a miniature calculator.

He took it out. Weighed it in his hand. Held it up towards the van.

The waving stopped. The sound disappeared before it had reached him. Future movements were put on hold.

A single button, slightly raised. Red. Almost luminous.

He pressed it, smiled faintly and climbed into the van.

A fiery blaze rose up behind the walls.

High, high up towards the sky.

No longer only walls behind him.

As the van gathered speed, the sound still hadn't reached him.

CHAPTER
THREE

"So you're on the committee for the Bajen Fans club?"

The man was in his thirties, and squinting as though the light in the darkened interrogation room was blinding. Behind his hangover, something else was going on. Watchfulness. The feeling that they would always be the accused.

"Yes," he said eventually. "Committee member."

"What is the Bajen Fans club, exactly?" Kerstin Holm asked.

"Not a violent organisation if that's what you're getting at."

"No one's suggesting that, not by any means. But a Hammarby supporter committed a terrible act of violence in a known Hammarby haunt, in the presence of at least one committee member from Bajen Fans. So it's relevant for us to ask."

He looked sullen. Remained silent. Glanced over to Hjelm, who was trying to look as though he was awake.

"I know roughly what it is," said Hjelm. "An independent supporters' group. Something that grew out of the Hammarby tribe in the early eighties."

"There you have it," said the man, with obvious pride. "We organise trips to the away games and our clubhouse on Grafikvägen is open on Thursdays and before every home game. We're the ones making sure it *doesn't* degenerate into violence. We stand for the only bloody bit of carnival colour in this monochrome country, and that's why suspicion automatically falls on us."

"The *club* isn't suspect. *You* are, Jonas Andersson from Enskede, *you*. You're suspected of withholding the identity of the Kvarnen Killer."

"The Kvarnen Killer . . ."

"The papers' name for you-very-well-know-who."

Jonas Andersson from Enskede met Hjelm's eye without hesitation.

"I was bloody well sitting there pressing a jumper to the guy's mashed head. I knew right away it'd be us who'd get the blame."

"Did you see the perpetrator?"

"No."

"Where were you?"

"In a group by the wall, a little way from the door. It was crowded and there were loads of people and I didn't see anything."

"You didn't see anything?"

Hjelm hung up his boots. It was the fourth time that day he had uttered those words. Kerstin Holm saw him throw in the towel and picked up the baton. To mix a few metaphors.

"Let's make it easy," she said, pushing a sheet of paper in front of Jonas Andersson from Enskede. "Here's a sketch of Kvarnen. When did you arrive, what did you see, and where?"

22

"I was standing here, against the wall where the door is, with about ten people who were aiming to grab some seats over towards the corner. We got there at quarter past nine and we'd already had a fair bit to drink. So we were standing there, pressed up against the wall."

"OK. Had that group at the bar already arrived then?"

"The bar was bloody busy. I don't know. I swear I don't know. It was packed, rowdy and noisy. A haze of disappointment. A 2–2 draw with Kalmar, at home. Last place confirmed. Everyone was pretty unhappy. Then suddenly it went quiet for a few seconds, the silence building like a little hole in the crowd. Then he was lying there. With a mashed head. I ran over and helped that Smålander hold the jumper to his head. It was all soft inside. Really fucking nasty. The only thing I saw was a whole load of people rushing for the door."

"A whole load of people?"

"Yeah, twenty people escaped for sure before the bouncers turned up. They'd probably been off doing drugs."

"Twenty Hammarby fans?"

"Others, too. Some managed to get out even though the bouncers were there. Talked their way out, probably, but I didn't really see."

"So what you saw was a flood of people heading for the exit?"

"I guess. Not what you'd expect. People normally react kind of like that group of dolled-up birds over in the corner did, screaming in panic and stuff like that. But quite a lot of people just rushed straight out."

"OK. Can you try to take us through where everyone was, using the sketch?"

Jonas Andersson caught his breath and groaned. He started pointing vaguely at the sketch, beginning with the row of tables by the window.

"The group of girls at two tables over in the corner. Three of them panicked and got hysterical. The third table, nearest the door: a group of IT types. They were all still there afterwards. The next row: a group of Hammarby fans in the middle, next to some kid who was reading. Staring right down into his book. On one side of them, by the wall, a gang of Slavs. On the other side, nearest us, a group of bookish-looking students. Then on the row nearest the bar: the Hard Homo. Two couples taking up one table, and the Hard Homo squashed onto the same table. On the next table: some drunks. Closest to us, a bit of a mixture. Then the table next to the door, along the wall here, a tough-looking group, not exactly skinheads but almost. They cleared out, all apart from one."

"This is getting complicated now. The tough guys, how many of them were there?"

"We were standing next to them, tried talking to them, but they didn't say a word, just sat there, pushed us if we got too close — one of them was even listening to music. Not the one who stayed behind, though. Slaphead. With a moustache. Five, there were five of them. One stayed behind."

"Who else? The Hard Homo? The drunks?"

"They stayed. You've got their names. The Hard Homo is Sweden's bravest fag. Always got his eye on

24

someone from the tribe. We're used to it now. He was just staring at that kid with the book, though. I didn't recognise the drunks, but they were the usual. Alcoholics, culture and media types, the kind who love their artsy Södermalm area. Probably haven't done a blind thing for culture these past thirty years."

"And next to the reader, you said 'a gang of Slavs'?"

"Yeah, three or four Slavs. Yugoslavs. They were talking. The guy with the book was sitting right next to them, he got pushed closer to them by the Hammarby tribe."

"How do you know they were Yugoslavs?"

"They looked like they were. They disappeared, all of them."

Kerstin Holm paused. Passed on the baton. Hjelm had returned. Recovered. He was ready again.

"So that entire group of 'three or four Slavs' rushed towards the exit as soon as Anders Lundström got the beer mug to the head?"

"Yeah. There was something dodgy about them, that's for sure."

"You saw a lot for someone who didn't see anything," said Hjelm with a vague feeling of déjà-vu.

"I'm on the committee," said Jonas Andersson, looking up. "I always try to keep an eye on what's going on. I'm just really bloody sorry that I was focused on the wrong things. I want to get the bastard just as much as you. He's ruined years of good work."

"The drunks," Paul Hjelm said carelessly to the four grizzled men dressed in worn-out corduroy jackets, each with flowing locks and greyish-white beards of various lengths.

"What do you mean?" said the one to the right.

"Pardon?" said the one to the left.

The two in the middle looked like they had been stuffed by an eager amateur taking a night class in taxidermy.

Hjelm pulled himself together and turned the tables.

"Did any of you gentlemen see anything of what the drunks by the bar in the Kvarnen were up to during the course of yesterday evening?"

"Unfortunately, at the time and place in question, we were deep in conversation about acutely important matters."

"Dare I ask which important matters these were?"

"Of course you may dare," said the one on the right. "*Quod erat demonstrandum.*"

"A self-answering question," said the one on the left.

The two in the middle leaned gravely towards one another, as though the seams were about to burst and the stuffing come out.

"Let's be serious now," said Paul Hjelm.

"We are the Friends of Vreeswijk, Cornelis Vreeswijk" said the one on the right. "Sweden's finest balladeer. We were having our annual meeting."

"We're trying to gain support for a Cornelis museum in the middle of Medborgarplatsen," said the one on the left. "The hope is that we'll be able to convince the Muslims to sing his 'Agda the Hen' from the top of the minaret."

26

"No, 'Felicia, adieu'," exclaimed the second from the right.

"No, 'Lasse small blues'," retorted the second from the left.

Following this, the duo in the middle fell silent.

"The multicultural society," said the one on the right, with a visionary glint in his eye.

"Did you see anything at all?"

The duo in the middle came back to life.

"'Grimaces . . .'" said the mid-left soberly.

"'. . . and telegrams'," the mid-right finished for him equally soberly.

"You saw grimaces and telegrams in Kvarnen yesterday evening?" asked Paul Hjelm, starting to think about claiming his pension. But the bright orange envelope containing information on the new pension system which had recently come through his letter box at home just outside of Stockholm made the thought impossible. He had miscalculated by thousands of kronor per month. Like all other Swedes of his generation.

The duo in the middle leaned forward over the table and simultaneously interrupted his ill-humoured thoughts about his pension.

"1966," said the mid-left confidently.

"An unsurpassed single," said the mid-right equally confidently.

"My moral sensibilities greatly enjoyed hearing such ambitious plans for partner swapping as those going on at the neighbouring table," said the one on the left, as the duo in the middle slumped back as though someone had let go of the strings.

"And *my* moral sensibilities equally greatly enjoyed the multicultural conversation which was going on at the table beyond that," said the one on the right.

"Can I just ask if you know why you're here?" said Hjelm, wondering where Kerstin had gone. "Fled the field" was the term which came to mind.

"You can, yes."

"Go right ahead."

"Do you know why you're here?" asked Paul Hjelm silkily.

"Unfortunately not," said the one on the right. "We expect to be questioned by the police authorities every now and then. It's in the nature of our societal role."

"Outsiders," said the one on the left solemnly, nodding.

"So you don't even know that someone was killed in Kvarnen yesterday?"

They fell silent. Exchanged surprised glances over the heads of the middle duo, who were now completely out of it.

"Naturally, we will do all we can to support you in your operation. But, unfortunately, we did not notice the event in question."

"Next to us, two not-exactly-youthful pairs were deep in an increasingly lively discussion on partner swapping. And behind them, the multicultural exchange."

"Besides which, we were pleased that Kvarnen was the venue for both listening to music and reading on a late Wednesday evening."

"Ovid. The blind king who murdered his wife."

"And then his mother. A significant cultural figure."

"I assume that you're alluding to Oedipus and Orestes respectively," said Paul Hjelm.

"Exactly. Or Ovid, as he was also called."

"Local variations."

"And the music?"

"An entire table over by the door, enjoying . . . could it have been a jazz concert? One of them had earphones."

"I recognised their way of listening. Attentively. Like jazz. Or a ballad. Cornelis."

"'Letter from the Colony'," sputtered the middle duo, instantly lapsing back into insignificance.

Hjelm stared at them, one after another, from left to right. He was having difficulty concentrating. He groaned slightly and fixed his eyes on the notes in front of him. "Multicultural exchange" it read in a scrawl that didn't seem to be his own.

"Why did you call the conversation which was going on behind the partner swappers 'multicultural'?" he managed to ask.

"Because it was clearly a Swede in conversation with some southern friends, let's say Turks."

"Or Basques."

"Basques?" exclaimed Hjelm.

"Or similar. Indians, perhaps. Probably South Mongolians."

"They were talking broken English on both sides. Fragments of the conversation reached our table."

"English? And they were sitting right next to the reader?"

"Exactly. Though they disappeared later."

"When the killing took place," Hjelm pointed out.

"Which we unfortunately missed. But suddenly they had all gone. Women were screaming, I remember. The pair of pairs didn't manage their swap since the women suddenly turned hysterical. Perhaps we should have reacted to that."

"Perhaps," Hjelm allowed himself to say. "Perhaps it should have invited a moment's consideration."

"Yeah, I saw him."

Kerstin Holm and Paul Hjelm glanced at one another and then turned to give the man with the shaved head and thin blond moustache a doubly searching look.

"You saw him?" asked Holm. "That wasn't what you said last night at Kvarnen. You told the Södermalm police night staff, and I quote, 'I didn't see anything.'"

"It was late, I was tired and a bit drunk, and we were just about to make a move. The others were already outside in the street. I was still inside, paying. It was my round. I was pretty mad that I was stuck there in Kvarnen while the others went on to the next place, so I wasn't thinking clearly. I've thought it over now, I saw him."

The bald man was in his thirties, wearing quite a stylish pale suit with a yellow tie; he was a real powerhouse. Hjelm wondered if his jacket sleeves were hiding a range of prison tattoos. He leafed through his files and found the record for Carlstedt, Eskil, 700217–1516. Born in Bromma, salesman, living in Kungsholmen, Stockholm. It was clean. Not one little traffic offence.

No prison tattoos.

"OK," said Kerstin Holm. "What did you see?"

Eskil Carlstedt paused briefly, taking in air like a boxer does smelling salts, before getting started.

"We had the table nearest the door. I was sitting with my back to the wall, so I was facing the bar. We got there pretty early, about seven thirty. The Hammarby tribe started to roll in just after nine. A bit surly, but hardly aggressive. One group took the last few seats, next to a little guy who was reading a book. Another group was standing next to our table. Then another gang appeared, six or seven people. They were a bit different. Aggression just beneath the surface, somehow. They were standing by the bar, the nearest section to us. Another bunch came in and found some space at the far end. The Smålanders, there were four of them, they were hemmed in between these two gangs. Then the Hammarby fans started attacking them. One of them prodded the biggest Smålander in the face with a rolled-up banner. He managed to run off with a friend. They got out onto the street, but two of them were left behind. It got all noisy and confused. One of the Smålanders pushed a guy over. He got back up slowly, and then suddenly he just hit the Smålander. I was busy paying. The guys had already gone, and the waitress was standing in the way, so I didn't really see it happen. But I saw him when he ran past. He still had the handle of the glass in his hand. He was wearing a denim jacket, a Hammarby T-shirt and scarf, and he had mid-length, dirty-blond hair and a little moustache."

"Like yours?" asked Hjelm.

Eskil Carlstedt stared at him, insulted.

"No," he said eventually. "Not at all. Like a country-bumpkin moustache. A mechanic's moustache, biker moustache. Went partway down to his chin."

"Would you recognise him if you saw him again?"

"I think so, yeah."

"How many of you were there together?"

"Five."

"But when the doormen blocked the door, you were the only one left?"

"The others had already gone. They were probably out on the street, waiting. We were going to the next pub. I was still there, paying. Like I said."

"Like you've said many times, yes," said Kerstin Holm. "Who were you with?"

Eskil Carlstedt unfolded his arms, cast a quick glance at his watch and, finally, rubbed his hand over his smooth head.

"Just a group of friends. A group of salesmen. We go out together a couple of times a week. Chase women."

"And listen to music," said Paul Hjelm.

Carlstedt groaned. "Music? Listen, how long's this going to take? I've already waited out there for a couple of hours, and I've got somewhere to be."

"We've got a witness who says that you were sitting in complete silence, not uttering a word, and that at least one of you had earphones in."

Carlstedt fell silent and looked at him furtively. Hesitant. He was thinking.

"All right, OK, I understand. Yeah, Kalle's in a band. Catwalks. Karl-Erik Bengtsson. We were listening to a demo. They could be really good. Record deal on the way."

"Were all of you listening?"

"I don't understand what this has to do with the killing."

"Were all of you listening?"

"Yes. We only had one cassette player, so we had to take it in turns."

"So you passed the earphones around?"

"Yeah. It took a while, so we didn't talk so much."

"And the others? Can we get hold of them?"

"Sure. They're not witnesses, though. They were already outside when it happened."

"You said. Do you remember anything else?"

"Like what?" Eskil Carlstedt sighed, staring demonstratively at the clock.

"Like who else was in the pub. We're looking for witnesses."

"It was packed, for God's sake. OK, OK, OK, fine. The people standing were mainly Hammarby fans. Before the tribe got there, everyone was sitting. The bar was empty, but all the seats were taken. Except next to the guy with the book. The first Hammarby fans sat there. Hen party at the tables over by the window. Next to them, nearest to us, a group of yuppies or IT types. Then the guy that was reading. Two horny-looking oldish couples. A gay guy on the prowl. A group of musician types. And a bit of a mixture nearest us, a group who looked like students."

"No one else?" asked Kerstin Holm.

Hjelm watched her closely.

"Not as far as I remember. But there must've been almost thirty Hammarby fans. Half of them disappeared before the doormen did anything, though."

"But your understanding is that there must be quite a few witnesses among the Hammarby fans?"

Eskil Carlstedt laughed gently.

"At least ten of them were staring right at it. They're not likely to say anything, though."

Hjelm stood up and leaned forward over the table.

"OK then, just two more things before you can run off to your eagerly awaited meeting. One: come with me to the police artist and help us with a picture of the perpetrator. Two: leave the names and details of your four friends with reception out there in the hall. OK?"

"OK," sighed Eskil Carlstedt, looking at the clock.

They sat quietly, each lost in the other's gaze. Or simply lost. A few years ago, they had slept together. Once. In Malmö. During the intense hunt for the so-called Power Killer. The A-Unit's biggest — and, on reflection, *only* — success. The media had proclaimed them heroes. The group was made permanent, "the National Criminal Investigation Department's Special Unit for Violent Crimes of an International Nature". Then along came the Kentucky Killer. Their relationship grew into friendship, deep friendship. They had been to the USA together, working with the FBI.

They had been called Jalm and Halm, like a wooden comedy duo from a variety show. It went well. They solved an old case. They captured a long-hunted serial killer. Then they made a wrong decision, and the story of the A-Unit came to an end. Bad blood always comes back round.

Though they would never say so again.

"We could stop right now," said Hjelm. "It's lunchtime. We could go out there into that waiting room where they're getting more and more agitated and say: sorry, come back tomorrow. No one would hold it against us."

He looked into her eyes. Searching. Trying to see what was going on. And she let herself be searched. Searching back.

"No," she said.

"No," he said.

In fact, each of them could probably see where the other's thoughts were heading. That this was no longer just a pub brawl.

Kerstin Holm pressed a button on the intercom, and a tall, gangly man in his fifties entered the room. Wearing a tracksuit, he looked like a jogger who had lost his way.

"Sten Bergmark — correct?" asked Kerstin Holm, holding out her hand to him. He took it and kissed it lightly, gallantly. He greeted Hjelm in a more masculine fashion. Absurdly so, Hjelm thought when he felt the pain, a second or two later.

"Hard Homo," said Sten Bergmark. "A real hit with the Hammarby tribe."

Their eyes must have shown a glimmer of surprise because he added, while folding his two-metre-tall body between the table and the chair: "They don't know that my name means stone, but they think I'm rock hard. Two birds with one stone, you could say."

"So you like to make eyes at the Hammarby tribe?" asked Holm. "And they take it?"

"I assume it appeals to their latent homosexuality, the kind which always pops up when men spend time with men."

"Has it ever worked for you?"

"More often than you'd think, policewoman."

"Though this time it wasn't the Hammarby tribe that you were eyeing up, was it?"

The tall man laughed.

"I have to confess that I was longing more for some intellectual stimulation this time. Or pseudo-intellectual, at least. Probably felt that the lack of it was getting serious. You know, of course, that the most threatening thing about homosexuality through the years has been its ability to cross class boundaries?"

"You live in Östermalm, the most exclusive neighbourhood in Stockholm, and you're a director in the Patent Office, yes?"

"Whose main dealings are with unemployed, working-class Hammarby fans from Bagarmossen and Rågsved."

"Pseudo-intellectual, by the way?"

"The chap with the book."

"But why 'pseudo'?"

"It seemed forced, with that book. Like he was sort of showing off with an education that really, deep down, he didn't have. And I wasn't alone in eyeing him up, as you so tastefully put it, policewoman. He was a tasty little titbit. You don't happen to have his address, do you?"

"Not alone?"

"Nope," said Sten 'Hard Homo' Bergmark. "A group of macho gays were staring at him the whole time."

"A group of macho gays?"

"You're acting like my psychoanalyst right now, policewoman. Five hundred kronor an hour to repeat what I've just said."

"The difference being that I don't earn five hundred kronor an hour."

"The table next to the door — how can I describe them? Skinheads who've passed the age limit. Thoroughbred Swedish bodybuilders. Five of them."

"And they were all staring at the reader?"

"Three of them, the ones with their backs to the wall. Two were sitting with their backs to the room. They weren't staring, for obvious reasons."

"And you're sure they were staring at the reader?"

"That's certainly how my competition-conscious desire interpreted it. I was jealous. Who'd choose an eel if he's got five beefsteaks within reach?"

"Who else would they have been able to see?"

"My God, policewoman. I only had eyes for him."

"Try."

Sten Bergmark sat stock-still. The scene loomed in his mind.

"I was sitting at the table nearest the bar. A group of past-it cultural types were sitting next to me, discussing which Cornelis song should be sung from the as-yet unbuilt minaret on the other side of the park. Two couples were sitting right in front of me, quite unashamedly discussing their sexual fantasies. Behind them, next to our reader and by the wall, some foreign gentlemen were speaking in English with a Swede who was sitting with his back to me. They must've been in the skinheads' field of vision. The student gang on the other side of our reader, too. And possibly some of the tipsy hen party by the window."

"Hmm," said Kerstin Holm.

"Hmm," said Paul Hjelm.

The Hard Homo clasped hands behind his neck and leaned back.

"But, noble police folk," he exclaimed, "wasn't it a death we were meant to be discussing?"

CHAPTER
FOUR

Arto Söderstedt had decided to stop driving. He didn't own a car, and drove only rarely on duty. Still, he had now done almost two hundred kilometres behind the wheel on a midsummer's morning which had defied all adverse weather reports, and as his tired service Volvo left the nourishing plains of Närke county and turned off towards the waste ground beneath Kumla prison, he could no longer deny it.

Driving was fun.

Since he was an active member of an association which wanted to drastically reduce traffic in the inner city, especially in Södermalm, and particularly on Bondegatan where he and his large family lived, that admission was made somewhat shamefully.

He eased off the accelerator, changed down to a lower gear, and turned to the passenger seat on which he was carrying horse feed.

A hay sack.

He poked the hay sack. It didn't move. He poked it a little harder. It came to life, reaching instinctively for its shoulder holster.

Viggo Norlander woke up.

A magnificent patch of white baby sick had dried onto the right shoulder of his leather jacket. Arto Söderstedt laughed.

"I've had five of them," he said in his clear Finland-Swedish accent. "Five babies have been sick on my shoulders. And still I never, *never* looked as wretched as you already do after your very first night."

"Shut up," croaked Viggo Norlander, trying to straighten himself up. Disturbing sounds were coming from his large body.

It was a strange night he had behind him. A manic-depressive night. Abrupt shifts between utter happiness and utter horror.

He had spent a night alone with his two-week-old daughter for the very first time.

It was a strange story. Like a dream. He was fifty years old and had lived the first forty-eight or so years of his life celibate, with the exception of a horribly unsuccessful month-long marriage in his youth, which had made all ensuing interaction with the opposite sex uninteresting. The thought of his own sex hadn't crossed his mind at all. He had been the dullest conceivable policeman, circumscribed by banal rules for conduct and behaviour.

Prematurely departed, that was what he thought of the old Viggo Norlander.

Then he'd had enough. His repressed soul had broken free, and he was off to Estonia on a curious mission which, unfortunately, ended with the mafia nailing him to the floor.

It had been the best moment of his life.

One that had changed his life completely.

He had thrown away all of his boring grey suits, got rid of his paunch and even had a hair transplant. He had updated his wardrobe, finding his own style, and ventured out into Stockholm's nightlife, where he welcomed even the sleaziest of approaches. He didn't refuse one single passion-seeking woman his services. Nor, for that matter, a servicing.

One occasion had been different. Last autumn, right in the middle of the ongoing hunt for the Kentucky Killer, a woman almost exactly his age had crossed his threshold with the clear intention of getting pregnant. Fifteen minutes later, she was back outside on Banérgatan. But when she turned round in the doorway, smiling at him, he really *saw* on her face that she *had* been impregnated.

He was plagued by feverish fantasies about a Nobel Prize-winning son tracking down his old policeman dad in the care home, to thank him for his near-superhuman intellect.

That wasn't quite how things had panned out. Instead, nine months later, a woman with a mewling little bundle in her arms appeared at his front door and said: "This is your daughter."

Viggo Norlander held out his hand and said: "Viggo Norlander."

The woman held out hers and said: "Astrid Olofsson."

After which Viggo Norlander said: "Come in."

"Thank you," the woman replied.

And Astrid Olofsson came in, not only into his tired old bachelor flat on the quietest stretch of Banérgatan, but also into his life. And she wasn't alone. The fourth thing she said was: "What should we call her?"

Strangely enough, Viggo Norlander didn't doubt for a second that it was true. Instead, he felt an immediate, contented peace. He *hadn't* imagined that pregnant smile nine months ago. His strange fantasies about the Nobel Prize-winning son *hadn't* been the first sign of dementia. He *had* become a father. And he *had* felt it, biologically, like pregnancy from a distance.

Besides, his little daughter, who he suddenly found himself holding, was so undeniably like him that every possible trace of doubt was removed. The same long, stretched-out face, as though the force of gravity was especially strong just around the forehead. The same lopsided, inward-backward-sloping mug, as Arto Söderstedt had cryptically put it.

"Charlotte" was the third thing that Viggo Norlander said.

He had no idea where it had come from.

This had been only a couple of weeks ago. They had been together every day since. He enjoyed Astrid's unexpected company, and found himself immediately dependent, like an addict, on the little person with the inward-backward-sloping mug.

Viggo Norlander, the man who had scarcely *seen* a photo of a baby before.

And now, for the first time, he had spent a night alone with Charlotte. A night somewhere between hope and despair. As a parting gift, she had vomited robustly

42

onto the shoulder of his leather jacket. Since he hadn't slept a wink the entire night, he had no energy to do anything about it, and went straight out onto Banérgatan and into the service Volvo which he had, despite repeated reprimands, refused to hand back. He sat down in the passenger seat, showing no surprise at seeing Arto Söderstedt behind the wheel, and was immediately transformed into a hay sack with bird shit on it. He was asleep before they even started talking.

"Something's happened at Kumla," said Söderstedt. "We're heading there as national CID officers. It's been a while. What was it that you rang in, by the way? Looking after a sick child, was it? Charlotte's not ill, is she?"

"No, me."

"It's best that I drive, then. Not that I really drive."

"Night."

And so Arto Söderstedt drove. Really drove. Since Viggo Norlander had transformed into a hay sack, he also had to manage the map reading himself. He kept one of his out-of-practice hands on the wheel and held the map in the other. It wasn't exactly easy. He looked up Kumla in the index of his road atlas, *Motormännens vägatlas över Sverige*, and found the answer "44 8E 2". Given that he was stuck in a disorderly queue at the turn-off to the main road out of Stockholm, that impenetrable combination of letters and numbers felt particularly cruel. When he finally started to understand how the system worked, he realised that he had looked up a little church village in Östergötland province. This reminded him vaguely of an earlier time when something similar had happened, and he realised that it must be the wrong Kumla and turned back to the index. To stop the atlas from closing as soon as he turned a page, he had to press the open book against the wheel with his left thigh, resulting in some difficulties steering. There were five further Kumlas. He sighed gently and went through them, one by one. Eventually, he found the right one. "61 10F 1". He needed to take the E18 via Västerås and Örebro, he realised, just as he passed the turn-off. He jolted onwards on the northbound E4, thinking positively. It was lucky that Viggo was asleep. See what luck he was having! He turned off by Kista, not losing too much time. No one had noticed a thing. He felt great. Nothing was as uplifting as discreetly correcting an embarrassment. One consequence of this cheerful mood meant that, as he finally pulled up to the security barrier outside Kumla prison, also known as the Kumla Bunker, even driving seemed fun.

"Good morning," said the guard.

Don't say shut up, Söderstedt thought to himself.

"Shut up," said Viggo Norlander.

The guard seemed more surprised than angry. He checked their IDs, confused.

"Local CID, Stockholm? We've got our own CID."

"We're national CID," said Söderstedt. "On loan to local. It's about an explosion," he added.

The guard made a few phone calls and got confirmation. The gates slid open.

"You can't say shut up to everyone who talks to you," said Söderstedt, releasing the clutch with pleasure. "It's an untenable life strategy."

"Shut up," said Viggo Norlander.

They parked the car in a carefully marked-out space, passed through a series of security checks and entered the Kumla Bunker. They wandered along corridors which would remain bluish-grey no matter what colour they were painted, and were shown into the prison governor's office. He was sitting in a leather swivel chair behind a highly polished, empty desk, and looked like male prison governors tend to. A special combination of civil servant, social worker and army officer.

It was 10.22 on Thursday 24 June, the day before Midsummer's Eve.

At this point, they still thought that they would be able to celebrate it.

The prison governor stood up to greet them.

"How much do you know?" he asked laconically.

"Not much," Söderstedt replied, equally laconically. "Just that it's obviously a matter of national concern."

"It involves class-A prisoners, so it's automatically a matter of national concern. But we don't even know if it's a crime we're dealing with."

"Looking after a sick child," Norlander thought aloud.

The prison governor looked at him, surprised, and came to the conclusion that it was Söderstedt he should talk to. So that was what he did.

"A powerful explosive charge went off in one of the cells this morning. The inmate was in the cell at the time, and had to be scraped from the walls afterwards. At present, we have absolutely no idea how it can have happened, what kind of explosive it was, how it was triggered, etc., etc. The inmate in question was Lordan Vukotic, if that rings a bell."

Söderstedt thought it over. Norlander didn't.

"Vaguely," said Söderstedt. "We brought the file with us but . . . er . . . didn't have the chance to read it on the way here. Drugs, isn't it?"

"Serious drug offences and aggravated assault. Eight-year sentence. He'd been in for three. Model inmate. Studying to become a business lawyer, and was going out on his first period of day release soon."

"Vukotic . . . Part of the group around Nedic?"

The prison governor nodded gravely.

"Definitely in the group around Rajko Nedic. One of the biggest drug dealers. Not that Vukotic has ever admitted it. Lordan Vukotic has never mentioned Rajko Nedic at all. It's that kind of loyalty that counts when you get out."

"Nedic has never done time, has he?"

"Never, and he was just about to get a personal lawyer of his own. Still, that's not how it turned out. They're still scraping bits of would-be lawyer off the walls."

"What happened? Was anyone else hurt?"

"The precise nature of the damage leads us to suspect foul play. A perfectly measured charge. It completely destroyed Vukotic's cell, but nothing else.

46

The cells next door are fine. An old friend of yours is in one of them, by the way. An old friend of the A-Unit."

"The A-Unit doesn't exist any more," said Norlander morosely.

"It did then. You were bloody good, as I understand it. The best. Though I never understood what happened with that Kentucky Killer."

"Who does?" said Söderstedt apathetically. "An old friend?"

"Göran Andersson. Another model inmate."

Neither Söderstedt nor Norlander could avoid a short laugh. The crime landscape of the past . . .

"Is he still alive?" asked Norlander.

No one uttered another word. Instead, they followed the prison governor out into the corridor, and were escorted to various areas of the Kumla Bunker by a couple of burly guards, noticing the walls changing colour. They grew successively greyer. Eventually, they went through the very last, almost spectacular security check, and found themselves in the inner sanctum. There were no inmates in sight. The long, concrete corridor was closed off, and an acrid smell of burnt rubber, plastic and meat was coming from the only place where life and movement could be seen. Forensics were running in and out of the doorway. The enormous door was wide open and seemed to be completely intact. Jet black, but intact. A fat civilian policeman was leaning against the wall, smoking a badly rolled cigarette. He was talking in a drawling voice to a well-dressed, fit-looking man who immediately registered on Söderstedt's Security Service radar.

The prison governor stopped and formally introduced them. Manly handshakes were exchanged.

"Arto Söderstedt and Viggo Norlander from national CID. Bernt Nilsson from the Security Service. And Lars Viksjö from our own Närke CID."

"First on the scene," the fat man said.

"What've we got?" asked Söderstedt, glancing in through the doorway. The devastation was complete. The entire room was black, and everything within was twisted beyond recognition. A macabre deep-sea aquarium. That enormous sea urchin might have been a bed, that sculpturesque coral a TV. Maybe those algae formations on the wall were actually the remains of a person. The forensics team were literally scraping Lordan Vukotic from the walls, packing the remains into small, well-labelled plastic bags. These were then being placed into a blue plastic box marked with the droll label "Pathologist puzzle". Söderstedt had a feeling that Qvardfordt, the forensic examiner, was behind this black humour; it was Qvardfordt who would be fitting all of the pieces together, in any case. Nowhere among the bags and boxes were any labels marked "Explosive" or "Detonation mechanism".

"Amazingly little," Bernt Nilsson from the Security Service eventually said. "We can't even establish the most basic of facts straight off. Normally you'd know what kind of explosive had been used almost immediately, but the technicians are at a loss."

Söderstedt prodded at an annoying, bright red patch of sunburnt skin on his otherwise chalk-white left arm.

The result of a hole in his shirt. He didn't cope especially well in the sun.

He turned to a feverishly working technician who was apparently *at a loss*.

"No news?"

"Nope, nada," the technician said, continuing to scrape the wall.

Söderstedt turned ostentatiously to the flabby Lars Viksjö from Närke CID.

"Do you have a sequence of events?"

Viksjö leafed through his little notebook.

"Woken up half six, breakfast at seven. Work duty for everyone who isn't studying from seven thirty. Vukotic was studying to become a business lawyer, so he was in his cell rather than in the workshop. We've got a statement saying that he 'skipped' breakfast, so presumably he hadn't left his cell at all. We haven't got a clear picture of what this 'skipped' breakfast means."

The prison governor looked anxious.

"We don't count people in to breakfast," he said apologetically.

"Who was it that said he 'skipped' breakfast?" Söderstedt asked.

Viksjö flipped frantically through his notebook.

"A guard," he eventually said. "Erik Svensson."

"OK. Go on."

"The explosion took place at 08.36. Apparently everyone in this section studies, so his neighbours were in their cells too. But it seems that the charge was so precisely measured for his cell that the walls weren't damaged. The four inmates closest to his cell are being treated for hearing loss in the infirmary, though."

"Difficult to interview them," Norlander chipped in, running his finger over the jet-black wall. The technician closest to him gave him a stern look. The black came off on his fingertips. It felt nauseating. Burnt cell remains — in both senses.

"Could he have been tinkering with his own charge?" Söderstedt asked, without turning to anyone in particular. "Was that why he didn't turn up to breakfast?"

"I find it hard to believe," said the prison governor. "Though that's just based on my personal knowledge of him."

"What do you mean?"

"Vukotic was the type who's a model of good behaviour while he's inside for the simple reason that he wants to get out as quickly as possible."

"And become drug baron Rajko Nedic's legal expert."

"Probably, yes. We were under no great illusions about rehabilitating him. Rather business law than aggravated assault, in any case. That's how we have to look at it."

"But the arm of the law isn't always especially long," said Söderstedt, repeating Norlander's blunder. The black stuck to his fingertips like glue. "As you know," he added, scratching his sunburn with his black, sticky fingers. He sighed deeply and withdrew into himself.

Viggo Norlander had, however, somewhat unexpectedly recovered and taken command.

"Are any of Rajko Nedic's other helpers in here? Who did Lordan Vukotic spend time with?"

"No one admits to any contact with Nedic at all," said Bernt Nilsson from the Security Service, the crime database in his head. "But there are a couple of other Slavs of the same kind here. Zoran Koco, Petar Klovic, Risto Petrovic."

"So these three people are 'a couple of other Slavs of the same kind'," Söderstedt said in summary.

This summary earned him a sharp look from Bernt Nilsson.

"Though you can't really say that he *spent much time* with anyone, really," the prison governor said. "He kept himself to himself."

Norlander retook the command.

"What we need are the following. One: an interrogation room. Two: the guards, especially Erik Svensson. Three: to get past the deafening ringing in the four neighbours' ears. Four: 'a couple of other Slavs of the same kind'. And five: constant updates from forensics and the doctors. Are Qvardfordt and Svenhagen in charge?"

Those present stared at the former hay sack, astounded.

After a moment, Bernt Nilsson nodded stiffly.

"Gentlemen," Norlander said formally while he picked the baby sick from his shoulder in paper-thin, white flakes, "tomorrow is Midsummer's Eve and I'm planning to devote it to my newborn daughter, not violent thugs in the Kumla Bunker. So let's get to work."

He cast one final glance into the burnt-out cell. He shouldn't have done so.

The crime scene technician was just coaxing a rough, burnt lump loose from the cell wall with a kind of large spatula. He weighed it in his hand, turning it round. For a moment, it ended up staring at Viggo Norlander.

The lump was staring. In the shapeless piece of unidentifiable material, a human eye was wedged. Completely unspoilt. As though it could still see.

He imagined that it was staring at him accusingly.

"False eye," said the technician, grinning.

CHAPTER
FIVE

It was time for a coffee break.

It was just after lunch, and for the third time that Thursday, it was time for a coffee break. They would manage to fit at least three more in before it was time to go home. To celebrate Midsummer.

Probably by having a coffee break, Gunnar Nyberg thought, staring down into his untouched mug of black coffee.

One of his ascetic's coffee breaks, as Ludvig Johnsson called them.

Johnsson himself wolfed down at least four Danish pastries a day; he was thin as a rake.

"It's your metabolism," Sara Svenhagen had explained a week or two earlier, on Saturday 12 June to be precise, just after half two in the afternoon. The paedophile hunters, as the group was unofficially called, were having a coffee break in the Strand café on Norrmälarstrand.

"You ruined your metabolism when you were Mr Sweden," she had continued didactically. "The anabolic steroids knocked the whole thing out of kilter. Ludvig's the exact opposite, he's got the build of a marathon runner. He probably ran his way out of his sorrow. Sixty kilometres a week."

"Sorrow?" Nyberg had asked, glancing with sorrow at the Danish pastry which had been bought for him. He had been in the middle of a strict diet, but seemed to keep finding Danish pasties and cinnamon buns and macaroons and almond cakes at his helpless fingertips.

Sara Svenhagen had looked at him, slightly surprised. He had looked back. She was stunningly beautiful. In her thirties. Her thick, dark blonde hair, shining like gold somehow, ran like a waterfall down to the thin, twisted shoulder straps of her top; shoulder straps which lay delicately against her freckled, golden-brown skin.

It was true, he always got a bit lyrical when he looked at Sara. He wasn't a dirty old man, he told himself time and time again, though two decades separated them. There wasn't any desire there. She was more like an angel of salvation, a luminary, always there to drag him back up into the light of day after he had been looking into the darkest depths of humanity.

Because that was what CID's paedophile hunters did: spent every day looking down into humanity's, and above all mankind's, worst conceivable depths. He could never have imagined anything so awful.

It had all been quite overwhelming for a while; things had only recently begun to calm down.

Gunnar Nyberg was the only member of the A-Unit who had emerged with his honour intact, even if this honour was internal and had never, under any circumstances, been allowed into the public eye. The lid

54

had been screwed on, and there it remained. But internally, within the National Police Board, he had been given a halo, and if the very thought of him, the man that a group of investigative journalists from the police newspaper had named Sweden's Biggest Policeman, as detective superintendent hadn't been so absurd, he probably would have been promoted. He ruled himself out right away, to save the National Police Commissioner having to make excuses. No promotion, but he would be glad of some stimulating projects.

And so, Sweden's Biggest Policeman ended up in front of a computer in the successful child pornography division of the CID. The man who had just started to live again, having been worn down by life in the muddy waters of shame. The man who had just found reconciliation with what he had believed to be irreconcilable. His children. His ex-wife. The witnesses and victim of his life's greatest crime. The unforgettable wife-battering of his bodybuilding period. It was more than twenty years ago, but every single day he remembered the sight of his children staring, wide-eyed, at his wife's split brow. He sang his pain away as the bass singer in a church choir in Nacka.

Then he had taken the step. Gunilla had long since remarried, in Uddevalla on the other side of the country. With shaking legs, he had made the journey down to visit her and Bengt. They had just sold their house and bought a place in the country on the island of Orust. That was where he went to visit them. She was completely different to how he remembered her, she had blossomed. She was a small woman, unexpectedly foul-mouthed, who, without hesitating, both forgave him and plied him with enough drink to make him cry through the night. A pathetic lump of meat. It did him good. Then he visited his daughter Tanja in Uddevalla. She was married and getting on in the world. Children could wait. She'd had a slightly more reserved, distant attitude, but even that went well.

But the best encounter of all had been with his son Tommy, living in Östhammar, just north of Stockholm. He was a farmer and had a son of his own called Benny. He spent as much time with them as he could; his fuel costs rocketing as a result. He didn't give a damn that his clapped-out old Renault used up an abnormal amount of juice. His grandson was going to be spoilt, whatever the cost.

And it wasn't only to his children he opened himself up, but women, too. Suddenly, after a twenty-year quarantine, he was able to think of himself as a sexual being. He started to look at women again, tentatively but without letting himself be overwhelmed by feelings of guilt.

And just then, both perspectives were twisted in the most terrible way.

Children and sex.

After the first few shocks, when Sara and Ludvig had found him slumped over the computer, sobbing, he went to work with the most enthusiasm imaginable. Since the collapse of the A-Unit, the group had been CID's A team of the moment. After a period of fruitless hunting, they were in the middle of a very successful spell, working closely with similar groups abroad.

Before Nyberg arrived, they had been working with fifteen other countries on Operation Cathedral, led by the British National Crime Squad, which had mapped out an enormous paedophile network online. The first thing he got to work on at the end of October was something disgusting called "Paedo University". In May of the previous year, the American police had begun an international effort called Operation Sabbatical, and at the end of October, there was a joint crackdown in the countries involved. At home, other parts of the group were working with all the tracks and networks that had come to light in connection with the twenty-two-year-old paedophile in Örebro who had recently been revealed as the country's most horrendous child molester ever.

And so it went on. Gunnar Nyberg felt, for the first time, that he really was doing something *important*. He was saving children. And he continued doing it in his spare time. For the past year, he had been giving increasingly well-regarded talks on doping in the city's schools. Free of charge, to the genuine surprise of the head teachers.

Who knew about the negative effects of anabolic steroids better than he did?

So, even though he spent his days focused on the most appalling sides of human desire, he felt that his life was shaping up quite well. Above expectations, considering what had happened with the Kentucky Killer.

He had looked out over Lake Mälaren. The lake in high summer. A few weeks into June, the weather didn't really know what it should be doing, but the sun had just broken through the clouds and was spreading its newly churned butter over the freshly baked bread of the water of Riddarfjärden, garnishing it with sails in all the colours of the rainbow. The air felt unusually fresh, which was only partly due to the absence of traffic. On Västerbron Bridge, the queues were now being caused by a growing troop of runners.

Gunnar Nyberg had turned back to Sara Svenhagen. Her expression had told him that she had answered something he had already forgotten.

"Sorry, what did you say?" he had been forced to ask.

"Ludvig ran through his sorrow over his family," she said. "Didn't you know? That he lost his family in a car accident a few years ago?"

"What? Christ. He's always seemed so . . . happy-go-lucky to me . . ."

"It's a front. He's literally running for his life, every single day. Wife and two sons, just like that. Gone from one second to the next."

"Were you already working together then?"

"Yeah, but not on this. It was before the police really understood how serious this child pornography was, how insanely widespread it is. No, we were working for Stockholm CID. He was my mentor, I suppose. It was Ludvig who built up the entire paedophile unit, and took me with him."

"And me, I guess."

"You knew each other already, didn't you?" Sara had asked. "How?"

58

Ground that had been so difficult to tread. Close to being erased by twenty years of agony. The past. *That* period. The steroid period.

It was no longer off limits.

"We were in Police College together," Gunnar Nyberg had replied. "We were really close back then, shared a room. But we grew apart, when he turned into a good policeman and I became a bad one. And I didn't even know that he'd lost his family."

"That's what time does," Sara had said, placing her hand on his.

He had smiled. Crookedly, he thought. He had smiled crookedly, and looked around the table. They were having a coffee. Five paedophile hunters. His new A-Unit.

Whose boss, the comet-careerist Detective Superintendent Ragnar Hellberg, generally called Party-Ragge, had suddenly stood up and pointed.

"The pack's coming."

They had left the Strandcafé and pushed through the crowds towards Norrmälarstrand and the water's edge. Nyberg could leave his pastry to the vigilant grey sparrows without a bad conscience.

The lead group of the Stockholm Marathon had just passed by when they reached the blue-and-white plastic barrier. Whenever anyone grumbled about them forcing their way through, they found a police ID shoved in their face. Nyberg knew that people had been suspended for showing their ID when they were off duty, and had let the apparently not-too-scrupulous Hellberg clear the path.

The marathon route became more crowded. About a hundred people had passed when Nyberg shouted: "How will we spot him?"

"You'll see!" Sara laughed.

And he had seen, you couldn't have missed it.

Ludvig Johnsson had passed them with a blue flashing light on his head. He was running incredibly fast and waved cheerfully to the happily cheering paedophile hunters.

Superintendent Ragnar Hellberg had ducked under the blue-and-white plastic tape and slipped through a small gap in the string of marathon runners. The group followed behind him. Party-Ragge had been openly waving his ID at the rapidly approaching stewards, who stopped dead in their tracks and allowed the group of police officers to go past on important business. They jogged up Polhelmsgatan.

"What's going on now?" Gunnar Nyberg had panted, his body not exactly made for jogging.

"Now he'll be bloody surprised to see us again, up on Fleminggatan," Sara had replied.

They had got there just in time to see the unmistakable blue light approaching. Sure enough, Ludvig Johnsson had laughed in surprise, pointed at the blue light and looked accusatively at them.

"That damned light weighs a couple of kilos," Hellberg had laughed sadistically once Johnsson had disappeared out of view.

Then they could relax and have *another* coffee, before it was time to catch Johnsson down on the other side of the shipyard on Norrmälarstrand. That time, he

60

hadn't looked quite so fresh, and when they saw him for a second time on Fleminggatan, the blue light had disappeared. They never did find out where it had come off.

The whole group had then jumped into a police car which, blue lights flashing, had set off for Stockholm Stadium, where they stood on the running track, all with blue flashing lights on their heads, cheering home their exhausted marathon hero.

Gunnar Nyberg had felt strange with the flashing light strapped to his head. It was almost five o'clock, and he had been doing his best to join in, to have just as much fun as the others seemed to be having, to avoid thinking that it was for *this* he had given up his weekend with his grandson Benny in Östhammar.

And when he saw his stick-thin old friend receive the fabulous Sara Svenhagen's heartfelt hug there in Stockholm Stadium, in the shadow of its fine old clock tower, he had felt like he could almost reconcile himself with it. Her golden hair wonderfully glossy in the gleaming late-afternoon sun.

That was then.

Now it was gone. Sara Svenhagen had chopped it all off. She looked like a different person. Just as appealing, of course, but in a completely different way. More interesting, maybe. Less of a luminary and more of a person. With everything that entailed.

"What got into your head?" said Nyberg, straight off.

Ludvig Johnsson didn't really seem to understand, sitting *stick-thin* in the café by the police station, wolfing down his third Danish pastry of the day. But Sara understood. She smiled slightly.

"A fresh start," was all she said.

Gunnar Nyberg stared down into his untouched cup of black coffee and had nothing to say. For his part, he'd had enough fresh starts for a while.

Though there was that thing with women, of course . . .

Ludvig Johnsson shifted in his creaky chair on the narrow pavement outside the pleasantly named Annika's Café & Restaurant by the police station on Kungsholmsgatan.

"Still going with your ascetic's coffee breaks, Gunnar?" he asked.

Johnsson looked almost too fit, with his wiry body and neat bald patch just above his monk-like band of black hair. He was wearing a thin, pale linen suit, a greenish tie and a beige shirt, and he looked at least ten years younger than Nyberg, despite them being the same age, just under fifty. It always grieved him so much to see such a fit and healthy man gobbling down unhealthy food so often.

On the whole, it had been a strange experience to meet Ludvig Johnsson again. They had been very close for a short time twenty-five years ago. Gone through Police College together, virtually lived on top of one another, day in and day out. The division had been clear even then: Gunnar spent most of his time in the weights room, Ludvig running amok down on the track. Gunnar became Mr Sweden and an ugly Norrmalm policeman with a baseball bat. Ludvig went out to the provinces and became a friendly local policeman in Vänersborg. And now they had been reunited. As paedophile police, as an evening paper had carelessly called them. And surprisingly little had changed. They had both lost their families, in completely different ways, and on the other side of the abyss, they had found each other once more. Again, more a result of differences than similarities. Ludvig was nimble, supple, elegant, European. Gunnar was big, strong, a fighter; out-and-out Swedish.

"I *have* to do it," said Gunnar Nyberg. "I've still got twelve kilos to go before I'm down to being Sweden's Second Biggest Policeman."

Ludvig Johnsson laughed. "Yeah, I read that story. Did they talk to you first?"

"Someone rang and asked if I still weighed a hundred and thirty-nine kilos. I said no, a hundred and forty-six. The entire story's built on that conversation. Sweden's Biggest Policeman."

"Well, listen," Ludvig Johnsson said abruptly, slapping his marathon-runner knees. "It's bloody well time for Midsummer. One day to go. May the country's paedophiles rest easy, at least for a couple of days. What're you all doing?"

"I'm going to see my grandson," said Nyberg without hesitation. "Dance around the Midsummer pole in Östhammar."

"I'm just going to relax," said Sara Svenhagen. "Unwind. There's been a lot on for a bit too long now."

"I'm going to renew myself," said Ludvig Johnsson cryptically.

Suddenly, a familiar voice could be heard on Kungsholmsgatan.

"Well, well! If it isn't Sweden's Very Biggest Policeman!"

A short-haired, medium-blond man dressed in a red T-shirt, jeans and sandals, a red pimple on his cheek, had appeared in sharp relief against the greyish facade of the police station. Nyberg allowed himself the trouble of standing up and spreading his arms. The two men hugged. When Nyberg let go, the other man looked as though he had just been embraced by an anaconda.

"Distinguished paedophile hunters," said Nyberg jovially, "meet the hero of Hällunda. The pride of the police force, Paul Hjelm. Ludvig Johnsson and Sara Svenhagen."

"Hullo," said Johnsson.

"Hi," said Svenhagen.

"Hi," Hjelm panted, regaining his breath. "Congratulations on your latest crackdown, it seems to have gone really well."

"Thanks," said Svenhagen. "Yeah, it was a little reward for our efforts."

"Finally, we should add," said Johnsson.

"What're you busy with nowadays?" asked Nyberg, patting Hjelm on the shoulder. "Where did you end up? Local CID?"

"In the mundane, you could say, yeah. Right now it's the Kvarnen Killer, if you've heard about that criminal mastermind."

"Pub brawl?" Nyberg said thoughtlessly. "Aren't you a bit . . . overqualified?"

"Don't say that," said Hjelm. "It's shaping up to be something really interesting. We'll see. I'm working with Kerstin by the way, Gunnar."

"That's right!" exclaimed Nyberg. "My old room-mate. She was meant to be going back home. So you ended up together? Good fit."

"A great fit," said Hjelm. "I've got to buy a couple of sandwiches from the delicious Annika's, then we're pressing on with the interrogations. It has its unexpected moments."

"What d'you say about Östhammar for Midsummer? Come up and meet the boy. Tommy."

"Thanks, but I can't. I think the kids've got a lot going on. We're renting the cottage on Dalarö again."

"Yeah, yeah, go and buy your killer sandwiches then," said Nyberg, "otherwise you'll get a telling-off from Kerstin."

Hjelm went in, bought a couple of well-made sandwiches from Annika's Café & Restaurant and, waving, started off in the direction of the police station.

Though his mind was in another place.

Elsewhere.

The Kvarnen bar at 21.42 the previous evening, to be precise.

He stopped on Kungsholmsgatan. The enormous police station complex towered above him. Turning to the right would take him up to CID on Polhemsgatan. Turning left would mean wandering through the leafy park, past the elegant entrance to local CID's building on Agnegatan, and out onto Bergsgatan where the City Police District had their considerably more humble entrance.

The right belonged to the golden past.

The left the more dull present.

Without really knowing why, he stood there hesitating at the crossroads like Hercules in Stiernholm's epic poem.

Only then was he forced to express what had been floating around, unexpressed, for several hours in the interrogation room that Thursday morning before Midsummer's Eve. He had read it time and time again in Kerstin Holm's eyes as, time and time again, they had looked searchingly at one other to make sure that their instincts weren't wrong.

Yes — this was a perfectly normal, boring, everyday crime in inner-city Stockholm. *But was that all?*

Was it just their intense hopes for a *proper* crime which meant that they saw something else looming behind this messy killing?

Paul Hjelm stood at the crossroads for a moment. He felt Nyberg's searching look on his back. Then he accepted the state of affairs and turned off to the left. Returned to the local police, to the violent crimes division of City Police District, and to the dull, raw, violent crimes.

But something within him suspected that a metamorphosis was approaching.

CHAPTER
SIX

Her stomach wasn't rumbling, it was roaring. Like when a lone Indian is sneaking through the jungle, his heart in his mouth, and suddenly hears the sound he knows he'll hear only once in his life.

Late in his life.

The roaring of a tiger.

On this occasion, though, the tiger was a far from terrifying female policewoman in her mid-thirties, and the Indian a young man from Kalmar, aged barely twenty, his eyes red and swollen from crying. And it was hardly late in his life.

It had been late in his best friend's life, though. The evening before. 23 June, 21.42, in the Kvarnen bar on Tjärhovsgatan in Södermalm.

Kerstin Holm was longing for Paul Hjelm. But even more — she had to admit it — for the sandwiches he would be bringing with him.

Her stomach growled again, even more murderously.

Not that Johan Larsson from Kalmar noticed. He was crying uncontrollably. He was completely lost, understood nothing. Nothing at all. Four high-spirited young men from Kalmar had followed their football team, Kalmar FF, the unexpectedly successful newcomers in the league, on an exciting little adventure to Stockholm. At 19.00 on Wednesday 23 June, they had been in the Södermalm Stadium, cheering the team on to a far from poor 2–2 result. Reasonably happy with their evening, they had made their way to Kvarnen, a pub they had heard about near Medborgarplatsen. It would be lively there, or so they had heard. But what they didn't know was that it would be packed with disappointed Hammarby fans, whose collective frustration over finishing last in the league was coming to a head. No one had believed them when, like St Peter, they denied, three times, any dealings with their champions. Instead, one of them had died. His blood had flowed out into Johan Larsson's hands, gushed out through the seams of his red-and-white football shirt, and life would never be the same again.

Maybe he would forget the sea of blood, maybe he would even forget Anders Lundström, his childhood friend. But he would never forget the blind hate, the inordinate rage. Those eyes that just *wanted to kill*. Those would be there until the very last moment of Johan Larsson's humble time on earth. That much he understood.

But nothing else.

Kerstin Holm did what she could. She tried to be motherly; she said to herself: I could be his mother, but it didn't really work. She wasn't exactly sure what being motherly involved.

She didn't have any children, didn't know if she wanted to have children. A year ago, she had known that she *didn't* want to have any, but now she wasn't even sure of that. Time had begun to run out for her. Her relationships hadn't really lived up to what had been promised. As a child, she had been sexually abused by a relative. Her engagement to a colleague in Gothenburg had been one long, drawn-out rape. Her strange, short, intense relationship with Paul Hjelm over two years ago was mainly a gilded memory from which the gold leaf had begun to flake away, and the most important relationship of her life, an equally intense love affair with a terminally ill sixty-year-old priest, had ended the way she knew it would.

He died.

She was with him when he died, and he had left memories behind that she didn't really know what to do with. They had an aura of *holiness* which she just didn't feel worthy of.

Paul Hjelm came into the room, brandishing a plastic bag. She gave a sigh of relief, and her stomach growled violently, as though it knew about the contents of the bag. He heard it, waved the bag once more, and got an immediate response from the tiger in her abdomen. He raised his eyebrows, surprised.

"The mysteries of biology," he said, sitting down and skimming through her notes. *"Gang of seven people,"* she had written.

"Blind hate. Three main figures, the perpetrator really a minor character. The one who helped (Jonas A): fucking furious. At us, because we'd gone there. At perp, because he'd ruined things.

69

Anders pushed him over so we could follow Hjalle and Steffe out. Completely unexpected. Unbelievably hostile looks, like there was nothing human in those eyes. The whole gang disappeared. In a flash."

She hadn't written anything else.

Hjelm looked up at Johan Larsson from Kalmar. He was hunched over, sobbing.

So-called meaningless violence.

For a brief moment, he felt sick to his stomach.

He looked at the new drawing, lying alongside the other two. Three police sketches of the perpetrator, completely independent of one another. So similar, and yet so different. Per Karlsson's, Eskil Carlstedt's and Johan Larsson's.

Dishevelled, mid-length, sand-coloured hair; a little moustache that went just past the corners of his mouth; blue eyes. On these points, the pictures were in agreement. But on the shape of the face, the nose and the eyes, here they differed on these most basic of points. It wasn't possible to come up with a single coherent picture from the three sketches. The question was whether they could even be used in the media.

Hjelm held up Eskil Carlstedt's drawing for Johan Larsson.

"Is this what he looked like?"

Larsson looked up, all red and puffy. Snot was running freely from his nose. Hjelm passed him a tissue without lowering the picture. Eventually, Johan Larsson managed to focus on it. He nodded. His head sank back down to his arms. Hjelm picked up Per Karlsson's sketch.

"So like this, then?"

The young Smålander looked up again.

"Exactly like that," he said.

Hjelm sighed and put the drawing down.

"How drunk were you?"

"Pretty," was all Johan Larsson said.

"And you didn't see anything else noteworthy in the pub?"

Kerstin studied Paul once again. He studied her back. When they returned their attentions to the young man, they saw that he had been studying them. It was getting a bit tedious.

"I only saw one thing worth mentioning," he said clearly.

They let him go.

Glancing at one another, they opened the plastic bags containing the sandwiches.

"The IT types," snorted Hjelm, muffled by mozzarella and Parma ham.

"I did them while you were gone, it was quick. They didn't see anything. And they were stockbrokers, not IT types. They were sitting nearest the door and saw absolutely bloody nothing. Apart from one thing: the hen party. I got the impression they were after some kind of complicated gang bang with the bride-to-be and her blind-drunk friends."

"And this hen party had absolutely nothing to add, I can tell you that. As far as I could see, a complicated gang bang wouldn't have been completely out of the question for them. So that means that the whole row over by the window, a table of stockbrokers and two tables of hens, are useless witnesses?"

"The best the stockbrokers had to offer was: 'A whole load of people rushed past right when the girls started yelling.' Both groups were just a bit too horny and drunk, simple as that. Just like that 'pair of pairs' who'd gone to Kvarnen for a partner swap. They'd never met before, just exchanged erotic emails where they indulged in shared fantasies about partner swapping and group sex. Their plans probably wouldn't have come to much, considering how drunk they were. Too horny and too drunk, all of them — even though it was only twenty to ten. Hen party, stockbrokers and the pair of pairs."

"Then let's go for the people who should have been *least* horny and drunk."

"But also the busiest."

"The staff. The waitresses or those thugs on the door?"

"The doormen, you mean. Which deserve to wait the longest?"

"Let's get the waitresses in."

They pressed a button on the intercom. A short conversation with the receptionist, and in trudged a group of slightly haggard-looking beauties. Five of them. They sat down and started to complain in unison. It sounded like the monkey house at the zoo.

"Naturally, we're very sorry that you've had to wait," said Hjelm courteously, not quite blinded by all their feminine splendour. "There are a lot of people to

72

interview, and none of you are missing work, since it's only ten past two and Kvarnen hasn't reopened yet."

"Are we *allowed* to open, then?" said the oldest-looking one. "Isn't it a crime scene?"

"We've secured everything that needs securing, so it's just a matter of going on as normal. Business as usual. It'll probably be full — lots of free publicity in the press. The same way that Tony Olsson can write a book and get any publisher he likes to print it."

"Tony Olsson?" the waitresses said in unison.

"The police killer who came home from Costa Rica a few days ago," Hjelm explained. "And announced that he was innocent."

"What's he got to do with us?" exclaimed one of the women.

"Nothing," Hjelm sighed. "Which of you was behind the bar when it happened?"

"Me," said a small, dark woman in her thirties. "Karin Lindbeck," she added automatically.

"How much did you see of what happened?"

"Not much. I was at the other end of the bar taking payment for a big order. It was crowded so it took a while."

"Care to tell us, just to be on the safe side?" Kerstin Holm put in.

"All right," said Karin Lindbeck, with a gesture of acknowledgement.

"So, did you feel the atmosphere was threatening?" asked Hjelm.

"You could say so . . . There was something in the air."

"And you'd served the perpetrator earlier?"

"Probably. But he was standing towards the back of that macho gang, and a bit shorter than the others, I think. A background figure. Not especially memorable."

"One of these three?" asked Hjelm, spreading the three drawings on the table.

The bartender Karin Lindbeck looked through them. With a quick, practised eye. Used to keeping track of faces.

"Hardly," was all she said.

"No likeness at all?"

"Only the hair and the moustache."

"Can you produce anything better?"

"I think so."

"And you've never seen him before?"

"I might've seen some of that gang before, but not him. Not that I remember."

"You can help us with a couple of drawings later, Karin. Do you remember anything else?"

"The Smålanders. A shy group who realised pretty quickly that they'd ended up in the worst place they could've. Too late. The one that died seemed nice, he was the one who ordered."

"OK, thanks. So the rest of you were waitresses? You're divided up, aren't you? By tables?"

"Yeah," the oldest waitress replied, a fake blonde of around forty-five. "I had the window. The hen party and the brokers. They were flirting with each other non-stop. And drinking a lot. I was working flat out to get them served. Also, I was having a break when it happened. He was already dead when I came out."

74

"More?"

"I was in the corner," said another. "Saw nothing, heard nothing."

"Very concise, but maybe not complete."

"I was further in. Not much happened there. Business as usual."

"More."

"I had the middle row," explained the young Asian woman. "A group of students were sitting nearest to the door, they were talking about a social anthropology exam, I think. Then there was the guy pretending to read, sitting alone, and a group of southern Europeans who had a Swede with them. They were speaking English."

"You didn't happen to hear what they were talking about?"

"I try not to eavesdrop."

"Like on the social anthropology students?"

She looked slightly embarrassed.

"Come on," said Hjelm. "You heard something."

"They were negotiating about something. They weren't friends. The opposite, I think. Distrust. They were trying to agree on something."

"On what? Try to remember."

"Weren't we meant to be talking about the murder? I didn't see that at all. I had my back to it."

"Just answer the question."

"No, I don't know. A meeting place, maybe. I don't know."

"But they left right away when the fight started? The whole gang? Did they go without paying?"

"If you're just drinking, you pay straight away. There wasn't any bill to pay, everything had already been paid. But yeah, they disappeared pretty quickly."

Hjelm thought. Something fuzzy was shifting in his mind.

"No bill? No, it's bloody obvious. *No bill to pay.*"

The waitresses regarded his curious little outburst suspiciously.

"Who had the table by the door? Along the wall by the door, I mean."

"Me," said the youngest of the waitresses, a short-haired, sturdily built girl.

"Who was sitting there, and what happened?"

"Five really serious, quiet types."

"Salesmen?"

"Not exactly, no, I don't think so. I guess you could say that you'd *expect* them to be the rowdy kind but they weren't at all. The opposite, they hardly said a word to one another. Just sat there, staring on the sly."

"Five macho gay men, staring at a kid who's sitting there reading," Hjelm said clearly.

"It wasn't him they were staring at, it was further away."

"Were they listening to music?"

"Hardly. One of them had a little earphone, but it looked more like . . . a hearing aid."

"And they *didn't* pass that earphone around?"

"No, it was just one of them that had it. He was sitting with his back to the room."

"And they *didn't* drink much?"

"A beer each at most."

"And *none* of them stayed behind to pay the bill?"

"No, no, same thing. There wasn't a bill. But one of them did stay behind. Shaved head and moustache."

"And the other four *hadn't* left *before* the killing?"

"No, but they left before anybody else. As soon as the glass broke. One of them pointed at the one who stayed behind and said something. Then he sat down again and waited."

"So they deliberately left Eskil Carlstedt behind?"

"If that's what he's called, yeah. It looked that way. I was standing in the middle of the Hammarby gang next to them, trying to take an order. It was slow. I was standing with my back to . . . the killing . . ."

Hjelm tried to catch Holm's eye. She was drawing heavy lines in her notebook. Eventually, she looked up. She looked composed.

"Shall we step out a moment?" he asked.

"Yes," said Holm. "But I just have one question for you," she added, pointing to one of the waitresses. Hjelm saw the underlined word: "pretending". Holm continued. "Why did you say that the kid was *pretending* to read?"

"What?"

"You heard me."

"He didn't turn a single page in that book."

"What was he doing, then?"

"Don't know. Thinking. Or listening."

They went out into the corridor.

"We're sending a patrol to Eskil Carlstedt right now," said Hjelm. "He lives here on Kungsholmen."

"We should've picked up on the music, the demo tape, the reaction when we asked," said Holm. "Christ."

"And the bloody rest," said Hjelm.

Holm went away to send a patrol car after Carlstedt. Hjelm returned to the waitresses.

"Well, ladies," he said, stretching. "We need the most exact descriptions you can possibly give us of the southern Europeans, the Swede, and the four who disappeared from beside the door."

The oldest of the waitresses stood up abruptly.

"What the hell is it you're working on?" she demanded.

"I don't have the faintest idea," said Paul Hjelm truthfully.

Three burly, traditional-looking doormen were sitting in a row, almost like the three wise monkeys who want to see, hear and say nothing.

Though only almost.

They actually talked quite a lot, even if it was exclusively about how heroically they had blocked the door despite everyone trying to get out. They described it as though they had been courageous UN troops, preventing genocide with nothing but their bare hands.

"Considering at least twenty people got out, maybe your reaction wasn't exactly lightning-fast," said Hjelm quietly.

They stared at him.

"There's actually a door between the cloakroom and the pub," said the oldest, insulted. "We can't hear everything that goes on inside."

"We had a pretty bloody rowdy queue to deal with," said the biggest. "Lots of difficult immigrants."

"Immigrants?" exclaimed Hjelm. It was clear that the man wasn't used to using any other word than "wog". He continued. "Still, you let thirty or so drunk Hammarby fans in, one of whom turned out to be a murderer."

"You know where you are with Hammarby fans," said the third one.

"I see," Hjelm said sourly, letting the subject lie. "Couldn't you have reacted a bit quicker when twenty men came running out of the pub all at once?"

"There was a hell of a crush then, so it wasn't exactly easy to move in the opposite direction."

"Anyway, our job's to check people going *in*, not coming *out*."

"We didn't know what had happened, did we? We can't just stop people leaving the pub."

"What kind of people were coming out?"

"Men. Just men. Hammarby fans, mainly, some older builders too."

"Builders? Like construction workers?"

"No, like bodybuilders. There aren't any construction jobs any more."

"Any . . . immigrants?"

"Eventually some wo — gentlemen with darkish hair, yeah," said the biggest. "I seem to remember that."

"But you must know all this," said the oldest. "You had a man there."

Hjelm stared at Holm. Holm stared at Hjelm.

"A man there?" they said in unison. It didn't exactly sound professional, but what can you do? What were they supposed to do with their surprise?

"Yeah," said the biggest of the doormen. "We'd just managed to push our way in and block the inner door. He hadn't quite made it out. I pushed him back. Then he flashed his ID and ran out."

"His ID?" they said in unison.

"His police ID."

They were paralysed.

Eventually, Kerstin Holm said: "You didn't think it was strange that a policeman wanted to get *out* after a crime had been committed?"

"I don't know how you work, for Christ's sake."

"And you can't remember what he looked like?"

"It was pretty crazy, to put it mildly. Some guy was lying in a pool of blood. Everyone was screaming, people were pushing towards the door. All I saw was a police ID being waved, and let him out."

"To freedom," said Paul Hjelm.

CHAPTER
SEVEN

Viggo Norlander was on great form. On the ball. With it.

To an external observer, he might have seemed like a highly ambitious policeman who wanted to solve a complicated murder case whatever the cost. He gave orders, directed and dashed around. He interrogated, bossed about and shone.

Arto Söderstedt *wasn't* an external observer. He was a *sceptical* observer. And Viggo Norlander *wasn't* a highly ambitious policeman who wanted to solve a complicated murder case whatever the cost. He was a highly ambitious new father who, whatever the cost, wanted to spend Midsummer with his baby daughter.

Söderstedt didn't find that quite as honourable. He thought back to all the times he had cancelled Midsummer celebrations, remembering the faces of his disappointed, sobbing sons and daughters, and felt a pang of envy for Norlander's purposefulness. He had never been so single-minded himself.

On the other hand, his fatherhood hadn't been as exceptional. On the contrary, he considered himself an unusually *normal* father. Anja's five pregnancies had passed with customary minor complications, and the children had plopped out a few weeks too early or a few weeks too late, completely healthy and white as chalk. His paternity could never have been in doubt. Unless there was another ghostly-white Finn living in one of the Söderstedt wardrobes, springing out like a jack-in-the-box as soon as he had cleared off to the police station.

Or the courtroom. Because Söderstedt's own little quirk had nothing to do with family life. It was the way his career had panned out that was the unusual thing. And the secret one. When he was very young, he had almost unconsciously raced his way through Finnish law school at record speed, become the young legal genius at a well-regarded law firm and, aged barely twenty-five, been defending the scum of the earth. The well-off scum of the earth, that is. Those who had the means to appoint a top lawyer like Arto Söderstedt in order to escape the long arm of the law. And to piss all over it just as naturally as a dog pisses on a lamp post.

Eventually, he had simply had enough. Cast his Hugo Boss suits and Armani ties aside, scrapped the Porsche, given up his Finnish citizenship and fled the limelight to Sweden, becoming . . . a policeman. In the stubborn, lingering belief that, despite everything, the system can only be changed from within.

And that afternoon, with the midsummer sun slowly starting to descend outside the walls, he was sitting in the Kumla Bunker with the other kind of scum of the earth. The kind that *didn't* have the means to appoint a top lawyer like Arto Söderstedt in order to escape the long arm of the law.

He didn't feel entirely satisfied.

But Viggo Norlander was in his element. Completely disinterested in formal rank, he had relegated Bernt Nilsson from the Security Service and Lars Viksjö from Närke CID to the sidelines. Or was it the substitutes' bench?

Norlander raised his inward-backward-sloping mug, beaming with energy, from the stack of papers in front of him, and peered out over the gathering in the cold little interrogation room.

"Shall we see if we can sum up before we let him in?" he asked, without waiting for an answer. "Erik Svensson, the guard, saw that Lordan Vukotic was still curled up in his bed after they were woken up at half six. Vukotic announced from under the covers that he wasn't feeling well and asked to skip breakfast, which he was allowed to do. When the bomb went off at 08.36, that meant he hadn't been out of his cell since the evening before. Can we draw any conclusions from that?"

Here — possibly — he paused for an answer.

"It's surely not out of the question that there's a connection between him missing breakfast and the explosion," said Bernt Nilsson. "But in that case, what kind of connection? Was he really tinkering around under the covers with a bomb of his own, one that went wrong and detonated by itself?"

"Hands above the covers," said Arto Söderstedt, receiving glances of the same kind that an orang-utan in a ball gown would receive.

"Alternative?" said Norlander coldly.

"We don't know enough," said Söderstedt, defusing the situation. "There could be any number of reasons why he chose to go without breakfast. Maybe he really did feel ill. Maybe Lordan Vukotic was telling the truth for the first time in his life. Let's keep going."

Norlander kept going.

"'A couple of Slavs of the same type', Zoran Koco, Petar Klovic and Risto Petrovic, they're keeping their mouths shut. All three of them are Rajko Nedic's men, just like Vukotic was, so they're not going to talk. Did anyone get a sense that any of them knew anything?"

Three shaking heads.

"They actually seemed quite jittery," said Nilsson. "Even a notorious war criminal like Klovic seemed worried. Vukotic was really close to Nedic, who was meant to be untouchable. You could call him Nedic's right-hand man. That much we know. Still, someone managed to get at that right hand, and in the very heart of the Kumla Bunker. Maybe we're looking at the start of a power struggle in the drug business. Maybe that's what Klovic and the boys think, anyway. Though there's nothing else to indicate that."

Söderstedt glanced furtively at Bernt Nilsson. He didn't exactly correspond to his — perhaps a touch unjust — picture of a Security Service man. No far-fetched conspiracy theories, no bind of absolute secrecy, none of the old nonsense that had almost scuppered the A-Unit's first case: the Power Killer. Maybe there was a shake-up going on within the Security Service. Though maybe *that* was just a far-fetched conspiracy theory.

84

"War criminal?" was all he said.

Nilsson looked at him.

"It's been confirmed that Klovic was a camp guard in Bosnia," he said. "He's a Bosnian Serb. Should really be in court in The Hague, but apparently there's not enough evidence for a trial. Petrovic was also involved in the ethnic cleansing, though in Croatia. Of Serbs. But under Rajko Nedic's protection, the former enemies have been united by a common love, the love of weapons."

"So Nedic happily works with war criminals?"

"They're brilliant workers, aren't they? Ready trained, as it were. Nedic's been in Sweden for maybe thirty years now; he got Swedish citizenship back in the seventies, but he seems to have a whole load of contacts from the paramilitary groups on all sides in the former Yugoslavia. A lot of the drugs are supposed to come from down there."

"But in this case, we can just put the Slavs on the shelf?"

"Probably. It's one of them who's the victim, after all."

"So," resumed Norlander, "we don't have much to go on. Our general enquiries trying to find out what Lordan Vukotic spent yesterday evening doing didn't give anything. It seems that the governor was right: he really did keep himself to himself. Ate dinner at half four. The time between then and lock-in at half seven is a blank, no one is saying anything about those three hours. And his deaf cell neighbours don't have anything to say but —"

"What," Söderstedt interrupted.

"What?" said Norlander.

"His deaf cell neighbours don't have anything to say but 'what'."

The stout Lars Viksjö burst out into roaring laughter. Bernt Nilsson and Viggo Norlander raised their eyebrows. Söderstedt chuckled to himself; irritating Norlander had its charms. Upsetting his energetic calculations.

Norlander continued, however, relatively unfazed — and more like his normal self. "They don't know anything except that their eardrums suddenly burst. Just like that, they sprang a leak."

"There's one still remaining," said Bernt Nilsson. "How does it feel to be meeting him again?"

Söderstedt and Norlander glanced at one another. Ties from the past. They didn't say anything, just let Göran Andersson in and looked at him. His tall figure clad in a bright green jumpsuit. Feet shoved into a pair of worn-out Birkenstocks. His face was completely different. Instead of the impeccable, neat-haired bank worker there was — well, what could you call it? A *thinker?* His blond hair was sprouting in all directions and he had an untidy beard which seemed to have been stuck haphazardly onto various parts of his face; but his gaze, that bright blue gaze, was crystal clear. The only thing spoiling the image of a fully-fledged artist were the two wads of bloody cotton wool sticking from his ears.

Leonardo da Vinci, thought Söderstedt.

Peter Dahl, thought Norlander.

The truth was somewhere in between.

How many people had this man killed?

Was it five? Or six?

"Hi," said Göran Andersson. "What've you done with Hjelm?"

It took a moment before they registered what he was asking.

"We don't work together any more," said Söderstedt.

"What?" said Göran Andersson.

Söderstedt chuckled. "His deaf cell neighbours don't have anything to say but 'what'."

"Can you hear anything at all?" he shouted.

Andersson chuckled too. "Just talk loudly. They say that burst eardrums heal, but that it'll take time and will probably leave scars that distort the soundscape for ever."

"How's your family?" Söderstedt asked loudly.

"Good, thanks," Andersson said just as loudly, as though he was listening to a Walkman. "Jorjie is almost two now. We've only met in here. Dad in the Kumla Bunker."

"Your son's called Jorjie?"

"He's actually called Jorge. Probably the blondest Jorge on earth."

Söderstedt and Norlander exchanged astounded glances.

"Jorge?" they said in unison.

"After the man who saved my life, yeah. Jorge Chavez. And Paul, after Hjelm. Paul Jorge Andersson. The two policemen who dragged me up from the underworld. Now Jorjie can continue the job. And

87

Lena, of course. She's waiting for me. She's holding me up with her frail arms all the time."

"I've heard everything now," said Söderstedt. "Do you still play darts?"

"Never again," said Göran Andersson calmly.

"Tell us what you know now," Viggo Norlander interrupted.

Andersson turned his clear gaze towards Norlander.

"Wasn't it you who got crucified?" he asked.

Norlander instinctively looked down at the circular scars on his hands. Stigmata.

"Just tell us what you know."

"Not much to say," said Göran Andersson. "Breakfast, back to the books, bang. The feeling of blood running from your ears is a deeply unpleasant sensation. Mystical, almost."

"You have the cell next to Lordan Vukotic, don't you?"

"Had. I think they've shut that section down. I don't know where I'll be tonight."

"What is it you're studying?" Söderstedt asked.

His eyes turned back to the fair-skinned Finland Swede.

"I've noticed a certain discrepancy between your respective interests," he said, good-naturedly.

"You could say that," said Söderstedt, equally good-naturedly.

"Art. Once I've studied art history, I'm going to start painting too. Theory and practice will become one."

88

"You keep yourself to yourself; Vukotic did the same," said Norlander. "Maybe that creates a kind of bond between you. Did you see him this morning?"

"No," said Andersson. "We normally see each other at breakfast, but not today."

"He was seen at dinner at about half four yesterday afternoon. From then until lock-up around three hours later, no one seems to have seen him. Did you see him during that time?"

"You've got to understand, I stay in my cell. That's what I do. I eat in the canteen, I'm let out into the yard for a few minutes, I study in my cell. Nothing else."

Söderstedt looked around. Was he the only one who had felt a slight hesitation in Göran Andersson's reply?

"You didn't answer the question," was all he said.

Andersson was silent. Unmoving. The way that he had waited for his victims. And yet not. He shrugged.

"If I was a different person today, if I wasn't the person I've become, this would've been a bargaining position. Then, my friends, I would've started asking if it wasn't time for release on temporary licence, or at least longer visiting times."

It was silent in the bare little room. Four pairs of police eyes trained on an apparently transformed murderer's.

"But I am the person that I am now," he said. "Just before lock-up, I heard a faint moaning out in the corridor. Short, like something escaping through gritted teeth. I peered out and saw Lordan Vukotic *dragging* himself into his cell."

"What do you mean, 'dragging'?" asked Norlander.

"He glanced towards my cell. His face looked the same as usual, but it was obvious that he was seriously injured. His legs were giving way under him. It was the look of death I saw."

"And you didn't do anything about it?"

"Look, I hate this world. I still don't understand how I could've ended up here. I don't want anything to do with it. If he chose not to report it himself, why should I?"

"You haven't changed as much as I thought," said Söderstedt.

"What's your understanding of why the injured Vukotic was blown up the next day, then?" asked Norlander.

"It's quite obvious," said Göran Andersson, stroking his thin beard. "Someone was covering his tracks."

And what tracks they turned out to be.

At about half five, a joint preliminary report from the forensic technicians and the medical examiner arrived. A long, difficult document came spilling out of the primitive fax machine in the little interrogation room in Kumla prison.

The medical examiner, Qvardfordt, had solved his autopsy puzzle. Viggo Norlander couldn't quite get away from the image of the staring eye in the lump of material which had been scraped down from the wall. It looked accusingly at him while he struggled his way through the medical examiner's report.

"I don't know how they've managed it," he eventually said, "but the fact is, they've worked out that

Lordan Vukotic's spleen was ruptured, his left tibia broken, and both shoulders pulled out of their sockets. In that condition, the explosion must've almost come as a relief."

"So he can hardly have been busy with his own explosive charge under the covers, then," said Bernt Nilsson.

"By no means," said Söderstedt, fishing out the other part of the report, the forensic report. "They've found a microscopic detonation mechanism. Controlled remotely. And the explosives are assumed to have been some kind of solution. Liquid form. Though they don't really know what it is, just that it's extremely volatile."

Four policemen, of different origin and different character, each digested this information.

The stout Viksjö, who evidently had the most well-trimmed digestive system, concluded: "Lordan Vukotic gets a real going-over yesterday evening. He *crawls* back to his cell and skips breakfast *so that no one discovers he's had a thrashing.* After that, he's blown into a thousand pieces with the help of a highly sophisticated explosive device. How should we interpret that?"

"It could be banal, some scumbag with good knowledge of explosives beats him up for some trivial reason and then covers up their crime with another crime," said Bernt Nilsson. "Silence the victim, who's also the only witness."

"Or it might not be banal at all," said Söderstedt. "That leaves us with two questions. Why did Vukotic try to cover up the fact that he'd been battered? And why was he killed, despite his silence?"

"He's got great backing in here, after all," said Nilsson. "He's Rajko Nedic's right-hand man, he's got at least three thugs from the former Yugoslavia as protection. Why didn't he turn to them?"

"Because he was hiding his injuries *from them*," said Norlander, nodding. "Why?"

"Because he's talked," said Söderstedt, nodding. "He's been tortured and squealed."

"On Nedic," said Viksjö, also nodding.

Eventually Bernt Nilsson also joined in, completing the nodding quartet.

"And that's what we weren't meant to find out. That's why he was wiped out so thoroughly. But they underestimated our technical competence."

"So why use such a sophisticated and clearly *expensive* explosive?" asked Söderstedt.

"If it's that *small* — highly effective liquid and microscopic detonation device — then it's presumably the only thing you can get into a high-security prison. Still, even now it should be impossible to smuggle a hydrogen bomb in behind the walls."

Söderstedt sighed and waved the fax.

"I can't help quoting our chief forensic technician Brynolf Svenhagen: 'Pearls before swine.'"

CHAPTER
EIGHT

Chief Forensic Technician Brynolf Svenhagen had a daughter. This daughter's name was Sara. Sara worked for CID's child pornography division. The child pornography division was, for the moment, unstaffed. Unstaffed didn't mean that no one was working, however. Working was precisely what Chief Forensic Technician Brynolf Svenhagen's daughter was doing.

Though she was working from home.

She had told her colleagues Gunnar Nyberg and Ludvig Johnsson, friends since childhood (and she quoted herself in the gloomy dusk): "I'm just going to relax. Unwind. There's been a lot on for a bit too long now." The last part was true, the first false. She had lied. All the same, it was a white lie.

She ran her hand over her newly cropped blonde hair, clicking away with the mouse. She was connected to the central police computer. The intranet. She would be working for hours yet. She knew herself that well.

Though she didn't *recognise* herself.

Suddenly, though not for the first time, she caught sight of her reflection in the computer screen. Yet again, her instinctive reaction was to think that she had ended up in the "Favourites" folder in Internet Explorer, landing on yet another paedophile site.

Reflected in the screen, she saw a young boy.

She stood up and started wandering around her little flat on Surbrunnsgatan. Was that why she had chopped off her long, golden hair?

To look more like a paedophile victim?

"What got into your head?" as Gunnar Nyberg had suddenly blurted out as they drank coffee and basked in the June sun at Annika's Café & Restaurant.

Yeah, Sara, what got into your head? she asked herself. Identification with the victims? Did your subconscious feel like you were just too far removed from the horrible reality of it all? That you were working from a distance? That the computer, and the incessant access to work it offered, meant that you found yourself in eternal cyberspace? That the computer itself gave the awful reality of paedophilia an air of unreality, and so a redeeming feature?

The distance *was* great. She herself had had a calm, tranquil, grey, patriarchal childhood in the suburbs, a childhood with a police-related slant. Brynolf, cut from a traditional cloth, had boldly drilled his children not to speak four different languages by the time they were four, to compose symphonies by eight, or be tennis pros by the time they were twelve, but in forensic methods. He would let the children into a room, meticulously cleaned by his wife, get them to look around, and then send them to the toilet where they would wait to be let out. Something in the room would be different when they came back out of the toilet, and

94

the children had to use empirical evidence and logic to work out what. These had actually been the only times that Sara had seen her father truly happy. Otherwise, he was neither good nor bad, neither warm nor mean, just austere. Like an old-fashioned patriarch.

No, the reason she pushed herself so hard couldn't really be found in her upbringing. Still, she was even less convinced by the genetic explanation. Of course there wasn't any kind of police gene in her, driving her towards the answers. There wasn't any compassion gene which meant that she shared the pain of the abused children, either. And of course — even though it was something that was claimed on a daily basis in the context of public debate — there wasn't any paedophile gene which caused whole family trees of men to expose themselves to children or sniff well-used nappies. A sickness, yes — a grotesquely sick world within a world. Genetic, no — there was no paedophile gene. She refused to believe that.

No, she understood the reason she worked her arse off about as much as she understood why she had suddenly chopped her hair off. The only thing she knew was that she had to keep going, that she had to get to the bottom of things whatever the cost, that she couldn't let her own or anyone else's laziness be the reason for any single child being sexually abused, if it could have been prevented. That was her driving force. Every little omission amounted to guilt, and that was why she took on an increasingly superhuman workload. "There's been a lot on for a bit too long now" was a statement that was more than true.

She had started having a recurring nightmare. It wasn't something she could share with anyone. Not her boss, the party animal Detective Superintendent Ragnar Hellberg; not with her mentor, the always running Ludvig Johnsson; not even with the new colleague she got on so well with, teddy bear Gunnar Nyberg.

No, she couldn't share it.

She would never be able to share it.

It's night. A woman is lying in a faintly lit hospital room. She's alone. Her face is in darkness. Only her large stomach is illuminated. It's as though it's glowing with its very own internal light. She can almost see something moving inside, she imagines she can see life itself. The sanctity of life. She strokes her stomach gently. Suddenly, it's no longer glowing. The delicate flame of life goes out. A shadow falls over her. At the same time, she feels a prolonged spasm of pain. She tries to cry out, but can't. She has no voice. Just the shadow which turns into a body, into a man, a penis. The pain increases, turns into one long contraction. And at the same time, the exact same time, the shadow forces its way into her. *She's raped while she's giving birth*. That alone would be enough to make her die several times over, but it *isn't* enough. The next insight is worse. *It's not her he's after*. She's just an instrument, an obstacle that needs to be overcome on the way. And then, just as his penis reaches the child, just as he's about to achieve that second penetration, she dies.

That's when she wakes up. At the moment of death.

She closed her eyes.

Where does lunacy start?

When has someone simply seen too much?

She hadn't even turned thirty yet, but she had seen everything.

An already shaky relationship had been obliterated as soon as she had been promoted and snatched up by Ludvig Johnsson and his paedophile hunters. Since that, there hadn't been anyone. She didn't even know if she believed in that kind of tenderness any more. She lived alone. Wanted to live alone.

She stood for a moment by the window facing out onto Surbrunnsgatan. The lights were going on in the building opposite. Private bubble after private bubble was being exposed.

Sara Svenhagen didn't want to see them.

It was like they weren't enough.

She returned to the computer, briefly glimpsing the young boy reflected in the screen, switched from the intranet to the Internet and clicked on "Favourites".

In this folder she had saved the addresses of hundreds of paedophile websites, each one worse than the last.

She looked at the clock. Two minutes twelve seconds left.

If it was right. If she really had cracked the code.

It was a Swedish website. She had found out that it existed through the Japanese police force. It revealed itself for ten or so seconds once every other week, before disappearing again without a trace. No policeman had ever been able to get hold of it, but everything indicated that the website was hiding an address book, the addresses of a huge international network of members who sent pictures to one another. If this was right, then an extensive list of addresses would appear on this page which, in turn, would appear at 19.36.07 on Thursday 24 June. In one minute and forty-eight seconds. One click on a website which would be visible for fifteen seconds at most, and the whole list would be downloaded.

The mysterious code had been discovered during a raid on a paedophile in Nässjö. It had ended up with her because it was thought to be uncrackable; she still didn't have party detective Hellberg's full confidence. Party-Ragge's. So she had been working in secret a lot. Never claiming any overtime. Spending hours and hours on cracking the code. And suddenly, she had done it. She thought. She hoped. It was quite a simple code. Once you found the key, the door opened wide. And from the cryptic Nässjö code, a Web address and time point emerged.

Not even Johnsson and Nyberg knew what she was working on.

19.35.40. Twenty-seven seconds.

She was completely motionless, her index finger resting perfectly still on the mouse button. It was now or never, there wouldn't be a second chance. It would be gone for good.

She could see the vague outline of a stomach, glowing from within.

She had entered the address. Quickly moved the cursor back to where she needed to click. Everything was ready. The clock was counting down. 19.36.00.

Seven, six, five, four, three.

Two.

One.

Zero.

Enter.

Then there it was. The home page. Simple. Impenetrable.

But with one line selected.

She moved the cursor to it. Click.

Save to disk?

Yup.

The hard drive whirred gently. She had it.

And then the page was gone.

Sara Svenhagen leaned back in her chair. She smiled faintly. She could allow herself that.

A large stomach gleamed fluorescent in the darkness.

CHAPTER
NINE

Up and down, back and forth, over and over.

Like the pendulum of a clock. Tick-tock.

Five or six boys aged about ten or twelve were skateboarding in Björns trädgård, a park in Södermalm. Two hardened police officers watched them from a bench.

The last time Paul Hjelm had been in Björns trädgård, it had been the city's shabbiest, most run-down public space. A playground for junkies and drunks. Now it was more like an oasis with its elegant little cafe, Viva Espresso, its abundance of greenery, its play area and skateboard ramp. And, soon, Stockholm's first mosque.

You really could talk about a metamorphosis there, Paul Hjelm thought.

And not only there. The whole area around Medborgarplatsen had changed character. Now it was the beating heart of Södermalm. The district around the crossroads of Götgatan and Folkungagatan was not only the area that newly arrived provincials first made their way to, was not only known as the most dangerous place in Stockholm, but was also the city's most pub-filled area. Within a five-minute radius from

Medborgarplatsen metro station, there were no fewer than sixty-five pubs. People were always hanging around the traditional hot-dog stand on the corner of Götgatan and Tjärhovsgatan. And opposite, on the other side of Götgatan, on the edge of Medborgarplatsen, the lavish establishment called London New York had a big outdoor serving area. On the other side of Medborgarplatsen, the queue to the always-packed pub with the rather more domesticated name of Schnapps snaked.

In other words, there must have been plenty of witnesses out there when twenty men came rushing out of Kvarnen, some ten or so metres away. The hardly stimulating task of finding them had been delegated to the Södermalm local police.

On the other hand, though, what would these potential witnesses actually have seen? A bunch of men charging out of the pub and running away? That wasn't anything especially remarkable in these parts. The local police had a fairly hopeless search ahead of them.

Hjelm sighed gently and tried to count the people. From the bench where he was sitting, on the edge of Björns trädgård, he managed to count around fifty.

With the summer solstice just a few days before, it was still light. It was eight at night, and the sun was still shining as though it was the middle of the day. The air felt fresh, the summer-evening scents not differing in any tangible way from those in the city's more rural districts. Birds were singing cheerfully and clearly. Rays of sunshine glittered on the windows of the buildings along the neighbouring street. Small children were still playing enthusiastically, watched over by drowsy parents. And the skateboarders would probably be there until darkness fell.

There was nothing to suggest that, less than a day earlier, a man had bled to death just a few metres away.

The general public's fear of the Kvarnen Killer was limited, despite the efforts of the tabloids to whip up a panic. Presumably people had simply had enough of panicking.

It had been a violent year so far. The acute stages of NATO's long bombing campaign against Yugoslavia, eighty days of ceaseless bombardment, were over. War from a distance. The ethnic cleansing in Kosovo had finally come to an end; the refugees had started to return to their mine-strewn homeland. Two American high-school students had celebrated Hitler's birthday by cutting down their classmates with all manner of firearms. The parents had been *bewildered*. In Sweden, a twenty-two-year-old in Örebro had been exposed as one of the country's worst ever paedophiles. Videotapes of rapes, an enormous collection of films and pictures and Web contacts. Within a few days, the trial would begin, but it was already clear that he would be sentenced to psychiatric care. Then there was the police murderer in Malexander. All three of the perpetrators had finally been caught. Three young men with Nazi sympathies who, cold as ice, had executed two policemen from Östergötland. One of them was a war veteran from Bosnia. Another had topped his acting career with a couple of shots to the back of a policeman's head. He had been in Lars Norén's deftly staged play *Seven Three*, where three Nazis advocated ethnic cleansing from the stage before the eyes of the powerless author, leading to a heated debate in the cultural pages of the papers. But hardly anywhere else. Not before the country united in horror over the Malexander murders, and placed the blame on the theatre.

A strange year.

Kerstin Holm turned towards him on the park bench.

"What did your family say?" she asked.

"They're at the cottage out on Dalarö," Hjelm replied. "I can paint the town red all night if I want to. Party all night with an old flame in Kvarnen."

"All in good time," Kerstin Holm smiled. "How are they?"

"Good. Danne's finally over the worst of his teenage madness. He's seventeen and wants to join the police, strangely enough. I'm hoping it'll pass. Tova's fifteen, and absolutely unbearable. Every cell in her body is unbearable."

"And . . . Cilla?"

Paul laughed and looked at Kerstin. She peered back. He could see the thin rings around her irises, giving away her contact lenses. Her upper lip, bulging like she had been mistreated. Though only by the tobacco company, Gothia Snus AB.

"Good, thanks," he said. "She's ward sister now, rehab at Huddinge hospital. Normal hours. And enjoying a long holiday at the minute, thanks to all the leave they owed her."

They sat in silence a while. The past moved like a ghost between them. Though it was like Little Ghost Godfrey. Or Casper. The world's friendliest ghost.

It was a time they both looked back on with an open heart. And completely without bitterness.

Eventually, Kerstin Holm said: "Shouldn't we feel guilty about not focusing one hundred per cent on finding the Kvarnen Killer?"

"We have been, by the book. We can just look at this as . . . a private investigation. Outside working hours."

"We don't dare put it down as overtime, then?"

"That depends on the result, I guess."

Kerstin sighed deeply, and stretched her arms out sideways. Her fingertips grazed the hair at the nape of his neck.

"Let's just hope there won't be any more violence this summer," she said, without seeming to believe her own words.

"We'll have to see whether the Police Olympics'll be enough to discourage them. World Police and Fire Games. You know there's going to be a party in a couple of days? You'll probably get to meet all of the others there, from the A-Unit."

"How embarrassed should I be that I don't really get the appeal of these games?"

"Very. You're police, you know."

They laughed for a moment.

"It's an American thing," Hjelm eventually said. "The world's police, prison guards, customs officers and firemen are getting together to compete against each other for the first time in Europe. The boxing in particular should see a lot of criminals in the spectators' seats. Watching the law going at one another."

A chilly breeze blew life into the evening. It quickly turned cold, sobering their thoughts. Focusing them on the task.

"It's probably time to say what we've been thinking," said Kerstin.

When the one concrete bit of action — picking up Eskil Carlstedt — had gone down the drain, there hadn't been much left to do. The barmaid, Karin Lindbeck, had produced a drawing of the Kvarnen Killer that seemed more reliable than the three earlier attempts. That was the one they had chosen to give to the press. It was already in the papers. There wasn't much more they could do at that point. All of the city's police districts were busy conducting their own separate hunts for Hammarby fans. The fate of the Kvarnen Killer was now in their hands. It was very much a regional case.

They had been listening to the interview tapes all afternoon. What was the sequence of events that was emerging? They had both been drawn to the same sections.

"How many parties are actually relevant?" asked Hjelm. "Is it two or three?"

"Instinctively, I'd say three," said Holm. "But the third is too vague. Still, I'm wondering what Per Karlsson was up to. He was reading Ovid and didn't see anything, but all the same, it turns out he saw a lot. He wasn't focusing on the book, that's clear. The only

105

thing he *didn't* see and *didn't* hear was the gang sitting closest to him, talking English right in his ear. It's not enough, though. He didn't run off after the killing so I'd say two. Two parties."

"Two gangs. One's sitting by the door, at the table next to the wall. The other's sitting at the middle table, furthest away against the opposite wall."

"The first consists of five 'macho homos', 'skinheads who've passed the age limit', 'thoroughbred Swedish bodybuilders' you'd expect to be 'the rowdy kind'. The other consists of 'three or four Slavs' or 'probably South Mongolians' having an English 'multicultural exchange' with a Swede who was presumably the man that waved his police ID to get out."

"And in this English-speaking gang, there's 'distrust', they're 'trying to agree on something', possibly about a 'meeting place'. Three or four 'southern Europeans' in discussion with a — real or fake — Swedish policeman. Nothing suggests they were aware of the five thoroughbred Swedes in the other gang who seemed to be watching them. Our friend Hard Homo said of our friend with the book: 'A group of macho gays were staring at him the whole time,' but the waitresses said: 'They weren't staring at him. Further away.' And then, further away, we have our little 'multicultural exchange'."

"And then there's the headphones."

"Then there's the headphones. And then the killing takes place. They react instinctively, realise the place is going to be crawling with police soon. So they run. Both groups blend into the Hammarby fans running

106

off. One man from each group stays behind. Should we assume that the 'policeman' stays behind so that he's not seen running off with the 'Slavs'? In that case, it's highly likely that he really is a police officer. Or someone who's aware of police work at least. He knows that the time around the killing is going to be looked at from all possible angles so he aims to slip out towards the end, when the 'Slavs' have already gone. But he's a little too late. The doormen have suddenly realised that something more dramatic than keeping the place free of 'immigrants' is required of them. So he weighs up the situation for a moment. Is it worth showing his police ID to get out? Or is it better to stay and make up a nice excuse? Act like a policeman should act, and take control of the situation. From his decision, maybe we can draw the conclusion that there's a lot at stake for him. He doesn't dare take the risk of being identified. He waves his ID in front of the stressed doormen and slips out. No one can identify him. He made the right choice."

"One man from the thoroughbred Swedish gang stays behind. He's ready to leave like the others but he's told to stay behind. Why? What was your first impression when you saw Eskil Carlstedt?"

Hjelm thought about it. The man with the shaved head and thin blond moustache walking into the interrogation room. He was in his thirties, wearing quite a stylish pale suit with a yellow tie; he was a real powerhouse. Hjelm wondered whether his jacket sleeves were hiding a range of prison tattoos.

"Mmm," he said. "Eskil Carlstedt was bait. All five of them probably looked just as dodgy, but Carlstedt must've been the only one without a criminal record. By staying behind, he drew our attention away from the fact that the gang, when you think about it, were acting damn suspiciously. They weren't talking, they weren't drinking; they were just staring, listening. It was real quick thinking. For a moment, he got us to believe that they were a group of salesmen out drinking and chasing women, even listening to a demo tape. And that was all he needed to go up in smoke, and with him the rest of his band of thieves. He was pretty experienced for someone without a record."

"They had the entire night to go through their strategy. Carlstedt's kept behind by the police, gives a short statement saying he didn't see anything, tells them his name and address and comes back to us in the morning. By then, his statement has changed. The whole thing was well rehearsed. The only time he slipped up was when we mentioned the earphones. But he dealt with that nicely."

"The four names he gave for his friends were pure fabrications. Not one of them exists in the real world. He was looking at his watch the whole time, they were going to meet and disappear together. He just needed to get out of the police station and then that was the end of it. So he was playing along, went to the police artist and put together a fake drawing, left four false names that he knew wouldn't be checked out for several hours, and left. And now the whole gang is lying low together somewhere. What for?"

108

"What we can say is that both parties were acting extremely professionally. But we can also say that they haven't actually done anything illegal. Not really. Not like killing someone with a beer mug."

They both stood up from the park bench. A hint of dusk had begun to fall over Björns trädgård, the playground had started to empty. Only the skateboarders remained, continuing to arc up and down, back and forth, over and over. Like the pendulum of a clock.

"Should we check, then?" asked Paul Hjelm. "If all of this is just a figment of our imagination, two frustrated CID officers who aren't happy with it being *just* a pub brawl?"

"Or if we're actually on the way to becoming CID officers again," Kerstin Holm nodded.

It wasn't far to Kvarnen, one of Sweden's last remaining beer halls. It had turned ninety the previous year. Never before had it been a murder scene, though it had been on the verge of it.

It had been built during the first decade of the twentieth century as a replacement for Källaren Hamburg, the legendary tavern where those sentenced to death ate their last meal and had a last drink for the road before they were taken up to the gallows in Johanneshov.

The same had happened with Anders Lundström from Kalmar.

The doormen recognised them and let them past the nonexistent queue of "difficult immigrants". The inner door opened and they entered the pub. The waitresses nodded briefly at them.

Sure enough, the pub was packed. Outside, it was a beautiful summer's evening, but inside, in the smoke-filled pub, it was jam-packed. They glanced to the right, towards the table where Eskil Carlstedt and his friends had sat. They looked over to the bar, where Anders Karlström from Kalmar had met his unexpected fate. They peered over to the middle table, where Per Karlsson and Ovid had sat. And they pushed their way over to the table against the opposite wall, the table where the multicultural exchange had taken place.

A group of a dozen twenty-year-olds sat squashed together around the table. They were laughing, smoking and drinking beer. They looked like they were having fun. Enjoying being in a place that was the object of so much rumour and speculation in the media. The centre of the action.

Hjelm guessed that seventy-five per cent of them dreamt of being TV presenters. The national average.

"Hi," he said, kneeling down.

They stared at him, instinctively moving their legs out of the way. He descended among the dewy young women's legs and bunched-up miniskirts. Their protests subsided as he ducked into the darkness under the table; he presumed that Kerstin had shown her ID.

Open sesame.

He crept further under the table. He hadn't needed to. A small gadget was stuck near the very edge of the table, so small that he had gone past it without noticing.

He pulled it loose, crawled out, heaved himself to his feet, brushed the ash and snus tobacco from his knees, and turned towards Kerstin Holm.

He waved the little microphone before her eyes.

And the figment of their imagination fell dead to the floor of Kvarnen.

CHAPTER
TEN

They're lying in bed. The sunset is reflected on their young bodies, still damp with sweat. It's the calm after the storm. The desire has subsided but it will wake again soon, it's never far away. It will always be there. Not even death can keep them apart.

But it's also the calm *before* the storm. That's how the saying really goes. And now, for them, the storm really is approaching.

The hurricane.

That's the insight that slowly begins to spread through them. The calm, the always temporary calm, gives way.

Trembles of unease ripple through their nakedness.

He sits up on the edge of the bed. He is pale, she is dark, and she can see, at that moment she can see where his mind has gone. Again. She leans over to him, her breasts softly grazing his back. Slowly and carefully, she pulls him back from the shadow of death. Like he has done so many times for her.

She knows that he can see the school playground. She knows that he has stepped out of himself. She knows that he can see a boy, a young, pale boy, lying on the desolate football field. She knows that he can hear

"If you get up, we'll hit you." One after another, they go forward. Stand there a moment. Peering down at him. Then they piss on him. One by one. Only the boys at first. The girls are in the background, giggling, thrilled. The brave ones leave, though none of them are brave enough to tell. It'll just keep going on. And on. Still, no girl has done it yet. A comfort in his distress. Then the last floodgate opens. A girl comes forward. She is wearing a skirt. She has already taken her knickers off, she is holding them in her hand. She squats over him, carefully. Slowly pisses on his body. She is dark.

He feels something soft against his back, and it brings him to his senses. He lifts off, floats, soars ahead. He is sitting on the edge of a bed, flying. He puts his hand behind his head and reaches her. Lets his hand move through her dark hair.

And she can smile again.

"I was hurt," she says, trying to stop herself from crying. "I was dead. You brought me back. You know that."

They sit there, their limbs strangely twisted. They're a sculpture. For ever united. By an eternal love.

"What do you want?" she asks.

It's a ritual. Neither can depart from it. He smiles, and says: "I want to sit on a veranda, reading. It'll be warm, but raining gently. The rain'll be pattering nicely on the roof of the veranda, and when I look up from the book, I'll see the steam rising between the raindrops."

She smiles. She knows it so well. She says: "D'you know what I want?"

He laughs. "No idea."

"I want to hear the dolphins singing. I want to see the foam along the edge of the pale blue water. I want to see the dolphins playing in freedom. I want to hear them talk to one another when there's no trainer there to drill them."

He turns round and gives her one last big embrace, stands up, pulls on his clothes and walks over to the backpack lying on the floor. He looks down into it.

She stands up too, slowly pulling on her clothes, going over to him and wrapping her arms around him. She too looks down into the bag.

Inside, there are two black, knitted balaclavas and two black pistols.

He bends down and pulls the zip shut.

Then he takes the car key from the desk, throws it up into the air, catches it and looks into her eyes.

"Let's go and arrange that, then," he says.

CHAPTER
ELEVEN

The man stands completely still. He has given up everything, and is standing completely still next to his car. In his hand he is holding a briefcase. It hangs, motionless, by his side.

It's dark but warm. As though the summer day was lingering behind.

As though there was still light.

Summer has hardly begun but already the nights are growing longer. It's Midsummer's Eve, he thinks, it has been for a few hours. The week began with the summer solstice, and it's ending with Midsummer's Eve.

What a way to celebrate the longest days of the year.

No lilies or columbines, as the folk song goes; no roses or salvia, no sweet mint.

No heart's delight.

All he really wants is to go to a place where the winters are shorter. That's all he wants.

That's what he is waiting for.

He stands completely still, looking out into the darkness.

It's not quite pitch black, it never is at this time of year. Not really, really dark. He can make out the shapes of old sheds and rusty, wrecked cars as he gazes out along the road in the cluttered industrial estate.

And right then, that's when he hears it.

At the same moment he hears the muffled explosion, he knows that it's all gone to hell. Everything. His entire life has gone to hell.

He stands completely still.

So that's how fragile it was.

The dividing line so thin.

The balance so delicate.

By the time he hears the third round of shots, he's sitting in his car. He sighs and drives away.

It's already too late.

Six men in a van. A metallic-green van parked up against an old industrial shed, windows glistening with condensation from their heavy breathing and involuntary perspiration.

It's a wait like they've never known before.

The night drags on.

Five of the men are moving slightly. Moving nervously. One of them picks non-stop at his thumb, one licks his lips so often he'll develop a cold sore; one pinches his nose, one bounces his knee up and down, one chews his thumbnail.

But one of the men is completely still. He is squatting down in the back of the van. It's as difficult as stretching; after a few minutes, the thigh muscles normally begin to twitch. But not this man's. He is completely still. In his left hand, his sub-machine gun is resting against his thigh, the barrel pointing up towards

116

the roof of the van. In his right hand, he's holding something that looks like a miniature calculator. Thin, black, and with a single, slightly raised button. A red one.

He looks at his watch and then surveys his men. He can see them sharply outlined in the faint darkness. Sweat is running from their thick, black winter hats, down over their faces. All are wearing these black hats apart from him; he is wearing a gold-coloured one. It sits, crown-like, on top of his head.

The sweat is flowing, but their faces are controlled. Tense, strained, concentrated. Everything as it should be.

"Three out," he says.

The three men in the back of the van transform their black winter hats into balaclavas, pulling the thick material down over their faces. Their eyes shine bright against the black. They take their weapons off safety and climb out of the van. Pressing close to the wall of the shed, their sub-machine guns raised. Clouds of steam rise from their masks.

He watches the movement of the second hand. Its calm, unaffected leaps. Step by step by step. Minutes of constant watching.

The clock strikes two. One second past. Two, three.

There, he hears the first sound of the engine.

It grows louder. Eventually, he nods slightly and pulls the golden balaclava down over his face. The two men in the front do the same, though theirs are black.

Behind the shed, headlights appear, illuminating the road. Only faintly at first, then more and more brightly.

Just as the front of the black Mercedes appears from behind the shed, he presses the red button.

It's not like an explosion, more like the car is lit up from within. An inward flash of light, strangely soundless.

The Mercedes rolls on for a few metres. Stops.

The three men by the shed are already on their way over to it.

The three still inside the van climb out. One of them is wearing a golden balaclava. He is the golden one and knows it.

When he gets there, the situation has already been determined.

The car is giving off a little smoke, no fire. Two men are standing on either side of it, leaning over the car. They're frisked, sub-machine guns pointing at them. Inside the car, a man. In the back seat. He is dead, his body blown to pieces. A chain coils from his wrist to a briefcase. It's intact. Explosion-proof. The golden one nods to the masked man next to him — the broadest of them all. The broad man takes out some bolt cutters, leans into the car and cuts the chain. He pulls back out of the car-turned-hearse with the briefcase in his hand.

The golden one nods to the broad man and looks fixedly at the men leaning over the car. Both have bleeding faces. Through the cloud of smoke, he catches the eye of the one furthest away from him. Blood is running down his dark face as he stands by the passenger side of the car. A dark, cold gaze which doesn't waver. A gaze the golden one has seen before, a gaze he himself wants. The gaze of a man who has

118

killed so many times that nothing else has any value any longer. The gaze of a man who knows he's going to die, who isn't afraid of it, and who just wants to take as many with him to the other side as possible.

Two sub-machine guns are pointed at the man by the passenger side of the Mercedes, two at the man by the driver's side. When the driver turns round, he looks like the passenger. Just like him.

The same cold gaze.

The golden one gestures with his gun and the broad one moves in front of the car, standing in its headlights. He lifts the briefcase up and opens it. The sub-machine gun hangs from a strap around his neck. He looks down into the case, then up again. Disappointment shines in his eyes.

"What the fuck is this?" he asks.

The golden one goes over, the shortest of the masked men with him. Three pairs of eyes gazing down into an open briefcase.

A momentary lapse of concentration.

In the briefcase, there is a key and a two-way radio, each in an individual holder. There is also a piece of paper. The golden one grabs it.

When he looks up again, the man on the passenger side of the car has a pistol in his hand. He shoots behind him, over his shoulder. The shot hits the man behind him in the face, just where the two white holes are gleaming in the black balaclava. For a moment, they gleam red instead. Then they gleam no more.

Never more.

It all happens in slow motion. The man by the driver's seat also conjures up a weapon, shooting in their direction. Misses. The sound of sub-machine guns rings out.

The broad man reacts instinctively. He doesn't have time to reach for his gun. Instead he runs, both hands grasping the briefcase. He is aiming for the nearest shed. It's just three metres away. Two. He feels the pain in his back. One metre. None. He is behind the shed. When he falls, he feels that the pain is gone. He doesn't feel anything at all. The last thing he sees is the briefcase, lying on the asphalt in front of him. It's covered in blood.

Then he sees nothing more.

And so, the summer evening is shattered. As though it exploded, as though the whole summer had been blown up into a thousand pieces.

Not much more fire is exchanged. Four sub-machine guns against two pistols. The golden one thinks to himself that the routine of war doesn't count for so much after all. Both of the men by the car are soon lying on the ground, motionless.

A moaning cuts through the night. When he turns round, he sees another of the masked men on the floor, shot. He watches him tear off the black balaclava, howling. His face is purple. His clothes are slowly turning red around his left shoulder. The golden one bends down over him and makes a gesture to the short one.

The short one heads off in the direction the broad man ran. Turns the corner by the shed. Stops dead.

Sees him lying in a pool of his own blood. Sees the pool of blood in front of him. Sees a rectangular island outlined against the blood.

The shape of a briefcase.

And beyond this, bloody footprints growing fainter until they're swallowed up by the night.

The short man swears. He follows the tracks until they disappear, gazing out into the night. Nothing anywhere. Just the pale, summer darkness. He charges around for a while, his gun raised. It's pointless. The briefcase is gone.

By the car, the injured man is shouting. His sweater is almost completely red. The golden one looks down at him, closes his eyes, and then presses a thick strip of tape over his mouth. The injured man's eyes widen fiercely. It looks as though they're about to burst out of their sockets.

The short man is next to the golden one. He has taken his black balaclava off. His face is pale. He shakes his head.

"It's gone," he says.

"What the fuck are you saying?"

"Esse's dead and the briefcase is gone. Someone's made off with it."

"Who?! Fucking hell! Spread out, get looking!"

There are only three of them now. Three people can't spread out especially well. Far in the distance, they hear the sound of a car starting. They realise that it's too late.

The golden one stops. Stands completely still. It couldn't go wrong.

It had gone wrong in several places, how the hell was that possible?

The short man passes him. He moves determinedly towards the still-smoking car. When he passes the golden one, he says: "Maybe we've still got a chance."

He bends down to Nedic's man, lying on the passenger side of the car. The man is coughing up blood, strange phrases in a strange language coming from his mouth.

"Frequency?" the short one asks in English, pressing the barrel of his gun to the man's forehead.

The man laughs. He laughs blood. The last thing he says is: "Fuck you, asshole!"

He gets a bullet in the face.

The short one looks up at the golden one's smoking gun. He goes pale, stares at him, shocked. He stands up. Regains his wits. Stands there thinking.

"The paper," he eventually says.

The golden one nods. He had forgotten about the piece of paper in the briefcase. Yet another mistake.

The golden one unfolds the paper. On it is a series of numbers.

The short one nods energetically.

"See," he says, "we're not completely screwed."

The golden one looks around. Nods briefly. He and the short one load the injured man into the van.

The golden one thinks about a conversation he had recently — in prison, with a murderer studying art. About the fabulous difference between theory and practice. He feels like a failure. Stands there for a few minutes for no particular reason. Then, he lifts his golden balaclava from his face and jumps into the van.

In the beginning there were six. Now, three and a half.

Though the others are nobodies, the golden one thinks, pulling himself together.

That's what counts, after all.

A rusty old Datsun is already on the motorway. It is filled with a flickering mixture of fear and elation. He is driving terribly. It's lucky there are no other cars around. It's early in the morning on Midsummer's Eve, probably the quietest day of the year. Usually.

This year it wasn't so quiet.

He is pale, she is dark, and he turns towards her. He can see that her wonderful legs are shaking. He lays a hand on her knee. Now his hand is shaking, too.

"Shit," she's saying. "Shit, shit, shit. Did you see? Shit, did you see?"

He nods, and his eyes move down her legs to the floor. To the bag resting by her feet. Two balaclavas and two pistols are sticking out of it.

Unused.

"We didn't do anything," he says. "They did it themselves."

"Shit," she says.

They're silent for a moment. Recovering. His gaze wanders, moving from the bag back up to her knees and further. To her lap.

To a briefcase, dripping with blood.

He can't hold it in any more. He lets go of the wheel. The car sails left and then right across the lane.

"Jesus Christ, we did it!" he shouts, putting his arm around her and giving her a kiss.

"Shit!" she shouts, raising her arms to the roof of the car.

CHAPTER
TWELVE

The porn police were wandering around in the clear morning light. The asphalt was covered with a layer of scented dew. It isn't often that dew has a scent, but on that morning, Midsummer's Eve, you could really smell the dew. Even the porn police had noticed it, though they had other things on their minds.

Their night's work made their uniforms feel like week-old underwear. All that effort instead of just sitting in the staffroom, watching high-quality videos.

The porn police enjoyed watching high-quality videos in the staffroom. So much so that someone on the outside had found out, and this person had told the tabloids. The result? The porn police were given their far from honourable nickname.

Maybe the night's events would wash it away. That's what they were hoping, in any case, as they wandered around in the clear morning light, growing used to the unusual sight which greeted them.

This should be able to wash away even the most stubborn of stains.

It was no later than five, but they had already managed to turn away five or six carloads of their friends from the tabloids. Not without a certain sense of *Schadenfreude*.

They went over to the blue-and-white plastic tape which was surrounding a square of the Sickla industrial estate. Another vehicle was approaching, one with TV 4's colourful logo printed on the side. Behind that, an old red BMW sports car came chugging along.

The porn police went over to the TV 4 vehicle and gestured very clearly that they should leave. The TV 4 people didn't give up easily; there was moment of fuss which ended with someone in the van blurting out their tired but well-known nickname, and the porn police started kicking the van. Eventually, it moved off and parked, slightly ruffled, next to the others in the designated space ten or so metres away. Still irate, the porn police moved on to the BMW behind them. When a short, dark figure stepped out of the car and, without a word, lifted the blue-and-white plastic tape, something inside the porn police snapped. They rushed over and grabbed the dark man in an iron grip.

"What the hell d'you think you're doing, you little Mediterranean shrimp?!"

"You see a nice car, you can be sure there's a spic in it! Clear off! As fast as you bloody can!"

They could already see that the man's mouth was starting to form the ominous words.

"The porn police, I assume," he said.

"Little prick!" the porn police snapped, twisting their grip.

"What are you doing?!" shouted a man dressed entirely in denim, running over from inside the

126

roped-off area. "This is Detective Superintendent Chavez from CID. Let him go immediately."

The porn police let go and dropped back without a word.

"It's not *that* nice a car," said Jorge Chavez, rubbing his upper arms. "Ancient. 1978 model. And I'm not Detective Superintendent."

Yet, he thought. But then, apparently there aren't any porn police.

The denim-clad man held out his hand and said: "Sorry about that. They've had a rough night. I'm Bengt Åkesson, local CID night staff."

Chavez managed to extend his aching right arm to return the greeting.

"Haven't we met before?" he asked.

"We met very briefly on the Power Killer case. I found a Russian called Alexander Brjusov when we busted an illegal poker club."

"Right," Chavez nodded. Åkesson.

He didn't normally forget people.

On the other hand, he hadn't had much to do with people lately. More with his books. After the strange resolution of the Kentucky Killer case, he had studied and studied and was now, theoretically, the most qualified policeman in Sweden. Even in terms of practical experience, there was a lot in his favour, despite all that had happened. All he was missing for a superintendent's job was years. Years *en masse*.

He was still little more than thirty years old.

"Well, Åkesson," he said, "the only thing I know is that I got a confusing phone call in the middle of the night, from Waldemar Mörner, a division head I know from the National Police Board, saying that I had to lead the investigation into, and I quote, 'an unbelievably grim mass murder'. Can you give me any more info?"

"We could always take a trip around the sights," said Åkesson, as they started walking. "A few hours ago, at 03.08 to be precise, we received a call from an old lady who was out walking her dog in the middle of the night. She had a mobile phone with her and she said she was standing in the middle of a slaughter site, that there were bodies everywhere. When we got here, it was already light, and this is what we saw. Five dead. All shot apart from one, who's been blown up. He's in the car here."

Chavez glanced into a burnt-out Mercedes, and regretted that he had wolfed down a quick sandwich on the way over. It felt as though it was just making a brief visit to his stomach. He spent a few seconds trying to prevent its reappearance, and then his professional side took over.

Sure enough, the man in the back seat had been blown up. Chavez didn't want to expand on that observation, the medical examiners could do that. The remains of a chain lay by the man's wrist.

Chavez was content with what he had seen. He looked up and glanced around the surrounding area. Sickla industrial estate. A worn asphalt road. A black Mercedes parked between two industrial sheds. Signs: "Rickard's Auto Repairs" on one of them, and "Sickla Boats and Building" on the other.

He looked further, along the left-hand side of the Mercedes. A man was lying face down in a pool of blood next to the driver's seat. Further away, there was a smaller pool of blood, this one lacking a body. He walked around the car. Here, on the other hand, there were two bodies. The one next to the passenger seat was riddled with bullet holes. The one slightly further away was wearing a black balaclava. Where his eye should have been, a fleshy mass protruded from the socket.

Jesus Christ, Jorge Chavez thought, allowing himself a few more seconds to keep the sandwich in place.

"You said there were five?" he said to Åkesson.

Åkesson rubbed his hand slowly and firmly across his forehead. For the first time, Chavez noticed how pale he was.

"The last one's over here," he said, pointing. "Round the back of Rickard's Repairs."

"A bit of alliteration never goes amiss," said Chavez, following him. Åkesson didn't comment.

They went round the corner of the shed in front of the Mercedes. Lying on the ground was a well-built man wearing a balaclava. He had been shot in the back. In front of him, a still-wet pool of blood had spread out. It was like an irregular frame around a perfect, dry rectangle. Beyond that, ten or so bloody footprints, growing increasingly faint the further they went.

"Hmm," Chavez said, like Sherlock Holmes. All that was missing was him reaching for a magnifying glass from the inner pocket of his worn old jacket.

Chavez and Åkesson exchanged a long look.

"OK then. Have you drawn any conclusions?" asked the former.

"Yeah," said the latter. "They're pretty clear. Make your own, then we'll compare them. Intuitive versus reflective."

Chavez gave Åkesson an appreciative glance, and said: "Two gangs. Those with balaclavas attack those without. The latter arrive in the Merc. They brought something attached to a chain, probably a briefcase. They're on the way to a meeting place, to exchange it for something unknown. Somehow, the robbers blow up the car and take the briefcase. Him with the chain, he's already dead. They cut the chain. The other two get out of the car. From their positions around it, we can assume they were frisked.

"Then it gets tricky. Something happens. The one whose face is oozing out of his balaclava is shot by one of the two next to the car, then they're shot. This lone pool of blood suggests that another of the robbers was shot, but only injured, since he's not here. The fact they've left the bodies behind means they don't care whether they're identified, and that worries me. It's hardly over. Then what? What's the robber behind Rickard's Auto Repairs doing so far from the others? Shot in the back. OK, so he's running off, but gets shot from behind. The shot probably went right through him, through his heart. The blood gushes out forwards, down his chest. OK. Should we assume that this blood pattern in front of him means he had the briefcase? He's running off to get the briefcase to safety when the fight breaks out and then, when it's over, the robbers

130

grab the briefcase from the pool of blood, take a couple of careless steps in the blood and clear off."

Åkesson looked at Chavez, raising his eyebrows in surprise, and said: "Completely agree, I'm afraid. I don't have anything to add. Other than that we've found the tracks of a van that was parked by the nearest shed, Sickla Boats and Building. And," he added, giving Chavez a furtive glance, "that the men from the Mercedes look obviously foreign."

"What about the robbers, then?" asked Chavez, unflustered. "Have you dared look under the balaclavas?"

Åkesson grimaced. "It wasn't pretty," he said. "But yeah, they seem more Swedish . . ."

Chavez looked at him. He seemed to have something else on the tip of his tongue.

"And . . .?" he asked.

"I'm not exactly happy with those 'careless steps in the blood'," Åkesson said eventually. "They don't seem the type to take careless steps in blood."

Chavez nodded for a good while. The weak link in the chain of his story, immediately laid bare. He tried to convince himself: "We can imagine they were in shock, I suppose. There'd been a slaughter. Five bodies. One injured. Three of them friends."

He looked out over the ugly scene. The woman with the dog and the mobile phone had said that she was ringing from the scene of a slaughter. She wasn't wrong, but *something* was. Here and there, the occasional policeman was walking around, looking at the crime scene. Otherwise, it was empty.

"Where the hell are forensics?" he exclaimed.

"On the way from Närke," said Åkesson, shrugging.

"Where?"

"From Närke. It's a province."

"Thanks," said Chavez.

"No doubt they've been flat out with the Kumla explosion. The whole force is there. And your friends."

"My friends?"

"Söderstedt and Norlander. We've been colleagues at local CID for a while."

Chavez allowed himself a smile. He was standing at the scene of a slaughter, smiling.

"Those white, middle-aged men," he said.

Though he was thinking about something else.

Hmm, he thought.

The Kumla explosion, he thought.

CHAPTER
THIRTEEN

In front of us is a house that very few policemen have ever seen. It stands alone by a lake with the unusual name of Ravalen. This lake is in Sollentuna municipality, just over ten kilometres north of Stockholm.

The fact of the matter is, only one policeman has ever seen this modest villa at the edge of the dense forest. And he's no longer a policeman.

He is the owner of the villa. He can say that in all honesty now. The last payment was made to the bank on the same day he retired, something that seemed like more than just a coincidence.

And isn't it him we see there now? Isn't he the sixty-two-year-old man we can see on that hilly little patch of land that's really nothing more than a parenthesis between the lake and the forest? Isn't it him dressed in the Hawaiian shirt and shorts which are a touch too small, pushing a lawnmower up and down the slope like Sisyphus?

Cutting grass is an endless job.

It has a tendency just to grow back again, after all.

As a policeman, this man had a defect. Former policeman, that is. Not a policeman, a *former* policeman. This defect consisted of not being able to tell grass from weeds. Obviously he could have taught himself that *this* little green tangle is grass and *that* little green tangle is a weed, but he had never, ever understood the more fundamental difference between grass and weeds.

Policemen should definitely be able to tell grass from weeds.

Not by looking in a manual which says that certain types of plants are grasses and others are weeds, but by *instinctively* being able to say what distinguishes grass from weeds.

That was where he was lacking.

He paused his Sisyphean work and bent down towards a little clump. He sighed, feeling the green strands between his fingers.

Grass or weed?

He stood up again and swung the lawnmower in an arc around the clump. Since he had retired, he regularly practised the mantra "Live and let live".

Who was he to decide what was grass and what was a weed?

None of his colleagues had ever visited him at home. He was known by most as "the man without a private life" and he never let anyone into his world. When he retired, he had relaxed his principles a touch, and actually spent time — even if it was never at his home — with an old colleague, his former boss, Erik Bruun from Huddinge Police. Bruun had also retired early, but following a heart attack rather than out of . . . necessity. They met once every other week at the

Kulturhus in Stockholm, drinking coffee and playing chess for a few hours. It was Bruun who, once upon a time, had picked out Paul Hjelm from the Huddinge police force to work in the A-Unit.

The pensioner's equally retired wife came out and sat on the porch with a cup of coffee and the morning paper, her hair in curlers. She waved at him. He waved back. Behind her, the waters of Ravalen glittered invitingly in the morning sun.

Everything was all right, it was just a matter of enjoying life. Fixed monthly outgoings at a minimum. Full supplementary pension. A tangible surplus in their account every month. A piece of land which, after thirty-five years, he had only just begun to find attractive. He would even be able to leave a decent inheritance to both of his adult sons.

Rowing boat and fishing rod down on the lake. Sauna on the shore. Binoculars hanging from a nail on a tree up at the edge of the forest. Two decent trips abroad per year. A healthy couple, retired early, who could be confident that they could be full of life for twenty years to come.

Fit as a fiddle, apart from the incontinence.

But that could be managed. The future was theirs.

The former boss of the former A-Unit, former Detective Superintendent Jan-Olov Hultin had, in other words, every reason to be happy with his life. He had no reason whatsoever to grieve over what had happened at the end of his career. He didn't regret a thing. Of course there were one or two less successful decisions to look back on in connection with the

Kentucky Killer, but there was absolutely no misconduct, nothing which should have forced him into early retirement. Nothing of that calibre at all.

He had nothing to dwell on.

There was nothing to dwell on.

He had no reason whatsoever to dwell on it.

And so on.

Day after day.

He paused in his doubly Sisyphean work. He could hear the crunching of gravel up by the garage. Not another grossly criminal estate agent who wanted to "make a fantastic offer" on the place? He pushed the lawnmower aside with a clang and trudged determinedly up the steep grassy slope.

The man who stepped out of the shiny new Saab certainly looked like a grossly criminal estate agent. Neat blond hair in a hurricane-proof style that looked confusingly similar to a toupee, artificially bronzed face, toned body, and even a thick gold wrist chain to go with his stylish, summery suit.

Still, Jan-Olov Hultin's jaw dropped.

"For Christ's sake, JO," the man panted, as though he had galloped the whole way like an elk and not driven in a luxurious, air-conditioned car, "there's something wrong with your phone. Some old cow was going on about how it's been disconnected. Haven't you paid the bill?"

"My name's not JO," said Hultin neutrally. "It's Jan-Olov. And the phone *has* been disconnected. We don't need a phone."

136

"Connect it again, for God's sake," said the bleach-blond man, who *wasn't* a grossly criminal estate agent but Head of Division from the National Police Board, and the Police Commissioner's right-hand man. His name was Waldemar Mörner, a man with a speciality for legendary blunders.

Waldemar Mörner's feet skidded on the gravel, he hopped delicately over the little fence that marked the divide between gravel and grass, and realised that his expensive Italian shoes weren't non-slip. He lost his footing on the dewy grass and suddenly his feet were pointing straight up in the air in an upside-down pirouette. He rolled unstoppingly and with gathering speed down to the porch, where his body hit the steps with a faint thud and his mobile phone flew out of his pocket, up onto the porch, and straight into Hultin's wife's coffee. Mörner got to his feet, bewildered, held out his hand to Hultin's wife, missed her by over a metre, sidestepped the entire porch, fell over the railing and landed, with a splash, in the waters of Ravalen.

Then his phone rang. Mrs Hultin fished it out from her coffee and answered: "Waldemar Mörner's phone. Yes, he'll be here in a minute."

No.

No, that wasn't what happened.

That was just what happened in Jan-Olov Hultin's vindictive mind. But Mörner had actually stumbled when he stepped over the fence onto the grass. He grabbed at Hultin's strong shoulders, keeping himself upright.

"Oops!" he said cheerfully, clapping him on the shoulder. "Good job there are some mainstays left in the force!"

"That's exactly what there aren't," said Hultin neutrally.

He hoped it wasn't obvious that his heart was pounding. At the same time, he knew he didn't need to worry about that. No one had ever looked deep into Detective Superintendent Jan-Olov Hultin's soul. It was so well hidden behind all his neutrality that he sometimes wondered if it hadn't disappeared back there.

It hadn't.

"Yes," said Waldemar Mörner.

The magic word.

"Yes," he continued, still panting. "There are, if you want it. We need you. I've talked the NPC into launching again. We've got a really nasty mass murder on our hands."

The NPC, Hultin thought to himself. Who the hell called the National Police Commissioner, NPC? It sounded like something from an old seventies crime novel. Instead, with emphasis on every syllable, he said: "Launching again?"

"Piling it on again," explained Mörner. "Checking the nets. Pulling out the aces we've got up our sleeves. Changing to winter tyres. Reactivating the potential. Taking our secret weapons off safety."

Hultin managed to keep up with the flood of metaphors. He replied clinically: "The A-Unit?"

138

"Yup," said Mörner, bursting into song with "Born to be Wild".

It was too much. Hultin stared at him blankly.

"In what shape?" he managed to ask. Utterly neutrally.

"In *good* shape," said Mörner, giving him a friendly little punch on his upper arm; against all odds, Hultin managed to ignore it. "In its good *old* shape."

"So its original shape, then?"

"Yep. Who'd dare to upset an old man's calculations?"

"And everyone agreed?"

"Even Chavez happily agreed to give up command. But only to you. Norlander just wants to spend Midsummer's Eve with his newborn daughter. And there's a bit of a question mark around Gunnar Nyberg — it's been going so well with the paedophiles. But he's coming to the meeting at ten, too."

Newborn daughter, thought Hultin. Those two words didn't seem to tally with the name Viggo Norlander. He said nothing. Instead, he looked at his watch. Ten past nine. Not much time to make a decision which would change his life.

"I need to talk to my wife," he said.

"Go for it," said Mörner. "But don't take too long."

"Can I borrow your mobile as well?" asked Hultin, taking it and walking down the slope towards the porch.

He went over to his wife, who listened neutrally — a family trait, apparently — before eventually nodding and putting in a few words. He went into

139

the house to change out of his Hawaiian shirt and too-small shorts into something more respectable, which turned out to be a baggy lumberjacket, a slightly frayed lilac shirt and an ancient pair of gaberdine trousers. The fact was, they were his old uniform trousers. He also phoned Erik Bruun, who listened patiently but by no means neutrally. It wasn't his style. When he eventually responded, Hultin imagined he could see the reddish-grey beard bobbing around the ever-present black cigar, which no heart attack in the world would manage to prise from his jaws.

"For Christ's sake, Jan-Olov. This is what you've been secretly dreaming about for ten months."

"Is it?" Hultin asked sincerely.

"Yes, stop pussyfooting around."

"So I should forgive and forget?"

"Neither. Ignore. To hell with them. It's not about them, it's about you. You've got a lot left to give. And you can start playing football with the veterans again. Just think how many of those ageing strikers have missed having a brute like Wooden-Leg Hultin to deal with. You can start splitting people's eyebrows with your headers again. It'll be like a rebirth."

Hultin's mouth was watering. He thanked Bruun and hung up.

He kissed his wife on the forehead; one of her curlers caught on the collar of his lumberjacket. Mörner untangled it for him.

"That doesn't make a good impression," he said.

"We've got a holiday to Greece booked for the end of September," said Hultin, looking with some surprise at the curler in Mörner's hand.

"No problem," said Mörner, throwing the curler like a champagne glass over his shoulder, opening the Saab's door in a smooth motion and adding: "By then, this little debacle will be dealt with."

As Detective Superintendent Jan-Olov Hultin stepped into the car, a luminous aura followed him.

The aura of a policeman.

CHAPTER
FOURTEEN

First it was French. A long, complicated conversation in French. There was a lot of smiling, a lot of laughter into the phone. The man standing motionless by the closed door, gazing across the large study, thought to himself that even his gestures had become French. He, who spoke two languages at most, had learned to distinguish between languages by the changes in his boss's body language. Long before he heard that a new conversation had begun, his boss's gestures had revealed it to him. The movements had taken on a different tempo now, they were slower but more distinct; slightly abrupt, perhaps. It was obviously a conversation in German. After a few sparing, solemn phrases, the speech took a new turn, which he could see because his chest puffed out, his back straightened and his jaw tightened. Since he realised that it was Spanish now being spoken, the man allowed his gaze to drift across the large study. The conversations in Spanish always took time.

Everyone in their line of business knew about this room. It was here that the big decisions were made, where the large transactions took place. The panoramic window out onto the bay; the large, digital globe on a pedestal next to the L-shaped oak desk; the walls covered in Miró paintings above the high dado rail; the thick Persian rugs on the shiny, mosaic-like parquet floor.

Everything was well known, legendary.

The man by the door knew that he shouldn't have been in this mythical room, that he wouldn't have even been allowed in if the circumstances hadn't been so extreme. The lack of staff was getting acute.

They had known one another for thirty years, came from the same little village in the mountains; they were childhood friends. Still, he had never won the great man's trust, other than as a friend, as a link to the past. Nonetheless, he accepted his role as a reserve without hesitation, his role as a substitute, as a surrogate. Even that was an honour.

He called him "the great man". It was natural. But he never said it aloud. Doing so sounded pathetic, corny. But in his mind, his boss was never called anything other than "the great man". There, it was anything but pathetic.

When the language changed once more, he decided that it was precisely this multilingualism which he admired most of all in his boss — it was there that he was "the great man". This multilingualism was a requirement for his sprawling international business.

On the other hand, there were parts of the business that he just couldn't come to terms with. The fact that the great man knew all too well how he felt about these areas was probably the main reason why he had never

143

been part of the inner circle. Before now, when there was no other choice.

When it was also those parts of the business which had caused the problem.

The language now being spoken was fairly familiar. The gestures had become cockily natural. As though it was his mother tongue.

It was Swedish.

He realised that it was the "security consultants" on the line.

"Yes," the great man said from behind the desk, spinning round in the leather chair to look out of the window. "I understand. And you have no idea where he is? No. OK. That makes the situation unstable to say the least. Yes, the material may well be on the way and then we'll have a real disaster on our hands. So in spite of everything, we've got to trust his greed. It's the most reliable thing we've got. We've got to trust that he's waiting until we've calmed things down. And that means we've got to find the briefcase fast. Number-one priority. Yeah, yeah, full throttle. Speak soon."

The leather chair span 180 degrees. For the first time, his eyes were on the doorway. When the next exchange began, it was finally directed at the man by the door. And the language was that which had, at one point in time, had the courage to call itself Serbo-Croat.

"Ljubomir," said the great man, waving him over. "No trace?"

Ljubomir strode across the large study, meeting the other man's piercing gaze and shaking his head.

144

"And the money's really stuck?" the great man continued.

"Yes. It was probably a mistake letting Jovan open the bank account. Now that he's dead, we don't have either the key or the identification papers. The money's stuck. Unless we rob the bank."

The great man frowned slightly; that didn't bode well.

"We may be childhood friends, Ljubomir," he said softly, "but remember that you should never, and I mean *never*, say what was or wasn't a mistake. That's way beyond your authority. You should just arrange everything I ask. That's your only job."

Ljubomir looked down at the desk.

"Have you got it?" the great man asked.

Ljubomir nodded and placed a backpack on the desk. He opened the zip and pulled out a two-way radio. The great man contemplated it, and said: "Frequency?"

"It's programmed. It's ready to go. Just press the button next to the microphone."

That gaze again. And then, ice cool: "I know how a two-way radio works."

The great man sat quietly for a moment, the radio raised. In the few seconds which followed, Ljubomir imagined that he saw the great man's true essence; it swept across his face like an icy north wind, tightening his features. The man about to speak was someone different. A ruler. A master. The most terrifying adversary you could imagine.

145

He pressed the button and changed languages once more. With clear, almost pedagogic emphasis, the great man began, in Swedish.

"This is a message for the person who stole my briefcase. You know that I will find you, and you know what will happen then. To know *roughly* what will happen requires no more than a minimum amount of imagination. But not even the most well-developed imagination is enough to know *exactly*. So give the briefcase back now. If you think about it, it's in everyone's interests."

Then he switched language once more, and repeated the tirade in English. Word for word.

Ljubomir shuddered.

He hoped it wasn't obvious.

They were in bed again. He was pale, she was dark, and they were finally sleeping.

After the longest night of their short lives, they had fallen asleep in an embrace, still joined, as one. The morning sun was shining through the lowered blinds, and although it was almost thirty degrees in the tiny flat, neither of them had rolled away from the other. They refused to separate.

But soon it would be necessary.

It wasn't what they had planned.

After they had practically danced over the threshold into the room, he had unpacked the champagne, torn off the foil, loosened the wire around the cork and prepared himself. She had gone into the bathroom and carefully cleaned the briefcase. Not a speck of blood could be left behind when they opened it. She came back out and they kissed briefly before she placed the briefcase on the table beside the champagne glasses. He was ready, holding the cork firmly in his right hand.

She lifted the lid of the briefcase.

No bundles of money.

Not a penny.

Only a key and a two-way radio, each in an individual holder.

The champagne cork popped by itself. It smashed the mirror in the hallway. Seven years' bad luck. As though to finish the job, he threw the bottle after it. The neighbours banged on the ceiling.

He cried.

But she thought.

She was already thinking. It had always been her only defence mechanism.

She lifted the key from its little holder, turning it over and over. There was a number engraved on it. 401.

"Safe-deposit box," she said. "Box 401."

"A safe-deposit box, for fuck's sake," he whined. "Where the hell is it, though? Kiruna? Paris? Guatemala?"

"Can you make a copy of it?" she asked, reaching for paper and a pen and jumping onto the bed.

His desperation was knocked off course. He could see the purposefulness in her, the thing which had led them there, and it put a stop to his self-destructive streak. Reorientated it. Towards something constructive. Like it had done so many times before.

"You know I can," he said honestly.

"Can you do it *now*?" she asked, starting to write a list on the piece of paper.

"Yeah," he said. "I can."

"Get going then," she said.

He took the key and went over to the walk-in cupboard where he had set up his workshop. Before he opened the door, he said: "What're you doing?"

"I'm trying to remember all the places he does business. It's our only chance."

He nodded and went into his compact little workshop. She stayed on the bed, writing. They worked like that through the night, each of them busy with their own task. Finally, the key was ready and the list was written. Then they could finally be united. And how they united. It was as though their bodies were meeting for the first time. All they had experienced on the longest night of their short lives took the form of desire. Of love. Love and desire were one and the same.

They fell asleep in an embrace. The list ran through her mind as she slept. All these places where escapism was in easy reach. This endless need for relief, for ecstasy, for expanding the senses. As though the senses we're born with weren't enough. As though their boundlessness wasn't boundless enough. But the demand for a change of circumstances was also endless, and that meant that access was endless, and the circle was complete. The vicious circle. And the person who represented access, the one who made sure that the circle stayed vicious, that was *him*. The centre. The viper. And she's a child again. It's a recurring dream. She knows it in advance, she knows every part of it, every little variation, but she can't stop it. It's as though the dream *has to have its turn*. As though, *for some reason*, it has to have its turn. That little awakening in the midst of sleep. An old, *innocent* dream being interrupted, never to return. One that she can't remember any more. That she won't ever be able to remember again. To begin with, it's just a flutter between the sheets. But then it's eyes, a gaze that belongs to someone else, or rather to no one, no one human. And her legs are forced apart and she doesn't know what is happening, doesn't understand, can't understand, hasn't got any chance of understanding what is being forced into her, can only understand the most basic of things, and that is that her trust has been broken, that trust itself has betrayed her, that the person she should be able to trust most in the world has treated her the worst in the world. And that was only the beginning.

It's only the beginning that she remembers. It's only the beginning that has become a dream. The rest went like clockwork. Became habit. Became the norm. A norm which meant that she was the first to split away from the girls and to piss on the boy on the floor.

All because of *him*. The viper.

And it's then, in the middle of the dream, that the *voice* appears. *That* voice. She got it into her head that suddenly there was speech in the dream, a dream which had always been so horribly silent, but the voice forced its way through the dream, from another place, a dark, dark place, and it was crazy, completely crazy, because when she opened her eyes and managed to orientate

149

herself in the room, she heard that the voice was coming from the briefcase.

She thought she had cleaned all traces of blood from the briefcase.

The voice said: "This is a message for the person who stole my briefcase. You know that I will find you, and you know what will happen then. To know *roughly* what will happen requires no more than a minimum amount of imagination. But not even the most well-developed imagination is enough to know *exactly*. So give the briefcase back now. If you think about it, it's in everyone's interests."

It was only when the message was repeated in English that she managed to stand up and stumble over to the table.

She knew *exactly*. But when she lifted the briefcase above her head to throw it towards the already-broken mirror, she started to think. Her only defence mechanism sprang to life.

He watched her from the bed. Eyes wide open, sheet instinctively drawn up to his chin. A futile defence. A little boy's instinctive defence.

"Was that *him?*" he asked after a moment. "The viper?"

She stood, the briefcase raised above her head. Reflection was fighting against instinct. And won. Eventually, thought won over feeling.

"Yeah," she said, putting the briefcase down on the table. "I think we need to hurry."

He sat on the edge of the bed and started to get dressed.

"Why didn't you smash it?" he asked. "Surely we only need the keys?"

"We can't throw away anything that could be a way out," she said. "We can use that to get in direct contact with him. If we need to."

He nodded, trying to understand. She went back to the edge of the bed and began to get dressed. She picked up the list from the bedside table and tore it in half. She held one half of the paper out to him. He took it from her, and looked at it.

"Do you remember how we'll stay in touch?" she asked.

He nodded.

"No direct contact," he said, pulling her close to him. They were united one final time in the middle of the bed. A long, terrible kiss goodbye. A last moment of direct contact.

All that they meant to one another rushed through them.

All of it hurt.

"Remember why we're doing this," he whispered. "For the dolphins' song."

She smiled, hugging him closer.

"And for the steam rising between the falling raindrops," she said, feeling the tears well up.

They stood in the hallway. It was time. They didn't want to, it didn't feel right. Still, they had no choice.

"Four hundred and one," she said, self-controlled. "If there's no box number 401, it's the wrong bank. Then you don't even need to try."

"Are you taking the briefcase?" he asked.

She nodded. "Pandora's box," she said, smiling wryly.

And so they went out, alone, into the world. As alone as they had sworn they would never be again.

There weren't as many of them as there should have been. It happens, he thought, glancing around the dingy basement. It's not the end of the world, he thought. You had to expect stuff like this. Losses, he thought, pulling off his gold-coloured hat and looking at it. Pawns, he thought. The biggest wins always involved victims. Apparent losses.

Though was Jocke really an *apparent* loss?

Esse was one thing — but *Jocke?*

He pulled on the hat and was crowned in gold once more.

He knew that the midsummer sun was already shining on the other side of the door. But in here, a cool, damp darkness prevailed. No windows, not even a little hole. Just a naked light bulb above a carpenter's bench where the only activity was taking place. In an armchair in the corner, a large man with cropped hair was cleaning a sub-machine gun. Rogge's always cleaning a gun, the golden one thought. If there were any more firefights, he knew he could count on Rogge. Always ready. And on the sofa next to him, Danne. Who he could normally also always rely on. Danne Blood Pudding. His prison name. Dark as a blood pudding. Purple face. How long would they be able to haul him around? The bullet must have gone right through him without hitting any bones or vital organs, but he was still bleeding. Left shoulder out of action. Maybe he would be able to use a weapon again. Not a safe bet.

And then Bullet by the carpenter's bench. The technical genius. Small and compact. Experienced with weapons and cool under pressure. *My man*, he thought, going over to him and placing a hand on his shoulder.

Bullet was hunched over a two-way radio. It was switched on. An oscilloscope lay next to it. Waves of differing shapes danced across the screen. He soldered a circuit card onto the side, turned a knob and the waveform changed shape.

"So we're not completely fucked?" he said to Bullet.

Bullet said nothing, just continued twisting the knob, eventually finding a waveform that he seemed to be happy with.

"Like hell we are," he said eventually. "It'll be fine. Assuming one thing."

"Explain it all now."

"OK. Shouldn't Rogge listen too?"

"He doesn't get anything anyway."

"Listen carefully then," said Bullet, leaning back in his chair. "The set-up was probably like this: they each had a briefcase, each a radio. They didn't trust each other enough to just hand the money over. It's in a safe-deposit box somewhere; we saw the key in the briefcase, didn't we?

"So the idea was probably that they'd contact each other on the frequency written on that piece of paper we got hold of and then, when everything had calmed down, the other person'd tell them which bank the money was in. The radio we saw in the briefcase was a special kind of police radio, I've seen one before. Since we know the frequency, we can find the radio. It's a frequency that's not in general use because they don't want to be overheard. This kind of radio always sends out a faint directional signal, so if we use this little monitoring device, we can track the signal down — and the briefcase, too. Though the signal's so weak that we can only find it if it's no further than ten, twenty kilometres away. I just have to calibrate it, then we can get going."

"And what's the *thing* we're assuming?"

Bullet looked up at him.

"That they haven't chucked the radio," he said quietly.

The golden one could feel himself grimacing.

"And why the hell would they keep it? Surely it's just the key they're interested in?"

"I think," said Bullet emphatically, "they got just as much of a surprise as we did, whoever they are. I think they're gonna have to *search* for the safe-deposit box. And I think they'll keep hold of the radio so that they're not chucking away any chances. Though," he added, "that's just what I think."

"It's good enough for me," said the golden one. "It's normally enough."

Just then, the waves began to dance on the oscilloscope. Bullet gave a start and shouted: "What the fuck, I'm getting something!"

The police radio on the carpenter's bench burst into life.

"This is a message for the person who stole my briefcase. You know that I will find you, and you know what will happen then. To know *roughly* what will happen requires no more than a minimum amount of imagination. But not even the most well-developed imagination is enough to know *exactly*. So give the briefcase back now. If you think about it, it's in everyone's interests."

Then it was repeated in English.

The golden one started to laugh. He laughed loudly for some time. Then he said: "That smooth-tongued bastard. I'm going to blow the fucking tongue out of him. That's a promise."

Bullet looked sceptically at him.

The man sat motionless. Everything had gone to hell. He was trying to make sense of his life. He couldn't, there was no way out. It was meant to happen smoothly, discreetly and silently. Instead, a bomb had gone off. An utterly real, clumsy, extremely visible and noisy bomb. Five dead. He couldn't believe it was true.

All he wanted was to get away to a place where the winters were shorter.

Well, that wasn't strictly true. He also wanted to put away a man no one had managed to put away. Capture the thing that had never let itself be captured.

He looked around the room. An anonymous room. Completely anonymous, in fact. He thought about the word: anonymous. I'm anonymous, he thought. All ties to the past were gone. What he was doing now had *nothing* to do with the past, it was pure future.

And it had gone to hell.

The kitchen table was cheerless and white. Plastic. That would have been impossible before. Now anything was possible. A terrible freedom. Even this was possible.

The man stood up to fetch a cup of coffee. The machine bubbled chaotically, like it did every time its job was done. First chaos, then the great calm.

The calm was death.

He poured the coffee, looking down into the pitch-black brew, as though into the kingdom of the dead, and heard a crackling from the kitchen table. He rushed over so fast that the coffee splashed out of the mug, throwing open the briefcase with such force that papers flew out of the brown folder. Among the piles of paper lay a sophisticated two-way radio; the kind that scans a large number of frequencies simultaneously. It said: "This is a message for the person who stole my briefcase. You know that I will find you, and you know what will happen then. To know *roughly* what will happen requires no more than a minimum amount of imagination. But not even the most well-developed imagination is enough to know *exactly*. So give the briefcase back now. If you think about it, it's in everyone's interests."

The civilised brutality of the voice. The almost-polished, refined cruelty.

Two things struck him. They went together, sort of.

First, that they were hunting the money. That meant that they themselves couldn't get at it. But they would presumably get it back, and in a way that would probably involve more deaths. And then perhaps everything would be possible again. So this was also a message for *me*, he thought. It said: "I know you're listening. Hold on, don't do anything hasty, wait, the money's coming. Whatever you do: don't do anything hasty."

What the hell had he started? A terrible snowball had been set in motion and he wouldn't have a hope of being able to stop it. It would roll in over Stockholm, taking down everything in its path.

Everything.

It was him and him alone who had set it in motion.

Second, he thought: danger. Before, he had completely ignored the personal risk. But when things had grown chaotic, when his colleagues had got involved, when everything had started to fall apart, that was when it had all destabilised, even for him. Maybe they would come after him now.

His insurance wasn't really valid any longer.

He was afraid of the pain, that was all.

When he finally lifted the coffee mug to his mouth, there was nothing left in it. The jet-black brew had spilled out over the floor and table.

It wasn't time to drain the bitter draught yet.

There were things left to do.

CHAPTER
FIFTEEN

The Supreme Command Centre. A name with a past.

Everything was the same in the sad old miniature lecture theatre which had, at one time, served as the temporary meeting place for CID's A-Unit, later known as its "Special Unit for Violent Crimes of an International Nature".

Now risen from the dead.

Maybe just as temporarily.

The dirty, yellow, windowless cement walls; the row of nailed-down seats you had to flip down to sit on, like a line of toilet seats; the table on the platform at the front, like a school-teacher's desk, crowned by what was now a fairly outdated computer; the clock on the wall, just past ten. And then the two doors.

The remains of the old A-Unit entered in dribs and drabs through the first. One after another, with almost tentative steps.

Paul Hjelm was first, like an overly eager student. He watched the others arrive. Trying to compare their outward appearances with those in his head. They never really matched.

They didn't even match when it came to Kerstin Holm, who was second to arrive. Even though they had worked closely the whole of the previous day, her appearance came as a surprise. He stole glances at her while she slipped over towards him. That wonderful woman. Always dressed in the simplest possible choice of clothes, but they always fitted her perfectly. A pair of loose, straight-legged linen trousers. A summery white blouse. That was all. And above: that dazzling face, ageing better than any burgundy ever had. Every hint of a wrinkle was an improvement.

Though he was a touch biased, of course.

She sat down and turned to him with a smile he was forced to call "spirited", a word he had always been suspicious of, but which had now undergone a metamorphosis.

"Have you got it?" she asked.

Hjelm nodded and took a small microphone from the breast pocket of his short-sleeved blue shirt. He waved it in front of her eyes. She nodded. He continued to wave it. She continued to nod. He continued.

"Yeah, yeah, yeah," she said eventually, laughing indulgently.

The door opened again. A thin, extremely pale man dressed in a striped T-shirt underneath an ill-fitting, light-coloured suit entered the room. He caught sight of them and spread his arms.

"My favourite people," he shouted in his clear Finland-Swedish accent.

They stood up and hugged Arto Söderstedt. He chuckled continuously.

"Well, we all had our hands full with those nice little cases yesterday, didn't we?" he said. "The media's already come up with names. The Kumla Bomber and the Kvarnen Killer. It didn't take long."

"And now they've been overshadowed by the Sickla Slaughter," said Kerstin Holm, grinning.

The door banged. Viggo Norlander entered, bluish bags under his eyes. They went nicely with the pink stigmata on his hands. He waved at them, taking the seat closest to the door and falling asleep immediately. On the way down, Hjelm thought.

Then Sweden's Biggest Policeman arrived. Gunnar Nyberg raised a cup of coffee to them.

"They sent me with my ascetic's coffee," he shouted incomprehensibly, sitting down next to the loudly snoring Norlander. "Hi, Kerstin," he said with a wave. "Welcome back to the right side of the country."

"Sweden's shithole," she shouted back.

Nyberg laughed, surprised, and placed the coffee on the little folding table in front of him. It could stand there until it cooled down. He had no intention of touching it.

A toilet flushed. Viggo Norlander woke with a start; it was a familiar sound. They waited while the taps ran. Eventually, the other door opened, and Detective Superintendent Jan-Olov Hultin entered the room from his private toilet, incontinence pad in place.

He nodded neutrally at them and sat down at the table at the front, a thick pile of papers in front of him.

Kerstin Holm went forward and placed a large bouquet of red roses in front of him. He stared at them. For a good while. Then he fished out the card from deep within their thorny depths. Silence. Absolute silence. They watched him. His expression was completely neutral, but his eyes were lowered. For a little too long. When he looked up, a couple of tears ran down his enormous nose.

"Thanks," was all he said.

"Just a little whip-round," said Kerstin Holm. "Welcome back."

"Thanks," Hultin said again, stiffly. Then he straightened up and turned the situation on its head. "But now we've got a job to do. Is anyone missing?"

They looked around the "Supreme Command Centre". The joker in the pack was missing.

The very energy source.

Almost on demand, the door opened. Energetically.

As if it's even possible to open a door energetically, Paul Hjelm thought to himself, watching as Jorge Chavez walked purposefully towards the front the steps. He sat down on the empty row of chairs nearest to Hultin, turned round and waved cheerfully to the others before standing up again and greeting the operative head of the A-Unit more formally.

"Welcome back, Jan-Olov," he said, shaking his boss's hand. Then he sat down and waited.

Hultin raised his eyebrows briefly, before regaining his wits and getting straight down to business.

"Fifty minutes ago, Waldemar Mörner pulled up on my driveway in his Saab. I was just about to finish cutting the lawn and take my first dip of the day when he told me what was what. I tried to get up to speed with things in the Saab on the way into town, but I know almost nothing about this damned Sickla

Slaughter. But Jorge does, so I'll hand you over to him right away. There you go."

Chavez was ready. He climbed up onto the platform and started fastening photographs to the whiteboard using magnets in the shape of sweet little ladybirds.

"You'll have to excuse the insects," he said. "Someone ordered the wrong thing down in the stockroom. Anyway, these are the pictures from the industrial estate in Sickla, down by Södra Hammarby harbour. From every conceivable angle. There's even a bird's-eye picture from a helicopter. Here. Five dead in what seems to be a typical underworld showdown. Unusually brutal, I have to say. One of the victims had twenty-four bullets in his body. Here. Another was blown up. His intestines were stuck to the roof of the car. Here.

"Let's start from the beginning. This was between two gangs. Gang One: three armed with pistols (1A to 1C on this sketch). Gang Two: six armed with sub-machine guns (2A to 2F). Gang Two attacks Gang One, probably with the aim of stealing a briefcase.

"*This* black Mercedes, registered to a car rental place in Örnsköldsvik and hired by a non-existent Anders Bengtsson from Stockholm two weeks ago, pulled up on *this* side road in the Sickla industrial estate at about two this morning. The three members of Gang One were in the car. A well-placed explosive charge detonated underneath it and killed the man in the back seat. The car kept rolling for a few metres before it stopped. The men in the front seat were injured in the explosion, but not fatally. They were forced out of the

162

car by Gang Two, who'd driven there in a van with new Continental tyres — we don't know any more about it than that at the moment. In all probability, they were frisked by Gang Two, though obviously not very well, since both men later managed to draw their weapons, killing two and injuring one member of Gang Two.

"Cartridges, the angle of the shots and the location of the bodies show that six of the nine available weapons were fired. Those not fired were the pistol belonging to the man in the back seat and the sub-machine guns belonging to the dead robbers. None of them had time to shoot before they died; otherwise, they'd definitely have done so. No one present seems to have flinched at the thought of using a weapon.

"Now look at the sketch. It seems to have played out as follows. One: the car explodes, person 1A is killed. Two: 1B and 1C are forced out of the car and frisked. Three: 1A is relieved, posthumously, of his briefcase, probably by 2A. Four: 1B and 1C take out their weapons. Five: 1B shoots over his shoulder and kills 2B, hitting him right in the eye. Six: 2A runs away towards the nearest shed with the briefcase, maybe because it's stopping him from using his gun. Seven: 1C shoots 2A in the back and kills him. Eight: 1B shoots and injures 2C. Nine: 1C is shot and killed by five shots from 2D, 2E and 2F. Ten: 1B is shot and injured by six shots from 2C, 2D and 2F. Eleven: 1B is shot and killed at close range by eighteen shots from 2D. Twelve: the briefcase is taken from the pool of blood in front of 2A, and bundled, along with the injured 2C, into the van. Thirteen: the van drives away.

163

1A, 1B, 1C, 2A and 2B are left behind. The injured one, 2C has AB negative blood. So that means that the people with the briefcase, whoever they are, are the surviving passengers from the van: 2D, 2E and 2F, along with the injured 2C.

"And now for the interesting part. We're pretty much in agreement that this is some kind of underworld dispute, right? So our fingerprint recognition software should be going crazy, but that's not the case. Of the five bodies — we obviously don't have any other fingerprints — there's just one who's got a criminal record. It's one of the robbers, Gang Two, the one who was shot in the eye. 2B. His name was Sven Joakim Bergwall, and he's been inside twice — the first time in Tidaholm and the second time in Kumla. A real first-class criminal. Bank robbery, manslaughter, attempted murder, grievous bodily harm and incitement to racial hatred."

"Incitement to racial hatred?" asked Hultin, when he finally managed to get a word in edgeways.

"Organised Nazi," said Jorge Chavez, letting his words sink in. "Was a member of the White Aryan Resistance, when it existed. Was also a member of the Nordic Reich Party, when it existed. Etc., etc. He was also active on the edges of the Maskeradliga, if you remember it. An armed gang carrying out robberies across the country. Military character. But the other four don't have records. No one from Gang One. Not 1A, 1B or 1C. Nor, for that matter, 2A."

"I'm a bit confused by all these codes," Gunnar Nyberg confessed. "So 2A was the one who ran away

164

with the briefcase and got shot in the back? The big guy?"

"Yeah," Chavez confirmed. "Though you're more of a big guy, if we're being accurate. The point of the codes is that we can pinpoint their positions and movements. We've got submachine-gun bullets with four different firing pin marks. Four sub-machine guns. Plus the two who never fired, but whose guns are still there: 2A, who was shot in the back, and 2B, who was shot in the face.

"2B was Sven Joakim Bergwall. He was alone on the right-hand side of the car. 2A took the briefcase and then stood in front of the car, from where he ran. 2D and 2E were also standing in front of the car. 2C and 2F were standing to the left, where 2C was shot and injured. 2D and 2F hit both 1B and 1C. What else can we say? Which of them went up to an injured man and put eighteen bullets into him? The group's crazy man, or the group's leader? Intuitively, I'd say: yes. The group's crazy man *and* its leader. I'd bet the leader is 2D. But we've got nothing on him."

"What about the explosion?" said Söderstedt.

"Well, that's our lead, other than Sven Joakim Bergwall. A couple of white, middle-aged men had just dragged the whole of the national forensic squad to Närke. Every single forensic technician in service is scraping walls in the Kumla Bunker."

"Get to the point," said the white, middle-aged Norlander gruffly.

"It's the same explosive and the same detonation device," said Chavez, letting the information sink in before he continued. "Both as yet unidentified, but the same. And it's obvious that if we put the details of the Kumla explosion together with the details of the Sickla Slaughter, then something not-too-pleasant emerges."

Söderstedt and Norlander glanced at one another knowingly. *Pattern*, they thought simultaneously.

When does a pattern start to emerge?

Arto Söderstedt suddenly felt alive. For the first time since he had driven Norlander's service Volvo to Kumla. It had been driven back by some rank-and-file officers while they took a plane from Örebro in order to make it back in time for 10a.m.

Suddenly it all made sense.

"We'd like to deliver a greeting," he said. "To all of you, but mainly to Paul and Jorge. From a two-year-old called Jorge Paul Andersson, nicknamed Jorjie."

There was a moment of confusion in the "Supreme Command Centre". Söderstedt smiled covertly. He liked confusing introductions.

"Göran Andersson's son," he continued, with dramatic precision.

Paul Hjelm and Jorge Chavez exchanged glances for the first time in almost a year. Was the old connection still there? They could read one another like a book, in any case. The serial killer Göran Andersson had named his son after the policemen who had sent him to prison. It felt peculiar.

Arto Söderstedt continued. "Andersson's eardrums burst in the Kumla explosion. At 08.36 yesterday morning, he was studying art history in his cell, the one next to Lordan Vukotic's. The night before, he'd seen

Vukotic stagger back to his cell with — as the post-mortem jigsaw puzzle later showed — a ruptured spleen, broken shin bone and both shoulders pulled out of joint. The next morning, he was blown up. Not into pieces, but into a bloody mess splattered all over the walls, and maybe by the same man who, about eighteen hours later, blew up the Mercedes down in the Sickla industrial estate. Which means that we were both right and wrong. Four policemen — the two of us, one from Närke CID and another from the Security Service — came to some fantastical conclusions yesterday, but we spent the evening on completely the wrong track. We assumed the following: that Vukotic had been tortured and talked; that that was why he didn't want to let anyone know he'd been tortured, least of all Nedic's henchmen in Kumla. Maybe he lay there in his cell all night, trying to put his shoulders back into joint. But why, you might ask, when he was just going to be blown up the next day? *Why* was he blown up the next day? That was the next question.

"Our conclusion was that the perpetrator realised his exploits would be discovered and so he got rid of all traces of his crime. So we were searching for inmates with a knowledge of explosives. We spent the night interrogating a whole range of people who had some connection to explosives. I've only just realised how wrong we were. If the perpetrator really wanted to 'cover up his tracks', as Göran Andersson put it, then we're assuming that he hadn't really understood the consequences of torturing Vukotic. But of course he had. He knew that Vukotic was Rajko Nedic's

167

right-hand man, that he was untouchable. Closest to what might be Sweden's most dangerous man. Of course he knew what he was doing when he got Vukotic out of the way. The explosion was hardly a display of regret or the result of some kind of fear of being discovered. It was more like a challenge, a statement. One which said: 'Pay attention, you fucking foreigner, we're coming!' But not just that. It also said: 'Pigs, I don't give a damn if you identify me, you can't catch me!'"

It was silent in the Supreme Command Centre. Once again, in the blink of an eye, it seemed to have lost the quotation marks around its name. Something unpleasantly — but also attractively — *big* was emerging.

"So," said Arto Söderstedt, "now you see what I'm getting at. Two points. First: the Kumla bomber wasn't a man rotting away in the clink, full of fear. He was someone *leaving* Kumla — guns blazing. Second: what we're looking at is a confrontation between neo-Nazi, professional, maybe even *paramilitary* attackers on the one hand, and one of Sweden's leading drug dealers, Rajko Nedic, and his group of war criminals from the former Yugoslavia on the other. Sounds nice, doesn't it? And maybe that explains why no one from Gang One — not 1A, 1B or 1C — left any identifiable fingerprints behind. They'd been imported directly from . . . well, maybe even from Kosovo. In any case, from the centre of the conflict in the Balkans."

"And all three die," Jorge Chavez said, breathless. He hadn't thought that far ahead yet. He looked at Arto

168

Söderstedt, languid, gangly and chalk white in appearance, and throwing out these horrible truths almost in passing.

Söderstedt continued, waving a piece of paper. "I've got the fax in my hand. It's from the governor of Kumla. At half eight yesterday morning a prisoner was released from the Kumla Bunker. Six minutes before the explosion. He'd been inside for three years, sentenced to six for grievous bodily harm, but got out halfway through for good behaviour. He's known on the fringes of racist and Nazi organisations, too. He beat up two Kurdish citizenship campaigners when they were taking part in a demonstration in Solna Centrum three years ago. There were explosives involved too, meant for a Kurdish cultural centre, but nothing could be proved. His name sounds so harmless, Niklas Lindberg. He's thirty-four and comes from Trollhättan. He trained as an officer in the army, quickly climbed the ranks, went on a few campaigns with the UN in Cyprus — and then joined the French Foreign Legion. Apparently — though this isn't confirmed — he has good ties with xenophobic organisations around the world. Not least in the US. My guess, if that kind of thing's allowed, is that Niklas Lindberg is your 2D, Jorge. The leader and the crazy man. The man who fired eighteen shots from close range into an injured person."

"Who, in all probability, was a war criminal from the former Yugoslavia," Jan-Olov Hultin nodded. "It's beginning to make sense now, even for an old pensioner like me. Jorge, you said that Sven Joakim Bergwall did

169

his last stint in prison in Kumla. Does the time frame overlap with Niklas Lindberg's?"

"Lindberg's name is new to me," Chavez confessed immediately, leafing through his papers, "but Bergwall was released from Kumla a month ago. So it's not exactly unlikely that two violence-prone Nazis like these met inside. Bergwall arranged things on the outside, Lindberg the inside. We can look at it like that."

"What is it they're up to?" Hultin continued. "The night before he was released, Niklas Lindberg tortured Lordan Vukotic, but it seems to be better planned than that. The night before. It surely must go further back in time. Six men in a well-planned attack — that surely wasn't something they decided on eighteen hours before?"

"I think," said Kerstin Holm suddenly, her chorister's vocal powers composed, "that they were double-checking something."

Again, a certain confusion spread through the concentration of the Supreme Command Centre. And, again, a new voice entered the chorus, altering the tune of the song and disrupting the harmony. All eyes were on her. She held her hand out to Paul Hjelm who, without hesitating, placed the little microphone into it.

She held it up before the A-Unit's collective eyes.

"This was taken from the underside of a table in the Kvarnen bar on Tjärhovsgatan yesterday evening. It's a discreet listening device."

"The Kvarnen Killer," exclaimed Gunnar Nyberg, who had been sitting in silence for too long and felt excluded.

170

"Not at all," said Kerstin Holm. "More like a result of him. During our interrogations with the witnesses from Kvarnen, something completely different emerged. Entire groups of people ran out of the place as soon as the killing had happened; something completely different was taking place in the background of all this everyday violence. Or maybe in the foreground."

"Double-check?" asked Jan-Olov Hultin, in an attempt to bring some clarity to a situation in which it was utterly lacking.

"Yeah," said Kerstin Holm, gathering herself. "The actual check, the real check, was taking place in Kvarnen on Wednesday evening. I think that all five bodies were there on Wednesday evening. Though living."

They stared at her. The room was completely silent.

"I don't know when patterns start to emerge," she continued, "but for me and Paul, they emerged early on. We had nothing at all to go on, really, except what we call a 'scent'. Something was emerging. We didn't know what it was, but it was there, in the middle of all the Hammarby fans. To make things a bit clearer: Gang Two were sitting listening to Gang One with this listening device. The penny's only just dropped."

"But Niklas Lindberg didn't get out until the morning after," said Hultin, trying to keep up. He felt rusty — but he could also feel it coming off him in large flakes as he sat at the front of the room. He was home. He was finally home again.

"That's true," said Kerstin Holm. "If we follow Söderstedt's reasoning then these were his men, the

171

ones who picked him up from Kumla afterwards, maybe led by the now-departed Sven Joakim Bergwall. It might also have been Bergwall who was clear-headed enough to leave a man behind on the crime scene, to divert our attention from the gang."

"What can you tell us about the unidentified bodies from the Sickla Slaughter, Jorge?" Paul Hjelm asked.

" 'Knocked about' is probably the best description," said Chavez. "Bergwall, 2B, was shot in the eye; it wasn't pretty. Without fingerprints, we wouldn't have had anything there. Same with the one who was blown up in the back of the car. 1A. Dark hair, that's the only definitive thing we can say. 1B was completely shot to pieces. Twenty-four shots. Eighteen from close range. There's no point trying to reconstruct his face. 1C looks best, and sure, he looks like he's from the Balkans. 2A fell like a log, face down onto the floor. There's not much left. Not much chance of putting out any reconstructions in the media."

"It's 2A we're interested in," said Hjelm. "The big guy who ran off with the briefcase and got shot in the back, the one who doesn't have a record. Powerful build?"

"No doubt."

"Thin moustache."

"Yeah."

"Shaved head?"

"Yeah."

Paul Hjelm fell silent. He left the rest to Kerstin. She had the notes ready.

172

"From what you've said, I think he's a match for a man called Eskil Carlstedt. Salesman from Kungsholmen. We spoke to him yesterday morning and bought his entire story. We let him go without suspecting a thing. So damn careless."

"Come on," said Hultin, slightly unexpectedly. "You had nothing to go on. You were looking for a man who'd crushed someone's head with a beer glass. You've got really bloody far on the little you had. If it's correct, that is; if it isn't just a good old Hjelm-Holm flight of fancy."

"Five men," Holm continued without seeming to have heard him, "at a table by the door. 'Not skinheads but almost.' 'Skinheads who've passed the age limit.' They ran off quickly but left Carlstedt behind, since he was the only one without a record. That's quick thinking. Carlstedt was interviewed briefly in Kvarnen by the night staff, but he identified himself and was told to come to the station the next day for a proper interview. Then he met up with the four who'd run off, and the five of them spent the night working out the best way to divert our attention. Carlstedt has to say that he saw the Kvarnen Killer. Sure enough, it diverts our attention enough to let him go without a fuss, not to his *four* friends but to the *five* of them, because the others have just been up to Närke to pick up the boss, Niklas Lindberg. Now the six of them are reunited. It's time to wait for the following evening. They've got the time and place from *two* sources now. From Lordan Vukotic in prison, and from the group in Kvarnen which, for the most part, is identical to Jorge's

173

ex-Yugoslav war criminals in Gang One: 1A, 1B and 1C."

"Why the hell would they discuss the meeting place in Kvarnen?" Hultin exclaimed, feeling his neutrality starting to slip. "It seems completely crazy."

"When it comes to the meeting place, there are two parties involved. They meet in Kvarnen. The briefcase that was going to be handed over at some later point presumably contains money or drugs. The two parties don't trust one another so they meet somewhere neutral, somewhere *public*, to decide on the meeting place for the handover. They're speaking English since, as we mentioned, they're probably recently arrived war criminals from Yugoslavia. That's probably also the reason why they chose such a public place to meet. The other party presumably has no desire to meet a group of crazed war criminals in a dark alley somewhere. Back to prison: Vukotic already knows about the provisional meeting place for the next evening, or at least that's what Niklas Lindberg assumes. He's taking a huge risk when — the night before he's released — he tortures Vukotic inside the prison walls. Maybe it's to *double-check* what his colleagues are soon going to find out in Kvarnen. Maybe just because it's fun, torturing a foreigner. It's a beautiful world."

"There's still one thing missing in our line of thinking," said the police aura still floating around Jan-Olov Hultin. "Whoever it was that was speaking English with Gang One in Kvarnen. The one who was supposed to receive the briefcase before it was stolen.

174

Where the hell did this *briefcase* come from, by the way? How do we know there even was a briefcase?"

"The imprint in 2A's blood," said Chavez. "Eskil Carlström's, if it turns out to be him —"

"Carlstedt," said Hjelm.

"It fits that it was a bag, a briefcase. That was the most likely."

"OK," said Hultin. "We'll accept that for now. Back to the other party in the English conversation in Kvarnen."

"I've been saving that till last," said Kerstin Holm. "It's not good news. We're probably looking at a policeman."

Sighs were heard in the Supreme Command Centre. Not surprised sighs, not agitated, more disillusioned. The previous year, PAN, the National Police Board's personnel department, had dismissed four policemen for criminal activities. A further four resigned rather than risk dismissal. Twenty-one policemen faced disciplinary action, of which seventeen were given a warning.

Holm continued. "A Swedish policeman. He showed his ID to get out of Kvarnen when the doormen blocked the door."

"Couldn't it have been a fake ID?" Hultin asked.

"Sure it could. But he was the only Swede in the gang. And the only Swede waved the police ID. Also, he seemed to be pretty familiar with police procedure. He *didn't* want to get stuck in Kvarnen when the interrogations around the Kvarnen Killer started up."

175

"Well then, it's time to ask what all of this is about," said Hultin. "If we accept all these rash hypotheses that have been flying around your rusty detective superintendent for the past half-hour. What's it all about? Rajko Nedic has to be at the heart of it. He's going to deliver something in a briefcase to a man who may be a Swedish policeman. What high-value object fits in a briefcase? Presumably money, since every policeman knows how difficult it is to dispose of drugs without being noticed at some point. It's obviously not a question of routine payment either, so it must be a handover. That means the 'policeman' must be scared, which means it must be a one-off payment. Why? Is a Swedish policeman on his way to breaking through into the drugs branch? That doesn't sound good. Blackmail? Mmm, why not? But about what? And how did this criminal, probably Nazi-tinged, gang find out that the delivery was going to happen? They've known it was going to happen for a while, the six of them were ready as soon as Niklas Lindberg got out of jail, but they don't know exactly where and when it's going to happen. That's what they find out, in two different ways, the night before. But how did they find out to begin with?"

"It seems likely that it happened earlier, via Vukotic," said Söderstedt. "Lindberg and Bergwall are in Kumla, listening to a secret conversation. They know that a delivery is going to happen, but where, when, how? Maybe Lindberg found out that the Kvarnen meeting was going to take place while he was still in prison."

"Lots of questions," said Paul Hjelm.

176

"Yes," Hultin conceded, looking up. "But lots of answers, too. Considerably more than I could've hoped for when I glanced through the anaemic information in Waldemar Mörner's air-conditioned Saab."

"So what have we got, then?" Chavez asked, summing up over by the whiteboard; he seemed slightly overwhelmed. "We've probably got three of the six men from Gang Two. 2A is Eskil Carlstedt. 2B is the Nazi, Sven Joakim Bergwall. These two are dead. 2D is the leader, Niklas Lindberg. Missing are the injured 2C, as well as 2E and 2F. As far as Gang One is concerned, we'll send the fingerprints from the bodies of 1A, 1B and 1C to Interpol — maybe to the ex-Yugoslav authorities too, if that's possible."

"And then the explosives," said Norlander. "What kind of highly volatile, liquid explosive is it? One that's set off by an electronic detonator? No one seems to have the answer, but it's probably important."

"Probably," said Hultin. "We'll keep working on it. Interpol again. Lots needs to be confirmed, too. We should take some fingerprints from Eskil Carlstedt's flat and compare them with the body of 2A, for example. And then we should think about how to handle Rajko Nedic. He's made a point of operating in the open, after all. Honest businessman. Restaurant owner."

"We should probably talk to him," said Hjelm, "though the question is, when? When should we reveal what we know? What do we stand to lose or gain by talking to him? Etc., etc."

Hultin nodded, glancing out over the room.

"And I suppose you want to know what's going on, don't you? Staffwise. You know what they said on TV yesterday. Police staff shortages are acute in the summer. The Justice Minister is openly talking about bad holiday planning. People have already set up vigilante groups in several places, to keep on top of the things we no longer can. Even if we've been called in specially, we still have to justify being here, seven police officers of differing rank, working on this. It's Midsummer's Eve. It's getting close to midday. Most policemen are on leave now, and will soon put down the bottle of schnapps to dance, legs unsteady, to Midsummer tunes with their children. But not you. On the contrary, you'll be costing the National Police Board more money because of all the overtime you'll be doing. Any problems with that?"

"I'd like to make a quick trip out to Dalarö, at least," said Hjelm.

"My kids will be waiting for me at Skansen at three," said Söderstedt.

"I'd really like to spend the evening with my newborn daughter," said Norlander.

"My son's carved a maypole for my grandson in Östhammar," said Nyberg.

Chavez and Holm said nothing.

"Forget it," Hultin said brutally. "We're setting up a new operation. There hasn't been one for almost a year. No one's complaining about holiday before this is wrapped up. *Right now*, you've got all the freedom you want to return to your previous work, but not in three hours' time, not tomorrow. You've really got to want this. As I understand it, this is also a chance to make the A-Unit permanent. The last chance. Unfortunately, it seems like they need us. That means: if any of you have developed a taste for the normal police life to such an extent that you don't give a damn about this, you're welcome to go. But only if you go right this moment. Anyone?"

Gunnar Nyberg looked up. Distracted, he took a sip of his ice-cold black coffee. It made him almost throw up. Drinking coffee had become a reflex.

"It's not the normal police life I've got a taste for," he said, in the midst of a bout of nausea. "It's the more *abnormal* parts. I'm in the middle of several ongoing paedophile investigations. I can't just chuck that all to the side."

"I know," said Hultin. "I've been keeping an eye on your careers. Jorge wants nothing more than to return from theory to practice. Kerstin has just come back from Gothenburg. Together with Paul, she's completed her part of the Kvarnen Killer case. Arto and Viggo's explosion in Kumla seems as though it can easily be incorporated into the Sickla case. For you five, it seems as clear as it does for me. It's you, Gunnar, you're the weak link. You're right in the middle of truly important work. What are your thoughts on that?"

Nyberg sighed loudly. "You don't have coffee breaks as often," he said. No one understood that this was the highest possible praise. He continued more clearly. "It's definitely tempting to get to work on a proper A-Unit case again. That feeling of free fall. But for me, it would be best if I could . . . I don't know, work half-time for a while, so I can work out what to do with the paedophile investigations. So that there aren't any delays. So that no one suffers for a moment longer than necessary. If you can understand that."

"I think we understand," said Hultin. "And as far as I'm concerned, that's fine. I haven't forgotten that it was you who was right about the Kentucky Killer, while the rest of us were wrong. Anyone else?"

No one else.

Hultin nodded and continued. "OK then. Before I start to deal out more distinct tasks, we should spend a bit of time, each of us, working out what we should do next. And what we can expect to happen now. We're assuming that Gang Two now has the briefcase. That could be an end to it. Nedic might have no idea who took the briefcase, but that's if we ignore the Vukotic explosion. How long will it be before he manages to link it all to Niklas Lindberg? And what'll happen then? A big showdown? Can we assume that Lindberg's gang is happy with the briefcase? Or do they want more? Might their Nazi links suggest that? Are they after an ethnic cleansing of the Swedish drugs trade? And why was this briefcase being delivered to a possible Swedish policeman? If there was money in the case, then why is the drug dealer Rajko Nedic, who has never been locked up by the police, giving money to them? Is that why he's never been caught? Etc., etc.

"What we need is the following. One: more information on the mysterious explosives; two: the identities of 2C, 2E and 2F; three: the possible policeman; four: to find out why Nedic is paying the

Swedish police money (if that is the case). If you come up with anything else, tell me right away. So. Let's keep working till Midsummer's Eve turns into night. No flowers beneath your pillows, no home-made schnapps, no Midsummer children being created. Nothing but work, work, work."

CHAPTER
SIXTEEN

Nothing but work, work, work. Though from home.

She looked out onto Surbrunnsgatan. Never before had her little corner of the world felt so abandoned. The midsummer weather was in two minds; sometimes sun, sometimes rain, occasionally lots of rain. And she was surfing. In cyberspace. Surfing the Web.

At that moment, the rain was beating against the window. Surbrunn's rain. One of those magnificent little showers. Short, intense, fleeting.

Sara Svenhagen had almost forgotten her public holiday anxiety. The kind that drives the suicide rate up during those very days when medical staff are paid holiday overtime. That notorious lump in the chest. The voice saying: you're alone, you know. Completely alone.

No one wants you.

She knew she shouldn't have felt that way. It was her who didn't want anyone, not the other way round, but public holiday anxiety didn't seem to discriminate. It sunk its teeth in. It spoke unwelcome truths.

No lights went on in the windows on the other side of the street. Not a person went by down on the pavement. Not one car engine started the entire day. The city was deserted. For once, it wouldn't be

Stockholm topping the violence statistics. It was missing both its perpetrators and victims.

They were in the countryside.

She could have celebrated Midsummer at her parents' villa in Tyresö. The family wouldn't have been complete, though. That was some comfort in her sorrow. She knew that for her dad, it was also work, work, work. The difference being that Chief Forensic Technician Brynolf Svenhagen was in seventh heaven. Two magnificent cases to crack. First the Kumla explosion, then the Sickla Slaughter. She imagined the strict, grey man being coloured in and given a carnivalesque sheen. She could just picture him dressed in a colourful grass skirt, little purple tassels spinning on his nipples. She smiled. The lump disappeared.

She looked around the small flat. It wasn't so stupid after all. Her inner sanctum.

She returned to the computer.

Since 19:36:07 on Thursday 24 June, she had allowed herself only a wink or two of sleep. Eighteen hours ago. That was when she had saved the address list from that strange, fleeting website.

Sure enough, it was an address list. An address list for paedophiles. A network which, to a large extent, certainly seemed to touch upon other known networks, but still: it was a completely new list. No names, of course. No real, physical addresses, but a list of email addresses, several of which she had never come across before. The fact was, her head was full of them. Overfull, maybe. About to burst, maybe.

Those short spells of sleep had immediately been invaded by the nightmare. The glowing stomach, the shadow, the penis, forcing its way into her and towards the child. She was convinced that the dream was trying to tell her something. Something vital. But she couldn't understand what. She only knew the fear she felt when she woke in the moment of death. She felt that the dream went *much too far* to be able to deliver a message. Any message was drowned out by horror.

Anyone can open an email address anonymously online. Hotmail was the favourite. There were millions of addresses ending in @hotmail.com. Access was unlimited. But there were always tracks; behind all the camouflage there was always an IP address, the computer's own fingerprint. Finding this IP address using the email address was sometimes impossible — when the person was particularly good with computers, for example — though sometimes, even if it was complicated, it was still possible.

But even if you managed to find the IP address, it wasn't by any means certain that you would find a physical person behind it. Most paedophiles were smart enough not to open these email accounts from their own computers, but from a public computer connected to the Internet, in the Kulturhuset or the Kungliga biblioteket, for example. That said, it was a bit more difficult to enjoy the forbidden fruits in these public places. Masturbating to babies who had been raped didn't exactly belong in the open spaces in the Kulturhuset. Normal practice was to check your mail on a public computer, transfer the images onto a disk and then enjoy them from the safety of your home. You were safe then. No tracks, other than the physical. Every now and then, material from this or that computer was downloaded in one place or another. When this happened, it was possible to link a physical person to that time frame and that computer, but it wasn't easy. The easiest to catch were the *blockheads*, those people who, every once in a while, let their impulses take over and risked downloading material to their own computers, using their computer's unique IP address. In that moment, the tracks were established.

So far, Sara had counted three *blockheads* on the latest list. Tracing them was a complicated process, one that involved several automatic elements, operations she could have carried out in her sleep. If she ever slept, that was. Through a complex interplay of the central police computer, Interpol, the Internet and the intranet, she had managed — having gone through around a third of the list — to find eighteen IP addresses already. Eight of them were Swedish. Five led back to public institutions. The others to private citizens in Boden, Lund and Borås.

She was starting to grow tired of cyberspace. Now and then, she caught sight of the crop-haired little thing in the computer screen. By now, she was no longer mistaking it for a young boy. It was her. The *living, breathing* Sara Svenhagen. That was how she looked. She was no virtual paedophile victim, but a real policewoman. She needed to get stuck into some practical police work soon. And so she was searching feverishly for a Stockholm number in the address list. None had turned up so far, but that was what she was looking for. So that she could strike right away. In person. So that she could physically look the man in the eye.

And confirm the old chestnut: that the paedophile didn't think of himself as evil. On the contrary, he was *nice*, he took the child's inherent sexuality seriously while the rest of the world misunderstood their nature and made them asexual. The paedophile gave the children the most important gift of their lives: he gave back the sexuality which had been taken away from them.

She had heard it all before. But she would never be able to understand it.

The question was whether the list was enough of a catch to begin a grand international offensive. That is, would she be forced to wait six or so months before taking action, alongside the Americans and Brits and Germans and French, not forgetting the Belgians? And what would happen during that time?

It was a question of conscience even before it existed in the material world; a classic moral dilemma, only in virtual form. *If* a physical Stockholm address turned up, one that Sara Svenhagen could go for immediately, should she do it? She was forced to weigh the risks and chances against each other. On golden scales. The risk that the virtual Stockholm paedophile would violate more children against the risk he would squeal to the rest of the network, therefore causing harm to considerably more children.

186

The chance of catching a man with even more information about paedophiles against the chance of catching an entire network.

Somewhere during the course of her calculations, she suddenly started to understand the basic principle of market economics. Everything had a price. Or rather: a price could be *put* on everything. Absolutely everything. Every relationship, every sign of life. The question of conscience she was struggling with was an economic calculation. It was simple: plus and minus. Minimising the losses. The least possible damage. The smallest number of sexual assaults on minors.

It felt disgusting.

Necessary, but disgusting.

A price could be put on *everything*. Commercialisation of the intimate sphere. The transformation of humans from physical beings to legal entities to virtual people. All that was left behind was a number, a value, a share price.

She suddenly knew precisely why she had chopped off her hair.

And just then, the physical address for the IP address appeared. It was in Stockholm.

But it felt strange. Fatburstrappan 18. Somewhere in Södermalm.

And then reality hit her. The moral dilemma was, on closer consideration, fictitious, or at least not hers. She had forgotten one important factor.

Rank.

It was almost two on Midsummer's Eve. Dancing around the maypole would already be well under way in many places. Friday. Followed by Midsummer and then Sunday. Weekend, with a minimal number of staff in the city. The majority were in the countryside. Her superiors would be dancing to Midsummer tunes. Ragnar Hellberg too, in all probability; comedy Superintendent Party-Ragge. But she had an emergency number. A mobile number.

The question was whether she wanted to contact Hellberg. There was no real hurry. The paedophile living at Fatburstrappan 18 might not commit any serious assaults during the Midsummer weekend. Though "might" wasn't enough for Sara Svenhagen. He *might*, on the other hand, celebrate Midsummer by indulging in a real orgy of sexual assault on minors.

What would Hellberg say? Maybe he would have already downed his first few schnapps and be wearing his party hat at a jaunty angle, rambling away. She couldn't really say how well she knew Hellberg. He was the police force's youngest and most up-for-a-laugh detective superintendent, though his was the kind of forced, businesslike fun. Everyone had to take part. That was an order. We'll wear blue lights on our heads at the Stockholm Marathon, right? All of us? Right? But sure, he was competent enough when it really mattered. Still, she couldn't really look past the way he had outmanoeuvred Ludvig Johnsson, the man who had already built up the entire paedophile division when the National Police Board brought in the more media-friendly careerist Ragnar Hellberg, and quickly promoted him. And Hellberg really did make a good

188

impression on TV. Party-Ragge, who called reporters by their first names and always had a joke ready.

But she didn't really know anything about him. Not whether he had a family, not where he lived, not whether he was hiding out at his place in the country, mobile phone switched off. Would the very fact that she had the cheek to contact him on Midsummer's Eve close all doors? Would she get a telling-off from a herring-munching, loose-jawed Hellberg, mid-drinking song?

It was either/or. Either she would get a green light or she would get a red one. At the moment, it was yellow. Changed according to the EU standard.

She rang. Hellberg answered almost immediately, as though he had been waiting for her call. He didn't seem to be in the midst of a paradise of schnapps and song; when his voice echoed down the line, she recognised, to her surprise, a hint of public holiday anxiety.

Was Party-Ragge sitting at home, just as lonely and abandoned as she was? Was his whole bon vivant attitude just a professional front? Inside, she felt quite surprised as she said: "I've found something."

"You're working *now*?" Hellberg asked, without the expected jovial tone in his voice which suggested that she should be rolling around in the Midsummer hay instead.

"Yeah."

"Me too."

"On what?" she exclaimed clumsily. Ragnar Hellberg didn't seem the type to take his work home with him, even on normal weekdays.

"Mmm," he said, seeming to chuckle. "Administrative stuff, I suppose you could say. What've you found, Sara?"

"A new network."

"What? Is it the Nässjö code? It seemed uncrackable."

"Yeah, the Nässjö code. A blockhead in Stockholm. Fatburstrappan 18. Several others, too. It's just a question of whether we should pick him up immediately, or wait for the rest and take them all together."

"Are there international numbers?"

"The majority, yeah. But also in Boden, Lund, Borås. So far. I've got lots left."

"How many other countries?"

"Three so far. The US, Germany, France. It'll take time to organise an international effort."

"Yeah," said Hellberg, seeming to think it over. "And you want to clip its wings immediately, if I've understood you right. So that they don't cast a shadow over the Midsummer blossoms?"

"I guess I do," Sara Svenhagen admitted, without really understanding Hellberg's flower analogy.

"Sigh and groan," Hellberg articulated. "We can't pick up Boden, Lund and Borås now. But we've got a chance here, I agree with you. OK. Two things. First, you need to find enough to arrest him and keep him. Under no circumstances can he make contact with anyone else who could warn the network. No conversations, no lawyers. Refer to the new rules. But — like I said — you *have* to find something in his flat."

"Are you suggesting that I —"

190

"No, I'm not. Just make sure you find something."

"And second?"

"This is between you and me. Solely."

"What? Why?"

"That's an order. OK?"

"I don't understand —"

"OK?"

"OK."

"Two rank-and-file officers from the local police to kick the door in. Give them only the minimum information. I'll fix the authorisation. Go straight to Södra Station and take a couple of assistants with you. Don't call ahead."

"I don't really understand what's —"

"You understand what you need to understand. OK?"

"OK," said Sara Svenhagen, confused, ending the call.

She looked at the receiver.

Was that really a green light she'd been given?

CHAPTER
SEVENTEEN

Certain traces had been left behind. A folder of invoices, order confirmations and booking forms lying here and there, looking lost. Posters, or rather the torn corners of posters, still pinned to the walls; almost all of the escapist kind. Images of paradise islands, fantastic scenes of virgin Swedish countryside, unobtainable archipelago idylls, endless Turkish beaches with bars at every turn.

The administrative staff had been told to give their room back to the A-Unit in a hurry, and each member of the team sat in their old room without really recognising it. Paul Hjelm came to a rash and not entirely objective conclusion: administrative work required a large dose of escapism.

Police work did too, though for completely different reasons. He didn't know if the things he dedicated his free time to could really be called escapism. He read, listened to jazz music and "played piano"; he always made sure that the quotation marks were in place around the last of them. But he had kept an old promise and bought himself a piano. He would check that his house — and ideally the entire neighbourhood — was completely empty before he started tinkling the ivories. But then he enjoyed taking liberties, experimenting with reckless harmonies, testing the limits, mimicking, taking out simple accompaniments and even humming, like Glenn Gould. Because Paul Hjelm never *sang*. He didn't know why, but he couldn't bring himself to sing. That was his limit.

When it came to reading, there were no quotation marks. He dared to assert that he did that straight out. He *read*. And he really *tried* to avoid shying away from anything, he tried not to stop where he instinctively felt he wanted to stop, but to venture into unknown territory. Maybe reading was actually some kind of midlife crisis. He didn't want to bloody die without having explored as many of life's opportunities as possible.

Recently, it had been Rilke. Poetry was still a challenge. He worked his way through the *Duino Elegies*, ten fantastic long poems, and he *felt* that there was something there, something absolutely fundamental, important, central, a point of contact with something he wouldn't manage to come in contact with by himself — still, he never really made it all the way there.

"For beauty is nothing but the beginning of terror, that we are still able to bear."

He had put the *Duino Elegies* to one side and promised himself he would go back to it. Instead, he picked up Rilke's only novel, *The Notebooks of Malte Laurids Brigge*, and found himself spellbound. He couldn't find another word for it. Spellbound. He couldn't put it down. This fantastic depiction of childhood had found a home in his borrowed office at the local police, it was there when he answered "Gunnar Löv's telephone" and received that strange pause in response, it was there when he waded through pools of blood in the city, trying to make sense of why the hell they'd had to pull out that knife and press it in between those ribs. It was only in the moment when the first contours began to emerge from behind the Kvarnen Killing that it felt like he had really finished reading the book. He imagined he could see something peculiar *behind* it that he wouldn't normally have noticed. He allowed himself to thank the literature for that discovery. Even though it sounded a bit idealised.

His relationship with his family was far from idealised, however. Danne had stopped being pubescent and moody. Instead, Tova was pubescent and crazy. Completely out of her mind. He didn't have the energy to even think about it. But Cilla was taking it quite hard, since she had always had a good relationship with her daughter. Now, suddenly, she was the most old-fashioned, awful individual who had ever lived, and it was the first time that Cilla had really felt her age. Which wasn't especially advanced, but now suddenly increased by roughly a year a day. She had now reached ninety-three, and was not especially inclined to marital interaction.

Behind Jorge Chavez's head was Delphi. An idealised ancient Greek landscape with shining gold drawing pins. Chavez's head was in the computer, however. Practically connected.

"It suits you," said Paul Hjelm.

"What?" asked Chavez, typing away.

"Delphi suits you."

Chavez stopped typing and glanced over his shoulder. He grimaced and began typing again.

"How are you?" Hjelm asked abruptly.

Chavez sighed and looked up. "Are we working or hanging out?" he replied brutally.

"Hanging out," Hjelm said, unflustered. "At least for a few minutes. Do you want a coffee?"

"No, I don't want a crap coffee with flakes of limescale in it."

"Racist," said Paul Hjelm, filling up two mugs from the old coffee machine on their shared desk. "You've got to integrate. Otherwise, you'll never fit into Swedish society. You'll never be let into any pubs."

"That's a little paradox about Swedish society," said Chavez, taking a mug. "Only the people who never go to pubs are let in."

They raised their mugs to one another. It had been a while.

"Oh yeah, that's pretty good," Chavez continued, pulling a face; you really could feel the flakes of limescale floating around in your mouth. "I've been on so damn many courses that I can't really distinguish them."

"Home-language lessons?" Hjelm said obstinately, smiling charmingly.

"*Soon*, when I become superintendent," said Chavez with the same charming smile, "that kind of thing'll be wiped out from the police force. And you'll be first of all."

Oh yes, they were back again. Everything was just the same.

"No women?" asked Hjelm.

"What's the name of that director, the one who did *Änglagård*?"

"Colin Nutley. Immigrant. Are you a couple?"

"Colin Nutley. When he came to Sweden, two things struck him. The women were completely fantastic."

"And the other?"

"But the men . . . That's it, word for word: 'But the men . . .' I think it's a great way to put it."

"And that's the answer to my question?" asked Hjelm quietly.

"Yup. Yes: women. Several women. But none in particular."

"Isn't it about time to settle down a bit?"

"Like Viggo?" exclaimed Chavez. "Did you hear about the thing with the baby? What a bloody story."

"The more shots, the better your chances of hitting. Even if there are a few accidental shots . . ."

"He seems to be living with that woman. One day she just turned up at his door and said: this is your daughter. And now they're both living with him. A normal, happy family."

"He avoided all the pregnancy madness," Hjelm said jealously. "Lucky guy."

"I know you don't believe it, but I do actually go home with women. It's that simple. Only, the *one* is conspicuously absent. So I'm replacing quality with quantity. You know your Marx, right?"

"Nope," said Hjelm, pointing to Chavez's computer. "Have you found anything?"

"Only thoughts. And you?"

"*If* that man in Kvarnen, the one who was overheard speaking English with the three dead Yugoslavs, if they were even Yugoslav, really is a policeman, then he's the key. He's the one who set the entire thing moving. It could be one of three things: bribe money, blackmail money or a purchase sum. The first would mean it was about a one-off payment, clearly a very big one. Not something regular. But it could also be some kind of initial payment, that's not so unlikely. The second is possible, but what could this policeman have on Rajko Nedic that no one else has? The third seems most likely. Maybe they're buying information, but it's most likely that they're buying drugs from him, simple as that. But if that's the case, we need to find a policeman with access to drugs. A confiscation, maybe? One that hasn't been accounted for? I think we should take a look at the drugs units across the country."

"In that case, shouldn't Internal be brought in?" asked Chavez.

"There's no guarantee that he's *actually* a policeman. The man who showed a police ID in Kvarnen *might not* even have been the person talking to the Slavs. But no one else seems to be missing. Kerstin and I'll have to get in touch with everyone from Kvarnen again to try to get better descriptions of both the policeman and the robber gang."

"2C, 2E, 2F."

197

Hjelm grimaced slightly, and said: "If you insist on using those names, yeah. 2A: Eskil Carlstedt, dead. 2B: Sven Joakim Bergwall, dead. 2D: Niklas Lindberg, annoyingly full of life. If we test 2C's blood type maybe we can get closer, not least if we do it through Kumla since he may well have been in the Nazi gang there. AB negative isn't *so* common, after all. Söderstedt and Norlander are still working on the Kumla case. They're going to interview the rest of the Slavs there, and the rest of the Nazis. Doesn't that sound enviable?"

"Not even slightly," said Chavez, pulling at a cuticle with an indifferent expression. "They'll be banging their heads against the cell walls."

"They can scrape one another off them, then. Well, all right. Now, Eskil Carlstedt. I've checked his background and been through his flat. Since he knew the flat would be searched, he's cleaned it meticulously. Not a trace. The neighbours heard the vacuum cleaner early in the morning on the twenty-fourth. Before he came here and allowed himself to be interviewed by a couple of idiots. The hard drive on his computer's been wiped. The technicians are working on it, maybe they can get something back. Something else for Svenhagen to get his teeth into. Have you seen his daughter, by the way? Might be something for you, Jorge. Gunnar's working with her. An unbelievable woman. Hair's too short, maybe."

"I don't believe in inbreeding," Chavez said darkly.

"It doesn't matter what you believe. It's about passion that throws all common sense and principles out the window."

"Shut up and go on."

"I can't do both," said Hjelm. "You'll have to choose one."

"Go on," Chavez said even more darkly.

"Carlstedt's past is about as empty as his hard drive. Kerstin's talking to his workmates at Kindwall's in Hammarby harbour. He sold Fords. Used-car salesman. Especially used now."

Chavez laughed, and said, in a silly voice: "'Would you buy a used car from this man?' I'm wondering most about Nedic myself. How the hell is it possible that he can live and work as an honest businessman when every single policeman in this country knows that he's one of the leading drug dealers? Most of these dealers are underground, after all, but he's playing a strangely precise double game. It seems to be built on an extreme, almost mafia-like loyalty. No one snitches on Rajko Nedic. That's just how it is."

"What kind of legitimate business?"

"Mmm," said Chavez knowingly. "A restaurant chain, for a change. Three restaurants. Great places to eat, apparently. One almost ended up in the Michelin guide. They've tried to go the Al Capone route, the back way, and do him for tax avoidance, but it doesn't work. He runs that part of his business impeccably. The most law-abiding man in the restaurant world, according to the finance division."

"Could that be what this is about?" said Hjelm, rubbing what he thought was the beginning of a bald patch.

"You mean that some policeman has found a back route and is trying to get a little extra in their pocket? Yeah, sure. Except there doesn't seem to be a back route. You said it yourself: what could one single policeman have found out that none of his colleagues have?"

"What's to say it's a single policeman?"

"The fact that a whole gang of criminal policemen sounds unlikely," said Chavez. "That's it. It just doesn't fit. Though it could be the porn police. *That* doesn't sound unlikely. The whole Mediterranean shrimp thing was really ingenious. It's an obvious lead."

"How're the arms?" Hjelm smiled evilly.

"Both shoulders are out of joint, tibia's cracked, spleen ruptured. They're going to blow me up tomorrow morning. You can have the honour of scraping me from the walls of the station yourself."

"What a privilege. But does it really have to be one single policeman?"

"Does it have to be a *policeman?*" asked Chavez, standing up, stretching and walking over to the window which faced out onto the inner courtyard of the police station. "Maybe we're focusing a bit too much on that. We shouldn't let it blind us."

"No," Hjelm nodded, "no, of course not. But more? The weapons?"

"Gang One had Russian Izh-70-300s. Do you want to hear the story about that pistol?"

"No."

"After the Second World War," Chavez began, like a storyteller in front of a log fire, "the Red Army's

200

classic Tokarev pistols were changed. An engineer called Nikolai Makarov designed a pistol that was eventually accepted by Stalin. Still, production couldn't start until after his death. In 1954, Izhevskij Mekhanikeskij Zavod started production of the apparently extraordinary Makarov pistol, which is still made today. After the Wall came down, the markets suddenly opened for the state-owned Izhevskij factory, and Russian pistols were hard currency. A new series, based on the Makarov, saw the light of day. The Izh-70 series. The Izh-70 and the Izh-70-100 use traditional Makarov ammunition, 9x18mm, with a magazine that holds eight and twelve bullets respectively. The Izh-70-200 and the Izh-70-300 are designed to use the more international Browning bullets, 9x17mm, eight and twelve respectively. In addition, there's also the brand-new Izh-70-400, which has been specially made for the enormous American firearms market's popular Parabellum ammunition."

"Unbelievably fascinating," Hjelm muttered. "Connection?"

"Sure enough, it's said to have turned up in the various Balkan wars. But, like I said, it's . . . popular."

"The sub-machine guns then? Let me guess."

"No."

"Military arsenal?"

"Yup," said Chavez, sitting down with a thud. "They've been traced back to a big arsenal in Boden where a great big break-in took place a year or two ago. Twenty-three standard-model sub-machine guns were stolen, as well as boxes and boxes of ammo. A feast for the eyes."

"Boden," Hjelm nodded. "I assume that Niklas Lindberg served there at some point during his military career."

"Both he and Bergwall did, actually. Bergwall did his service there. Lindberg was a cadet. If that's what it's called."

"No idea. More, more, more."

"Well," Chavez sighed deeply, "I'm going to work on the Nazi organisations. With Gunnar Nyberg as a backup, if it all works for him. Someone somewhere must know about this organisation, and someone somewhere must know what's going to happen next. I don't think this is the end. They've got the briefcase, they've got the money — or drugs, if that's what this is about — but they're going to do something particular with them, I'd bet my bloody life on it. So it'll be like this: me and Gunnar working the Nazi racket, Arto and Viggo on Kumla, you and Kerstin the 'policeman'. I don't think it's a good idea to go straight for Nedic, it's never worked. Plus, it's not him behind the Sickla Slaughter. It's Niklas Lindberg and his gang. We've got to get them."

"Great," exclaimed Hjelm. "That's that, then, Detective Superintendent. There's just one thing missing. A pensioner by the name of Jan-Olov Hultin."

"Yeah, yeah. He can have some kind of therapeutic job. Basket weaving, maybe."

CHAPTER
EIGHTEEN

Jan-Olov Hultin didn't weave any baskets. He went straight for Nedic.

Why not? he thought as he parked the service Volvo he had just signed out on Granitvägen and strolled the last few metres through the most luxurious parts of a deserted, Midsummer Danderyd. The weather couldn't make its mind up. At that moment, the threatening rain clouds had decided to take a break, drifted apart and exposed a confused sun which didn't seem to know what it should do with its rays of light. They fell capriciously over the waters of the Edsviken inlet, glimmering sporadically, now here, now there, and this strange, unsteady sparkle had a hypnotic effect on the former pensioner. For a moment, he imagined that he was back on the other side of Edsviken, and that it was his lake, Ravalen, that was shimmering. He had once again failed to tell grass from weeds, made the customary arc around the innocent little plant with the lawnmower, and continued up the slope. No luxurious Saab had pulled up on the gravel driveway. No man, looking like a gravely criminal estate agent, had come to meet him. Life was as normal. A constant Sisyphean task.

The moment passed.

It wasn't everyone who could call themselves a "former pensioner". It struck him that it was probably one of the country's most unusual titles. He would have to live up to it.

Why not? he thought, but not quite as recklessly as it might have seemed. The A-Unit had expressly left the question of Rajko Nedic open. Should they allow Nedic to remain ignorant of their knowledge of his involvement in the Sickla Slaughter? How would that make things better? Wouldn't it be preferable to make sure that he toed the line and didn't cause another, even worse slaughter? Wouldn't it be better to show that they knew, so that he didn't think he could do whatever he wanted?

Rajko Nedic wasn't the kind of man to do anything if he thought it would get him into trouble; he would hardly carry out an enormous massacre leaving a whole load of tracks behind him, he would rather cajole the bag back to him using threats and professional investigation. Still, Hultin felt — and again, it was a kind of instinctive feeling rather than any kind of logic or reason which guided this — that it was good to put some pressure on Nedic, to establish personal contact, to show a presence and his own, personal interest in the course of events.

Plus, he was the one who decided.

With that incontestable argument on the tip of his tongue, he trudged up to an enormous, locked metal gate set into a long brick wall. A surveillance camera

204

zoomed in on him, and before he had even started to look for a doorbell, a voice said: "Name and business."

Jan-Olov Hultin cleared his throat and said, authoritatively: "Detective Superintendent Jan-Olov Hultin from CID. I'd like to speak with Rajko Nedic."

There was a moment of silence. Then the gate slid open and he walked into a gardener's paradise. A man dressed in dungarees and a filthy cap was fiddling with some flowers on a magnificent, exceptionally pretty bush. All around him, the garden was in full bloom. Hultin who, as we know, couldn't tell grass from weeds, felt an instinctive jealousy. He walked over to the man in the dungarees and hat and said: "I'm looking for Rajko Nedic."

"An unusual plant," said the man without looking up, still fussing with the pretty purple flowers. "But in this garden, you'll find everything."

He took off his gardening gloves and held out his hand. "Rajko Nedic."

"Jan-Olov Hultin," said Jan-Olov Hultin, shaking the man's hand, surprised. He really did look more like a gardener than a leading drug dealer. Though what do leading drug dealers look like? Maybe like a slightly furrowed but healthy-looking man without a single grey hair, dressed in dungarees and a cap.

"I think it must be my poor childhood in a barren country that's caused this abundance of flowers," he said, without a trace of a foreign accent. "I come from a little mountain village in eastern Serbia. Maybe you know that already."

"I wish I had such a green touch in my garden," said Hultin, looking out over the display of colour.

"I must admit, it's not just a matter of a *touch*," said Nedic, smelling the flower in his hand. "Unfortunately it's also a matter of money. Some of these plants are rarities, but not this one. My favourite flower. It's in almost every Swedish garden, flowering nicely. Completely normal columbines. My goodness. The first time I saw it, I thought I was seeing proof of God. Look at the shape of the flowers. These four fantastic cupped petals arching around a common point. As though they'd found the centre of the universe."

Hultin looked at the columbine. It really was exceptional.

"A masterpiece," he said honestly.

"Yes, it really is. Well, Detective Superintendent, what can I do for you? Yet another baseless accusation? I've made a real effort to explain that I'm just a normal restaurant owner. A restaurateur."

"I'm not here to accuse you," said Hultin, lifting his gaze from the columbine. "More to express my condolences. Four such devoted colleagues."

Rajko Nedic's gaze didn't falter. He remained the good-natured gardener showing off the results of his green-fingered patience.

"I'm afraid I don't understand," he said.

"Vukotic in Kumla and the three war criminals on the Sickla industrial estate. Really tragic."

"You've lost me now, Detective. I really don't understand what you're talking about."

206

"Haven't you heard about the Kumla explosion and the Sickla Slaughter?"

"Unfortunately I don't have time to follow the gambols of the press too closely. I work rather hard."

A mobile phone rang somewhere within his dungarees. Nedic fished it out and answered: "Hello . . . *Ja, ja, guten Tag. Leider können wir uns jetzt nicht sprechen . . . Ich rufe zurück in etwa zehn Minuten . . . Ja. Tschüß.*"

"*Zehn Minuten?*" asked Jan-Olov Hultin.

"An estimation," said Rajko Nedic, shrugging. "It might be sooner if you would get to the point, Detective."

"German contacts?"

"Suppliers. Most of my time is spent in negotiation with suppliers."

"Suppliers?"

"Of Mosel wine in this case, yes. Direct import. It's lawful nowadays, as you know."

"Then I'll use my allotted ten minutes economically. This time we know more than normal, and it's not the usual drugs or finance police who are involved, but it'll be me and my group that you'll be dealing with, Mr Nedic. It's a good group. Specialists. We know that the contents of a briefcase were stolen from you down in Sickla, and that you lost four of your key staff. Maybe you'll start to feel the loss, even if you can bring in as many replacement war criminals as you like, whenever you like, from the former Yugoslavia. We also know who robbed you, if it's of interest. You were delivering money or drugs in that briefcase, to a party who never received it. That party will be annoyed by this time. Maybe that's a risk factor. We know that you'll do all you can to get the briefcase back, and we'll be here the entire time. Is there a case of blackmail that you'd like to report?"

Rajko Nedic regarded the elderly man with owl-like glasses perched on his enormous nose.

"No," he replied.

"Fantastic," said Jan-Olov Hultin, turning on his heels. "But remember that this isn't the normal situation. From now on, everything will be more difficult."

He began walking towards the gate. After a few metres, he turned round.

"One more question," he said. "What's the difference between grass and weeds?"

Rajko Nedic chuckled faintly.

"It's easy, Detective Superintendent," he said. "Weeds are the things you clear out of the way."

CHAPTER
NINETEEN

As Sara Svenhagen stood outside, looking up, she realised why she hadn't recognised the address, Fatburstrappan 18.

It was the address of Söder Torn, the high-rise which loomed over Södermalm.

In 1980, the redevelopment of the Södra Station area had begun in Stockholm. In practical terms, this had meant that a completely new quarter would be built. An architectural design competition was announced. HSB, the cooperative housing association, suggested that a "Södermalm Manhattan" be built, covering the entire twenty-five hectares with skyscrapers. Their suggestion gained support from a surprising number of camps, but it was the beginning of the eighties, after all. A time of accelerating madness. Naturally, their outlandish suggestion couldn't go through. Instead, in 1984, an alternative proposal was made by the Town Planning Office, a plan where one tall building remained; a compromise that was meant to ensure both that the quarter's traditional character was retained — with one high tower, a campanile or a church tower — and that those clamouring for skyscrapers wouldn't be left empty-handed. Later the same year, yet another competition was announced, focused on the tower that would be built close to Medborgarplatsen. Seventy different entries flowed in, the vast majority suggesting a pseudo-American skyscraper with around fifty floors. One of the judges was hardly neutral. His name was Sune Haglund, the city planning commissioner for the Moderate Party. He argued enthusiastically in favour of an extremely high and bulky office block, ideally with a rotating restaurant at the top. No winner was announced from the competition, but several commended entries were allowed, two years later, to take part in a new competition to design a considerably slimmer high-rise than Haglund had suggested. The Danish architect Henning Larsen won with a plan for a circular tower of forty-three floors. Its nickname was "Haglund's Stick". This was in 1986. After a couple of years of consideration by the committee, it was decided that forty-three floors was abnormally high, that the tower would rise like a distorted phallus up out of Södermalm, with the large, round testicle of the Globe Arena a sorry addition in the visible distance. And so the tower was lowered to thirty-three floors, which then became twenty-three, which, after the Stockholm Party vetoed it, eventually became eleven. The hand was reduced to nothing but a thumb. In 1990, a hardly impressive office block of eleven floors was officially approved. By then, the Söder Station area was almost complete. The stalls and boutiques of the Södermalmshallarna, the flats in Bofills båge, the areas of Fatburstrappan and Fatbursparken. But this was the start of the nineties, the property crisis a reality. All

210

further building projects were put on hold. Until 1992. Then the authorities decided that it was no longer offices that were needed, but residences. So, from the office block of eleven floors, Henning Larsen created a residential building of twenty-three floors; sixty-six metres high, home to around one hundred flats. In the spring of 1995, these new plans were approved. Building work could begin.

After all of the toing and froing, protests and attempts at compromise, "Haglund's Stick" came to be known as "Haglund's Semi", though in order to remove Sune Haglund's name from the tower once it was complete, it was officially named Söder Torn. That name hadn't quite caught on.

People lived there in any case. The flats were abnormally expensive, but people lived there.

A man named John Andreas Witréus lived there, for example. He was a paedophile.

Sara Svenhagen stood between two uniformed police officers, looking up at the strange enormous metal ring which floated like a halo above Söder Torn. At that moment, she thought to herself that Haglund's Stick really was beautiful. Perhaps her view was slightly coloured, but it really wasn't so bad.

On the other hand, the combination of phallus, halo, semi and paedophile seemed to be telling her something that, for the moment, she couldn't piece together. She had other things on her mind.

She looked out over Medborgarplatsen. It was strangely empty. Usually Stockholm's busiest square, it was largely deserted. It was overcast and dreary. And completely deserted.

A caretaker let the trio into Söder Torn. The elegant stairwell smelt new and faintly perfumed. They thanked him and stepped into the lift. The taller of the policemen was carrying a short, black cement battering ram with handles. He held it ostentatiously in one hand. Sara thought that maybe she should give him an impressed look. Just to make sure of his goodwill.

It didn't quite work.

The lift took them to the sixteenth floor. They wandered through a corridor, exquisitely adorned with flowers, and came to a door marked "Witréus". Is that really a name? she wondered to herself, pointing silently at the door. Just to be on the safe side, she took her pistol out. The policemen positioned the battering ram just beneath the door handle, and glanced at her. She nodded. They broke the door open and rushed in.

By the window in the flat, which was shaped like a slice of cake, a grey-haired man in his sixties was sitting, dressed in a thin summer suit with a mauve tie. He lowered a long-lensed camera to stare straight down the muzzle of Sara Svenhagen's pistol.

"My God," he said quietly.

She could see clearly in his eyes that he knew what their visit was about.

"John Andreas Witréus?" she asked.

"Yes," the man whispered.

"Put the camera down and raise your hands above your head."

John Andreas Witréus did as he was told.

212

"Lie flat on the floor," she continued, nodding to the assistants who had begun frisking him with a slight touch of brutality.

She wandered around the flat. It was fantastic. And pedantically clean. There were countless antiques. Old, elegant objects everywhere. The view out over the city was magnificent, in several directions. And in the bedroom, which had the atmosphere of British colonial India, the computer was on.

When she saw that, she felt a wave of complete, ice-cold calm. She had him. She returned to the living room.

One of the assistants was, for some reason, sitting on Witréus's back. She heard it cracking and crunching.

"I think that's enough now," she said, taking the camera. It was a Canon, press photographer standard. Easily twenty thousand kronor's worth.

The police assistant climbed off John Andreas Witréus.

"Thanks," she said ingratiatingly, turning to the man lying on the floor. "What is it you take photos of?"

"I'm very interested in photography," said Witréus, trying to sit up. The cracking continued.

"I can see that," said Sara Svenhagen. The rest could be saved for the secluded interview room. She turned to the assistants. "Take him with you. Put him in an interview room; I'll be there soon."

They packed up and disappeared. She stood by the window, waiting until the police car had driven away. To the right, she could see the Södermalmshallarna and their cineplexes, and the edge of the enormous, strangely curved building which went by the name of Bofills båge. Straight ahead, Medborgarplatsen stretched out, full of empty cafes and bars, and then the old civic hall with its public baths and library. To the left, Götgatan and the right-hand corner of the Björns trädgård park.

She turned back to the expensive flat. She was doing her best to make the undeniable elegance of the place tally with the sleazy business of paedophilia.

Still, the officers in Auschwitz had lived in nice places, too.

Almost immediately, she found a whole series of child-porn films in the video cabinet. That dilemma was over and done with, at any rate. There was a great case for an arrest. She continued through the flat. In the bedroom, she found three extensive albums full of images of children.

The smaller of the two bathrooms had been turned into a darkroom. She switched on the red light and stepped into a strange world of pictures. Newly developed photographs were hanging from a clothes line. Veritable piles of photographs were strewn across the room. There must have been five, six thousand. And, for the most part, they all had the same subject.

She had expected a monstrous sight, the kind that changes the very core of a person. Thousands of pictures of children being sexually abused. Söder Torn as a kind of Tower of Babel, the reason God had turned His back on man. The flat as the country's worst paedophile den. John Andreas Witréus as Dr Mengele.

214

But that wasn't the case. Sure, there were pictures of children, but they all seemed to have been taken from the windows of Haglund's Stick. Spring, summer, autumn and winter. Children skating on Medborgarplatsen's artificial ice rink. Children running through the rain on their way from the cineplex. Children playing with hula hoops in the summer sunshine. Children skateboarding between dirty piles of snow. Children with little paper flags, on their way from the McDonald's on the Götgatan-Folkungagatan crossroads. Children, children, children. And most of the photographs were fantastic. Beautiful pictures of children. They gave off a palpable affection for the existential form of children. In its own right. She felt deeply surprised.

They were black-and-white photographs, the date printed at the top. It was like a long documentation of the place, seen through a child's eyes. She thought of the film *Smoke*, where Paul Auster lets Harvey Keitel document his own little corner of the world. There was nothing more to it.

John Andreas Witréus had documented his own sick little corner of the world. With a child's eyes.

She looked up at the photographs hanging from the clothes line. The most recent date was 7 June. In a jam jar on the toilet seat, there were many more undeveloped films. She took the jar with her, together with a random selection of photographs. She made her way into the kitchen and found a carrier bag into which she put everything. She went back to the bedroom and picked up one of the albums, then back to the living room where she also placed the camera and a couple of the videotapes into the bag.

She went over to the computer and checked whether it was password-protected. It was. She switched off the password protection, shut the computer down and packed it up. Every single disk went into the carrier bag.

Then she pulled the broken door closed, taped a sign to it explaining that the flat was a crime scene, and waited for one of the uniformed officers to return.

"Have you called for a locksmith?" she asked.

He nodded.

She nodded.

"Take the computer," she said, heading off.

She strolled down through Fatbursparken, past Bofills båge, glancing up at the enormous clock above Södra Station. Then she arrived at the police station at Fatbursgatan 1. Without further ado, she walked through reception and followed the police assistant's extended forefinger to the interview room. John Andreas Witréus was waiting; he looked like a bank manager on summer holiday. Without a word, she placed the things on the table. The pile of photographs, the jam jar filled with rolls of film, the album of pictures, the videotapes, the camera. She looked at him.

He squirmed. Caught.

Like a child.

"I'm sorry," he said courteously.

"I don't actually think that you're a *practising* paedophile," said Sara Svenhagen. "But on the other

216

hand, you know that the laws regarding possession of child pornography have become stricter recently."

"I know," he said quietly, looking down at the table. "Was it the Internet?"

"We'll come back to that. You had a really successful firm down in Varberg that produced some kind of filters for Volvos, right? Subcontractor. You started the firm sometime in the sixties, and after you won the Volvo contract, the value went through the roof. When you sold it five years ago, you got countless millions for it. And now the Volvo contract's been cancelled, and the firm's collapsed. Nicely done."

"Is this about my business?" John Andreas Witréus asked, completely confused.

"No," said Sara Svenhagen. "I'm just summarising. You sold the firm and became financially independent. You blew a couple of million on the flat in Söder Torn, bought yourself a magnificent set of furniture, and then spent your time sitting in your window, peeping and taking photographs of children from the sixteenth floor. Why?"

He was silent, gazing down at his bright white knuckles. He looked up, and said: "I like children."

She held up a videotape. She opened the photo album, and held one of the pages a few centimetres from Witréus's face.

"No," she said. "You don't bloody *like* children. You *desire* children. There's a hell of a difference. Why do you take these pictures?"

He was staring at his knuckles. After almost thirty seconds, she took the album away and was met by a completely defenceless gaze. A defenceless, *questioning* gaze. One which actually seemed to be looking for an answer to her question.

"I think," said Sara Svenhagen, "that you hate your sexuality, that more than anything else, you'd like to be castrated. You think that you like children, but you really just *want to be* a child. You want to be a child. You sit up there in Haglund's Semi and tell yourself that you're taking photos from a child's perspective, but really you've put a distance of sixteen floors between you. As if to emphasise the distance. Unobtainability itself. By definition, it's an impossible project. You're sitting at a safe distance, manically taking pictures. Five, six thousand pictures since you moved in just a year or two ago. You're looking for the perfect picture of childhood, but you've made it impossible yourself. You've placed yourself, completely intentionally, at such a distance that it'll be impossible to take the perfect picture, the one which would make you a child. The whole thing is about your never-ending, unconditional longing to be a child. And so when the desire sets in, you punish yourself by violating the most precious thing: the child inside you. Like all paedophiles, you don't give a damn about actual children, real children. It's always all about you. When you're sitting there, getting off on children who've been mistreated, it's the child inside you that you're punishing. That's what's mocking you, by never being able to show its face in the light of day. The one with a grip around your testicles, about to split you in two."

218

John Andreas Witréus stared at Sara Svenhagen. She felt almost sweaty, as though her voicebox had been for a jog.

"Yeah," he whispered. "Could be."

"But I don't care about you," she said bluntly. "I want to know how you ended up in a paedophile network online."

Witréus blinked. His entire being seemed to be a wall, closing in and closing in until there was nothing left to close in. Until there was nothing but wall. He couldn't relinquish his very self. He was completely stuck in himself.

"I don't actually know," he said eventually. "I was looking at pictures on some site. Then the pictures started flooding into my inbox. I don't know how. They must've got hold of my address on some site."

"Don't lie to me."

"I'm not. I never lie. But I keep myself to myself. For fifty years, I've carried my secret with me. I've never, ever acted on my desires; it isn't real, it's virtual, and I've never, ever met any of . . . my kind. That's the last thing I want. I'd despise them. Pigs. Swine. The ones who travel to Thailand to buy children. Never. I don't want that, it's not that I want. I swear I don't have any idea how I ended up on that list. My inbox is overflowing with pictures and I have no idea how it happened."

Sara Svenhagen paused to think. If this was true, then it was a new strategy. It would mean interesting new opportunities. Was it possible to capture the email address of every visitor to a website? If so, how the hell did you do it?

She watched John Andreas Witréus closely. He was shaken and moved and thinking about one thing only. The only thing he had thought about his entire life. Himself.

And he was telling the truth.

She was convinced of that now.

But she couldn't feel sorry for him. She hadn't come that far.

Or so she told herself.

CHAPTER
TWENTY

"Shit, I had it!"

Bullet's face scrunched up as though he'd had a mouthful of acid. He adjusted the headphones, twisting and tuning a device in front of him. The LEDs on it remained black.

He had found the signal three times now.

And lost it.

The first time, they had stormed out of the cellar and into the metallic-green van. Bullet first, spinning like a ballerina with the antenna in the air, eyes on the device in his hand and headphones around his neck. Then Rogge, carrying Danne Blood Pudding. Then the golden one himself, still sceptical.

"Still got it!" Bullet yelled, jumping into the passenger seat. Rogge pushed Danne in through the back doors and ran round to the driver's seat. They sped off.

"Try the E4 southbound," Bullet continued. "That's where it should be."

Then it was gone. The signal tone disappeared from the headphones, and the LEDs went dark.

"Fuck," said Bullet. "Keep going on the E4 anyway. We've got to find it again. We've got the best chance there."

They kept just at the upper edge of the speed limit. 118 kilometres per hour, max. To be stopped for speeding would be a death blow. Since it was Midsummer weekend, it wasn't impossible that the pigs had put a few extra traffic checks on. Though, on the other hand, it wasn't exactly likely.

The first dilemma arose in Södertälje. There was no signal, and they were approaching the turn-off for the European highway. The E20 westbound or the E4 south? Bullet gestured with his hands.

"Gothenburg or Malmö?" he asked. "Right or straight ahead?"

The alternatives coursed through the golden one's mind while the damn junction rushed ever closer. If the thieves had got hold of the money, the E4 would've been the obvious choice. They would have been on their way to Europe. But now they probably had to test the key, so there was no reason to choose Malmö over Gothenburg. Gothenburg was bigger, after all. But then, maybe they'd realised that it was a foreign key and, in that case, wouldn't heading south, towards Copenhagen, be more likely? What was closest if they kept going straight? Nyköping, Norrköping, Linköping? And to the right? Strängnäs, Mariefred, Eskilstuna, Örebro. Christ, no, not Kumla. That settled it.

"E4," he said, and Rogge had just enough time to turn left and continue southwards.

The second signal came soon after Norrköping. They had just passed the second turn-off onto the European highway and opted against the E22 towards Västervik and Kalmar. A brief signal they couldn't determine the direction of. Still, they were on the right tracks. Bullet shouted and screamed in frustration.

"Fucking hell, can't we step on the gas a bit?" asked Rogge.

"No," said the golden one.

Nothing happened on Vätternvägen. They passed Gränna and Visingsö. They were close to giving up. Not a squeak. Had they lost the signal for good now? Did Bullet's bloody handiwork even work? They knew that Jönköping would be the test. A meeting point of roads going in all directions. The 33 towards Nässjö, Vimmerby, Västervik. The 30 towards Växjö, Kalmar and the whole of Blekinge county. The E4, continuing on to Värnamo, Ljungby and Skåne county. The 40 towards Borås and Gothenburg. Was it Gothenburg after all?

"Nothing?" asked the golden one.

Bullet shook his head. They were in Huskvarna. The last descent down towards Jönköping.

"We'll have to fill up soon, Nicke," said Rogge. "The warning light's on."

"Bullet, you bastard, can't you speed that thing up somefuckinghow?" Danne moaned from behind. "Turn it right up?"

"You don't know a thing, you bloody idiot," Bullet snapped.

"Shut up," the golden one said calmly.

Everyone shut up.

Not Gothenburg. He had decided against that. He stuck to his guns. Not Västervik. Also dropped. Växjö? That way, they would have a whole load of places to choose from: Karlshamn, Ronneby, Karlskrona, maybe Kristianstad. Though that would have been the E22 anyway.

"Stay on this one," he said.

They stayed on the E4. In Skillingaryd, the fuel was dangerously low.

"Stop here," he said before they pulled up into the petrol station staff's line of sight.

"We've gotta fill up," said Rogge.

"We need money," he said, pulling on the gold-coloured hat, taking his pistol off safety and jumping out of the van.

"Are you going alone?" said Bullet through the window. "Is that a good idea?"

"It's not good, it's the *best*. Wait here."

They waited. After five minutes, he came back, a plastic bag in his hand.

"You can fill up now," he said, pulling off the hat. "I don't think you'll need to pay."

They filled up. Back out on the E4, Bullet suddenly shouted: "I've found it again. Christ, it's here. They must've stopped. I've got the direction. They're going south on the E4. Not far ahead."

"Step on it?" said Rogge.

"Stick to the limit," said Niklas Lindberg calmly, shoving the gold hat into the glovebox.

Bullet's face scrunched up again. He shouted: "Fuck, I had it!"

CHAPTER
TWENTY-ONE

The unexpected flaw in their plan dawned on them much too late. Two cars, each on a different course through Sweden. A rusty old Datsun and a dazzlingly white Ford Focus, one of last year's award-winning models. Not until six hundred kilometres separated them did the fact that it was Midsummer weekend cross their minds. Not a single bank would be open in the whole of Sweden. They were left to their respective ghosts. The ones they had told themselves they would never have to be alone with again.

It would be a Midsummer weekend that neither of them would ever forget. And never again have to repeat.

He was lying in a sad hotel bed just outside of Orsa, listening to the distant Midsummer celebrations from down on the shore of Orsasjön. The sounds were being sent like severely distorted electrical impulses from his eardrums to his brain. They pierced almost mockingly. A sound that cut and ripped. Orsa's musicians were stabbing at the taut strings of his nerves with their bows. Pressing a pillow to his ears didn't help, either. The sound was being distorted from *within*, that much he understood. It echoed like festivities do for someone on the outside. He wondered how long the little boy would have to be tied to the tree while the party continued down by the beach. Midsummer. They were letting him take part. For the first time, he had been invited. He had actually been invited.

He had trembled with happiness as he walked through the stretch of woodland by the waters of Edsviken. This would be the turning point. He took the route past the den. He stopped, standing motionless alongside the pathetic little patchwork of boards that had shielded him from the world whenever everything collapsed in on him. When had it done anything else? He had sat there, whittling boats from bark with an urgency that blocked out everything else. He had filled the den with increasingly elaborate bark boats until there was almost no room left for him. He was like Emil of Lönneberga, carving away in the woodshed. Though utterly devoid of all humour and warmth. And now, he was on his way to a Midsummer party with the rest of his class. He had been invited and finally, finally, finally been accepted.

He stood in front of the den and knew that it had saved his life. He went up to it and pulled it down. It didn't take much. A couple of kicks and it fell like a house of cards. A steady stream of bark boats came tumbling out. He said goodbye to that part of his life and welcomed another. A better one. Because it was impossible to imagine a worse one. He set off through the wood. He caught sight of the party down by the water. They were drinking. He stood still for a moment at the edge of the wood. Took a few deep breaths, straightened his new summer clothes and trudged over

226

to them. They welcomed him with laughter and shouting. He welled up with happiness. They took hold of his arms, held them behind his back, tied him to a tree and forced him to drink until he was sick. He stood there like a half-dressed maypole, his smart new summer clothes covered with bright green vomit. The maypole was ready.

He turned over in the sad little hotel bed and fished a newspaper, *Expressen*, from the bedside table. He read the article that had caught his eye once again, drawing rings around the words in ballpoint pen. The headline said: THE SISTERS THAT VANISHED INTO THIN AIR. He picked up his mobile phone.

She was lying in a sad hotel bed in Falkenberg, on the other side of the country, and couldn't hear a sound. The little west coast town seemed to be completely empty. Not a sound. She stared up at the ceiling and then at the briefcase, lying open on the floor. Imagine if she made contact. But there was no contact to make. There was only her and a bed. For several years, she hadn't been able to sleep in beds. They had scared the life out of her. Almost literally. She could still hear. Something within her could still hear the footsteps on the stairs. Though the sound was faint now, almost gone, as though the hearing was the last thing to leave her. She didn't hear the door opening in that unmistakable way that should have been soundless but wasn't; on the contrary, it echoed through her, and she knew that it would echo through her for the rest of her life. That was why it was going to be so short. A short life. That was why she experienced such immense

227

pleasure from *not* hearing the door open. She couldn't feel the sheet being pushed to one side, either. Not that first scream, the quiet, almost silent scream of mad desperation, nor the other, more shrill, more wholehearted, but also more self-reproaching.

Actually, she didn't hear anything at all before she suddenly glanced down at her near-naked body and saw that it was covered in clotted blood. She saw the bandages around her wrists, the bag of blood hanging from the stand — and she realised that she had failed. That was why she started to cry. Her family were gathered around her, and it was obvious, it was immediately obvious that they thought they were tears of joy. But they were tears of sadness. Sadness at still being alive.

He stood up and went over to the window. The musicians seemed to have halted their accordion playing. Perhaps someone had silenced them with a generous glass of schnapps. He could see right down to the shore of Orsasjön. If she had been by his side, it would have been a fantastic evening view. Now, it was quite unimportant. Like everything had been for so long. When had the turning point come? Was she the only turning point, or had there been other, smaller points along the way? He had left them behind once his compulsory education was over. No more school. He had continued tinkering about with things with the same all-consuming intensity as he had with the bark boats. He started to feel a certain pride over being able to fix anything, anything at all; being able to take something apart and then put it back together again.

228

And he continued his whittling, though no longer making bark boats but abstract wooden sculptures. He hadn't even understood that they *were* sculptures until someone told him. It was a kind of life, in any case, so long as he kept the others at a distance. Everyone else. And then that strange invitation had turned up. Class reunion. Meet his old classmates. As though they hadn't already invited him one time too many.

He was convinced they had sent the invite by mistake, that he just happened to have been left on a list from which he should have been crossed out. Still, he felt like he really *should* go. He was almost twenty. It was far enough back in time that it didn't bring him down. He would show them that he existed as a purely physical indictment. You didn't manage to kill me. No hate, just his very presence as proof. He went, convinced that he would be mocked or left on the outside, if not tied up, abused and pissed on. But that wasn't how it was. All of the old tormentors were there. All of them. And none of them seemed to have the faintest memory of how they had tortured him. They treated him well, even laughed at their memories. Together. Cheerily. Like happy children. And he realised that the torture had taken place almost incidentally, without much thought, that they actually had no idea what they had done to him. Worst of all would be meeting the girl that had been the driving force. The boys he could live with, but the degradation of meeting the girl who had been the first to come forward and piss on him would be awful, he had also been firmly convinced of that. He was wrong there, too.

229

And then some. She had grown into a wonderful young woman. It was clear from her eyes that she was the one feeling guilt and shame, not him. She was the only one who touched upon the forbidden part of the past.

"Shit, we treated you so badly," was the first thing she said, and he was able to meet her eyes as she said it. What he saw was something even *worse*. It was the first time he had seen anything like it. His eyes didn't leave hers that entire evening. He sat, reading a terror beyond comprehension deep within her dark eyes. And in that moment, he knew that he wanted to know everything. Absolutely everything.

She stood up and went over to the window. People had slowly begun to return to Falkenberg. The town was no longer completely deserted. If he had been by her side, it would have been tempting to go out into town. Now, it was quite unimportant. What had stopped her from taking the step for so long? For the first time, a glimmer of light was peeping through from the past. There was someone she went to, someone she could tell anything to, someone who listened. Uncle Jubbe.

She remembered his expression, how his face had clouded over in that special way, the awkwardness in the way that he stroked her hair while she sobbed silently, how his tears fell into her hair and slowly made their way down to her scalp. But eventually, even Uncle Jubbe wasn't enough. She had slashed her wrists, lengthways rather than crossways, not as a warning but as a final solution. One which turned out not to be final at all. She was invited to the class reunion while she was

230

in hospital. It was almost like a taunt. As though the last part of her mask had been ripped off, exposing a corroded skull. The toughest girl in the class. Her wrists had healed, but she refused to leave the hospital. Every day, she begged the doctor to find a new complication, and her doctor had done it, with an increasingly troubled expression. Until finally, it couldn't go on any longer. She went to her old school's reunion party. At the far end of the bar in the unbearable golf club, she saw the person she wanted to meet least of all, the person she had vented her self-loathing on. He looked different. So alive, as though reborn, and so awfully, wonderfully different to the others. They were all the same. At the very moment she uttered her first words to him, she knew that they belonged together. She said: "Shit, we treated you so badly."

The rest, as they say, is history.

CHAPTER
TWENTY-TWO

They had agreed to meet in Sundberg's Konditori down by Järntorget. Though it was Midsummer, it was still open. She assumed it was because of the Germans. Not the Germans who had built Järntorget five hundred or so years ago, but the Germans strolling up and down Västerlånggatan that very day, wondering why everything was closed. Even the restaurants.

But not Sundberg's Konditori, Sweden's oldest coffee shop. As a result, the cafe was chock-full of Germans looking for shelter from the rain. It was a gloomy Midsummer's Day in Stockholm. The magnificent summer weather which had held for almost all of June was clearly a thing of the past. The rain was pelting down over Gamla Stan, washing Germans out from the alleyways. The fortunate ones washed up in Sundberg's Konditori.

He was sitting, cramped, at the back of the cafe. She thought to herself that he looked like Stalingrad. Surrounded by Germans.

He gave her a slight wave. Normally, when you had arranged to meet Party-Ragge, Detective Superintendent Ragnar Hellberg, he would stand up abruptly, smile broadly, wave enthusiastically and shout loudly. But not this time. Just that restrained little wave.

He was wearing a faded green T-shirt, jeans and tattered sandals; this wasn't how he normally looked. And his dark, mid-length hair above his little black Lenin beard, she had definitely never seen it look so dishevelled. There were hints of purple beneath his eyes. What had he been doing over Midsummer? Working? On "administrative stuff, I suppose you could say"?

Sara Svenhagen thought that he looked younger when he was serious, hardly thirty. That wasn't the case with men in general. They almost always looked younger when they *laughed*. Though, on the other hand, they only laughed when they were young. Properly laughed.

A little paradox in the midst of the Midsummer rain.

He was sitting at the very back of the cafe, next to a door she soon realised was the toilet. It slammed shut with high frequency. She shook the water from her clothes and sat down next to him with a little cup of coffee. No Danish pastries. It wasn't the time.

"Hi, Sara, everything OK?"

"Yeah, pretty good. I always feel a bit shaken when I've been talking to one of them. They seem to be on a completely different planet. A parallel universe."

"How did he seem? What was his name? Wirsén?"

"Witréus," she said. "John Andreas Witréus. And he seems . . . well, out of it. Here but not here. In some parallel existence, almost. You talk to him, but he's not there. Not really. He wanted me to act as a therapist.

233

Quite damaged, but quite harmless, too. A passive paedophile, I guess. Had quite a bit of porn but mainly took pictures. Loads of seemingly innocent pictures from his window up in Söder Torn. Of kids on Merborgarplatsen and the area around it. Hardly criminal."

"Have you had a chance to look at his computer?"

"Yeah. What he said is probably true. He doesn't seem to have any address lists himself, and doesn't seem to have sent any pictures. Just received them. En masse. There must be about five hundred pictures in his inbox alone. No proper sender details, of course, but it should be possible to find that out. Witréus unwittingly ended up on an address list. It might not be a network."

"What could it be, then?"

"I don't know. I'm not really a computer expert. We'll have to see what the specialists say."

"I'd rather the computer didn't end up there."

"What? Why?" Sara Svenhagen exclaimed.

Ragnar Hellberg leaned towards her. She guessed that he hadn't brushed his teeth for some time.

"I could pull rank on you, Sara. Say 'just follow my orders' and nothing more. But I don't want to. You've got to trust me. Let's keep this between us. No one else."

She scrutinised him. The young, comet-careerist superintendent. The party policeman. So subdued, so serious, so deflated. She didn't understand.

"OK," she said. "I won't ask."

"I know that you know a hell of a lot about computers, Sara. You'd be able to get a lot from it yourself, right?"

"Probably," she replied honestly.

"And what? What is it if it's not a network?"

"It's a list of addresses. It showed up for a few seconds on that temporary website on Thursday, at 19.36.07. I've got that address. But it stopped being of interest as soon as it revealed itself. It's a free, anonymous American site. Since I'm convinced Witréus is telling the truth, I don't think it's a network. The addresses, they don't know one another, they aren't sharing pictures in the usual way. The list is a way of expanding the circle without risking anything. Everyone that's visited a certain site — which is still unknown at this point — is bombarded with emails full of child porn.

"Without having *given* their email address?"

"I think so, yeah. They must've found a way to quickly identify a person's email address. Something that we'd find very useful. Since most of the people who want an anonymous email address use Hotmail, I think it's the key. You quickly identify the number of the phone line, check it off against the Hotmail users, and find an email address. It probably only takes a few milliseconds. I'm assuming it's something new."

"So this means that there's no alert risk, at least? If we let Witréus go, or let him talk to a lawyer, he won't be able to warn the network?"

"No. Because there is no network to contact. Theoretically, I suppose you could imagine him sending out general warnings via the paedophile sites, but it doesn't seem likely. He's staying in the closet. But are we really talking about letting him go?"

"No," said Hellberg, leaning back. "No, of course not. We've got enough with the child porn. And we're seizing the computer. Can you take it *home* and work on it there?"

"Yeah, if necessary."

"I'm afraid I'll have to be stubborn and say it *is* necessary. Anything else?"

"Witréus had a jar full of undeveloped films. And a film in his camera. Is it OK if I take them home and develop them? Can I get the darkroom equipment from the stockroom?"

"Buy it," said Ragnar Hellberg. "And give me the receipt."

"No tracks?" said Sara Svenhagen, watching her boss.

"No tracks," he nodded.

CHAPTER
TWENTY-THREE

Sunday afternoon. Time to sum up the blood-soaked Midsummer weekend. Unusually high levels of drunkenness. Unusually high numbers of rapes. Unusually high levels of violence. Unusually high levels of Midsummer.

Though that wasn't their concern.

Paul Hjelm hoped that there wouldn't be a repeat of the meeting the day before. It had been a painful affair. Partly because half of the team was missing, with Söderstedt and Norlander at Kumla and Nyberg piecing together the remains of his ongoing cases, partly because it had taken a far from heroic course. Hultin had come in through his mystical old side door, dumped some papers on the desk, sat down and looked out over the gathering. No one in the unimpressive little congregation — Hjelm, Holm, Chavez — wanted to be the one to begin. All were going to say the same thing anyway: that nothing had happened. Hultin didn't want to say it openly, either. And so they had just left, somewhat bewildered.

Their chances seemed slightly better today. Everyone was there, and the cat seemed to have loosened its grip on their tongues. There was small talk in the Supreme

237

Command Centre, a faint murmur. Jan-Olov Hultin regarded them through his owl-like glasses, silencing the small talk with: "I have an confession to make."

A strange opening line. They let him continue.

"I warned Rajko Nedic."

They looked at one another.

Chavez wrinkled his nose; otherwise, the outcry failed to materialise.

"I thought it would be best to keep him under a tight rein. Also, I just wanted to introduce myself. I visited him at his house out in Danderyd. He wasn't celebrating Midsummer. On the contrary, he was pottering about in a garden that looked like Eden."

"The toilet paper?" asked Söderstedt.

"Not Edet," Hultin retorted neutrally. "Eden."

"East of Eden," Hjelm alluded silkily.

"What did he say, then?" asked Chavez.

"Nothing really," said Hultin. "He was talking about columbines being proof of God. Denied everything."

"How unexpected," Nyberg muttered.

"So, ladies and gentlemen," said Hultin. "Time to go over the weekend's successes. Anyone feel inclined?"

"I've been thinking about something," said Chavez. "Something Åkesson said, out by the slaughter site in Sickla. About those bloody footprints next to the dry spot left by the briefcase. Eight prints, as it turned out. Four-year-old Reeboks, size 7."

"Four-year-old?" Norlander asked, perplexed.

"Apparently," said Chavez, glancing down at one of Brynolf Svenhagen's forensic reports. There were a lot

238

of them. Svenhagen was in ecstasy. The reports were flooding in. He had gone mad with excitement.

"You can work it out from the model," Kerstin Holm said, in the know. "The soles look different every year."

"Get to the point," said Hultin.

"One: the tracks are going in the wrong direction," said Chavez stringently. "Two: Niklas Lindberg's men don't exactly seem the type to take any careless steps in blood."

"They were careless enough to get shot," said Hultin, shrugging. "Actually, half of them were shot, and by men they'd already frisked, judging by appearances. Maybe we're overestimating their professionalism. And the fact that the footprints were going in the wrong direction surely only means that the person who picked up the briefcase and saw it covered in his friend's blood was nervy. He took a couple of careless steps in the blood. In the wrong direction. By then he'd walked the blood off his trainers. He turned and went back. Let's not make a mountain out of a molehill."

"It was just an observation," Chavez mumbled, thinking about basket weaving and other stimulating activities for pensioners.

"Size 7," said Hjelm. "Is that a small man? Or a woman? Eskil Carlstedt was at least a 12."

"11," said Chavez, his eyes on Qvardfordt's forensic report.

"There's no real correspondence between shoe size and body size," said Holm. "Or any other anatomical size, for that matter . . ."

"What else?" asked Hultin. "Kumla?"

Söderstedt and Norlander looked at one another. Both seemed to to be leaving the next word to the other. Eventually, Norlander said: "Everyone's keeping their mouths shut."

"That's because you always tell everyone to shut up," said Söderstedt. "I'm holding you personally responsible for all the shut mouths."

"Shut up," said Viggo Norlander.

Söderstedt continued, egged on by his own quick wit. "According to the guards, there was some kind of Nazi clique in Kumla. Nothing new, I know. Organised criminals always seem to be either immigrants or Nazis nowadays. Maybe what we're seeing in the underworld is some kind of nasty prelude to a wider development in society. Or rather, some kind of clearer, less veiled version of the polarisation which is becoming more and more obvious in society.

"I mean, what's it really like when it comes to racism, if we really ask around in society? If we scratch the surface a little. At the moment, we don't need to be especially worried about any political parties with Nazi tendencies or anything like that; but on the other hand, we should be more vigilant than ever when it comes to the enemy within. The enemy within ourselves, I mean. That's where attitudes seem to have changed. A barrier has been lowered. It's not easy to detect, but it's a change from a few years back. It suddenly seems to be much easier to think of people as *objects*. As non-people. As people whose blood isn't quite as red as our own. Is the ethnic cleansing in Kosovo and Bosnia really a strictly internal, historical Balkan affair, or does

240

it have something to do with the wider change in . . . well, enlightened mentalities after all? How big a difference is there between sending all the immigrants to the outskirts, to Rinkeby or Hammarkullen or Rosengård, and driving people out of their home towns?"

"Back to Kumla," Hultin said, remaining completely neutral.

Söderstedt changed tracks without much of a problem.

"Niklas Lindberg and Sven Joakim Bergwall were both part of this Nazi clique. Lindberg might've been the leader. Otherwise, we've scraped together about twenty or so names. Eight of them are out now. Some of the other criminals might be part of this eight, but at the moment we can't say for sure. As many as *three* of the men released have AB negative blood: Christer Gullbrandsen, Dan Andersson and — no joke — Ricky Martin.

"On the other hand, we've got a rookie like Eskil Carlstedt, a used-car salesman, in their gang. Linking this too closely to the Kumla Bunker is probably a mistake. The question is whether we're right to link it to these Nazis at all. We'll see. We spoke to several members of this clique, the ones that're still inside. Viggo's laconic description fits well there: they're all keeping their mouths shut. Our ex-Yugoslav friends are keeping their mouths even tighter shut. No one is saying a word. They pretend they don't understand a single word of Swedish. Still, they listened carefully to our account of Lordan Vukotic's torture. And Göran

Andersson didn't have much else to say. He did tell us quite a lot of interesting things about how Fra Angelico played with different shades of blue, though."

"What else?" said Hultin.

"I spoke with Eskil Carlstedt's workmates at Kindwall's Ford garage in Hammarby harbour," said Kerstin Holm. "With his old mother out in Bromma, too. A picture of a man with quite extreme opinions when it comes to racial issues is emerging, so we can keep that Nazi connection for the time being. Violent tendencies aren't lacking, either. His workmates described a pretty scary paintball game, the start to some company party, where Carlstedt gave two of them a beating under the cover of darkness. He'd gone berserk. Actually, no one there really seemed to like him at all. A couple of them said he was a strange character, impossible to get to know. But on the other hand, he sold cars better than anyone else. Easily the best. It was this car-seller trait that Sven Joakim Bergwall trusted when he let Carlstedt stay behind in Kvarnen. And now both of them are dead. All that trust was in vain.

"We've also tried to recall the witnesses from Kvarnen to get some better descriptions of this so-called 'policeman' who was sitting with Gang One. News of his existence came so late that we didn't have time to ask earlier. Most of the witnesses had left the city for Midsummer, and the ones who'd stayed behind didn't have anything useful to add. So we don't have any description of the 'policeman'. The same's generally true of Gang Two. Everyone remembers

242

Carlstedt clearly, the broad one with the shaved head and moustache. A couple thought that they recognised Bergwall when we showed them his photo. Someone mentioned a man with a purple face. Otherwise, nothing. The man with the earphones was neither Carlstedt nor Bergwall, so we can assume this means that the technician in the group is still alive and well."

"Speaking of technicians, our own have gone through Eskil Carlstedt's hard drive," said Hjelm, glancing down at yet another forensic report. "The problem is that it was empty. Completely empty, I mean. Which means it was new. The computer wasn't new, but the hard drive was. As far as we can tell, it was replaced for our benefit. Which, again, tips the balance in favour of professionalism. The night before Carlstedt came and let himself be interviewed by us, the same night that they cobbled their story together, the hard drive seems to have been swapped. They realised we'd be making a visit. Scrapping the whole computer was too risky; there's always the chance of someone finding a scrapped computer. So they swapped the hard drive so that they didn't leave any evidence. That means there must've been something on the hard drive, in all probability of a racial character. Now we've got a swapped hard drive, a sophisticated listening device in Kvarnen, and two utterly subtle bombs. They don't seem to be lacking technological competence."

"Can you commit a crime without technical competence nowadays?" asked the technologically minded Chavez.

"Meat cleavers and penises are still popular," said the less technologically minded Kerstin Holm. "The latter have worked especially well as instruments of crime for millennia."

There was a moment of silence. Everyone seemed to be thinking about their penis as a potential crime tool. Kerstin Holm smiled covertly.

"I suppose that's a kind of technique, too," Hultin said eventually.

"Speaking of those two ingenious bombs," said Norlander, glancing briefly at Kerstin Holm's notes. "In one of Svenhagen's reports, I've finally managed to find some information on the bombs. It's a case of highly explosive, highly concentrated liquid, like nitroglycerine but more effective and easier to handle. It's detonated by electricity *alone*; not warmth, not impact, just that little microscopic trigger that sends a short, sharp burst of electricity through the liquid, causing it to explode. Works brilliantly with a remote detonator, as we've seen. It's an explosive that hasn't been used in Sweden before, but there are certain hints of something similar in the US. They've not found a name for it yet, though."

"In any case, we can probably assume that Niklas Lindberg's stock isn't empty," said Chavez. "Do you want to hear a bit more about him, by the way? I've devoted my life to him for the time being. Searched all the databases I could think of, interviewed a whole load of former friends and colleagues over the phone, even been down to Trollhättan to talk to his parents and ex-wife.

"He was married for a while when he was still living there, even though he was mostly away on military exercises and in UN service in Cyprus. Just as his relationship was breaking down, he left the army and joined the Foreign Legion. Apparently you can still do that. His ex-wife is still called Lindberg, which might suggest that it wasn't an acrimonious divorce. It didn't sound that way, either. She got tired of him being away all the time, she had lovers, he had lovers among the nurses over in Cyprus. Popular with women in general. But let's start from the beginning. Niklas Lindberg was born in January 1965, took the science route in high school in Trollhättan, leaving with good grades in 1983. Did his compulsory military service in a commando unit in 1985, went through that with top grades, started officer training in autumn 1986, was a cadet in Boden in 1988, an officer in Cyprus in 1990 and 1992, climbed up the ranks and had just become a major with the commandos in Arvidsjaur when he left in 1994. Twenty-nine-year-old major, pretty good, no?"

"Yeah," said Hultin. "That's great."

"A couple of friends from school talked about him as a fun-loving guy who it was generally going well for," Chavez continued. "A high-flyer. A golden boy, you could say. Loads of women. His friends saw the thing with the commandos as a way to . . . get good grades in his enlistment, too. He liked getting good grades. His friends didn't take it seriously. There was nothing soldier-like about him. He doesn't seem to have done his service with his eye on a regular officer's career, either. And his childhood seems to have been a comfortable, small-town, middle-class one. His parents seem nice. A sweet couple, you could say. High-school teacher and occupational therapist. No racist tendencies, and believe me, I can normally get an instinctive feel for that. They were talking about a little tow head who had always landed on his feet, always been happy, always taken care of those weaker than him. The pictures from his childhood didn't suggest anything else. His parents really were immensely sad about his inexplicable transformation into a violent offender. A deep, internal sorrow. He stayed in Trollhättan even once he'd become an officer, married an old flame and seems to have been a nice enough guy. Smart, handsome, kind, or thereabouts. Then there seems to have been some kind of breakdown linked to his divorce five years ago. Spring 1994. A critical point.

"I've been talking to two of his superiors from the commando unit in Arvidsjaur; no one understood why he quit. There were no complaints. From either side. He just quit and went straight into the Foreign Legion. Two weeks later. It must've been well planned. But why? I haven't managed to get in touch with any of his Foreign Legion colleagues, they're a bit secretive after all, but I'll keep working on it. He quit that after a year, in any case, went to Stockholm and took part in a failed bomb attempt against a Kurdish cultural centre. There'd been a party there, but the bomb went off when everyone had gone home. It turned out there was something wrong with the timer. The bomb was meant to go off right in the middle of the party, and it was powerful enough to kill a lot of people, a hell of a lot. It

246

was generally assumed that Lindberg himself was behind the bomb, but they never managed to pin it on him. There was no doubt the day after, though, at a Kurdish demonstration in Solna Centrum, where he violently assaulted two Kurds. In the investigation, it transpired that he had good contacts with Nazi organisations in both Sweden and the US, and presumably elsewhere, too. So we can assume that his departure from the army had its roots in some kind of Nazi conversion."

"In that case, the Foreign Legion sounds like a really strange choice," said Hjelm. "Isn't it a truly multicultural army?"

"Maybe that's what he discovered," said Chavez, shrugging. "But he had a year-long contract. All he wanted was to make war, for real. And maybe his racial hatred reached unexpected heights among all of those foreigners. Well, from my conversations with the police and lawyers involved, I got a picture of an unusually cold, violent man, with a great love of bombs. Acute lack of empathy, that's what his own defence lawyer said off the record."

"He always wants to be best," said Kerstin Holm, thoughtful. "Could he really be *challenging* the man he views as best? Sweden's smartest drug dealer, Rajko Nedic? Who's also an unusually well-integrated foreigner."

"There's probably only *one* who's better assimilated," boasted Jorge Chavez. "Sweden's best-educated police-man."

"Let's not get cocky now," Hultin said neutrally. "Anyone else have anything?"

"One strange thing which might not be that important," said Viggo Norlander, deep in the reports, one of which he waved in the air. "Forensics' report from the crime scene in Sickla. The dead men, Bergwall and Carlstedt, they were wearing black balaclavas. The same brand. A whole load of black fibres from other, similar hats have been found there, too. But also some gold-coloured ones."

"Gold?" an uncoordinated chorus exclaimed.

Chavez smiled and said: "Aha. The golden one . . ."

"What're you talking about?" Hultin asked, irritated.

"Could it be possible that Niklas Lindberg marks his dominance over the others by wearing a golden balaclava?" Chavez asked.

There was a momentary pause in the Supreme Command Centre. Suddenly they felt that they knew Niklas Lindberg much better.

"Of course it could," Hultin nodded.

After yet another pause, he continued.

"How're you getting on, Gunnar?"

Gunnar Nyberg had been sitting in silence. He was torn. Was this his team? Or was it Sara Svenhagen, Ludvig Johnsson, Ragnar Hellberg and the others? He felt deeply and sincerely torn.

"I've been switching between paedophile and Nazi sites online," he said, "and I haven't been able to work out where I belong. I'm starting to get a feel for the extent of these secret networks, in any case. And for how they've grown massively since the Internet became commonplace. But I can't find Lindberg online. Or Carlstedt, aside from as a seller at Kindwall's. Bergwall's name crops up on certain racist home pages. He seems to have been the group's ideologue."

"So now they're ideologically homeless," said Söderstedt.

"But no less dangerous for it," said Hultin. "Let's keep going as before. Don't forget that there's a little party tomorrow afternoon for the Police Olympics. They need all the support they can get. So, 16.00 in the Police Board's assembly halls, Polhelmsgatan. You're guests of honour. Waldemar Mörner hinted subtly that you've got orders to be there. Anyone missing will be kicked out, quote 'arse first'."

"Good job his priorities are in order," said Paul Hjelm.

CHAPTER
TWENTY-FOUR

Four hundred and one. An inscription on a small plaque above a key, a hand shaking slightly. It had done the same several times already. It would probably stop shaking soon. It would just be a matter of routine.

He had even found himself a little ritual.

Four hundred and one, another one gone, he sang to himself, pushing the key into the lock and turning it.

No. He didn't turn it. It wouldn't turn. It was the first time the key had even gone in. That's a bit strange, he thought, taking a piece of paper from his pocket and marking it. Why had the key gone in? Was that a hint that the safe-deposit box was in another branch of Föreningssparbanken? Maybe. But it didn't make a difference. He had to check them all anyway. Every single place on the list had to be checked off.

Every place. Every bank. And the places were banks. And the banks were places.

Postbanken, he thought, distracted, walking over to the branch of SE-bank on the other side of the road.

Four hundred and one, another one gone.

The woman was one of Systembolaget's summer temps, and she was alone in the shop. Monday. A good day to start. Quiet. Sales of the number-one drink, for the most part. Bottles of Renat Brännvin vodka. But if any madmen came in asking for something like a French wine called Château Montpellier-montreusechargot, 1991 vintage, there wouldn't be much she would be able to do. She was slightly anxious. The only customer was on their way out. Another came in. A handsome young man wearing a little hat, despite the summer heat. She felt a certain Château Montpelliermontreusechargot-risk. He didn't look like a Renat Brännvin man in any case.

No, he didn't ask for the number-one drink. Not for Château Montpelliermontreusechargot, either. Instead, she got a pistol in her face.

She emptied the tills at once and when the man left the shop, he was carrying six thousand, nine hundred and twenty-four kronor in a carrier bag.

The woman was lying unconscious on the floor.

Four hundred and one. Wasn't that a darts game?

No, that was 501. That belonged in a completely different story.

She raised the key and sighed. She thought. She tried to work out the probability of this particular safe-deposit box being the right one. Tiny, she thought. Negligible, she thought.

The key didn't go in.

Well, wasn't that unexpected?

She groaned and considered their method. Was this really the best way? How reliable was it?

Yup. No more banks in Kinna.

Next stop, Borås.

There should be a couple of 401s there.

But first, contact. It had worked well so far. It was like he was with her the whole time. The advantage of the Internet. But also its disadvantage.

Virtual closeness.

"Nothing?" asked Niklas Lindberg. He was starting to get tired of asking the same question.

Bullet shook his head.

"Do we have any reason to assume that the thing hasn't just died?" Lindberg continued.

"It's fine," said Bullet. "We've got to read it as a sign we should keep going north. The last contact was in Skillingaryd. It suggested we were going about the same speed. Then we sped up a bit. If they'd gone on to Helsingborg, we should've found a new signal somewhere along the way. The only thing I can think is that they turned off somewhere between Värnamo and Örkelljunga. So we're working our way further north."

"Where are we now?" Danne groaned from the back of the van. He was looking paler and paler. Would he really make it? Wasn't it time for him to pull his weight a bit more? A slightly bigger robbery, maybe?

Just then, Rogge climbed into the van and sat down in the driver's seat.

"Go well?"

Rogge nodded, handing a carrier bag backwards and turning the key in the ignition. Niklas Lindberg peered down into the bag while the van swung out onto the E6.

"Good," he said.

"Good?" said Rogge, putting his foot down. *"Good?* There's gotta be twenty thousand in there."

"A slight exaggeration, but OK. Great."

"That's more like it," said Rogge.

"Can't one of you bastards tell me where we are?" Danne shouted. He sounded wheezy. He was losing blood the whole time.

"Ängelholm," said Bullet, turning the dials.

The great man beckoned him over, gesturing disdainfully with his index finger. He would never have thought of doing so in his private moments. He played two different roles, two main roles, and these main roles each contained a number of minor roles. Ljubomir wondered how many there were. The great man was a cornucopia of roles.

Ljubomir strolled over to the desk. On the way, he tried to avoid looking at the beckoning finger — he couldn't say that he liked it. Instead, he fixed his eyes on the large electronic globe. He had never seen it in action. It must have been impressive. There were rumours that the great man entered coordinates into the computer, and the best route for transporting drugs between them was automatically illuminated on the surface of the globe. He didn't know. He hadn't ever seen it in action.

Ljubomir reached the desk. The great man stared fixedly at him. More so than usual. Something would happen now. Some kind of test of loyalty. Again.

"Have you come up with anything?" the great man asked.

Come up with thought Ljubomir.

"Not exactly," he said. "The police claim to know who they are. That means they're probably Swedes. Some mob. They've interviewed Zoran, Petar and Risto in Kumla. Some white detective going on about Nazis."

"Some *white* detective? They're all white, aren't they?"

"White-haired. Snow-white skin."

"More specifically?"

"I don't know what he's called. The other had stigmata on his hands. Spooky, like Petar said. The strange return of Our Lord Jesus Christ."

"*Nazis*, more specifically?"

"Don't know. I'll check with Zoran."

"For God's sake, 'don't know'! It's your job to know. It's about the man that killed Lordan, and you're saying 'don't know'. Wake up, Ljubomir, otherwise I'll replace you."

"Sorry."

"Don't say sorry. How's the surveillance going?"

"They said everything's quiet. No one has gone into the bank with our briefcase. It's more difficult if they've got rid of the briefcase. But no one has been in the box, that much we know."

" 'They said'? Haven't you been yourself?"

Ljubomir was silent. It was a silent obstinacy. He had no intention of going there. He refused to go to *that place*. That was where his limit lay. The great man

254

could see it. He could see it in Ljubomir's eyes. And he was content. For the time being.

"Fine," said the great man, gesturing with his index finger again. Though in the other direction.

It meant "clear off now", that much Ljubomir had learned.

The great man never made that gesture in his private role.

But in his private moments, he wasn't the great man.

Privately, he was Rajko, the childhood friend. From the little mountain village in eastern Serbia.

Four hundred and one. Shit, no. The numbers stopped at two hundred here. Shitty little bank. Ugh.

It was a drudge. Like a nine-to-five job.

Whatever that was. He had never had one.

Four hundred and one, another one gone.

He could hear how hollow his song sounded.

CHAPTER
TWENTY-FIVE

Party time! It was 4p.m. on Monday 28 June, and everyone was bursting with excitement about the obligatory PR party being held for the World Police and Fire Games.

The so-called Police Olympiad would take place between 16 and 24 July, with an opening ceremony in Stockholm Stadium on Saturday the 17th. Twelve thousand police officers, firemen, customs officers and prison guards from all corners of the world would compete in sixty-eight different sports. One thousand, nine hundred medals would be dealt out. It would be the biggest sporting event that Stockholm had ever hosted, the 1912 Olympics and 1992 World Cup included.

Paul Hjelm couldn't quite see the appeal of watching all of these more or less mediocre sportsmen and -women in action. It screamed mutual admiration society. Unless you had friends or relatives taking part, it couldn't be much more stimulating than a sixth division football match.

But it was a question of taste.

There were other problems with the games, and they weren't.

For days, the media had been reporting what everyone on the inside already knew: that the finances were a mess. Those in charge of the budget for the World Police and Fire Games had presented the most hair-raising, overly optimistic calculations to the city of Stockholm — and with the help of difficult-to-explain PR trips to various holiday destinations, they had sent the budget far past the verge of bankruptcy. Stockholm's taxpayers had been forced to step in with large sums of money so that the thirty thousand visitors wouldn't arrive to a complete bankrupt mess.

And now they were having a party. A PR party for the glorious event. All while the Sickla Slaughterers went free. It felt a touch embarrassing.

Hjelm followed a waitress's back with his eyes. It disappeared out through the door of the interrogation room where all of the Kvarnen-related questioning had taken place. She was the last to be seen that day: the Chinese waitress who had served Gang One and the "policeman" in Kvarnen on 23 June. They couldn't show her any pictures of 1A or 1B — the first one's face blown to pieces, the second full of bullet holes — but she could look at 1C. They had tried to make him look as though he were still alive. It hadn't worked too well. The waitress had screamed immediately. Once she had calmed down, she nodded and said: "Yeah, I think he was there."

About the "policeman", she said: "I don't remember him very well. Compared to the others, he was pretty plain. The others were tough guys, that much I know.

Gangster types. I think he had dark hair, wasn't too old, not more than forty."

And now she was gone. A back which had soon disappeared from memory.

Hjelm looked at Holm.

"Should we go and party, then?" he asked, swinging his arms playfully.

She looked at him indulgently.

"The Police Olympiad," she said, pulling her black leather jacket on over her black T-shirt. Her tone of voice wasn't to be messed with.

"Positive thinking," said Hjelm, pulling on his worn old linen jacket. "Apparently there's free booze."

"And as we all know, sport and booze do go hand in hand."

"Sport, drink, corruption, doping, oxygen tents and Bingolotto."

They walked through the police station. It had been eerily empty for the past few days. An empty building. *Das öde Haus.* Forgotten by God and by man. A ruin by Caspar David Friedrich. Today, it had slightly more life in it. Though only slightly. The first proper holiday week had begun.

Holiday, Kerstin Holm thought. That thing that others had.

She had slowly begun to readjust to life in Stockholm. Her time in Gothenburg hadn't been especially successful. She had been on loan to her old police district where her ex also worked. Her former fiancé; a man who, in the not too distant future, would play a crucial role in her life. Though she knew nothing

258

about that yet. All she knew was that, during those wretched few months in Gothenburg, their icy relationship had eventually covered the entire police station in frost, and she had been forced to leave. Move on. To a district in the suburbs. To Angered. Rowdy but hardly stimulating. She went about her work among criminals who laughed at her. Called her an upperclass police whore and other such niceties. She didn't even bring herself to contact her old church choir in Haga. She was just *on loan* after all. She could be called back to Stockholm at any moment.

She got a sense of how professional hockey players must feel. You could be flung from one side of the continent to the other between one day and the next. The difference — again — was the money. For several million, you could put up with a lot. She was back now, in any case. She had managed to find a small flat right in the centre of things. On Regeringsgatan. She could feel her spirits rising. She had started jogging through Stockholm's City district. She had gone back to her church choir. She was on the right track again. But a National Police Board PR party? No. That was more like a problem on the tracks. Or even a derailment.

They came to the A-Unit's room. Hultin had gone, Söderstedt had gone, Norlander had gone, Nyberg had gone, Chavez was still there. He sat, jabbing away at the keyboard.

"Ten past," said Hjelm, jabbing at his watch. "Remember 'arses first'."

Chavez looked up, as though from another planet. He stared blankly at them. His eyes looked like little computer screens.

"Hello yourself," said Kerstin Holm, smiling.

"Damn," said Chavez, confused. "What time is it?"

"Are those meant to be party clothes?" asked Hjelm.

Chavez looked down. During the summer months, he always wore an utterly plain, permanently crumpled linen suit. Hjelm had to confess that he had copied him. Though only the jacket. Jeans or shorts would do on the bottom half. Today it was jeans.

In conclusion: none of them was dressed for a party.

Though Kerstin always wore the right clothes, both men were in agreement about that. She had an impressive ability to always seem well dressed, regardless of what she was wearing. At that very moment, both men wondered whether it was discriminatory to think that.

"What were you doing?" she asked.

"Yeah," he said, making a few final jabs at his keyboard and pulling on his jacket. "I was reading all I could find about the Sickla Slaughter online. I found a chat, a conversation group, which devotes all its time on it. The Sickla Chat."

"Like FASK?" asked Hjelm.

"Exactly. Fans of American Serial Killers. A cheery club!"

"Aha," said Jalm and Halm, exchanging knowing glances.

He looked at them, confused, as they went out into the corridor. They understood one another so well, in a

260

completely different way from him and Hjelm. Not like two well-functioning policemen of slightly different generations, but like . . . well, like yin and yang.

"Yup," he said, "there's a countrywide discussion about Sickla going on. It's not completely free from racial aspects, that much I can say. You can have a printout of the entire chat tomorrow morning, if you want. It's very informative."

He glanced furtively at them as they wandered on through the labyrinthine corridors of the police station. He couldn't help wondering what had happened while they were over in the US together. They were close in a way that implied there had been intimacy. He delved further back in time. Hadn't it been there already, during the hunt for the Power Killer? Various overlooked signs? Small, fleeting touches? Loaded glances? Furtive hints of tenderness? A hole emerged in the wall he thought he had built so carefully between his professional and private lives. His job on the one hand, the music, the jazz, the double bass on the other — and the women. When he saw Hjelm and Holm deep in relaxed conversation in the corridors of the police station, he thought, to his surprise: imagine if you're lacking something essential as a policeman if you don't embrace your private side. Imagine if all of those small agreements, the caring, and instances of forethought which went into cultivating and holding a loving relationship together were actually necessary for being a good policeman. Even though he wouldn't readily admit it, Paul Hjelm was still his role model as an officer. The way that Paul and Kerstin had worked out

261

what had gone on between Gang One and Gang Two in Kvarnen, how they had come up with *something* from all that background noise — would that have been possible for anyone else other than those two? Would it have been possible for Jorge Chavez and Paul Hjelm? Or did the whole thing depend on that partial hint of patience and gentleness normally seen in relationships? The hardships of a real relationship were relatively unknown to him, however; he still put his faith in the easy freedom of looser unions.

His thoughts drifted some distance before they were pulled back. The trio had reached the rooms which had been temporarily transformed for the party. Each of them was handed a glass of champagne from somewhere, and they heard some sporadic applause, following the noise to see Waldemar Mörner climbing down from a rostrum. They had definitely missed a high point. Mörner looked incredibly happy, a broad grin revealing his brilliant-white teeth. He put his arm around Jan-Olov Hultin who, faced with the National Police Commissioner, managed to crack a smile; they could see him simmering behind the smile, and turned sharply away.

The rooms looked like completely normal police-station offices. The only extravagance was a couple of banners on the walls, proclaiming the "World Police and Fire Games". Quite a few policemen and -women had managed to tear themselves away from the stacks of unsolved cases piling up more and more uncontrollably in the country's increasingly unmanned police stations. A familiar face or two slipped past; the

262

trio nodded now and then, blurting out something amusing from time to time, saw Söderstedt talking to a few people, and saw Nyberg with a group to one side, coffee cups in hand: a thin, well-dressed man with a black ring of hair around his skull; a younger man with well-groomed hair and a small, black beard. And a short-haired woman that caused Jorge Chavez's Latin heart to skip a beat.

They joined the end of the conversation. The thin man said to Nyberg: "Yup, the holiday starts in a couple of days. I'm going out to the cottage to recharge the batteries. Do you remember the cottage, Gunnar?"

Then their peace was shattered.

"Paedophiles!" Paul Hjelm shouted. "Are you having a coffee?"

"We. Are. Not. Paedophiles," Gunnar Nyberg said emphatically, looming menacingly over the trio. Then he made introductions in all directions. It was utterly incomprehensible, so they took matters into their own hands.

"Of course," exclaimed Kerstin Holm as she greeted the thin man with the bald head. "The Marathon Man! Where did you come this year?"

"Ludvig Johnsson," the Marathon Man said politely. "I came ninety-sixth, my first time under a hundred. And you're the miraculously resurrected A-Unit, I assume?"

"Part of it," Holm nodded.

Hjelm greeted the younger man with the little beard, and gave a start when he said: "Detective Superintendent Ragnar Hellberg."

He didn't look more than thirty. A superintendent younger than Chavez? Was that possible? Was this really Party-Ragge?

"I tend to give the title to see people's reactions. They're often like that," Hellberg added, laughing, when he saw the reaction.

"Sorry," said Hjelm. "I can normally keep a neutral face."

"That's not exactly true," said Holm, giving him a furtive glance.

Hjelm started to wander deeper into excuse territory.

"I knew that there was a Hellberg and that he was young, but we've never met before, so . . ."

"Give up," Kerstin Holm whispered, and Hjelm gave up.

Chavez gave the considerably taller woman a kiss on her hand. She looked sceptically at him while Gunnar Nyberg said: "Don't lick the lady's hand, you ruffian."

"Sara Svenhagen," said the lady.

"Jorge Chavez," said the ruffian, adding: "Svenhagen?"

"That's also a standard reaction," said Sara Svenhagen. "Yep, Chief Forensic Technician Brynolf Svenhagen is my dad. Just so that's out there."

"Unexpected quality from the chief technician's gene pool," Chavez said clumsily.

"Give up," Kerstin Holm whispered, which Chavez took as a hint to keep trying.

"You don't expect someone investigating paedophiles to look like this."

At which point someone should have shown compassion and removed him from the stage, throwing

264

him out of a side door. That didn't happen, however. The conversation was already under way.

"How come you recognised me?" Ludvig Johnsson asked Kerstin Holm.

"I've started running a bit myself," she said, receiving a surprised glance from Hjelm.

"Are you getting anywhere with the Sickla Slaughter?" Ragnar Hellberg asked Paul Hjelm. "It seems to be a real hornets' nest."

"You could say that. We've started to close in on a few leads, but no arrests are imminent."

"Christ," said Hellberg. "You sound like a press release. And now you're going to steal Gunnar from me, too."

"We'll see," said Gunnar Nyberg. "I'm struggling to tear myself away from all those nice web pages on the Internet."

"Gunnar working on a computer seems like a contradiction to me," said Hjelm. "He's the most earthbound policeman I've ever worked with. He once wrote off a car by tackling it. With a bullet in his neck."

"He seems to have lots of strings to his bow," Ragnar Hellberg laughed.

Sara Svenhagen, meanwhile, had been left at the mercy of the strange Latino man. Her thoughts were elsewhere, and the terrible introduction had been followed by sluggish distraction. Not from his side, though. Quite the opposite. Through sheer hard work, he had eventually managed to find a common interest, the Internet, strangely enough, and suddenly they were the only ones left, giving one another tips on how to deal with JavaScript. He was also *courting* her ceaselessly. Swapping her firmly rooted coffee mug for a champagne glass, toasting her, looking at her attentively, giving her compliments of a kind she had never heard before, incredibly aware of her reactions. And the strange thing was that she started to feel *seen*. Really *seen*. Appreciated. Valued. Things were so distorted.

The Internet made her virtual, faint around the edges; paedophilia hardened her against erotic feelings, and so when she successfully cracked a complicated code, tracking down a paedophile all by herself, she had no one to tell. She had painted herself into a corner, cut off her hair, let herself be held back by a horrible nightmare. She had disappeared among the invisible. The only person who saw her was Gunnar Nyberg, but as nothing more than a shining light, she knew that. And now, suddenly, she was standing before this passionate little man who was looking at her non-stop, really looking at her in order to uncover her true feelings, and she just wanted to let her hair down, like young, single women sometimes did. Even though she had no hair to let down. She did it anyway. Allowed her cropped hair to flow. He seemed to be spellbound, enchanted by her very existence, and she liked it. She had to admit that she really did like it.

They stayed behind until the catering staff started circling them like hungry hyenas. They hadn't even realised that they were the last to leave, that the party had ended long before, that the police station was as good as empty for the night. When they finally did

266

realise, she heard herself asking: "Do you want to come for a cup of coffee?"

They kissed in the taxi on the way to Surbrunnsgatan, engaged in a spot of light petting in the stairwell, threw off their clothes in the entrance, made love in that utterly uninhibited way, starting in the hallway, continuing in the bedroom and finishing on the floor; starting over again somewhere else. When they came to their senses, they were in the kitchen. Neither of them knew how they had ended up there. The contents of the bin were strewn over the floor. Neither of them knew why.

Sara felt as though she had thrown the windows wide open, as though air was rushing into a vacuum, as though her short hair was blowing wildly in the intense breeze. She threw her arms around him, holding him tightly.

Jorge felt as though something had shifted. Sex was no longer the end of something: it could also be the beginning. This was a radical mental shift. He wondered what it meant. He lay, curled up *in her arms*. She had thrown her arms around him, and he lay curled up, with his cheek against her chest.

It was a fantastic feeling.

A feeling. A shared feeling.

An enormous void in their lives which had suddenly been filled in.

He was woken by the sun's rays. Nature's own alarm clock. Though, on closer inspection, they weren't completely natural. They were being *directed* at him. By a crack in the blinds.

In the slanting light, she was a glorious outline. As though enveloped in a waterfall of light. He reached out for her. She came no closer. She was completely still, surrounded by light. Completely inaccessible.

Ah, he thought. A nightmare.

"I've got something you should see," she said.

Ah, he thought. Not a nightmare. An everyday dream. A dream of happiness turned everyday. A bit early, surely.

"Come on," she said.

Apparently not, he thought. Apparently not too early.

He stood up and accepted that he was awake after all. He went over to her, through the waterfall of light. She was wearing a large T-shirt which hung down below her hips. He was naked. He reached for her body.

"Put something on," she said.

He put something on, and followed her into the bathroom.

For a moment, he felt sceptical. Had he misjudged her so badly? What could she be so keen to show him in the *bathroom*? A positive pregnancy test? A collection of death's-head moths? Shrunken heads in linseed oil?

No, he was being unfair. What he entered was a darkroom. A faint red light glowed in place of a normal bulb. From the ceiling, strings of black-and-white photographs dangled from clothes pegs. On a board covering one half of the bathtub, three differently coloured trays of various stinking liquids stood. In the other half of the tub stood an enlarger. She closed the door.

Everything looked new. All of the equipment seemed to be brand new. A pile of wildly unsuccessful prints lay on the floor. If he hadn't been so tired or so happy, the detective in him would probably have set to work. He would have thought: Hmmm, and then: New equipment, unfamiliar with darkroom techniques, keen to share. Which meant: Some kind of secret task.

The slumbering detective inside him was soon put to the test again.

Sara Svenhagen said: "A couple of days ago, I caught a paedophile living in Söder Torn."

Pause. He was expected to say something, to react, if not with a "Eureka!" then at least with a "Hmmm". No, the detective within him was still sleeping soundly. She continued.

"Söder Torn, Haglund's Stick."

Nope. The detective within him was unavailable.

"Haglund's Stick towers above Medborgarplatsen."

"Go on," was all he said.

"This man spent his entire life taking photographs of kids in Medborgarplatsen and the surrounding area. He did it every day. He had a jam jar full of undeveloped films at home. I've developed them."

"Why?"

"Wake up, Jorge. Daily. Medborgarplatsen. It was just a hunch. I've developed twelve of the films, and now I've found it."

"What time is it?"

"Six thirty. I've been working since half four."

"Ah, hell. So I've been brought here as a policeman?"

"Shut up. Look here."

His eyes followed her finger up towards the photographs hanging from the ceiling. Skateboarders in Medborgarplatsen. Crossing between the square's restaurant tables and park benches. In the bottom corner, a series of small digital numbers. 21.43 23.06.99.

The detective within him woke with a start. For a moment, he looked around in the darkness without understanding where he was. But he said: "Ahh."

"Exactly," said Sara Svenhagen.

"Do those numbers mean what I think they mean?"

"It's a sophisticated camera. It prints them on every image. Twenty-third of June, 9.43 in the evening."

"Christ!"

His eyes moved along the series of images hanging from the washing line. One after another. In the second image, the skateboarders were moving towards Björns trädgård. In the third, they were in the middle of Götgatan; above their heads, a forest of moving legs was visible. In the fourth image, the skateboarders had disappeared behind the trees, down towards the ramp in Björns trädgård; the top of Tjärhovsgatan could be seen instead. There was chaos on the pavement. In the centre, a young man was running wildly in the direction of the camera. He was surrounded by others, carrying banners and wearing striped scarves. All looked agitated. Some were shouting. The man in the middle had unkempt blond hair and a moustache which went just past the edges of his mouth. He was holding something in his hand. Chavez pointed at the object. Sara pointed at the next picture. It was an enlargement of his hand.

He was clutching the handle of a beer mug.

"The Kvarnen Killer," Chavez said breathlessly.

He ripped down the photograph, sending the clothes pegs flying. He studied it. Closest to the wall was a group of four men. It was impossible to distinguish their faces. But a familiar face was pushing his way out of the door. He looked better living than he did dead.

It was 1C. The driver of the Mercedes from Sickla.

Two men were waiting for him. They were just as swarthy-looking, and visibly different to the clusters of Hammarby fans.

Chavez ripped down the last photo. The Kvarnen Killer was gone. The three men were gone. Gang One had made off as soon as 1C had come out. Now, the group by the wall was more visible. One of the figures was familiar. Chavez recognised his face from the prison photographs. His name was Sven Joakim Bergwall. 2B. He was dead, too.

Gang One and Gang Two.

Group portraits.

In the pale red glow, Sara Svenhagen took some photographic paper from a packet, placed it into the enlarger and let a faint light fall on it for ten or so seconds before lifting it up with a strange plastic pincer and pushing it down into one of the liquid-filled trays. She turned it over. A picture developed before their eyes.

In it, Gang Two was also gone. One last man was leaving Kvarnen. His entire figure was nearly concealed by the Hammarby fans. Only certain features were visible.

" 'The policeman'," Jorge gasped.

"What?" asked Sara.

"You're a genius, I said. You, Sara Svenhagen, are nothing less than a genius."

He placed both hands on her cheeks. She was glowing deep red in the darkness. He kissed her, sinking down to the floor. He crept in underneath her T-shirt, his face gliding upwards, over her stomach towards her breasts. He lapped up the taste of her skin.

Sara Svenhagen looked down at her enormous stomach, touching it lightly.

She imagined that it was glowing with its own, internal light.

CHAPTER
TWENTY-SIX

Paul Hjelm was sitting on the sofa. It had been a long time since he had last done so. It had been a long time since he had been home at all. He could hardly remember what it was like. A strange calm settled around him, as though a glass bubble had closed in over him.

Not that his surroundings were especially calm. His family was dashing all over the house in Norsborg. He could hear the familiar melody of the evening news drifting over from the neighbours' house. It was nine in the evening, and they were all going out. For the first time in a long while, he felt a moment of surprise at how big his children had grown. No more hugs. No more intimate family moments. No more reading aloud. Just their long, drawn-out departure.

Danne was seventeen and heading out to play football. "At ten in the evening?" Paul the father had asked. Training times were limited, Danne had replied pedagogically. Nowadays, their conversations went no further than that. Would they have time to make amends later, or was it already too late? Was it all too late? Would he suddenly, one day — like those nice Lindberg parents over in Trollhättan — be informed

273

that his previously well-behaved son had become a violent criminal with Nazi tendencies? How would he react? Would he survive that? He could see unpleasant parallels — the well-behaved Niklas Lindberg had become an officer, his own well-behaved son wanted to be a policeman.

But at that moment, he was running around like a madman, accusing everyone — the family's new parrot included — of deliberately and spitefully hiding his shin guards. Eventually, he found them, wrapped up in his own putrid old towel. Slightly embarrassed, he left the house.

Tova was still there. Fifteen years old and crazy. Beyond all reason. Paul had no siblings of his own, and teenage girls were brand-new territory for him. He was amazed by the role that hormones played. Right now, she wanted to go to a club. For the third time that week. He didn't know how worried he should be. A club sounded better than a rave, in any case, and her mother, Cilla, reassured him that they were organised by teetotal youth groups. As though that would be worth any bonus points with a daughter who seemed to hate her mother more than anything else in the world. It had only recently occurred to him that it might be a matter of love, rather than hate; certain glances exchanged between the two of them suggested that. Like they were playing a game just for him. He didn't understand it.

"Twelve!" Tova shrieked in her most piercing voice. Wasn't it meant to be sons whose voices broke?

"Twelve," the parrot cawed, its voice definitely breaking. Normally, that would have caused Paul to reach for a slipper to throw at the disgusting creature, but today he was immune. He was sitting in his little glass bubble, watching their performance from another planet. It was splendid.

"Eleven!" Cilla shouted, sounding precisely like both daughter and parrot. "You know, you could tell her too, Paul, rather than just sitting there like a dolt!"

A dolt? Did those still exist? Paul wondered to himself from inside the bubble. He didn't lift so much as a finger.

The door opened and Tova slipped out, Cilla running after her, shouting from the doorway: "If you come back later than eleven, I'll kill you!"

Hmm, Paul thought to himself from inside his bubble. Was that good parenting? Was that a model of tolerance and understanding?

"Dolt!" Cilla repeated in the direction of the lump of jelly on the sofa, as she pulled on her coat.

"Dolt," croaked the parrot.

"Aren't you head of ward?" asked the dolt. "Don't they have normal working hours?"

"Do you think I'm cheating on you?" shrieked Cilla, "Is that what you think? Do you think I'm running off to fuck some doctor?"

That was something that hadn't even crossed his mind. But it would be lodged in there now, that much he knew. There was just one way to get rid of it. Temporarily. He glanced in the direction of the piano, which had been shoved into a corner, detested by all except him. As compensation, he had been forced to accept the parrot, something they had been desperately asking for without success for years.

The worst thing was when it mimicked his mediocre piano playing. A real nightmare.

"No," he said, holding back the rest.

Cilla sighed deeply and made a slight conciliatory gesture.

"Sorry," she said. "Tova's driving me crazy. And work. I have to go in and do the night shift sometimes, you know. Otherwise everything'll fall apart. We're on our knees, you know that."

"I know," he said. "Go on. Have as good a time as you can."

A quick kiss on the cheek. Nothing more.

He sat in the glass bubble for a while longer. Waited until it was safe. Then he smashed it. One hit, and it broke into pieces. He went over to the piano and lifted the lid. Sat down. Let his fingertips touch the keys. Enjoyed it for a moment.

He started playing. A little tune he had learned. "Misterioso". Monk. Strange, beautiful notes. He fell into dangerous improvisation. Eventually, he started to hum along. He didn't sing, though. He hadn't come that far yet.

He wondered why. But not now. Now, he was just playing.

Instead, the parrot sang. With an awful breaking voice.

Paul Hjelm laughed and continued to play.

He didn't sing.

276

CHAPTER
TWENTY-SEVEN

It was Wednesday morning. Or, to put it more dramatically: it was the last June morning of the millennium.

Jan-Olov Hultin preferred to call it Wednesday morning. There was hardly any reason to go over the top. Their investigation was going surprisingly slowly. He still felt rusty.

Hultin was sitting at the desk at the front of the room, waiting. While he waited, he went through the latest documents from Brynolf Svenhagen's overexcited forensic technicians. More about the weapons. An Interpol list of places where the Russian Izh-70-300 pistols had been found; it was endless — Bosnia, Croatia, Serbia and Montenegro were just a few among many.

There was also a list of places that the sub-machine guns from Boden had ended up after they were stolen a few years ago. Sure enough, several had been recovered from right-wing extremist circles around Europe; two had been found with a fascist group in Bulgaria, two more with a Danish motorcycle gang. It didn't seem unlikely, though it was far from certain, that Sven Joakim Bergwall and Niklas Lindberg had carried out the break-in at the weapons arsenal in Boden themselves. Then there were the explosives. New indications suggested that the highly explosive liquid had been developed by the South African security services during the final years of apartheid, apparently with the intention of using it at one of the ANC's international mass meetings. But this was all still unconfirmed.

Hultin looked up and sighed. It still wasn't time. The A-Unit could wait.

He had tried to look at the case from above, to summarise it and tie all of the threads together, but it hadn't quite worked. Something was missing. Swedish-Yugoslav drug cartel, a lone Swedish "policeman", right-wing extremist techno-robbers, sophisticated explosives from South Africa, dead war criminals from the former Yugoslavia. It stank — he couldn't stretch his analysis any further than that. The guesswork went much further. Wasn't there a whiff of *continuation* in this crime? Was the crime they were investigating really over — or was it ongoing? Were the fascist robbers really just out to steal from the drug dealer? Was that all? Wouldn't the money, or whatever was in the hypothetical briefcase, ultimately be used for some specific goal? By this point, he was skating on increasingly thin ice.

He read on, turning to a compilation of the kingdom's ongoing crimes from the National Police Board. A violent spring had turned into an equally violent summer. Further attacks on the police had taken place after the Malexander shootings, most recently in Malmö, where a policeman had been called to an abandoned car following a report of a theft. When he opened the door, the car exploded. He was left blind. It was an attack aimed directly at the police. This was something new, Hultin thought to himself. A new, incomprehensible trend. Why were they focusing on the police? He thought about the World Police and Fire Games for a moment. Twelve thousand competitors from every corner of the earth, coming to a country where policemen were being executed and blown up . . .

What else? A Norwegian with links to international alcohol and cigarette smuggling had recently been found murdered in a van to the south of Stockholm. A string of robberies was taking place on the west coast, from Ängelholm northwards. An investigative journalist specialising in Swedish Nazism had, along with his son, been blown to pieces in his car in Nacka. Everything seemed to be curiously linked to everything else. But only vaguely.

Hultin looked up again. No. Still not time.

He was starting to feel annoyed. The after-effects of the day before were still lingering. Mörner's speech to the police Olympians, the embrace which had followed — all had left a bitter taste in his mouth. And now this meeting which he hadn't even called — and then the idiot had the cheek to not even turn up. As though Detective Superintendent Jan-Olov Hultin had nothing better to do.

They still hadn't had any response from the authorities of any ex-Yugoslav states other than

Slovenia, where none of Gang One had left any traces. Considering the circumstances in Serbia and Kosovo, they couldn't expect any answers from there. They could hardly expect anything from Bosnia or Macedonia either, both of them preoccupied with their own problems. He was still hoping for Croatia to come through.

He was on the verge of cancelling the meeting when the lead character came trudging in, a triumphant smile ready to burst across his face. Jorge Chavez went straight to the whiteboard and attached, on top of all the earlier pictures, three black-and-white enlargements. Each of the photographs required eight of the absurd ladybird magnets to hold it in place.

Eventually, Chavez said, pointing: "Especially for you, ladies and gentlemen, I would like to present a curious breakthrough in the investigation. Three photographs of Tjärhovsgatan by Björns trädgård at 21.43 on Wednesday the twenty-third of June. A week ago. Pictures without parallel when it comes to the concentration of crooks."

Hjelm and Holm looked at one another.

"In other words, the pictures were taken a minute after the Kvarnen Killer smashed a beer glass on the head of a poor Smålander inside the bar, the entrance of which can be seen here in picture one," said Chavez, pointing. "In the middle, we have the Kvarnen Killer himself. To the right, by the wall, we have Gang Two. Minus Eskil Carlstedt and Niklas Lindberg who were, at that time, inside Kvarnen and Kumla prison, respectively. Up to the left, we have Gang One,

280

complete with 1C here in the doorway. The driver of the Merc."

It was completely silent in the Supreme Command Centre.

"Picture two," Chavez continued in the same slightly irritating, triumphant tone. "Gang One is gone, the Kvarnen Killer is gone. But you can see Gang Two more clearly here. And here, beside 2B, Sven Joakim Bergwall, we've probably got our three unnamed robbers. Carlstedt, or 2A, the other one who died at Sickla, is inside Kvarnen, waiting to deal with the police. These three should all still be alive, though one's injured. So, these are three of the four Sickla killers that we're looking for. The picture's good enough to identify them, and I spent yesterday doing just that. It wasn't easy, but we should have enough to release the identities of all four robbers now, *if* you want to release them."

He stopped talking for a moment, glancing around the silent room. Sure enough, he had their undivided attention. Then he began to draw red circles around the four faces, one after one.

"*This* is Sven Joakim Bergwall, the man shot in the face. He's followed by *this* man, a real jailbird called Dan Andersson, often called Danne Blood Pudding because of the burns he suffered as a young offender when a large chunk of his skin turned purple. I'm not sure how they got to blood pudding from that. Andersson's thirty-eight and has been convicted of — wait for it — eighty-six crimes, mainly bank robberies, since the age of fifteen. He left Kumla in February and

281

was a member of that so-called Nazi clique in there, even if the right-wing extremism has never been one of his main activities. He's a professional criminal, simple as that.

"*This* man is Roger Sjöqvist, the only member of the gang convicted of murder. Thirty-three, bodybuilder with a military background. Killed a drug dealer ten years ago, escaped when he was on leave from Tidaholm a year ago, and has been lying low ever since. He appears more frequently in right-wing extremist circles and was probably involved in a number of bank robberies. He's a wanted man.

"Finally, *this* man, the shorter of the well-built men, is the technician in the gang. Agne Kullberg, called Bullet because a tough guy can't have a name like Agne. He's only been inside once, for assault and battery. Was released six years ago. He beat up and blinded a Turkish pizza chef in Hagsätra. He's thirty-six and trained as a civil engineer when he was inside, specialising in telecommunications. He's never had any work as a civil engineer, though. Doesn't feature directly in a right-wing extremist context, but he's a member of a dodgy shooting club which also had two of our more notorious colleagues from Norrmalm's police as members, as well as Bergwall."

"Where the hell did these pictures come from?" Hultin exclaimed, staring at the enlargements.

"Can't we wait a minute before going into that?" Chavez asked, continuing: "We've still got picture three. In this one, Gang Two have disappeared as well. It's from when the doormen managed to block the door in

Kvarnen. The Hammarby fans are still there, talking; they know it'll be a few minutes before the police arrive, that there's no rush. The queue, apparently full of 'difficult immigrants', didn't exist, as you can see. Just fans. Apart from *this* man, who's sadly almost completely hidden behind the fans and who, in all probability, is our so-called 'policeman'."

They looked at the figure. He could hardly be seen at all. Only the very left edge of him. He might have been dark-haired. Maybe he was wearing jeans. His right shoe was clearest. Nike Air trainers.

"We'll see what the technicians can do with the picture," said Chavez. "They're working flat out."

"Where are the pictures from?" Hultin asked, mustering his best ice-cold neutrality.

Chavez looked at him. There was a pause which seemed to go on for an eternity. A trial of strength. Hjelm sensed that he was looking at the beginnings of a future power struggle.

"They were taken from a high spot nearby," said Chavez, telling them nothing in particular.

"Haglund's Semi," exclaimed Södermalm inhabitant, Arto Söderstedt.

Chavez was silent.

"Where are the pictures from?" Hultin repeated, iciness intact.

Chavez broke free from the clinch hold and leaned back against the ropes, catching his breath.

"I can't say for the moment," was all he said.

"My room," said Hultin.

Chavez nodded. Then he said: "Just let me sum up first."

Hultin allowed him to sum up first.

"Times," said Chavez, following the Hultin model and drawing a kind of flow chart onto the whiteboard. "Where does this story start? What comes first? The 'policeman' prepares an attack on Nedic? Why? Does he have something to sell? Is it blackmail? Is it the start of a future collaboration? In any case, he makes contact with Nedic, and Nedic goes along with delivering whatever was in that famous briefcase. It's looking more and more like money.

"Somehow, someone in what turns out to be Gang Two finds out that a handover is going to take place. Considering Niklas Lindberg seems to be the driving force, we can assume that it was him, or at least his so-called 'Nazi clique' in Kumla, who found out about the delivery. Probably via Nedic's righthand man, Lordan Vukotic. Sven Joakim Bergwall and Dan Andersson are part of this gang. Andersson is released in February, so he's probably already out when the information reaches the 'clique'. Bergwall, who was released in May, and Lindberg, who was released on the morning of the twenty-fourth of June, were still inside. Maybe they happen to overhear some part of a conversation that Vukotic is having with someone inside. They realise that it's about something *big* — probably just *a lot of money* — and they bide their time, join forces with their prison friend Dan Andersson plus Bergwall's mate from the shooting club, the civil engineer Agne 'Bullet' Kullberg, and a

284

couple of right-wing extremist friends — the as-yet-clean Eskil Carlstedt and the murderer Roger Sjöqvist.

"Bit by bit, they work out that a meeting's going to take place in Kvarnen. It turns out it's going to happen the night before Niklas Lindberg gets out. He probably thinks this seems like a happy coincidence, so he pulls Lordan Vukotic's shoulders out of joint the same evening, to get the information out of him or just because he enjoys it. But the fact that Vukotic keeps quiet about it suggests it wasn't just a bit of fun for Lindberg. In other words, Lindberg manages to get information out of Vukotic, probably the *provisional* meeting place for the handover; the other details are going to be decided in Kvarnen by the 'policeman' and Nedic's men: Gang One.

"The 'policeman' has picked a public place like Kvarnen because he's afraid of Nedic's men; he obviously knows what they're capable of, after the genocides in the former Yugoslavia. Maybe they're also working out some kind of insurance policy, so that both the 'policeman' and Gang One know they'll be leaving the meeting place alive. Maybe that's what their conversation in English was about. Anyway, we've got five men led by Sven Joakim Bergwall there, too. Eskil Carlstedt, Dan Andersson, Roger Sjöqvist and Agne Kullberg are there, the latter wearing an earpiece. He's managed to plant a microscopic listening device under the table where the 'policeman' and Gang One are sitting. When the Hammarby fans start flooding in, they're about to reach some kind of negotiated solution. Even though it starts getting crowded, they keep going. And Gang Two sits there, listening from the table against the opposite wall, even though they're constantly being disturbed by the Hammarby fans. They must've reached a solution — at two the following morning in the Sickla industrial estate — just before one of the Hammarby fans decides to smash a glass on a Smålander's head. Both Gang One and Gang Two realise they've got to leave as quickly as possible. Still, both manage to rapidly think the situation through. Everyone in the pub suddenly becomes a witness. Neither of the gangs can go unnoticed any longer. They know their presence is going to be remembered. That the police are going to be analysing every single detail of the scene in Kvarnen. The 'policeman' makes sure the Slavs leave before him, so that they're not linked to one another; he stays behind for a few seconds longer and is forced to show his ID to get out. We can assume that Bergwall makes sure that the only one without a record, Carlstedt, stays behind to take the questioning, and turns the mysterious gang with an earpiece into a group of salesmen out chasing women. It works. They spend the night going through their plans. Carlstedt will wait in Stockholm and come up with a nice story for the police while Bergwall, Andersson, Sjöqvist and Kullberg drive to Kumla to pick up Lindberg. They're probably not expecting him to blow up the bunker while they're out in the open, but he does it not least to show them who's boss. Power markers are always important in the criminal world, as you know.

"Then they pick up Carlstedt; maybe they park their van outside the police station and wait for Paul and Kerstin to finish their interrogation. Maybe the six of them make off to their hiding place immediately, and go through their plan for the evening. They get to Sickla just before two, planting a microbomb on the way, and then they wait. At two, the Mercedes arrives. Somewhere nearby, the 'policeman' is waiting. He probably hears the explosion. He realises it's gone wrong and leaves. Lindberg, Bergwall, Carlstedt, Andersson, Sjöqvist and Kullberg go over to the blown-up car. Just like in Vukotic's cell in Kumla, it's a precisely measured explosion. It goes off right under the back seat of the car. There were three men talking to the 'policeman' in Kvarnen, so they're presuming it'll just be those three coming again. One of them will be sitting in the back seat. He'll probably have the briefcase, and since it'll contain the money, it's likely that it'll be bombproof. And it is. The man in the back seat, 1A, is blown up. The two survivors are forced out of the car and placed either side of it, 1B by the passenger side, and the driver, 1C, by the driver's seat. They're frisked. Bergwall walks around the car and stands on the other side. Carlstedt takes the briefcase from the back seat and clips the chain with some bolt cutters which we've found, by the way. It gets messy here.

"Something happens to make them lose their concentration. The weapons-fixated war criminals, 1B and 1C, have — and this has been confirmed by forensics — some kind of device in their jacket sleeves

287

which means they can hide their Izh-70-300 pistols and whip them out in a flash. Like Robert De Niro in *Taxi Driver*. A firefight breaks out. 1B shoots *over his shoulder* and hits Bergwall in the eye. Carlstedt, who can't get hold of his weapon because of the briefcase, chooses to run. 1C shoots him in the back. Carlstedt's hit in the heart and dies at the very moment he reaches safety. 1C probably already had a number of bullets in him by that point. He keeps shooting anyway, and then drops down dead with five bullets in him. 1B is also on the floor, six bullets in him. Maybe dead, though probably still alive, since Niklas Lindberg (or maybe Sjöqvist or Kullberg) then goes over and puts eighteen bullets into him. A man wearing size 7 Reeboks takes the briefcase, and finds it covered in Carlstedt's blood. It's Kullberg, the smallest of them; he has size 7 feet. The one who's shot and injured is Dan Andersson, Danne Blood Pudding, with AB negative blood. The amount of blood suggests it's a serious injury, but he's not in hospital anywhere, so if the group hasn't split, if it's planning something else, then Andersson's still with them. If they didn't just kill him, that is. Maybe he's starting to be a burden by now.

"So, the Sickla Slaughterers who are still fit and healthy are: Roger 'Rogge' Sjöqvist, Agne 'Bullet' Kullberg. And Niklas Lindberg, of course. What about on the other front, then? There are two other fronts. The 'policeman' and Rajko Nedic. Will the 'policeman' do anything? Most likely not. He's probably waiting until Nedic's got the money back, or maybe he's demanding new, clean money. It's not his fault that

Nedic was careless, after all. Nedic *isn't* careless. He hates the thought of being careless. He conducts his illegal business with clockwork precision. He manages to run an enormous drug business and seems to enjoy working openly as a legitimate restaurateur. Not much else can have gone wrong in his life. He's probably fuming right now. But the situation isn't the same any more, for Nedic or for the 'policeman'. The 'policeman' has ended up in a nightmare situation; he can hardly have predicted that five men would die for his money, and he can hardly be comfortable with the enormous police investigation focusing on his little transaction. Nothing can take place in secret any more. Nedic knows we've got him in our sights, too. He knows we know more than the media are claiming. He needs to find a solution which gets him his money back, punishes the bandits *and* makes the 'policeman' happy. Otherwise, he could take out the 'policeman', who must realise that that risk has grown. He's safest if he's got a rock-solid insurance policy. Presumably he has. What must be happening *right now* is this: Gang Two is hiding from Nedic, he's hunting flat out for them, and the 'policeman' is nervous but passive. End of story."

Hultin's room. The high-school student, taken down a peg or two, facing his head teacher. And yet not quite. Not mutinous or career-driven. *Nyet. A proud man.* A proud man asserting his rights — actually, not even his rights — against supremacy.

Supremacy felt tired.

Jorge Chavez was Jan-Olov Hultin's best find. His own, personal find. The rest of the A-Unit had been put together based on tips and advice from various quarters, but he had found Chavez himself. Working as Norrland's only immigrant policeman, as he labelled himself, on a nightmare duty in Sundsvall. He had proved himself to be a real success. The most energetic policeman Hultin had ever come across. And now this — what was it? Insubordination. This direct refusal to obey orders. A fantastic find, the photographs, but then this incomprehensible refusal to reveal their source.

He looked at Chavez, waiting him out. Expecting him to talk any moment. Eventually, Chavez said: "It's complicated."

Nothing more. Hultin waited. It continued in the same fashion.

"It's a moral conflict. An ethical dilemma. The photos have helped us with the identification, we don't need them any more. It's a thing of the past."

"Not exactly," said Hultin. "We have to give the Kvarnen Killer's picture to the press."

"But we can do that without giving a source." And then, almost pleadingly: "Just as I'm saying it to you, Jan-Olov, I'm also saying it to Mörner and the Police Commissioner and the entire bloody force."

"Not necessarily," said Jan-Olov Hultin neutrally.

"Yeah," said Chavez, looking him in the eye. "You can't afford to keep anything from Mörner after the Kentucky Killer. You've been given a second chance and you're not planning on throwing it away."

Hultin met his gaze without hesitation.

"That's where you're wrong, Jorge. It's the opposite, I have nothing to lose. Nothing at all."

Chavez swallowed and came to a decision. He said: "They were taken by a paedophile living in Söder Torn. Haglund's Semi, like Arto said. Sara Svenhagen arrested him, if you've heard of her."

"Of course," said Hultin. "I've known her since she was little. Brynolf's daughter. A great policewoman."

"But Sara has been given orders by her boss to investigate that case *in private*. She can't, under any circumstances, reveal anything related to her investigation. Not even internally."

"Hellberg," said Hultin, feeling weary. "A more *modern* detective superintendent than me. Why?"

"I have no idea," said Chavez. "All I know is that Ragnar Hellberg has sworn her to absolute secrecy. She broke that already when she showed me the photographs. She developed them herself. At home. Because of a *hunch* that the paedophile might actually have captured the aftermath of the Kvarnen Killing. A hunch which was spot on."

"At home?" Hultin asked knowingly.

Chavez was silent. Silent and proud. Proud of his silence.

"Why are you going to such trouble for Sara Svenhagen?" asked Hultin, though he was starting to understand.

Jorge Chavez took a step towards him, leaned over the desk and said clearly: "Because I love her."

CHAPTER
TWENTY-EIGHT

And she loved him. It felt a bit pathetic.

She knew how it was meant to work. That love had to develop slowly and be carefully nurtured, that it took time and effort to create a relationship, that it wasn't something that just popped up all of a sudden, ready-formed. She definitely didn't believe in love at first sight. It hadn't been very first sight, anyway.

Though almost.

She had thought herself immune. Thought that she had seen and heard far too much to be susceptible to Cupid's arrows. She had thought that the paedophiles' arrows had caused irreparable damage to her emotional life. But then she realised how *strong* people are, despite everything; how much we can really endure.

She put all of the critical questions to herself. Was this really love? Hadn't he just turned up at a moment when her emotions were in turmoil? Hadn't he used his thoroughly silky tongue in a pretty dishonourable way? Hadn't she just fallen victim to a classic Latino seduction ritual?

But this questioning didn't last long. She found herself thinking about him all of the time. She felt happy, expectant, longing. A new energy had grabbed

292

hold of her, and she found herself working with a completely new drive.

Because, strangely enough, love didn't have a *paralysing* effect on either of them, as it had done during their teens. Maybe this could be called a more *mature* love, one that seemed to have a positive effect even at work. Both were working harder than before, which seemed impossible, and both imagined that they were thinking more clearly. Jorge had neatly summarised the whole Sickla Slaughter, and Sara was able to take stock of her own situation with great clarity.

She had two things to do. First, she had a list to work through: the address list on which she had found John Andreas Witréus's name, the one which had appeared so briefly on that temporary web page. Second, she had a computer to work through. John Andreas Witréus's computer. By using the clues she found on his computer, she would try, first and foremost, to find the website which had detected his email address and added him to the list she had mistaken for a network. It was a *potential* network, after all. Someone, somewhere, was compiling the addresses of everyone who visited a certain website. This website had to be found and, in time, maybe the people behind this new means of gathering paedophiles could be identified.

It was a difficult job, but she was in full swing, without any kind of professional, technical help. Though by this point, she had become a kind of technical professional herself. She began to think that she could do anything at all with just a computer and a phone line.

How was it possible to live with your head held even slightly high in a world like this? Everything was for sale. Everything was possible for the right money. How many people across the globe were really active in this underground business? What had she come across? Was it . . . Hell?

For a moment, she imagined that it really *was* Hell. The proper, biblical Hell. The one which had always run like an undercurrent through normal human activity, finding ways to drag susceptible people down in keeping with the times. What was it that made people susceptible?

She was starting to contract the global conspiracy fever which infected all hackers from time to time. Most believed the theory that the American government was covering up UFOs in a secret vault somewhere, and was also responsible for producing Aids in laboratories and testing it in Africa. Others still believed in communism and the domino effect. She had got it into her head — and then she had started to keep an eye open — that these theories *themselves* were part of the conspiracy. The great conspiracy obviously didn't consist of an elite group running the world from their headquarters somewhere, like in a cheap crime novel — it was about an *invisible ideology*. It didn't need any physical border guards; it was about internalising them, making sure that the ideology was active in people's minds. The twentieth century had been the age of democracy, but it was also the century in which it had been most fiercely challenged, above all from within. How could you — where the "you" was essentially the market, the biggest and ultimately only ideology of the age, a completely uniform and utterly inflexible system of thought which built upon nothing other than maximising profits — how could you get people to believe that they had power while, at the same time, taking it away from them? By preventing them from thinking, of course.

All marketing is about getting people to stop thinking and to focus on different kinds of carefully crafted ideals instead. About selling an image. And what else? A massive accumulation of things like intellect-dulling entertainment television, causing every single teenager to want to be a presenter; celebrity obsession, porn, sports hysteria, thinking in terms of ethnicity, forcing people to spend their time making absurd choices about refuse-collection companies or electricity suppliers; the limitation of all economic thought to the personal sphere, which had increasingly started to become blurred with the stock exchanges, and biological determination, which Sara Svenhagen understood as being the crown on the idea which had to be spread *whatever the cost*: that we have absolutely no control over our own lives. Our brains were finally spongy enough, our self-confidence so lacking, for the death blow to be dealt: the thought that, actually, it doesn't matter what we do or are subject to — our entire lives are controlled purely by our genes. That was the death blow, and it was now being suggested from all sides, in all manner of ways, all at once. Whatever you do, don't believe that you can do anything about your lot: it has already been determined by an infinite number of generations before you.

If you've got an older relative who is a paedophile, then you know that you'll become one yourself. There is no real reason to resist temptation. It would only be in vain.

She began to get agitated. It was time to return to reality.

There was an enormous collection of paedophile sites on Witréus's computer, most of them known to her, some of them unknown, some well hidden behind faked headings like "Calendar of activities at Gothenburg University" or "Spitfire aeroplanes: a historical outlook". It could be anything at all, anywhere at all, any time at all. These hidden pages opened on Witréus's computer, revealing, once again, a parallel universe. Everywhere, she came across address lists of varying types.

Above all, she was confronted by a series of pseudonyms she hadn't come across before. They were mentioned in various strange presentations and, as a rule, appeared alongside email addresses of a certain type: "xxxxxxx@hotmail.com". From these previously unknown websites, she compiled a list of pseudonyms: "crushy_tomboy", "limmeystone", "rippo_man", "sweetfacepowder", "lungan" and "brambo". From these she went further, searching for IP addresses. It wasn't easy. These figures hadn't made the same mistake as John Andreas Witréus. The IP addresses belonged to official institutions from around the world, the pseudonyms to Swedish numbers.

She logged into the central police computer and searched the paedophile unit's material for those six pseudonyms. Three of them had already been found and arrested. Remaining were: "rippo_man", "sweetfacepowder" and "brambo". In the more extensive material from the international Operation Cathedral, she eventually found both "rippo_man" and "sweetfacepowder". Both had been traced back to Sweden, and they had managed to find the computers from which these pseudonyms were used.

Then things got really complicated.

Following an extremely thorough search of the material, she realised the following: that *some policeman* had already been to all these home pages. The name "rippo_man" *only* appeared alongside "brambo".

But now "brambo" was gone.

This "brambo" was nowhere to be found in the files.

Yet the policeman who entered "rippo_man" into the reports *must* have known about "brambo". Adding "rippo_man" to the report without also adding "brambo" was gross misconduct.

She saw that "rippo_man" had already been arrested for distribution of child pornography and for sexually assaulting children. He was a twenty-four-year-old medical student from Linköping who had, in April, earned himself a four-year prison sentence in Hall.

But why the hell, why the bloody hell was this pseudonym "brambo" missing from the investigation?

The more she searched, the clearer the pattern became.

The investigating officer had deliberately left "brambo" out of the reports. *And the investigating officer was from her own group.* From CID's own division for paedophile cases.

A deep, heartfelt unease coursed through her.

She clicked the up arrow and watched the text fly by. She was heading for the top of the document.

To the investigating officer's name.

The doorbell rang.

She knew who it was. She had been waiting for him all day. She loved him.

But she couldn't talk about this. Not right now.

The text scrolled past. The bell kept ringing.

She had to find the name. Now.

Come on, please; come on!

She shouted, desperate: "Hang on a sec, I'm coming!"

The bell kept ringing.

The text stopped. She saw the name.

It was as she had thought.

Detective Superintendent Ragnar Hellberg.

She closed the document and ran towards the door.

Jorge Chavez would never forget the hug she gave him when the door finally opened.

CHAPTER
TWENTY-NINE

On Friday 2 July, Hammarby's losing streak ended. 3–0 at home to Norrköping. Hans Berggren's goal-scoring dry spell was over. Kennedy Bakircioglü scored his very first league goal.

Perhaps as a result of what happened earlier that day.

Just before ten in the morning, two shabby-looking young men wandered into the police station on Agnegatan. They asked to see Paul Hjelm and Kerstin Holm. Since they had gone to the county police station, there was a certain hesitation at reception. The detectives' names were unfamiliar. During their long wait, the older and taller of the two men stood with his arm around the younger and shorter one.

Eventually, the receptionist managed to track down Paul Hjelm and Kerstin Holm. She phoned them, and asked the two men to take a seat on a nearby sofa. Neither man sat down. It was something they were physically incapable of doing.

Hjelm and Holm arrived together. They immediately recognised the older and taller of the men. It was Jonas Andersson from Enskede, committee member of the Bajen Fans club. After a while, they also recognised the younger and shorter of the two. From a black-and-white photograph, attached to a whiteboard with ladybird-shaped magnets. The unkempt blond hair and the drooping moustache slightly past the edges of his mouth were, by this point, well known.

What they hadn't expected was the Kvarnen Killer's eyes, puffy and red from crying.

"He was sitting outside the clubhouse this morning," said Jonas Andersson from Enskede. "He said he didn't want to do any more damage to Hammarby."

They nodded at him.

"Thanks, Jonas," said Kerstin Holm.

Jonas Andersson smiled faintly and trudged off.

"What's your name?" Paul Hjelm asked the Kvarnen Killer.

"Conny Nilsson," the Kvarnen Killer said faintly. His vocal cords seemed to have tied a knot in themselves.

"Why are you coming forward now?"

"I saw my picture in the paper. Not the drawing, the photograph. It was enough. It hasn't been fun."

"I understand," said Paul Hjelm, sitting down on the visitors' sofa. He patted it. Conny Nilsson sat down next to him. He was small, compact. And completely broken.

"Where have you been hiding?" Kerstin Holm asked, sitting down on the other side of the Kvarnen Killer.

Without a word, they both mentally decided never to use that name again.

"At home," said Conny Nilsson. "I live with my parents in Haninge."

"How have you been able to stay hidden? Are your mates that loyal?"

"My mates . . . I don't know them, they don't know me. I just followed a group after the game. They didn't seem to know I was there. They were so bloody angry. A draw against Kalmar at home. They started mouthing off against some Smålanders in Kvarnen. The atmosphere was really heated. The Smålanders were lying, saying they didn't support Kalmar. One of them pushed me. I don't know what happened, it's completely black. I guess I must've wanted to show I was there, that I wasn't some worthless little shit you could just push around. I'd already passed the metro when I realised there was a bit of bloody glass in my hand. I chucked it away and ran. I took a bus from down by Stadsgården. That's it. I've been ill for a week."

"Off sick?"

"I don't work. I don't have any job to be off sick from. My mum's the only one who realised I was sick. I heard her talking about that Kvarnen Killer one night. She was wondering what kind of sick world she lived in."

"Now she knows."

"She'll know soon," Conny Nilsson nodded. "Jesus Christ."

They didn't have much else to say.

They left him to the local police.

They felt ill at ease.

CHAPTER
THIRTY

Arto Söderstedt dropped his children off at nursery. In the summer, he enjoyed dropping the children off. He liked to watch their attitude change, how they transformed from daddy's girl into just one of the group. A real little metamorphosis.

Though in the winter, he didn't see it. There wasn't enough energy then.

As he hugged his little Lina goodbye, it struck him that time was running out. He had five children and had been dropping them off and picking them up for almost fifteen years without ever thinking that, one day, it would be over. After next year, he would no longer be dropping children off at nursery. He would *never* drop the children off at nursery again.

Grandkids, maybe. Though hopefully not too soon.

Lina, the little blonde, disappeared, skipping off towards the other children. When he saw her hug a little boy called Rutger, she was no longer daddy's little girl.

He stood for a moment, watching her. His youngest.

When he stepped out into the hesitant summer morning, he imagined that it would be a good scene for a crime novel. He was a detective, dropping his kids off at nursery. People would recognise themselves in it. Though, obviously, he would be a woman . . .

No, Arto Söderstedt decided. This wasn't a crime novel. This was reality.

He wandered along Bondegatan, the sun making a half-hearted attempt to peep through the thick patches of cloud. The street was strangely mottled, an ongoing battle between sun and shade. He came out onto Götgatan, right opposite the tower block which housed the tax authorities. It shimmered in the same strange, mottled, constantly shifting light. Anja would already be inside, checking over tax returns. At the breakfast table, she would give daily reports on the most astounding attempts at tax evasion. So he didn't need to feel too bad about letting the children spend their summer in day care, the youth centre and summer camps. The married couple shared the tax burden fraternally — or was it sororally?

Down on Götgatan, the newly assigned service Audi was waiting. Without a parking ticket. He had started to learn the complicated parking rules. The accelerator pedal felt well oiled and the clutch elastic. He sat for a moment, *pretending* to drive. He secretly hoped that no one had seen him cross the line as the Safari Rally's most brilliant winner of all time.

He turned the ignition and drove towards Kungsholmen. He knew what he would be doing first today. True, he and Viggo would be going to search through Roger Sjöqvist's and Dan Andersson's flats in the southern suburbs, but that wasn't the first thing he was planning on doing.

The first thing Arto Söderstedt would be doing was buying a car. On the Internet.

It was a decision that had matured, if not slowly, then . . . quickly, in any case. A decision which had matured quickly. He had gained the support of the family using hardly democratic means. Anja, who had been nagging for a car for two years, looked at him sceptically, trying to work out his hidden motives. He revealed nothing, just sat there, poker-faced, spouting altruistic motives like fake playing cards: they could go on trips to Skåne, take day trips to the Kolmården Animal Park, drive around the Bay of Bothnia to Vasa and see whether they had any friends left in Finland.

After all, he couldn't reveal what the real reason was — that it was fun to drive.

What the enormous family needed was a so-called family car. As he turned off into the garage beneath the police station, he pondered over the term "family car". They were minibuses, but you couldn't call them that. It sounded unsophisticated. The European Commission for Traffic Safety had recently presented the results of a large safety test on family cars. It was especially welcome in Sweden because the last year had seen a couple of catastrophes where family cars had burst into flames following collisions. Fortunately, the tests revealed that there were safe models.

He came to his office, nodding absent-mindedly in greeting at Viggo Norlander who, once again, looked like something the cat had dragged in. Today, he looked like a ruffled and tattered old great tit. Söderstedt sat down at his computer and launched the browser.

"We've got to go," said Norlander sullenly. "To Handen first, and then —"

"The foot," said Arto Söderstedt, entering his password.

"Shut up," said Viggo Norlander.

"So you had Charlotte again last night? Did it go well?"

"Christ, it's hard work."

"Are you getting cold feet?"

"No. No, I love it. Really. But it's hard work. I'm convinced she's dead three times a night. Sudden infant death syndrome."

"What about Astrid?"

"Thursday night. Astrid meets her friends then."

"Sewing circle," said Arto Söderstedt while he waited for his password to be approved.

"What?"

"They listen deeply to one another. No, it used to be called a sewing circle. Nowadays it's called a girls' evening or a girls' night in. If you've woken up on the wrong side of the bed, you could call it a hen house, too. Though you should keep that to yourself. How's it going with her?"

"Well, vitality's the word. Astrid's born again. She got her baby in the end. She's bubbling. You say that, right? 'Bubbling'?"

"You can say that. If that's what you mean."

"It's what I mean. What the hell are you up to? I've been waiting quarter of an hour. We've got to go."

"What do you mean by 'bubbling'? It's only three weeks since she gave birth. No complications?"

"She tore a bit. Not that it's slowing her down."

"Sexually?"

"That's our business, isn't it?"

"Exactly," said Arto Söderstedt, typing the address for *Gula Tidningen*'s home page. "Your business is the kind of thing you share with your friends."

"Shut up," said Viggo Norlander.

Söderstedt turned towards him.

"Come on, Viggo. You're in your first monogamous relationship in God knows how many decades, and I want to know how it's going. It's called a social network. *I'm* your social network."

Viggo Norlander's facial expression changed dramatically. His gloomy, lopsided, inward-backward-sloping mug was replaced by a dreamy smile.

"Got it," said Söderstedt, smiling. "That was quick work. Go down to the car, then, I'm coming. This will only take five minutes."

Norlander disappeared. That's a robust great tit, Söderstedt thought to himself, glancing over the headlines in front of him on the screen.

Gula Tidningen had, for the past few decades, been Stockholm's main paper for free advertisements. Maybe also for the stolen goods trade. You could buy anything you wanted second-hand. No questions asked. Cars, for example. Family cars, for example. The paper also had a website. The system wasn't fully developed yet, but it was more than enough.

He found seven items of interest, above all a Renault Espace and a Toyota Picnic. Terrifying prices, of course, but it was just a case of facing the music. He sent off seven messages showing his interest. That was enough. He returned to the home page.

The headline, THIS WEEK'S "I LOVE YOU", woke his easily aroused interest. Arto Söderstedt loved reading personal ads, declarations of love and intimate messages. He couldn't really explain why — maybe it was just a perversion of his; maybe these small, concentrated phrases held *the longing of our times*. In tightly constrained form. A person's entire complicated emotional life reduced to no more than a few lines, and that meant that the results were normally highly interesting. He thought for a moment about Norlander, seething as he waited down in the garage. But only for a moment. With a voyeur's overexcited feeling of shame, he glanced through the entries under THIS WEEK'S "I LOVE YOU". Some of them really fuelled the imagination.

"Stallion Harald. I'm passionate about your rut. Your filly, Edna."

"BK is CF. 3 12 13 18 24 28 30. DL."

"Stefan. Come back. All is forgiven. Even the freezer incident. I L Y, Rickard."

"3+3=5. Still waiting. D & the gang."

"Eurydice. 'No crime is worse than bitter betrayal, the Florento sisters said.' 82 12G 14. Orpheus."

"Saturday 3rd. You know where. Licking Jack."

"Hard-ons are fun. Secret(ion) Services."

He lost interest, closed the window and ran down to the garage. Viggo Norlander was fuming. He was standing by his rusty old service Volvo, stomping.

"Bastard," said Norlander.

"Söderstedt," said Söderstedt.

They drove to Handen, twenty or so kilometres south of Stockholm. Norlander drove like a ruffled and tattered old great tit the cat had dragged in. Dan Andersson's flat was in the centre of Handen, a flat which wasn't a bomb site but a surprisingly well-cleaned one-bed. Precision-cleaned. Forensics probably wouldn't find even a fingerprint. It was exactly like Eskil Carlstedt's flat in Stockholm. They went through the few books and files. Everything was in impeccable order. Even the tassels on the rug had been combed out. A scent of soap still lingered beneath the deep-rooted stench of smoke in Danne Blood Pudding's flat. On a shelf there was a photograph. Dan Andersson in Mallorca, smiling broadly and with an enormous beer in his hand. His face actually was slightly purple in colour. There wasn't much else to see. Here, too, all traces of right-wing extremism were conspicuous in their absence. Here, too, they were standing in a flat which had been expecting a visit from the police, and had been made as bland as possible.

Arto Söderstedt did his duty but little else. Somewhere under the dull, routine work, something was niggling. He wondered what it was.

A grain of sand, waiting to become a pearl?

They drove north to Hökarängen. Roger Sjöqvist's last-known haunt. Sjöqvist had fled on his first unsupervised period of release from Tidaholm prison, having served nine leave-free years. Back then, he had given this address as his residence. It turned out to be his parents' flat, though he hadn't been there in ten

308

years. Both Söderstedt and Norlander were convinced by the wretched Sjöqvist parents. The father — if it was in fact his father — stank so strongly of alcohol that the smallest of sparks would have sent the entire high-rise up in flames. They left the danger zone rapidly.

"Well, that was worthwhile," Norlander said in the car on the way back to Stockholm. "What a difference we're making. How meaningful it all feels!"

"Shut up," said Söderstedt.

Norlander looked at him in surprise.

Arto Söderstedt was thinking. The niggle was growing more and more intolerable. The grain of sand was *demanding* to become a pearl.

He had seen, heard or thought something. At some point during the morning, something had crept past and should have caught his attention. But it had slipped away, and now it was rubbing, like a grain of sand in a mussel. Or rather like a fly which has worked its way behind someone's eyeball, and can't be reached. Without resorting to surgical methods.

Söderstedt's surgical methods were of the orthodox, clinical kind. He went through the entire day, from the moment he woke up. When he opened his eyes, Anja was gone. She had already dragged herself to work to scrape excess fat from tax returns. Next, he went to the toilet. No memorable thoughts. Irritated by his constipation. Breakfast. Lively. Four kids. Minor fight between the eight-year-old and the ten-year-old. Catfight, he recalled thinking. The fifth kid at summer camp north of Uppsala. Dropping off three of the kids, the thirteen-year-old staying at home: the first two at the youth centre, the smallest at nursery. Pondering over dropping the kids off at nursery in summer and winter. The lightning-quick realisation that soon he would never have to drop them off again. Watching the shadow play on Bondegatan and on the tower block. Strange fantasies about being in a crime novel. Pondering the parking regulations in inner Stockholm. His clear victory in the Safari Rally. Thoughts of buying a car. The term "family car". European crash tests. Viggo. Discussion on sudden infant death syndrome, sewing circles, hen houses, the word "bubbling". Viggo's dreamy expression. *Gula Tidningen*. Expensive family cars. Seven messages of interest sent by email. Then the shamefulness. The feeling returned. Why the shamefulness? The headline THIS WEEK'S "I LOVE YOU". Exactly, "Secret(ion) Services". It was here. Somewhere here. A message.

What had it said? Your filly, Edna. The freezer incident. Licking Jack. Still waiting. Nope, they didn't set any bells ringing.

"No crime is worse than bitter betrayal, the Florento sisters said." That must have been it. The Florento sisters? A small bell rang. A *crime* of some kind which had recently been discovered . . . Weren't the Florento sisters criminals? They were in the US, weren't they? A couple of prostitutes who had stolen a load of money from some mega-pimp? Though surely that couldn't have been so important?

Why were criminals being quoted in THIS WEEK'S "I LOVE YOU", in a message posted on *Gula Tidningen*'s home page?

Yeah, yeah, so what? It was their combination with something else in the same message that was crucial. What had it said? Orpheus and Eurydice? Yes, that was it, but it wasn't all. Weren't there some numbers? Some combinations?

How had it gone in THIS WEEK'S "I LOVE YOU"?

"BK, CF, DL. 3 12 13 18 24 28 30." No, those sounded like lottery numbers. There were seven numbers when you played Lotto, weren't there? Initials and a row of numbers.

"3+3=5." No that was "still waiting". One of the six was missing. Two groups of three. Maybe two love triangles joining together. Two smaller group-sex gangs joining forces. But one didn't want to. You could call that group pressure.

More. "Saturday 3rd." Nope, meeting. "You know where. Licking Jack." Classic adultery. Meeting between woman and tongue.

He normally remembered things. Memory like an elephant. Orpheus and the Florento sisters and — a combination of numbers.

"Eurydice. 'No crime is worse than bitter betrayal, the Florento sisters said.' 82 12G 14. Orpheus."

"82 12G 14." Exactly. *That* was it. That was what had been nagging him, and continued to do so. Why? How could he be supposed to know what that combination meant? It was just numbers and a letter. Impenetrable. Give up, as Kerstin Holm would say.

He couldn't give up. It was nagging him. "82 12G 14."

"82 12G 14." "82 12G 14."

A car emerged in his mind. *This* car. Viggo Norlander's half-stolen service Volvo. Why? When? *Hard to steer.* Yeah? Why hard to steer?

Because he had to hold a book open using the wheel.

Kumla. A little church town south-west of Lake Tåkern in Östergötland.

E18. Missed turn-off on the way out of Stockholm.

Arto Söderstedt grabbed the atlas from the compartment in the car door. *Motormännens vägatlas över Sverige.* He ripped the loose red plastic cover open and leafed frantically in the index. Kumla. "44 8E 2."

Shit. It was right and not right.

"82 12G 14."

"44 8E 2."

At the start of the index, there were instructions on how to read the combinations. First page. 82 and 44. Then a square on that page: 12G and 8E. After this, the quarter of that square: 1 was bottom left, 2 bottom right; 3 was top left, 4 top right. It was that part which didn't make any sense. The last number in the combination could only be 1, 2, 3 or 4. Not 14.

Arto Söderstedt didn't really understand what he was doing. Was this just a mental workout? Brain-training? So that it didn't go rusty when he was seventy-five?

Conclusion. Criminals are quoted in THIS WEEK'S "I LOVE YOU". Why? Combined with something which seemed to be a geographic location, but wasn't quite. Was it a red herring after all? Did "82 12G 14" have nothing to do with the atlas, despite the similarities?

"How common is this?" Söderstedt asked, holding up the red plastic book.

Norlander stared at him so long that he became a real road hazard.

"You've gone mad," he said eventually. "You've finally lost the plot. It was just a question of time until the little bells started ringing."

"Just answer me."

Norlander caught sight of the oncoming lorry just in time to swerve out of the way.

"It's the standard road atlas in Sweden," he said after a while. Their pulses were racing.

Söderstedt nodded. OK, if you were looking for a geographical location in Sweden, then it wouldn't be entirely unreasonable to assume that you would use this particular atlas. He continued from that hypothesis. The last number, 1, 2, 3 or 4, referred to the division of each square into four identical squares. It had said 14 in *Gula Tidningen*. If you imagined a *more precise* division of each of these new squares into four further squares, in this case "12G 1", you would end up in square 4 *in* square 1. 14.

From the square labelled "82 12G 14", he created the square "82 12G 1", and from this square, he made another four, choosing square number 4 from them, "82 12G 14". He turned to page 82, square 12G, and then square 1, to the bottom left, and *inside* that square, square 4, in the top right. He ended up in Avesta, a town on the border between the counties of Västmanland and Dalarna. That didn't seem unlikely. Right in the middle of a town.

Orpheus was sending Eurydice a message to tell her that he was in Avesta, and also took the opportunity to quote those criminal Florento sisters from America.

So what? The A-Unit was in the middle of one of the most important murder investigations of late — why should that little message be of interest to him? He couldn't describe it as anything other than a hunch. That indescribable feeling of being onto something completely unknown.

Criminals, location, mythology . . . There was something there.

But, of course, it couldn't intrude on the rest of the investigation. That much was clear.

When they returned to the office, Söderstedt went straight to the computer. He had received four messages on the family cars: sold, sold, sold and sold. Not much variation.

There was, however, variation on *Gula Tidningen*'s home page. Under the title THIS WEEK'S "I LOVE YOU". It now read:

"Orpheus. 'But the sisters vanished into thin air.' 41 7C 31. Eurydice."

Söderstedt had smuggled the atlas with him into the office. He looked up "41 7C 31".

It was the other side of the country, Alingsås.

He had found something, but he had no idea what.

All he had was his hunch.

CHAPTER
THIRTY-ONE

Ljubomir was there. There. He knew perfectly well why. It was a test of loyalty.

The two Swedes had been in the study. "Security consultants" dressed in Hawaiian shirts and shorts. They had sat cumbersomely on the L-shaped desk, talking to the great man. Quietly, so that Ljubomir wouldn't hear. He had been standing by the door, as usual. He heard everything. His hearing was good.

"Do we know who they are?" the great man asked gruffly.

"Not really," said one of the Swedes. "We're working on it."

"It seems racial," said the other. "That's top of the list. Wog money. Royal straight flush. Can't get any higher."

"Who the hell blew Lordan up?" the great man demanded.

"Like we said, we can't access that information. It's not possible."

"You're ex-police," said the great man. "So what the hell *can* you actually access? What're you doing to earn your money?"

He paused, gathered himself, and continued.

"Could we get to any of the investigators?"

Both of the "security consultants" shook their heads.

"They're difficult. We've had a bit to do with them . . ."

"Dyed-in-the-wool types. Tight, smart, a bit eccentric. Untouchable."

"No one's untouchable," said the great man. "The one who came here. Hultin?"

"Forget it," said the first of the Swedes, looking troubled. "A rock. Old school. You'll never get to him. You could kill him, but you can't squeeze him."

"Fuck the police," said the other. "Just stay ahead of them. Like normal."

"Nothing from our man?"

"He's lying low. Isn't it time to squeeze him a bit now?"

"Absolutely not. His insurance is watertight. If anyone's going to squeeze him, then it'll be my people doing it. Understand?"

That was the end of the discussion. The Swedes had left without even giving Ljubomir a glance. Then the great man had just dragged Ljubomir along with him, without a word. He dragged him out, through the paradise garden to the garage door. They stopped. Three men had immediately come rushing out of the guardroom and followed them, close on their heels. They went past Ljubomir and the great man, entered the garage and started the car. Everything was fine.

These three men tested everything. They shielded him with their bodies, they entered all rooms first, they tasted his food, they opened his post, they started his car, and they *drove* his car. That's what they were doing now. Ljubomir was squashed in between two lumps of meat on the back seat as the car raced into town.

And now they were *there*. In *that place*.

It was disarmed. Disinfected. Not a trace of its disgusting past left. An empty flat. Apart from two additional, almost identical men. Like parodies of gangsters. The civilian look.

But they simply didn't know how civilians dressed. They had been recruited to various armies and paramilitary forces since they were young. Since before they had learned how to dress.

But they knew how to follow orders.

No one said a word.

If you ignored the precision binoculars in the window, it was a completely normal flat.

If you ignored the screams which bombarded Ljubomir's ears from the soundproofed walls.

Those clear, piercing screams.

Ljubomir imagined that they had been absorbed by the porous walls, which looked like they had golden foam cushions fastened to them. All the screams. They bombarded him in unison, like a terrible, piercing accusation. He was overwhelmed. He could feel that he had turned pale. He stepped over to the window, tried to open it. No fresh air blew in. It was stuck.

The great man came over to him and put his arm around him. It wasn't a gesture of friendship — he saved those for outside of working hours. It was a test. To see how much he was shaking.

To see if he was about to throw up.

They stood together, childhood friends from the little mountain village in eastern Serbia, looking down at the bank on the other side of the street. You could almost believe they were friends.

A short, well-built man wearing a hat had just entered the bank.

A short, well-built man wearing a hat had just entered the bank. He scratched his forehead as he walked, scratched it so that his hand covered his face. He looked around for a moment. Big, inner-city bank. Not yet converted into an open-plan office. Half ten, mid-morning: low traffic. Four customers, none of them potential heroes. Three cameras. He worked out their range, pulled the black hat down over his face, and peered out through the balaclava's eye holes. As the others came running into the bank, he pulled out a pistol and shot the surveillance cameras. Three shots were all that was needed.

One of the others stood guard by the door. He could hardly lift his gun. Two went over to the counter, weapons raised. One of them was wearing a golden balaclava. He said, clearly: "We know you've pressed the alarm. So we're asking you to fill these two bags with money as quickly as you can. You've got thirty seconds, then we'll start shooting customers."

The bags were quickly filled. No one screamed, no one made a sound. A strange silence spread through the room. As though everyone had instinctively understood that he had meant it.

318

On the way out, they took off their balaclavas, wrapped a chain around the door handles and locked it using a padlock.

The four men walked calmly down the street, the two bags over their shoulders, turning off into a side road. No one paid any attention to the fact that one of them could hardly walk.

The short, well-built man wearing a hat had just left the bank in the company of a young blonde girl. He put his wallet into the inner pocket of his jacket, and ruffled the girl's long hair before they hugged and parted ways. The great man pointed at him.

"He's probably just seen his daughter in the bank. A chance meeting. His *daughter*. Do you understand, Ljubomir?"

Ljubomir met the great man's gaze. It bored into him. The great man continued.

"This flat is for surveillance and nothing else. You've got to forget everything else, Ljubomir. We can see *everything* from here. Sooner or later, they'll come here, and then we'll catch them. It's that simple. *No one* cheats Rajko Nedic, Ljubomir, and *no one* lets him down. I really want you to understand that."

Ljubomir nodded. He understood. He understood *exactly*.

And still, he didn't want to forget.

CHAPTER
THIRTY-TWO

They were as close to one another as they could get. Though the blinds couldn't stop the sun in its tracks, they lay pressed up close to one another, as much of their bodies as possible touching the other's. The heat could never be oppressive.

It was forty degrees in the little flat on Surbrunnsgatan.

They had done something that neither of them had done before. They had skipped work. Suddenly, as if following a simultaneous, shared impulse, they had just gone home and made love. As though they had been following orders from some higher and more important being than the National Police Commissioner.

Both realised — around the same time — that they had wandered into an emotional wilderness of work, work and nothing but work, and that they had only now found an oasis; not another mirage, but an oasis. That was where they planned to stay. That was where they planned to settle down.

Nothing else would have been able to tear them from their duties.

Only this. A higher calling, a higher right.

They would get to know one another inside and out, out and in. Nothing would be kept secret any longer.

Still, that was exactly what happened. Two walls were raised between their tightly entwined bodies. Walls of sworn secrecy, built from both sides. And between them, a strange minefield.

They tried to convince themselves that the walls didn't affect *them*, that they didn't have anything to do with their being together — only with their jobs. But it didn't quite work. Their jobs were a part of them.

There are, essentially, only two real attitudes to work. Either you can take any job at all, so long as the pay cheque falls into your hands at the end of the month, or you can deliberately look for a job that, in some way, chimes with your character.

Both Sara Svenhagen and Jorge Chavez had done the latter. When they worked on their investigations, when they slowly but surely worked their way towards hidden truths, they were also doing something else. Something more important. They were restoring an order, finding patterns in their environment, exposing hidden structures, slowly approaching the *meaning* itself. They were *devoted*. There was no other word for it.

And now they were also devoted to one another. Two devotees in an embrace.

Jorge agonised over how ungrateful he had been. Determined "only" to help find the Kvarnen Killer, Sara had given the A-Unit photographic material which had enabled them to identify the whole of Gang Two and also provided them with pictures of all of Gang One. It was like a token of her affection. Unfortunately, the picture of the "policeman" was as good as non-existent, and it was ultimately this policeman that was the reason behind his ungratefulness. If a policeman really was involved, then the strictest possible secrecy was absolutely essential, and that meant it was impossible to discuss any of the main points of the Sickla Slaughter. He was convinced that an exchange of ideas about Niklas Lindberg and Bullet Kullberg really would help move the case forward; he would have loved to hear Sara's thoughts on Rajko Nedic and Lordan Vukotic, on Danne Blood Pudding and Roger Sjöqvist, Sven Joakim Bergwall, Eskil Carlstedt and a gang of probable war criminals from the former Yugoslavia. And, above all, on the "policeman". But he couldn't. A wall was preventing it.

Of course, Sara had wondered what the strange cry of "The policeman" had meant, the thing Jorge had blurted out when the photograph of the hidden man was developed. But it had quickly disappeared behind a dilemma of her own. *Her* wall. Her boss, Detective Superintendent Ragnar Hellberg, had silenced her investigation, classified it as top secret — and the question was whether that was a case of misconduct. Or even a crime. He had deliberately erased all traces of an email address that had appeared quite frequently on various paedophile websites: "brambo". Judging by all appearances, "brambo" was a paedophile, active online. She had two possible options. Either she could confront Ragnar Hellberg, or she could keep searching for "brambo's" identity. The only thing she couldn't do was talk to Jorge. That was *her* wall and no one else's.

And so they lay there, as close to one another as they could possibly be. But still oceans apart.

Between them, a strange minefield.

CHAPTER
THIRTY-THREE

Sure enough, the Florento sisters were criminals. Arto Söderstedt managed to find them fairly quickly in the news archives. The story had gained lots of column inches, particularly in the tabloids, over the few days around Midsummer — it was uncommon for any story to last longer than that.

The sisters were prostitutes in Atlanta, Georgia. They had been part of an enormous brothel controlled by a mega-pimp called Big Ted Curtis, who treated his whores badly even by pimp standards. Under challenging circumstances, the sisters had set up an Internet connection, gained access to Big Ted's bank account, emptied it, and then vanished into thin air. Penniless, he had committed suicide, and the whole brothel was set free.

A few weeks ago, the sisters had broken their silence. They communicated with the press via email, telling their story. But still, no one knew where they were.

Söderstedt pondered their story. Each second he neglected to spend on Niklas Lindberg and Rajko Nedic gave him a guilty conscience. Though less and less so. He couldn't let it go.

Two people, presumably lovers, were calling themselves Orpheus and Eurydice — the ancient musician and his beloved, whom he had sung back from the kingdom of the dead. They were quoting two criminal sisters who had also made their way back from the dead and, on top of that, managed to sink their tormentor and become rich. They were sending messages about their respective positions in different places across Sweden using *Gula Tidningen's* THIS WEEK'S "I LOVE YOU" feature. Something outside the bounds of the law was probably going on here.

Söderstedt sat at his desk with the extensive investigatory material on the Sickla Slaughter in one hand, the measly printouts from *Gula Tidningen* in the other. The strange thing wasn't just that they seemed to weigh the same amount, but that they were also being pulled together like magnets.

Two positions: Orpheus in Arvika, Eurydice in Alingsås. Two citations, quotation marks and all: "No crime is worse than bitter betrayal, said the Florento sisters." "But the sisters vanished into thin air." He had a brainwave, phoned *Gula Tidningen* and spoke to the webmaster.

Yes, the paper had backups for the last six months' ads.

Arto Söderstedt clenched his fist for a brief moment. He asked whether he could have the last month's entries for the THIS WEEK'S "I LOVE YOU" feature sent to him. He could. It took just under an hour.

He searched through the extensive material on his computer. As "Orpheus" after "Orpheus" popped up on his screen, he was struck by how drastically this little

325

computer function had aided their police work. Eventually, he was left with a cluster of similar messages on the screen in front of him. They all looked alike. First, the name of the recipient — Orpheus or Eurydice — then, in quotation marks, a short phrase which was more or less obviously connected to the Florento sisters; then, the position marker from the atlas which, without exception, referred to an urban area; finally, the sender (Orpheus or Eurydice). Always exactly the same form.

The first message was sent on Midsummer's Eve, 25 June. Söderstedt could feel the two piles of paper being pulled even closer together. The Sickla Slaughter had taken place on the night of the 24th.

He looked more closely at the first message. It had come from Orpheus. The code from the road atlas said Orsa in Dalarna county. There was no quotation, but a reference: "Expr., 24.06, p.12 top". The reply from Eurydice had come just under two hours later, along with a code that pointed to Falkenberg on the west coast. Here, there was a quotation: "The sisters were just spiritual sisters."

"Expr."? And then "p.12 top"? That must have been a reference to the top of page 12 in the previous day's issue of *Expressen*. There weren't any tabloids on Midsummer's Eve, were there? Maybe Orpheus had got hold of the day before's number — and found . . .?

Söderstedt rang the police station's library. A woman answered, and five minutes later, a girl brought him a copy of *Expressen* from 24 June. Most articles were about the Kvarnen Killing, but at the top of page 12

326

was one with the headline: "THE SISTERS WHO VANISHED INTO THIN AIR." It was a follow-up article on the Florento sisters. Partway through, it said: "The sisters were just spiritual sisters." Towards the end, it read: "No crime is worse than bitter betrayal, said the Florento sisters."

And the article ended with the words: "But the sisters vanished into thin air."

He went through the rest of the messages from THIS WEEK'S "I LOVE YOU". All were quotations from the *Expressen* article.

Reconstruction, Söderstedt thought to himself, leaning back. Orpheus finds the article about the Florento sisters. In his first message to Eurydice, he refers to it. She replies after two hours, during which time she's presumably gone out in Falkenberg, where everything's closed for Midsummer, to get hold of a copy of *Expressen*. She then replies with a quote from the article: "The sisters were just spiritual sisters." The pair must have agreed in advance to call one another Orpheus and Eurydice, those who escaped the kingdom of the dead. They find an article on a couple of spiritual sisters who have done the same thing — and who have also got hold of an enormous sum of money. They identify with the sisters, so they send a quotation from the article each time they communicate. They're moving through Sweden, each in a different location, and they've decided in advance to keep in touch using *Gula Tidningen's* most harmless, well-hidden page: THIS WEEK'S "I LOVE YOU". That implies that they have access to the Internet. Wherever they are, the pair seem

327

to have immediate Internet access. How? And why the Internet? Why not direct contact? To avoid the chance of being traced? Hmm.

The server, Söderstedt nodded. It must be possible to find out where the messages to *Gula Tidningen* were coming from.

He contacted the webmaster again. Yeah, Orpheus and Eurydice were using the same server. A free Spanish server called Virtud. He found it online. After some linguistic confusion and general resistance, Virtud's Spanish webmaster finally accepted that Arto Söderstedt was calling from the Swedish police and, very reluctantly, gave him Orpheus and Eurydice's details. They were registered as Baruch Spinoza and Elton John. That didn't mean a great deal. The most important thing was that there were two phone numbers.

Two mobile phone numbers.

In other words, Orpheus and Eurydice were connecting to the Internet using their mobile phones.

He looked up the numbers with the provider, Comviq. Both were registered. At the same address. A restaurant.

The Thanatos restaurant in Östermalm, Stockholm.

He contacted the Patents and Registrations Office. What could they tell him about the Thanatos restaurant?

Eventually, Arto Söderstedt found the name of the owner.

The Thanatos restaurant was owned by a man called Rajko Nedic.

Arto Söderstedt suddenly felt completely, completely calm.

328

CHAPTER
THIRTY-FOUR

The weak link between Sara Svenhagen and Jorge Chavez was called Gunnar Nyberg. A few weeks ago, he and Sara had been working as a pair. Now, the other half of the pair was Jorge.

Though "pair" was maybe a bit much. They didn't take it in turns running up dingy stairwells, service weapons raised; they didn't cover one another as they crept down some dark alley; they didn't play good cop, bad cop in any dark interrogation rooms. No, they sat at their computers. Through no fault of his own, the once boorish bodybuilder policeman had been thrown from one computer nerd to the next and, as a result, had actually become quite good at working online.

Though enough was enough.

Moving back to the A-Unit had somehow breathed life into old habits. Or maybe they were bad habits. He went out into the underworld, into the old Gunnar Nyberg territory. Suddenly he'd had enough of virtual cyber-Nazism, and put a surprising number of rank-and-file officers to work, hunting the only line of business which never took a break.

First of all, there was a gang of robbers. It was primarily made up of relatively young right-wing extremists, but also of more out-and-out professional criminals like Danne Blood Pudding. Nyberg organised an extensive interrogation of professional criminals, bank robbers and skinheads. He followed up leads, above all on Danne Blood Pudding and Roger Sjöqvist.

So far, it hadn't led to anything.

Then there was a drugs ring. Rajko Nedic really did seem untouchable, but in the long run there must be something to go on. Anything at all.

And that was what he was currently busy with. The old intimidation techniques were like reflex. He heaved his irritatingly constant 146 kilos towards the thin figure of a man named Robban, a known big-time pusher in Hjulsta. Robban was in his flat, gaping with surprise at the broken front door which was hanging in scraps — not splinters, not pieces of wood, but *scraps*. Robban thought: How the hell did he manage to break the door into scraps? But that wasn't what he said. Instead, voice shaking, he said: "I don't know what you're talking about."

"Think again," said Gunnar Nyberg.

"Shit, man," Robban half sniffed. "You know as well as I do that it's an idiot-proof system. You don't know anyone else! There's a delivery, you pick it up. You deliver the money, they look happy. When they don't look happy, you're dead."

Nyberg heaved himself a little closer. His grizzly bear's face was only a few centimetres from Robban's, which was more rabbit-like than anything else. The grizzly's breath *didn't* smell of raw meat and fresh blood — it smelt of coffee.

"Yugoslavs?" the coffee-scented predator barked.

"Could be," Robban panted. "I dunno. They look southern, they do. Ruthless guys. Always speaking gibberish together."

"What d'you mean by that?"

A sudden burst of kamikaze bravado: "Go fuck yourself, you bastard."

The grizzly bear grabbed the rabbit's neck, pressing hard. The rabbit shook violently — a trembling piece of second-rate fur.

"I learned this through close contact," Gunnar Nyberg informed him pedagogically. "It really works."

"Wait. Christ! Wait," Robban trembled.

Nyberg loosened his grip, feeling ill at ease. He had said he would never again use violence in his work. It had just happened. As though his grizzly role demanded it.

Robban stared *admiringly* at him.

"Wow, man!" he shouted, massaging his neck. "What a grip!"

"Get to the point now," Nyberg muttered, ashamed.

"OK. I've heard about a drug dealer who's made a thing of it. All his men speak gibberish between themselves. It's a way of disguising the entire thing."

A way of disguising the entire thing, Gunnar Nyberg thought to himself before asking, as he should: "Which dealer?"

"Rajko Nedic."

"And you think it's Nedic making deliveries to you?"

"No idea," said Robban, lighting a cigarette and trying to look calm. "And above all, I didn't say that."

Nyberg returned to his worn-out old Renault, sitting for a moment with his hands on the wheel and looking out over Hjulsta's utterly homogeneous seventies architecture. The July sun reflected listlessly in the identical, greyish-brown rows of windows.

Well, Gunnar Nyberg thought to himself. It was the warmest day of the year, he was dripping with sweat, and his thoughts were heroically trying to crawl up out of a day which had turned into quicksand. Once again, he thought: Well . . .

And: Well . . .

His thoughts broke free in a short, sharp burst.

If Rajko Nedic's men always spoke Serbo-Croat between themselves, how could those Swedish Nazis in Kumla have worked out that a handover was going to take place?

Niklas Lindberg surely couldn't have tortured Lordan Vukotic twice. Someone would have noticed. And yet Lindberg knew two things: that a big handover was going to take place, and that there would be a meeting in Kvarnen. How had he known?

Nedic's empire was built on perfect discipline. No one ever blabbed. That was the mainstay of the entire operation. That was how he managed to act as a law-abiding restaurateur with such precision. Quite simply, his word was the law.

Did that mean he had suddenly discovered a crack in Nedic's walls?

One of his men in Kumla had squealed — even before Vukotic had done it. A leak in the watertight system.

Gunnar Nyberg saw the chance to sow some weeds in the carefully pruned garden. Wasn't there a chance that the whole organisation might start to bleed information if news of a leak reached Nedic?

Nyberg sat in his car. His hands had turned white at the wheel. Drops of sweat ran between his fingers, loosening them.

Three men in Kumla. What were they called? Zoran Koco, Petar Klovic, Risto Petrovic. He would talk to them. Right away.

He was already halfway there. Hjulsta. He tore off in his rusty old Renault, along the E18 towards Örebro. Between Bålsta and Enköping, he passed a place called Grillby. The name set a little bell ringing in his head. Grillby? He had been to Grillby. When? How? Though he didn't know why he was thinking about it now. Probably some kind of failure to adjust to a slower speed.

After Örebro, he sped across the Närke plain towards Kumla. It didn't take much more than an hour. He made his way to the prison governor and immediately found the trio's collected works in front of him in an interrogation room.

Interpol's material was extensive but, ultimately, not especially comprehensive. There were lots of blanks, especially in relation to the Yugoslav war. Zoran Koco was a Bosnian Muslim from Sarajevo and had apparently been one of the leading black-market sharks during the Bosnian war. Petar Klovic was a Bosnian Serb and had been a guard in one of the concentration camps for Muslims. No crimes — if you ignored their

333

crimes against humanity. Risto Petrovic was a Croat, the former commander of a paramilitary group which had also been involved in the ethnic cleansing. Though of Serbs in Croatia.

An utterly unholy alliance.

When it came to Niklas Lindberg, the blank was his year in the Foreign Legion. May '94 to May '95. Koco and Klovic were already in Sweden by then, but not Petrovic. On the contrary, there was a very significant gap in the material from that time. In July 1995, Petrovic had come to Sweden and joined Rajko Nedic's gang, something which was, of course, unconfirmed. By September, he had already been nicked for peddling drugs, and had been inside, awaiting deportation, ever since.

Nyberg contacted CID's Interpol group. They, in turn, contacted the Foreign Legion and, within an hour, had produced a number of possible names from '94 to '95.

During that hour, Gunnar Nyberg had tried to make sense of it all.

A Croatian who had taken part in ethnic cleansing. There was a musty stench of Ustaša, the fascist organisation which had exterminated Serbs during the Second World War, about the whole thing. It wasn't unlikely that Risto Petrovic had arrived in Sweden by way of the Foreign Legion, under a false name, in order to avoid arrest. There, he had met a kindred spirit, the ex-commando major Niklas Lindberg. Petrovic had then ingratiated himself with the Serbian-Swede Rajko Nedic, who wasn't especially interested in ethnic purity, in order to supply Lindberg with information on the imminent transaction between Nedic and a Swedish "policeman", for example. But was Lindberg really powerful enough to have planted a spy in Nedic's organisation? Or were there larger organisations of right-wing extremists at work in the background? Directing both Petrovic and Lindberg? And if so, did that mean there was an even greater motive behind the Sickla Slaughter?

Gunnar Nyberg sat in the little interrogation room in Kumla, and felt like the walls were closing in. What kind of strange connection had he come across, thanks to a rabbit-like drug pusher called Robban?

The fax machine rattled into life. Three extracts from the Foreign Legion register for 1994 to 1995. Three Yugoslav names, and three mediocre but clearly discernible photographs.

Gunnar Nyberg rang Jan-Olov Hultin. He explained the situation, and was given various orders. All sounded good.

Risto Petrovic was brought into the interrogation room. A certain contentedness spread through Nyberg's enormous body as he immediately recognised the man's face from one of the pictures.

Petrovic sat staring at him. He was large, compact, with the kind of solid, bulging muscles that only prisoners have. A body which doesn't do much moving but, instead, spends hours pumping iron. His gaze was ruthless, on the verge of inhuman. Exactly as Nyberg had hoped.

When he opened his mouth, he was fully aware that, by doing so, he was sentencing Risto Petrovic to death.

"Jovan Sotra?" he read from one of the three faxes.

Petrovic froze. Suddenly, the consequences were clear to him. As soon as Koko or Klovic or any of the others close to Nedic found out about the link, he would be a dead man. Power was coursing through Gunnar Nyberg at that very moment. Pure power. He understood right away what it means to have a man's life in your hands. It was unbearable.

Perhaps he should have stayed at his computer. In the safety of cyberspace.

"I don't know what you're taking about," Petrovic eventually said in English, though his eyes told a different story.

Nyberg switched to a rusty-sounding English.

"Shortly after the end of the war in Croatia, you went from being commander of a paramilitary group to a private in the French Foreign Legion. During that time, you met a Swede, a former officer called Niklas Lindberg. When you later met again here in Kumla, you gave him information about a large transaction that would be taking place between your employer, Rajko Nedic, and another party. Lindberg used that information to kill Nedic's closest man, Lordan Vukotic, as well as to rob and kill three other Nedic men in the so-called Sickla Slaughter, where whatever was being handed over was stolen."

Petrovic stared at Nyberg. His eyes were searching for a way out. He didn't know whether he could find one in the large, bear-like policeman. Maybe. He repeated, mostly because it was expected of him: "I don't know what you're talking about."

It sounded so hollow that Nyberg simply ignored him.

"However," he said, nodding, "there is a way out."

They looked at one another for a moment. The paramilitary commander and Sweden's Biggest Policeman. The Foreign Legionnaire and Mr Sweden. It felt masculine to the point of absurdity.

"We're waiting for a policeman called Lars Viksjö. He'll take you to a safe place. You'll be a Crown witness, get a new identity, and be placed wherever in the world you want to go. In exchange, we want to know the following. One: the connection between you and Lindberg. Two: everything imaginable, and unimaginable, about Rajko Nedic's organisation. Three: what kind of handover it was. Four: who was going to receive it. Five: what Lindberg was going to use it for. Six: where Lindberg and his men are now."

Risto Petrovic closed his eyes. He was completely still. When he opened them again, the decision had been made. It was obvious.

"I don't know where Niklas Lindberg is," he said.

Then he said nothing more.

After fifteen minutes of absolute silence, Lars Viksjö arrived, taking Petrovic with him. Once again, the former war criminal had changed lives.

It would be interesting to see how Rajko Nedic reacted.

Gunnar Nyberg allowed himself a moment of quiet contemplation. No, he admitted to himself, not contemplation; that was saying too much. Rather, it was a moment of pure self-righteousness. He felt very pleased with himself.

He rang Hultin and updated him.

Hultin said: "Bloody good job, Gunnar."

Nyberg said: "Not at all."

He climbed back into his rusty old Renault and pottered homewards. Just after Enköping, he came to the little village called Grillby. He was forced to stop. What was it with this Grillby? Why was it demanding his attention in his moment of triumph?

Grillby. A little cottage. An aunt's cottage. Youthful feeling of freedom. Police College exams. Twenty years ago. Five men and a van full of six-packs.

What was it he had said? "I'm going out to the cottage to recharge the batteries."

Why not try? Gunnar Nyberg followed a twenty-year-old internal map. Grillby mustn't have changed much, because he found it without a problem. He came to a narrow gravel road which led out of the little community into the forest. He drove a couple of kilometres along an increasingly vanishing road. The sun turned the old Renault into a baking oven, and Gunnar Nyberg into a slow-cooked meatloaf. He was doubting his memory more and more, along with his sense of direction, when a glade finally opened up in the sparse forest, and the little cottage came into view. It was the same, exactly the same. It stood by the edge of the trees and looked like it had been abandoned. A little red labourer's cottage from the turn of the

338

century. Many beers had been transformed into urine here.

Ludvig Johnsson was leaning against the veranda, stretching. He looked up with an utterly surprised, almost terrified gaze. He obviously wasn't used to visitors.

Nyberg waved to him. His face lit up, and he jogged over to the Renault, peering in through the wound-down oven window. He recoiled.

"Jesus," he said. "You've been sitting in there a while."

"It's quite warm," said Gunnar Nyberg, squeezing out of the entirely-too-small car. He stretched, and held out his hands towards the cottage.

"So it's still standing," he observed.

Ludvig Johnsson nodded, returning to the veranda and continuing to stretch.

"It's still standing," he said. "No electricity, no running water, no phone. I come back when I want to get away from the world. It's happening more and more."

Nyberg nodded. "I know what you mean," he said. "I go to my son and grandson's in Östhammar, though it hasn't happened so often this year."

Johnsson stopped stretching and looked at him.

"That's not so relevant for me," was all he said.

Nyberg bit his tongue. Much too late.

"Sorry," he said.

Ludvig Johnsson walked over to Nyberg and put an arm around him. It turned into a hug. They stood in the blazing hot sunshine by the little cottage outside of

339

Grillby, Uppland county, hugging. The power of the past.

"It's OK," Ludvig Johnsson eventually said. "It was a long time ago."

They sat in the shade on the veranda. Johnsson fetched two beers. They disappeared quickly. Two more appeared.

"Gas fridge," said Johnsson.

"That's enough," said Nyberg. "I've got to drive home later. We've had a breakthrough in the investigation."

"From paedophiles to Nazis," Johnsson nodded. "Anything you want to talk about?"

"I think so. Later. Is this still your aunt's place?"

Ludvig Johnsson laughed and scratched his bald head.

"She had senile dementia even then, when we were here celebrating the end of exams. She still does. She's in the same home and looks the same, though she's closer to a hundred. Like the dementia preserved her."

He grimaced and continued.

"Then, when I got a family, I almost forgot about it. Hanna and I travelled a lot. With the boys once they'd arrived, too. They were nine and seven when they died, and they'd been to fourteen countries. They bragged about it at school. Fourteen countries! Then one day they were just gone. All three. Hanna, Micke, Stefan. Just like that, gone. I don't know if it's possible to understand it."

It was completely silent. Gunnar Nyberg imagined he could hear the sun shining. A tiny, tiny whirring in the background. He had nothing to say. There was nothing to say. He had managed to put the broken pieces of his past back together. Ludvig Johnsson hadn't even had the chance. The irrevocability of death.

"Mmm," Johnsson said after a moment. "Then I remembered the cottage. I can just be myself here. I need it. Recharge my batteries before taking the paedophile world head on. No one knows that this place is here. Well, they didn't until now."

"I won't tell," said Gunnar Nyberg, thinking he had made a mistake. He had barged onto holy land. He had populated a world which should never have been populated. Without consideration, he had forced open a door to an intimate world with such force that it was hanging in *scraps*. He felt awful.

Ludvig Johnsson leaned forward over the table, placing his hand over Nyberg's, and looking into his eyes with a clear, searching look.

"It's OK, Gunnar," he said quietly. "Maybe it's what I needed. I can't be a hermit any more."

They looked at one another. In some way, they were still living together in their shared flat, twenty years ago. Neither of them had ever really left it. The way you never really leave a place. Everything always remains. Those had been important years in their lives. The worldly Ludvig and the sulky Gunnar. There they were again.

And so it happened that Gunnar Nyberg made a mistake. He talked about the case. He needed a sounding board more than ever, and his sounding board needed to be one, too. That was clear. For a moment, Gunnar Nyberg imagined that they were about to solve the case together. Like they had done in Police College.

He began with the breakthrough, with the leak around Rajko Nedic: Risto Petrovic. Then he went back to the very beginning, to the events in Kvarnen and the Kumla Bunker, before moving on to the ex-Yugoslav mercenaries and Niklas Lindberg and the Foreign Legion and possible right-wing extremist umbrella organisations, and then he was done. It was a long and complicated story. One which, thus far, had no ending.

"I'll be damned," said Ludvig Johnsson.

That was all.

When Gunnar Nyberg left Grillby, it felt like a weight had been lifted from his shoulders. An old friendship had been revived, properly revived, and he felt like he had found a sounding board for life. It felt good. As though yet another stray piece from the past had fallen into place.

He pulled out onto the E18 and returned to Stockholm.

CHAPTER
THIRTY-FIVE

"Yes, yes, yes!" shouted Bullet. "Got it again!"

It was the second time that day. The first had come and gone. A brief signal which might have been, though probably wasn't, a false alarm. But this time it was clear. Bullet felt extremely pleased. Even he had stopped believing.

Niklas Lindberg could see it in him. His short but broad body almost quivering with sudden, unanticipated expectation. Like a soufflé, he surprised himself by thinking.

He looked down towards his parents' home. It was so still down in the valley. The cute little rows of houses where he had come into existence. Undisturbed by foreigners. A clean and healthy childhood where everything was as it should have been. Trollhättan — so typically Swedish. And now? Shady pizzerias on every corner, mafia gambling joints, dishonest southerners' shirker mentality. A world of rapists, drug pushers, madmen with knives, benefit scroungers; of Arabic-Jewish-Catholic corruption and weakness dressed up as machismo. At least he knew what he was fighting *against*. It was more difficult to say what he was fighting *for*.

"Gone again," Bullet said, subdued, turning the dials.

"Did you get a direction?" asked Niklas Lindberg.

"Yeah," said Bullet. "Eastward. Either on the 44 or the 42."

"What's out there? Rogge?"

Roger Sjöqvist leafed through the atlas.

"Hard to see. Right between pages. The 44 splits in two. Continues as the 44 up to Lake Vänern, Lidköping. As the 47 it goes to Falköping. But the 47 meets the E20 which goes up to Skara and Skövde. What else did you say? The 42. It doesn't go anywhere. Vårgårda. Fristad."

"We need another signal," said Bullet.

Niklas Lindberg thought. "Take the 44," he said. "And put your foot down."

"The speed limit, though?"

"Fuck it. We're close now."

"What are you thinking, Nicke?" asked Bullet.

"That we'll get another signal," Niklas Lindberg replied. "And then we'll know."

CHAPTER
THIRTY-SIX

Detective Superintendent Jan-Olov Hultin wasn't at all happy that Jorge Chavez was sitting on his desk, swinging his legs. Not happy at all. Though he didn't really know why.

Probably because he couldn't be seen.

It was Friday 9 July, and time was passing quickly, quickly. They had no real hot leads to go on. Lots of new information all the time, but nothing really hot, really important. Maybe things would start looking up today.

Why this sudden optimism?

The past few meetings in the Supreme Command Centre had actually been dominated by a kind of hopeless resignation. So much information, and so little room for action. Nedic was lying low, and the inevitable nationwide alert for Niklas Lindberg and his men was drawing closer. If they released their identities, the tabloids would blow the Sickla Slaughter up into something enormous, Lindberg would be depicted as the Antichrist and the three others his apostles of darkness. They wanted to avoid that at all costs.

So far, Hultin had Mörner, the head of CID and the Police Commissioner on side when it came to keeping the lid on Lindberg, Sjöqvist, Andersson and Kullberg's identities, but the longer the investigation failed to produce any results, the more the demand for disclosure grew. Soon, they would no longer be able to avoid bringing PC General Public into the equation — increasing Rajko Nedic's room for manoeuvre considerably by doing so; he would suddenly know exactly who had robbed him. Soon they would have no other way to go. Hultin dreaded that moment. It would paralyse their investigation, they would end up in a hopeless period of checking tips, and any chance of giving the team a free rein would disappear.

And what was the A-Unit without a free rein?

The sight of the free-reined Gunnar Nyberg down in the depths of the Supreme Command Centre was one of the reasons for Hultin's sudden optimism, but there were others. *Everyone* looked so psyched up — perhaps with the exception of Viggo Norlander, sleeping open-mouthed and dribbling. A nice titbit for the tabloids. "A behind-the-scenes glimpse into how the hunt for the country's most dangerous criminals is being run." Accompanied by a close-up of his dribbling mouth. Nice.

He had learned to read the facial expressions of the A-Unit well enough to know what to expect. Jorge looked lively up on the desk — that boded well. For the past few days, he had been noticeably absent; infatuation — but also a kind of visible pressure, as though there were unwanted obstacles in the way of love. Paul looked as though he was in real high spirits — which, actually, he had done since he was paired up

346

with Kerstin, and Hultin suspected that there were certain complications. Kerstin, in turn, also looked charged. But she always looked good. Still, it was Arto who caught his attention the most. The corners of his mouth were taut in a way that Hultin hadn't seen for a long while. He'd be damned if Arto Söderstedt hadn't gone and cracked the whole bloody thing. It certainly looked that way.

So, it was not without expectation that Superintendent Jan-Olov Hultin handed over to the A-Unit.

A television and VCR stood by alongside the desk. Chavez pressed play on a remote control. A sequence of a few seconds played. A short, broad man wearing a hat entered a bank. Experienced, he hid his face from the camera using his hand, stepping out of frame. Only his legs were visible. He was wearing boots, and stood for a few seconds next to a table. Then the picture disappeared into static. Chavez played the sequence once more.

"Bank robbery in Gothenburg," he said. "Before the CCTV cameras were shot out. Look at his feet. Measurements at the scene showed that they were size 7."

"Though those aren't four-year-old Reeboks," said Arto Söderstedt.

They looked at him, waiting for a continuation which never came.

"No," Chavez admitted. "They're not the four-year-old Reeboks that walked through Eskil Carlstedt's blood in the Sickla industrial estate. But it is possible to change shoes. Such things have actually happened."

A defiant glance at Söderstedt. No reaction. Chavez continued.

"This bank robbery yesterday was the crown on what, with hindsight, is clearly a real string of raids in south-west Sweden. Everything from shops to banks along the west coast. It started on Midsummer's Eve, with a petrol station in Skillingaryd, between Jönköping and Värnamo in Småland. The Sickla Slaughter took place in the early hours of Midsummer's Eve."

"Skillingaryd isn't on the west coast, though," said Kerstin Holm.

"Of course not," said Chavez. "That came later. Six further places have seen raids: Ängelholm, Mellbystrand, Halmstad, Varberg, Ulricehamn, and the culmination, yesterday, in Gothenburg, where they took 420,000 kronor. Since the evidence from witnesses is basically non-existent, we still don't know if it's the same gang behind all of these raids. But with the combination of experienced behaviour in the bank in Gothenburg and size 7 shoes, it's not entirely unlikely that it really is our boys in this gang on the west coast. There were four bank robbers, after all, of which one was apparently injured. I want to say that it *is* our boys. And there's one more thing."

"What's that?" Hultin asked patiently.

"Witness statements from the bank," said Chavez. "Four robbers. Three wearing black balaclavas, one in another colour. Gold. Maybe you remember the gold thread from Sickla . . ."

Hultin nodded but objected all the same. "First, they steal a nice, juicy amount from Rajko Nedic, probably

348

millions, and then they continue with a series of small, risky robberies on the west coast? The smallest of these generated 4,212 kronor. Sounds unlikely."

"It *is* unlikely," said Söderstedt.

Again, all eyes turned to him. He was *holding something back*, that much was clear.

"It's unlikely for the very reason that the premise is all wrong," he explained. "If we change the premise, then it's not only likely, but true."

His clarification didn't exactly help to clarify the matter.

"I'd like to come back to the matter," he ended, staring at the wall.

Chavez felt that he should be angry. To his surprise, he wasn't. Curiosity had taken over. He jumped down from the desk, and returned to his normal seat.

"Kerstin?" Hultin said.

"Yup," said Kerstin Holm, climbing up onto the podium and attaching a large photograph to the whiteboard using the ladybird magnets. "This can be a little interlude while we wait for Arto's revelation. As you know, we've caught the Kvarnen Killer; a timid, invisible little man called Conny Nilsson. Hardly a bloodthirsty killer. I don't know how to explain it, but it's almost like he was just a pawn in something bigger going on at the same time. A young, slightly apathetic man who suddenly, without knowing *how*, realises that there's a blood-soaked handle in his hand. I don't know, but there's something awful there that I can't quite put my finger on. Anyway, the fact that we've caught him hardly makes it any easier to get hold of the

349

witnesses from Kvarnen again. The whole lot seem to have gone on holiday or been scattered by the wind. Paul and I have been trying to find something on the 'policeman'. A couple of the witnesses seem to have disappeared from the surface of the earth, it took a lot of effort to get hold of some of the others. We're finally starting to get somewhere. It seems increasingly likely that the 'policeman' was dark-haired and had a beard. They all seem sure he was under forty. The witness with the best memory, the so-called 'Hard Homo', insists that the 'policeman' had a little black beard; you know, the kind that sort of circles the mouth. And if we look closely at the most accurate, cleaned-up enlargement of the photo, where he's almost completely hidden behind the Hammarby fans, then we can — *here* — clearly see a bit of such a beard."

"And then," said Paul Hjelm, "we asked ourselves where we last saw a policeman with that kind of beard. Still under the assumption that he really is a policeman, of course. It wasn't so long since we last met a dark-haired policeman, just the right age, with the right beard. Though there must be a lot of them."

"Oh God," Chavez exclaimed. Sara loomed in his mind. The wonderful Sara Svenhagen. Walls raised between them. He continued with good speed: "Sara's boss."

Gunnar Nyberg started, staring sceptically at him. Was that really his figure of light being alluded to? What did she have to do with Jorge? And his own — other — boss? Party-Ragge?

"Let's keep very, very calm," Jan-Olov Hultin articulated, slowly and explicitly. "No one, and I mean *no one*, is throwing any rash accusations about colleagues around before we've had time to check the facts very, very thoroughly. Do you understand? Is there any reason at all that we should suspect Detective Superintendent Ragnar Hellberg? Just because he has a small, dark beard? I think we need a bit more than that."

"Are you talking about Ragnar Hellberg?" Nyberg exclaimed. "Party-Ragge? But he's completely . . . harmless."

"You can't claim that any of CID's superintendents are completely harmless," Hultin said curtly, glaring at Nyberg. "But Gunnar is essentially right: there's no reason at all to suspect Ragnar Hellberg or any other policeman in particular. Let's get on with the real business. Right, Gunnar?"

Nyberg was still completely taken by surprise. First, this business with Jorge and Sara — then Party-Ragge. In his eyes, Party-Ragge was the make-up plastered onto the face of the paedophile group, a figurehead who would adorn a sturdy but unspectacular vessel. Signed Ludvig Johnsson.

The Party Policeman versus the Hermit Policeman.

He regained his wits and began, in a distant tone, to deliver his own triumphant little speech.

"Niklas Lindberg can't have eavesdropped on any conversation between Rajko Nedic's men in Kumla, because they *always* speak Serbo-Croat among themselves; that's a characteristic of the entire gang.

351

That means *someone* must've squealed. First, *someone* blabbed that a big handover was going to take place, and that there'd be a preliminary meeting in Kvarnen on the twenty-third of June, the day before Lindberg would be released. Then, Lindberg tortured Vukotic to find out where the delivery was going to take place, while his men found out the same thing by eavesdropping on the meeting in Kvarnen. A double check, as you said. *But* — what started it all was someone else, something unique, a leak within the Nedic circle. This snitch, having performed his duties in the ethnic-cleansing business, enlisted in the Foreign Legion, where he met a Swede sharing his extreme right-wing ideology. This Swede was Niklas Lindberg. When the two of them, for different reasons, ended up in Kumla, the snitch became Lindberg's link to the Nedic empire. This snitch's name is Risto Petrovic."

"'A couple of Slavs of the same kind'," said the newly woken Viggo Norlander energetically. The others were convinced he was talking in his sleep.

"Risto Petrovic," Gunnar Nyberg continued, "is now being guarded as a potential Crown witness in a secret location. In all likelihood, he could tell us a lot about his ideological kinsman Niklas Lindberg and about his employer, Rajko Nedic. On the other hand, he doesn't have any idea where Lindberg and his men are now."

"But Arto does," said Hultin neutrally, while the others continued to stare in amazement at Nyberg, who had already slumped back into his chair.

"We should've checked their backgrounds," said Söderstedt, soul-searchingly.

"It wouldn't have helped," said Nyberg. "Petrovic used a false name in the Legion. Jovan Sotra. And also, Niklas Lindberg wasn't in the picture yet."

"Still," Söderstedt persisted meaninglessly, standing up. He went over to the whiteboard, and shook his head in disappointment before fastening an enormous map over the top of all the photographs, arrows and notes. It showed half of Sweden. The southern half. Three squiggles, each a different colour, had been drawn onto different places on the map — like streamers left behind after a crayfish party.

"Well, everyone," he began distractedly. "I've found something really strange. It might be a coincidence, probably not. The other day, I noticed — after some serious thinking — a series of cryptic messages on the THIS WEEK'S "I LOVE YOU" page of the online version of *Gula Tidningen*. Two parties, exchanging information about their location, using references to the literary masterpiece that is our nation's favourite atlas. The thing that caught my attention was that they were quoting the Florento sisters. Do you remember them?"

"Yeah," Kerstin Holm nodded. "Sex slaves who rebelled and stole a whole load of money from their pimp."

"Roughly, yes. Why would you quote criminals on the THIS WEEK'S "I LOVE YOU" page? In any case, I contacted *Gula Tidningen* and they sent backups of the entire series of messages. Since Midsummer's Eve, they've exchanged information sixteen times each. Which has given us two routes. The yellow one, *here*, goes through two counties: Dalarna and Västmanland.

The blue one, *here*, goes through two more: Halland and Västergötland. The yellow route goes from Orsa to Köping, the blue from Falkenberg to Skara. Messages about Köping and Skara were posted online only a couple of hours ago. Ten minutes before we gathered here, we also had a message about a new robbery, a petrol station in Falköping. According to witness statements, the robber was wearing a coloured balaclava that could best be described as gold. And if we turn the robberies that we know of — Skillingaryd, Ängelholm, Mellbystrand, Halmstad, Varberg, Ulricehamn, Gothenburg, Falköping — into a route — this red one, *here* — then we can see that the red route is getting closer and closer to the blue one."

Arto Söderstedt paused, turning round to stare at their utterly uncomprehending faces.

"They're hunting Eurydice," he explained.

Again, his clarification didn't exactly help to clarify the matter.

"As soon as I realised that, everything was clearer. As Jan-Olov rightly pointed out earlier: why would the Sickla Slaughterers set out on a mediocre string of robberies in western Sweden *if they had robbed Nedic?* It's this 'if' which changes the premise. *If* they had stolen say . . . ten million from Nedic, they wouldn't be robbing petrol stations for a couple of measly thousand notes. Because *they haven't robbed Rajko Nedic*. They tried but failed. Someone else stole it from under their noses. A little man with four-year-old size 7 Reeboks. The bloody footprints going *away* from Eskil Carlstedt's body. Orphei bloody footprints. When I put some pressure on the technicians, they admitted that the prints had with, and I quote, 'certain but not absolute likelihood' been left by a *lightweight* man, not by Bullet Kullberg, who weighs eighty-eight kilos. Or, perhaps, by a woman."

"Orphei?" asked Paul Hjelm, casting a glance towards Kerstin. She cast one back.

"Genitive of Orpheus," Söderstedt replied, sounding like a high-school teacher suffering from senile dementia. "Orpheus' footprints, in modern Swedish. They call themselves Orpheus and Eurydice. Let's keep going. Orpheus and Eurydice grab the briefcase. They split up and head out into the countryside, each in a different direction. Why? It's complicated, but probably because they know, for whatever reason, that they're being hunted. They know that our Gang Two is on their tracks, so they're trying to lie low. I don't know, maybe they've hidden the money somewhere and they're hoping that at least one of them will get away. Because Gang Two is coming. Slowly but surely, they're getting closer. Maybe they've got some kind of tracking device, that's not clear. We can draw a few conclusions, in any case.

"One: Gang Two did want the money for something in particular; they're gathering a new, albeit smaller, amount of money everywhere they go. A contingency fund. They need the money for something particular.

"Two: this is our mystery. I've found Orpheus' and Eurydice's phone numbers. The messages on THIS WEEK'S 'I LOVE YOU' always come from the same numbers, two mobile phones. Both of these phones are registered to a restaurant right here in Stockholm. The Thanatos restaurant on Östermalm, owned by . . . Rajko Nedic."

"So Rajko Nedic's meant to have stolen his own money?" Hultin asked, confused.

"Like I said, it's a mystery. I've been in touch with Nokia, and these are the most modern mobile phones imaginable. Prototypes, almost. You can go online with them. As soon as Orpheus and Eurydice arrive in a new place, they send a message to *Gula Tidningen*'s THIS WEEK'S 'I LOVE YOU'. In all probability, it's a man and a woman, and in all probability, they're in love. Maybe this really is just some kind of subtle double-dealing from Nedic, or maybe the young pair have given his organisation the slip."

"There seem to be quite a few holes in his tight organisation," said Chavez.

"Let me see if I understand," Hultin said neutrally. "The whole of this far-reaching theory is built on a certain geographic correspondence between your red and blue lines? From a love-sick pair exchanging addresses on the Internet, you managed to come to the conclusion that they're the ones who robbed Nedic?"

"The mobile phones belong to Nedic," said Söderstedt, pointing. "And look at the lines. There's also a certain time factor involved, that's why I'm being obstinate before I'm really sure. If we look at the speed that the red and blue lines have been moving thus far, Lindberg's gang and Eurydice, that is, and look at their last-known stopping places, Falköping and Skara, then it's very likely that they're going to collide tomorrow morning. In Skövde."

"So you think that —" Hultin asked, finding himself cut off.

"That we can catch Niklas Lindberg, Roger Sjökvist, Dan Andersson and Agne Kullberg in Skövde tomorrow. Yes. And also get hold of this mysterious Eurydice. Two birds with one stone."

Hultin was silent. He was thinking. What would happen if Söderstedt didn't know what he was talking about? Not much, a failed crackdown, no risks on the scale that there had been with the Kentucky Killer. It was quite vague, and God knows how Söderstedt had found the mystical Orpheus and Eurydice. The Florento sisters? *Gula Tidningen?* THIS WEEK'S "I LOVE YOU"? Could it be Nedic behind it? Throwing them off the scent using the restaurant's phones? But would Hultin ever forgive himself if he let the chance go by? And would the A-Unit be able to forgive him?

He looked at the crooked red line on the map. Was it really Lindberg's men? A golden balaclava . . . Småland, Skåne, Halland, Västmanland . . . It was true, it was no chance route. They had turned. A bend down by Ängelholm, and then northwards. They were in pursuit. And taking the chance to get hold of some titbits on the way to the real trophy. It made sense. And the blue line? Zigzagging through western Sweden. Why? And the yellow? Dalarna? But the dates fitted perfectly. They had all begun at the same time, all three of them. The robberies and the messages in *Gula Tidningen* had begun the very same day, Midsummer's Eve, the day the Sickla Slaughter had taken place. And, sure enough, the red and blue lines were going to collide. For the first and surely the last time. And, of course, Eurydice had to be protected. She — if it was a she — would, in all probability, die.

Jan-Olov Hultin nodded. Briefly. Neutrally.

"OK," he said. "We're going to Skövde."

CHAPTER
THIRTY-SEVEN

It was 10.26 on Saturday 10 July.

He was lying in a flea-bitten bed in a little campsite cottage just outside Arboga, beginning his third weekend alone. He wondered how much longer he would be able to bear it.

Four hundred and one, another one gone.

The rhyme was mocking him. How many safe-deposit boxes with those now-hypnotic numbers — 4, 0, 1 — had he tried the key in? Fifty? Even more? He didn't know. The weekdays were like a haze. All he did was drive the car and go into banks and find his position using the road atlas and send short messages over the Internet. There was nothing else.

Until the weekends. Then it all came crashing down on him. The longing. The hopelessness. The knowledge of defeat.

Their dreams would remain dreams.

But worst of all was the longing. His entire being — body, soul, spirit, everything he could imagine — was screaming for her. The weekends were a long, drawn-out agony. A walk to Golgotha.

Hymenaeus has been called to Thrace in vain.

He hugged the flea-bitten pillow until the feathers started slipping out and floating around the room. His eyes fell on the small digital clock. It had just turned 10.31.

That was when he felt the jolt.

The jolt passed through his entire being like electricity; a violent impulse which shot through every nerve cell in his body, out to the more ethereal connections of his soul and his spirit. All was pain. There was only pain, and pain was all. Apart from a short, brief realisation:

Without knowing it, he must have turned round.

Orpheus must have turned and thrown a glance over his shoulder.

And Eurydice sank back into Hades' shadowy depths.

It was 10.26 on Saturday 10 July.

She was lying in a flea-bitten bed on the ground floor of a hotel in Skövde, beginning her third weekend alone. She wondered how much longer she would be able to bear it.

Had she made a mistake after all? Had the viper not actually headed out into the country to put the money in a rural safe-deposit box? Was something missing from her calculations? Wasn't there something she should remember — something she should take into consideration? Something she was blocking out?

She thought. It had always been her only defence mechanism. And she felt, at that moment — when the weekend arrived and almost drowned out the overactivity of the past week — that her thoughts took her a step closer to the truth.

One factor was missing from her calculations.

Uncle Jubbe . . .? Wasn't there something there?

Shouldn't she *know* where this bank was?

Time to be seized by misgivings . . .

He was pale, she was dark, and she missed him. That was the only thing that was crystal clear. That was the only unquestionable fact of life. The only pure, utterly unblemished part.

They wouldn't be able to stay apart for much longer now.

She hugged the flea-bitten pillow until the feathers started slipping out and floating around the room. Her eyes fell on the small digital clock. It had just turned 10.31.

That was when she felt the jolt.

The door opened. She hadn't even locked it.

Three men in balaclavas, two black and one gold, strode into the room, closing the door behind them. A fourth clambered in through the door out onto the little terrace outside. All four had pistols in their hands, and all four were dripping with water.

She froze.

"Bloody rainy," said the golden one, pointing his pistol at her.

She stared into his icy blue eyes. That was all that could be seen behind the golden balaclava.

She couldn't breathe. It didn't work. She couldn't get any air.

"There, there," the man continued, "just breathe nice and calmly. You should be pleased with yourself. Two weeks you managed to stay hidden. That's pretty good, considering your opponents. Are you alone, by the way?"

She still couldn't breathe. She could feel herself turning blue. And in her terror, in the middle of it all, she was *thinking*. Defence mechanism. She was thinking: I've felt this way before, there have been other times in my life when I haven't been able to breathe.

The man in the golden balaclava moved closer and slapped her hard. She could breathe again. Every breath was painful. She was elsewhere. On the way to *another room*.

"Are you alone?" the man repeated. The other three stood as though to attention behind him. One of them seemed to be injured. She had seen them before. In the same clothes. She had seen the injured one get his injury. And she had seen four others shot. A briefcase had been lifted from the blood of one of them. The golden man with the pleasant manner struck again. Abruptly. He hit her again. Harder. Shouting: "Answer, fucking little foreign whore."

"I'm alone," she said faintly. She could feel herself starting to fade. Slowly dying away. As though she were sinking back down into the kingdom of the dead. To Hades' shadowy depths.

The man's disposition changed again.

"Thanks," he said politely. "We won't need any help finding the briefcase."

362

He turned, gesturing, to the shortest of the masked men. He had headphones on top of his balaclava, a small device in his hand. He went over to the wardrobe, lifted up three blankets and pulled the briefcase out. He handed it to the golden one, who opened it and nodded.

"Radio and key," he confirmed. "Great. Now tell us as much as you can about this. First of all: who are you?"

The second biggest of the men had opened her bag. He took out a mobile phone with a large display.

"Look at this," he said, holding it up. "You can go online with it."

"Yeah, those exist," the smallest said expertly. "Prototypes. Expensive as hell. Small inbuilt computer. Nokia, of course . . ."

"Wallet," said the second biggest, digging around in her bag. "Driving licence for Sonja Karlsson. Passport, too. Same name. Loads of cash, must be five thousand."

"A passport," said the golden one. "Were you thinking about running off abroad, Sonja Karlsson?"

She sank deeper and deeper. Reality started to disappear. Another reality replaced it. It was like a cave, a vertical cave, a funnel down into the ground, and she sank down between cave walls, stalactites, stalagmites, and somewhere deep down, there was an opening, a door. The door to Hades.

"You can talk now, you know," the man with the golden balaclava persisted. "Sonja? *Karlsson?* Nah. Hell, you're a wog. Fake name. I hate fake names. Like when John Bengtsson turns up for a job interview, and he's a bush nigger. That's the worst kind of infiltration. No, you're not called Sonja Karlsson. What are you? Iranian? Or Slav, of course. What's your connection to Rajko Nedic?"

She sank further. She could feel her arms and legs moving slowly. Like the air was water.

She felt a blow. Not another slap, a punch in the stomach. The pain was somewhere on the the edge of existence. Only vaguely perceptible.

"She seems out of it," the injured man said breathlessly from over by the door. "Make sure you don't lose her."

The golden one looked at him. Nodded.

"You're right. Let's get the essentials. Did you find the safe-deposit box, Sonja?"

She looked at him vaguely. Only those steely-blue eyes against the gold. Boreholes. Cavities, she thought, confused.

Her thoughts cleared. To tell would be to stay alive, after all.

"No," she said. "I've been looking, but haven't found it."

"Why are you looking *here*?"

"He sells his drugs in three areas of Sweden," she said clearly. "This is one of them. The others are Dalarna and Västmanland, and then Norrbotten and Västerbotten. Those are his territories. He doesn't have Stockholm, Gothenburg, Malmö. He's trying to get in there, but it's slow work. Certain suburbs."

364

"See," said the golden one, "she speaks Swedish like all those immigrants up in Rinkeby."

He turned to the shortest of the three men.

"What d'you think?" he asked, subdued.

"She's looking herself," he replied, equally subdued. "She's probably done a runner from Nedic's organisation somehow — whore, receptionist, pusher, what do I know? — and she probably thought there'd be money in the briefcase just like we did. I don't think we'll get much else from her."

"But we've got the key," said the golden one. "That's a big step forward. I've got to let our supplier know. Try to find out as much as you can. Check which banks she's checked and which are left. Find out if she's got an accomplice. You know what to do." Then he added, significantly louder: "Do whatever it takes."

The second biggest man rubbed his hands together. The injured one gave a kind of hollow laugh.

The golden one left the room.

There were three of them left. She started to sink again. It happened quicker and quicker.

The smallest said: "Your last defence is gone now, Sonja. Me, I'm not a great fan of rape, but sometimes needs must. We've been on the road for two dry fucking weeks now, because of you, and my friends here are really starting to fancy a bit of pussy. The more you talk, the better your chances of avoiding it. This is what we want to know: What's your relationship to Nedic? How did you know the handover was going to happen on the Sickla estate? Are you really alone in this? Where else were you planning on looking for the safe-deposit box?"

She was no longer sinking, she was falling. She struck the door to the kingdom of the dead. It was a door. A normal front door. She was standing outside. Her body was almost squeezing through it, slowly, painfully.

The short one shrugged and stepped to one side.

The injured one made his way over from the door. His baggy army trousers were bulging at the flies. He leaned forward. She could see the pain in his eyes as he grabbed at her trousers. He yanked them down, ripping them off with such force that her shoes came off. She could feel her left foot twisting strangely. Then he pulled down his own trousers. His pants. She was staring at his erection. He climbed onto her, pushing it towards her face. The stench of sweat and unwashed genitals washed over her.

She was through the door. She was there. In *that place*. Hades' shadowy depths. She saw his penis coming towards her. She could smell the stench of sweat and unwashed genitals. She could see the flash bulbs. She could see pictures of children. She could hear screams that must have been her own. And she turned away. She wasn't there. Looked out of the window, thinking. Defence mechanism. The street outside the window. Cars passing by. Number plates. AGF. Agfa film. BED. English for where you sleep. DTR. Dithyramb, whatever that was. EID. Eider. Or first eid. Though that wasn't how it was spelt. And in

366

the background, behind the dark clouds, the flower shop, the video shop, the barber, the bank.

The bank.

The door flew open. She heard shots. The man on top of her was hit, bellowed and fell. A sticky liquid ran onto her.

Chaos everywhere.

And in chaos was the beginning.

The police station in Skövde was what you might call understaffed. The duty officer was the only one there. The rest of the little force were in town. Two were taking care of a break-in which had taken place at a supermarket warehouse the night before, the others were on patrol. As a result, the duty officer found it quite strange to have seven plain-clothes officers inside the station.

He was sixty-one years old and eagerly anticipating retirement.

"Are you sure you shouldn't call the National Task Force?" he asked for the fourth time.

Though his question touched upon an unpleasant truth, Jan-Olov Hultin had started ignoring him.

He considered his team. All members of the A-Unit were in place. They were gathered around two maps. The first was a town map of Skövde. The second was a detailed plan of a building.

"Let's start from the beginning," said Hultin. "The hotel's here, on the edge of town. The lone young woman who signed herself in as Sonja Karlsson, and who's probably our Eurydice, is in a room on the corner on the ground floor. Here. There are two ways in, one from inside the hotel, one via the terrace. Besides that, there are windows on the opposite wall, though we don't really know how high up they are. Two go in via the terrace, Hjelm and Holm. Two standing by the window, Chavez and Nyberg; take pallets to stand on. Three go in via the main door, myself, Norlander and Söderstedt. Everyone in flak jackets.

"First, we're going to check what's going on inside. Contact via walkie-talkie. If Lindberg's gang is there, Norlander's going to kick the door down. Everyone else wait until you hear the door break. Then you storm in. Exercise caution. It might be a hostage situation. Which *could* mean calling in the National Task Force. But that'll take time. The best thing's obviously if we can catch them off guard. We know they're not likely to give themselves up without a fight. Any questions?"

"Neighbours?" asked Söderstedt.

"The hotel's clapped-out and not very popular. It's almost empty. The adjacent rooms are empty. Any neighbours are a long way off. We can't evacuate them all without drawing attention to what we're doing. If they're there, anyway. My feeling is that we can carry this out without putting anyone other than ourselves in danger."

"And Eurydice," said Söderstedt.

"Though if they're there then she's already in real danger. OK. Let's go."

They went out to two rental cars and drove slowly and carefully through Skövde until the built-up area began to thin out. They soon arrived.

It was 10.26 on Saturday 10 July.

It was a miserable day. The rain was pouring down. The kind of bad weather that seems to want revenge on all those halcyon days, to even out the statistics. Visibility was nil. They switched their walkie-talkies on, put their earpieces in, and set off.

All headed in the direction of the unassuming little hotel's entrance apart from Hjelm and Holm, who made off around the building. Nyberg and Chavez split off by the stairs, each with a pallet in hand, and crept carefully along the hotel wall to the corner by the garden; they were heading for the windows on the corner. Hultin, Norlander and Söderstedt entered the hotel lobby. A budget version of a bellboy was loitering by the reception counter.

"Room 12," said Hultin, showing his ID. "A young woman. We spoke on the phone a few hours ago."

The bellboy barely reacted to the sight of the detective superintendent's ID. All that happened was that he dropped his gaze to the register lying open on the counter in front of him.

"Karlsson," he drawled. "Sonja Karlsson. She's got visitors."

"Four men?" asked Hultin.

"Three. One just left."

"How long ago?"

"Five minutes, maybe. Ten."

"Car?"

"I heard one start. But it wasn't parked outside."

"OK," said Hultin. "Lock yourself in the office for a while."

The imitation bellboy opened his eyes fully for the first time. That was his only reaction. Then he disappeared into another room.

Hultin, Söderstedt and Norlander entered the corridor through double doors, drawing their service weapons. Slowly, they moved towards room 12. The number glimmered like a mirage from the door at the end of the corridor.

Hjelm and Holm took the back route. They came in from the opposite corner of the hotel, working their way past a row of unoccupied terraces, each marked off with high fences covered in climbing plants. At the last fence, they stopped. Hjelm nodded, Holm peered around the corner.

"Hard to see," she whispered. "Fucking rain."

"We're in position," Gunnar Nyberg whispered into the walkie-talkie. "There are curtains. We've got movement, but not much else."

"We can't see a thing," said Holm. "We've got to get closer."

"They *should* be there," whispered Hultin. "We've got confirmation that three of them are there. Repeat: *three* are there, one's missing."

"Eurydice?" asked Nyberg.

"Her too. They've probably got their weapons on her. Extreme caution advised. We're right outside the door, we need to know *exactly* what's happening. Paul, Kerstin?"

"We're moving closer now."

Kerstin Holm crept forward first. The saturated grass squelched loudly. Hjelm was hot on her heels. Only when they were halfway there could they see the door properly. It was a classic terrace door: wooden bottom half with glass on top, and a small set of steps below it. They crept over to the steps, keeping low. They were soaked through, wiping the water from their faces. Hjelm pointed at himself. He rose slowly. Forehead, eyes, up over the edge of the window. Water was streaming down the glass.

Through the veil of water, he could see three men in balaclavas and a girl in her underwear. One of the men was pulling his trousers down and climbing on top of the girl, his penis in her face. He had a pistol in one hand. The other two men had their pistols jammed into the waistbands of their trousers.

Hjelm grimaced and sank back down. He whispered into the walkie-talkie: "She's about to be raped. The rapist's got a pistol in his hand, the other two have them in their waistbands. The head of the bed's in your direction, Jan-Olov, immediately to the right, behind the door when it's opened. You won't really be able to reach him. We've got to take him out from the terrace. When you come in, Bullet, the ace shot, will be straight ahead. The third man's to the left, right underneath your window, Gunnar."

"OK," Hultin whispered. "Can you see anything, Gunnar, Jorge?"

"Nope," Chavez whispered. "We'd have to break the window first, then open the curtain. It's tricky."

"OK, it's us and you, Paul," said Hultin. "Kick or smash?"

Paul looked at Kerstin. She looked strangely tense. Like another person. Her lips formed the word "smash".

"Smash," said Paul Hjelm.

"Everyone ready? Viggo will kick in the door. Three, two, one."

The door flew open. Hjelm saw it through the window. He saw Norlander tumble in, almost in slow motion, and take a shot to the chest from the man on top of the woman. Hjelm shot him. From behind. Through the window of the terrace door. The bullet hit the man's chest from the right-hand side. He fell down on top of the woman. Blood was pouring out of him. The other two men raised their arms instinctively in the air. The window above them broke and they were showered with glass. Nyberg's face and pistol poked through. Hjelm kicked the shot-out terrace door open. The woman sank down onto the floor. The injured man on the bed fired again. Right over Hjelm's shoulder. Hjelm shot him again. Two bullets in the face. Right through his balaclava. Hultin entered the room. Norlander stood up, examining the smoking hole in his chest. Hultin, Söderstedt and Nyberg up from his window all pointed their weapons at the two men with their hands in the air. Chavez ran over, around the edge of the building, and immediately shouted: "Kerstin!"

Hjelm turned round and saw Kerstin Holm lying on the terrace, her hands pressed to her head. Blood was running between her fingers. Chavez was on his haunches beside her. Hjelm staggered towards them. Just then, the big man beneath the window decided to reach for his pistol. He pulled it out and shot straight ahead. Hjelm felt himself being thrown forward, out onto the terrace, landing beside Holm. The pain hit him in waves.

Hultin shot the man. Four shots right in the heart, without mercy.

"Jesus Christ," exclaimed Gunnar Nyberg from up in the window.

Hultin went over to the short man standing with his arms in the air. He yanked the balaclava upwards, jamming his gun into the man's mouth, and pushing him back against the wall. His face was completely white. His eyes bulging.

"Jan-Olov!" Söderstedt yelled.

His trigger finger was twitching. The barrel of the gun rattled against the man's teeth.

"Don't do it, Jan-Olov," Söderstedt persisted. "Walk away."

The barrel remained in the man's mouth. Hultin was forcing it further and further down the man's throat. The short man was crying and sniffing and sobbing. Then his gag reflex took over and he was sick right down the barrel of the gun.

"Walk away," Söderstedt repeated. "Check what's happening with Paul and Kerstin. That's what counts. Now! Go!"

Hjelm lay on his back, staring up into the rain. He could see the raindrops growing bigger and bigger. All of them growing bigger and bigger. They *didn't* change character. He *wasn't* about to die. He turned to Kerstin. Jorge was pressing his jacket against her head.

He was shouting. Jorge was just shouting. A vague figure crept past Paul's back. He stared at Kerstin's face. It moved. It was forming a word, and that word was: "Paul."

"Yeah, Kerstin, I'm here. It's going to be all right."

"Paul, I love you."

"It'll be all right, Kerstin, it'll be all right."

Hultin tore his gun from the short man's mouth, taking a couple of teeth with it, leaned towards him and headbutted him. He could afford to do that.

From up in the window, Nyberg trained his gun on the short man; Söderstedt did the same from inside the room. He shrank back, sniffing, into the corner.

Norlander was sitting on the bed, furiously ripping off the bulletproof vest. Smoke was rising from his chest.

"Fuck, it hurts," said Viggo Norlander.

"Shut up," said Arto Söderstedt.

"Hultin lifted the mask of the dead man by the window.

"Roger Sjöqvist," he said, disappointed.

He went over to the bed, and lifted the mask of the body with its trousers around its ankles. The face oozed out onto the bed. One which had once been violet.

"Dan Andersson," he said, even more disappointed.

Only then did he see Jorge, Paul and Kerstin out in the rain on the terrace. Blood was running from the arm of Paul's linen jacket. Kerstin's head was wrapped in Jorge's jacket. Jorge was bellowing.

Hultin went over to him and gave him a slap. He fell silent.

"How's she doing?" asked Hultin.

"She's been shot in the head, for fuck's sake," said Chavez, subdued. "How do you think she's doing?"

Hultin took out his mobile phone and called an ambulance. Norlander came out with Bullet Kullberg in handcuffs, knocking him over and pushing his face down into the mud with his foot.

"Stop it," said Hultin neutrally.

Nyberg came round the corner just as Söderstedt came out. He sank to his knees next to Kerstin.

"Jesus Christ, Kerstin," he said quietly. "What have you done?"

"Much too little," she said, straining to smile.

Söderstedt jammed his pistol into his holster and sighed. "Imagine what would've happened if Niklas Lindberg had been here too . . ."

"Where the hell's Eurydice?" asked Paul Hjelm before fainting.

Jan-Olov Hultin was thinking about grass and weeds. Then he threw up.

CHAPTER
THIRTY-EIGHT

In Stockholm, meanwhile, it was a sunny Saturday, 10 July. In fact, it was the highest high summer imaginable. The city was almost panting under the blanket of heat enveloping it. People were sprawled on every available patch of grass as though expelled from the city itself — the city's sweat. The clouds had disappeared in an attempt not to wither away, and the sun seemed to have taken a few steps closer to earth, as though to get a better view. It couldn't believe its eyes, drawing ever closer.

Sara Svenhagen was sitting, along with a busload of Germans, in Sundberg's Konditori on Järntorget in the city's old quarter. Since the busload of Germans could barely fit into the cafe, it was a bit of a tight squeeze.

She wanted it to be that way.

As tight as possible.

She was waiting, and while she waited, she went over the past few days. Keeping track of the latest chapter of her life. Could she have done anything differently? She turned the events over and over in her mind, but found no obvious mistakes. Her steps had been clear and distinct and they had irrefutably led her here. To this point.

"Brambo" had led her here.

An online pseudonym. The word appearing before the @ symbol in an email address. She summed up.

Via the passive paedophile of Söder Torn, on John Andreas Witréus's computer, she had found a number of child pornography websites previously unknown to her. They had been well hidden behind harmless title pages, thereby making themselves impossible to find using search engines. On these pages, she had found a whole range of pseudonyms, several of which were Swedish or could at least be traced back to Swedish IP addresses, which wasn't exactly the same thing.

These pseudonyms had done their best to remain untraceable but could, when all went well, be identified after closer inspection. It became apparent that all these pseudonyms appeared in the extensive investigation material, a small part of which had been written by CID's child pornography unit, of which she herself was a member. All the pseudonyms apart from one: "brambo". Wherever this "brambo" appeared online, another pseudonym, "rippo_man", was also present. This "rippo_man" turned out to have been convicted of sexual assault on children, among other things, thanks to the Swedish policeman who had put him away. This Swedish policeman should also have sent "brambo" to prison, or at least tried to trace him, since "rippo_man" and "brambo" always appeared together on the hidden pages she had found. Yet that wasn't the case. "Brambo" had been deliberately deleted from the report. And in each instance, one man had been behind the investigation. Sara Svenhagen's own boss, Detective Superintendent Ragnar Hellberg.

She had two choices: either go straight for Hellberg, or try to find out more about "brambo", if for no other reason than to have more of a leg to stand on in any direct confrontation with Hellberg. She had chosen the latter. It hadn't been easy.

"Brambo" was an incredibly well-disguised figure. It was obvious that he had no intention of having his hidden desires revealed. He made use of a couple of extremely advanced, illegal computer programs which could be downloaded online, and which completely concealed the source. If you connected these programs, something which required professional knowledge, you could be entirely anonymous online. All the experts she spoke to were in agreement about that.

Then it struck her that Hellberg might simply have committed a minor breach of duty: he had deleted "brambo" because the person behind it was untouchable.

But she didn't stop there. She knew that the real Internet experts were hardly those employed by the police. Or by anyone else, for that matter. The real experts were the hackers. Often teenagers. Completely up to date. And so she had made her way into a number of online forums. With deliberate naive femininity, she threw her questions to the most advanced chats she could find. Chats where Chen, 18, was discussing the Pentagon's new security system and the slow finance routines on the New York stock exchange with Bob, 16. She presented herself gallantly as a sexy nobody with problems, and received pubescent, testosterone-fuelled, virginal responses. Sure, those programs were old, several-month-old upgrades; they were crackable, but only by guys, people with dicks. You just do this. And suddenly she was through. As she saw the IP number appear on the screen, she thought about the perils and possibilities of the information society.

"Brambo's" IP number could, after lots of toing and froing, be traced to a restaurant. To the Thanatos restaurant on Östermalm, right here in Stockholm.

Thanatos, she thought, as she searched the registry of businesses for an owner and manager. Wasn't that the ancient Greeks' kingdom of the dead? The deepest depths of Hades?

The deepest caverns of Hell.

Strange name for a restaurant.

Wasn't it Freud, too? Eros and Thanatos? Our two strongest urges. The sex drive and the death drive?

The Thanatos restaurant was owned by Rajko Nedic.

Rajko Nedic, she thought to herself. Wasn't he the drug dealer who always managed to get away? He had never figured in any child-porn context, had he?

She checked the times. "Brambo" had been online at all manner of times. It was difficult to imagine anyone in the restaurant busying themselves with child porn down in the kitchen while the lunch rush was on. She checked with the network, Telia. The IP number had been subtly and secretly diverted. She would have to use all the police tricks she could think of to crack their wall of confidentiality.

Yes, the number was diverted. *Home* to Rajko Nedic in Danderyd.

Suddenly, it all started to make sense. Rajko Nedic wasn't in the child-porn business. It was much simpler than that.

Rajko Nedic was a paedophile.

She started to collect all the images linked to "brambo" that she could find online. It was a cavalcade of the usual kind. So normal, and so unbearable. Always the faces. It was always the children's faces that grabbed hold of her and which she couldn't let go, which held onto her, accusing her; accusing her for having escaped, for being able to have lived her childhood in peace, for not helping them right then and there, for being removed from the actual event. A terrible, silent, dampened scream of horror which rose towards the horizon and swept over the world, taking her with it and leaving her with nightmares about an awful double penetration in the middle of giving birth. Those eyes. Always so dark — ruined, but always crystal clear. Their acute prematurity. Their stolen childhoods. The inconceivably grotesque act.

Sara Svenhagen tried to calm herself down. She recognised the situation so well. She tried to become a policewoman again: objective, critical, chasing clues. It was always the same procedure, the same narrowing of the field of vision. It worked in the end.

Though through a haze of tears.

For the most part, it was a question of *one* child in the pictures, a dark little girl at different ages, but there were others, too. It was always the same room, the same background. The walls were clearly soundproofed — it looked like golden foam cushions had been stapled to the walls. Otherwise, there were no distinctive features. The perpetrator's face could never be seen, and of his body, only his penis was visible. There was nothing special about it — aside from what it was doing.

In all probability, it belonged to Rajko Nedic.

OK, she thought, stretching. She looked around the flat. Traces of Jorge were everywhere. The sight of his boxer shorts on the bedside lamp filled her with warmth. It rose from her toes up to her hairline.

OK. Ragnar Hellberg had never seemed particularly comfortable online; his speciality was making jokes for the press. Still, he had obviously cracked the utterly complex code that she herself had cracked — with the help of the master hackers. He had realised what he had stumbled across: a way to trap the man who had never let himself be caught. A back route into the untouchable Nedic's organisation. Why hadn't he used that back route, then? Why had he made sure that not even the faintest trace of it was left in the investigation instead?

Because he had gone after Rajko Nedic in private?

Because Detective Superintendent Ragnar Hellberg had been blackmailing Rajko Nedic for money?

Taking a sober view of it, there were two alternatives: either Hellberg had simply felt a certain shame over not being able to crack the "brambo" pseudonym and erased it from the reports, or else he had used his knowledge of Rajko Nedic for blackmail purposes.

Sara Svenhagen was about to find out which of the two was correct, because through the hordes of German tourists, Detective Superintendent Ragnar Hellberg, also known as Party-Ragge, was pushing his way towards her. He stroked his little black beard as though deep in thought, and sank into the chair opposite her. He gestured, and asked: "Why here?"

"I want it this way," was all she replied.

Ragnar Hellberg nodded. As though he understood.

"Let's hear it, then," he said.

"Rajko Nedic," she said.

He looked at her. His gaze was sharper than she had ever seen it. Otherwise, there was no reaction.

"Go on," he said.

"The 'brambo' pseudonym is the drug dealer and restaurant owner Rajko Nedic. And you deliberately left 'brambo' out of the investigation."

He smiled. Ragnar Hellberg actually smiled. He laid his hand on top of hers and looked into her eyes.

"Thanks," he said.

"For what?" she asked, pulling her hand from beneath his.

"For it not being you," he said.

She could feel herself staring at him in disgust.

"What's going on here?" she asked.

"I'm sorry," he said. "I had to test you. First of all, I wanted to make sure that all new material was kept from the group; that was why you had to work in private, Sara. Then I realised that it could be the litmus test. In all probability, you'd come across those hidden websites, and maybe even decipher them. Though that was more of a side issue. Most important was whether you'd accuse me or not."

She could feel that her gaze had become murderous. He continued.

"A couple of weeks ago, I was looking — for an entirely different reason — through my old investigations linked to Operation Cathedral. I found considerably more files with my name on them than I'd written. Someone had been producing material *in my name*. I managed to separate the unfamiliar files from my own and go through them. I looked through all of the web pages where the pseudonyms appeared. And I found — just like you — the unmentioned 'brambo'. But I had no chance of cracking his identity."

"And you want me to believe all of this?" she exclaimed loudly. A large number of Germans looked sceptically at her.

Ragnar Hellberg continued unperturbed. "What I did manage was to narrow down the possible culprits. It was between two people. One of two of my subordinates had been submitting incomplete investigatory material in my name. Someone who wanted to frame me, I thought. I realise it was more of a side matter now. The main reason was blackmail. All the material on Rajko Nedic the paedophile is now with this subordinate, and if anyone decided to investigate it, they'd end up with . . . me. And you, Sara, you were one of the two possibilities."

"How long have you been preparing this?" she asked. She didn't know if she had actually asked him. She didn't know what to believe. But she had realised where it was heading.

She felt herself growing pale.

"I can't prove anything," said Hellberg. "He's made sure of that. It's his word against mine, and I know that my word's worth very little in the group. Figurehead, Party-Ragge. Who am I against Ludvig Johnsson? The man who lost his family in a car accident and then built up the entire unit. And who then had his leadership stolen by . . . me. The lightweight party policeman."

"So it was between me and Ludvig?" Sara asked. She felt that she should have said something else. Here sat the man she saw on TV more often than in the police station, accusing her mentor, the only policeman she really admired. Ludvig Johnsson. Along with Gunnar Nyberg, he was the only man she really dared to call a colleague.

"Yes," said Hellberg. "It was you or Ludvig. Look at it like this: would I really have managed to identify this well-disguised 'brambo'? Would I really have been able to blackmail someone as notoriously dangerous as Rajko Nedic? Would I have dared go anywhere near his mob of torturers and war criminals? Party-Ragge? Think about it."

Sara Svenhagen closed her eyes.

She was convinced.

And overwhelmed with sorrow.

Ludvig Johnsson. Her surrogate father.

She gave her coffee cup a shove, causing it to splash onto the Germans.

Ragnar Hellberg sat still, flecks of coffee on his suit. She gave him a resounding slap.

CHAPTER
THIRTY-NINE

"Kerstin's doing well."

There was a moment of silence in the Supreme Command Centre. Then the rejoicing began. Briefly, intensely, a lid which lifted for a short moment. Then it closed again.

Paul Hjelm continued. "They just let me leave the hospital. I crept up to see her on my way out. The bullet caught her just above the ear, taking a bit of bone from behind her temple with it. It hit a blood vessel, so it looked a lot worse than it was. She's got concussion, but sends her regards."

"How are you, though?" Hultin asked from the desk at the front.

They exchanged a glance. The first since they were in Skövde. A glance between *two men who had killed*. Both realised at that moment what a strange threshold they had crossed. Neither of them had given much thought to it during the last twenty-four hours. Now it hit them with full force.

Both of us have killed another human being.

There was nothing to say.

"Fine, thanks," said Hjelm. "The bullet went through my arm and hit the vest. One slightly fractured rib, but my arm's fine. Just flesh wounds, but it hurts like hell."

Hultin nodded and asked straight out: "Have all of you spoken to Internal?"

They nodded. All had spoken to Internal Affairs. Hjelm had already been confronted by an old tormentor named Niklas Grundström while he was in hospital in Skövde. It had been surprisingly painless.

No one had mentioned Hultin's gun handling. It was as though it had never happened. He himself seemed to be remarkably unaffected.

"Well, listen," he said, stretching. "There are both pluses and minuses in all of this. The biggest plus is that we saved Eurydice. The biggest minus that she escaped. That Niklas Lindberg had just left his friends was hardly our fault. Maybe we could've been fifteen minutes earlier, but it was out of our hands. A quick-thinking member of the group" — Hultin cast a grateful glance in Söderstedt's direction — "made sure the ambulance was diverted to minimise attention. Still, that wasn't enough to get Lindberg to return. He must've smelt a rat and vanished into thin air.

"The shooting of Roger Sjöqvist and of Dan Andersson must be seen as just. Obviously, it was a blunder that Sjöqvist had the chance to shoot Paul, and that Andersson managed to shoot Kerstin, but there was absolutely no misconduct. It all went so quickly. What we do have is Eurydice's shoes, size 7 brown sandals, the briefcase and a safe-deposit-box key, and then Agne 'Bullet' Kullberg. Besides that, we've got the right-wing extremist Risto Petrovic in safe keeping. Thorough interviews with both these two should give us some kind of idea about what Niklas Lindberg has

387

got planned. Both are keeping surprisingly quiet at the minute. What we *don't* have is Niklas Lindberg, the van and the loot from the robberies out west which, all told, should add up to about a million. If Lindberg is planning something, then he's not likely to have shelved it. Unfortunately this wasn't the end."

"The safe-deposit-box key is the Swedish standard," said Chavez. "It could be from any bank anywhere. If we're going to reconstruct the entire thing, then we've got to assume that the mistrust we've already talked about, between Nedic and the 'policeman', was so great that Nedic didn't even dare to hand over the money. Instead, he gave him a key and a top-of-the-range police radio. Presumably the 'policeman' was going to be told which bank was holding the money as soon as something had happened. Exactly which that was is, for the moment, unknown. Anyway, it meant that the civil engineer, Bullet Kullberg, could make an electronic tracking device to find the briefcase stolen by Orpheus and Eurydice. They don't have the key any more, so their role in the drama must be over. They'll have to make do with still being alive and having one another. We can also add that, amazingly, we've managed to keep the entire thing out of the press." Chavez added with a sidelong glance: "Also largely thanks to Arto's quick thinking, which was what led us there, after all."

Söderstedt looked completely dumbfounded by this unexpected praise. He leafed through his papers, confused.

"I'd been planning to tell a story," he mumbled. "About the metamorphosis of metamorphoses."

388

They looked at him. This unlikely policeman went from clarity to clarity. They waited tensely for the next step.

"It's Monday today," said Arto Söderstedt with great precision. "Monday morning, the twelfth of July. Two hours after our Skövde incident, at one on Saturday, a short message appeared on *Gula Tidningen*'s THIS WEEK'S 'I LOVE YOU' page. Since then, no other messages have appeared. We've got to assume that our young couple have now been reunited. The message went like this: 'Philemon. Starting point. Baucis.'"

They stared at him.

"Now, if the police had been mythologically ignorant," he continued, "then this cryptic little message would have passed us by. That's not the case, though. Philemon and Baucis are another classical pair of sweethearts from antiquity, though in some ways the opposite of Orpheus and Eurydice. Instead of being stormy and dramatic, their relationship was settled and peaceful. If we weave the two stories together, it's roughly as follows. The god of marriage, Hymenaeus, is called to Thrace, where Orpheus is going to marry his Eurydice. But Hymenaeus comes in vain, because Eurydice is dead: 'ran joyful, sporting o'er the flow'ry plain, a venom'd viper bit her as she pass'd; instant she fell, and sudden breath'd her last'. Orpheus, the divine singer, makes his way to the kingdom of the dead and appeals to Hades: 'all our possessions are but loans from you, and soon, or late, you must be paid your due'. Even Sisyphus stops his eternal rolling of the stone up the mountain. The entire kingdom of the dead

389

allows itself to be seduced, and Eurydice is carried up from the shadows. *As long* as Orpheus doesn't turn round and look at his bride before they've left the underworld, then he'll have brought her back to the world of the living. But he couldn't resist; in his care for her, he glances back over his shoulder anyway. Obviously it's impossible for us to know what kind of hell our young pair has been through, but just as Eurydice is on her way back into the kingdom of the dead, just as Orpheus is on his way to return to be torn apart, alone, by the Thracean women, just then — they transform the transformation. The metamorphosis undergoes a metamorphosis. Instead of being Orpheus and Eurydice in Thrace, they become the industrious pair of Philemon and Baucis in Phrygia. A couple of gods in human form go there, to test the population. Everywhere they ask, they're refused a room. Everywhere apart from with Philemon and Baucis. The penniless pair offer the gods everything they have, and they're given their reward. The gods reveal themselves:

'The neighbourhood, said he,
Shall justly perish for impiety:
You stand alone exempted; but obey
With speed, and follow where we lead the way:
Leave these accurs'd; and to the mountain's
    height
Ascend; nor once look backward in your flight.'

Philemon and Baucis' old hut is transformed into a golden temple, and the couple become its keepers.

Asked by the gods, they have just one single wish: to be able to die together. And eventually, both are transformed, simultaneously, into trees. 'At once th' incroaching rinds their closing lips invade,' or '*ora frutex*' in Latin."

Söderstedt broke off, looking out over the dumbfounded congregation.

"I hope you appreciate the subtle transition. Just as Eurydice is on her way back down into the kingdom of the dead, she's saved and becomes the poor but industrious Baucis instead, the woman who, together with her husband, follows the gods up to the top of the mountain, and eventually dies at the same moment as him. '*Cura deum di sint, et qui coluere colantur.*' Maybe you could call it maturity."

"Dare I ask what it is you're citing from?" asked Paul Hjelm.

"Of course," said Arto Söderstedt. "It's Ovid's *Metamorphoses*."

CHAPTER
FORTY

Gunnar Nyberg had successfully managed to give himself tennis elbow when he broke his way in through the hotel window in Skövde, and pointed his gun at the robbers. He had probably been grasping it too tightly — several strange dents in the butt of the gun suggested as much.

Or maybe he had just developed mouse elbow.

Mouse elbow, or repetitive strain injury, affected computer nerds. A new national disease was on the approach. No more occupational lung disease, no more crippled backs, but RSI? Of course. Societal progress can be read on different scales.

He looked around his office. It felt so empty. No Kerstin Holm to sing duets with. Nothing at all. How long had it actually been since he had visited his grandson Benny in Östhammar? He was afraid the boy would forget his grandad.

On the other hand, his son, Tommy, hadn't forgotten him in twenty long years. They had become reacquainted in a surprisingly unforced way. Life returned. The blood, the viscous liquid, started flowing its marathon distances around Sweden's Biggest Policeman once more.

Now it was thickening again. He remembered how he had felt, sinking to his knees in the mud next to Kerstin Holm's bleeding head. How fleeting life was. It felt as though life itself had broken free from him and sailed away through the rain-filled sky. It was a moment he would never forget.

He was close to Kerstin Holm. They shared a love of choir singing which sometimes grew to abnormal proportions. People who sing together, who stretch the voice to its limits and create the greatest harmonies possible — could you come any closer to God?

During his twenty-year vacuum, there had been only one other woman who had been as close to him, and who, as he sat there stretching his enormous mouse elbows, came into his office. He thought for a moment about mystical correspondences.

Sara Svenhagen wasn't herself. She looked haggard, worn out, as though she hadn't slept for days. Her white T-shirt had several large coffee stains on it, and her shorts were absurdly crinkled.

"Gunnar," she said, stroking her newly cropped golden hair, "I need your help."

He stood up, walked over to her and put a protective, fatherly arm around her shoulders. It felt both right and wrong. On a purely professional level, *she* was his parent; it was her who had carefully guided him into the hell of child pornography. Her and Ludvig Johnsson.

He led her over to Kerstin Holm's chair and helped her down into it. He sat on the edge of the desk. He didn't care that it buckled alarmingly.

"What about Jorge?" he asked. "What can I do that he can't?"

She looked at him with what was, at least, mock surprise.

"You know about that?"

"I guessed," said Gunnar Nyberg, feeling like a crook. "Was I wrong?"

"No," said Sara. "No, not at all. I love him. He loves me. We've come to life, both of us. But we've also built walls around our cases, without really knowing why. Presumably it's some kind of absurd protective instinct. Spare him. Spare her. No, Gunnar, the only real connection between these two cases is you. And also, it affects you personally."

A sense of foreboding ran through Nyberg.

"Personally?" he asked. "Privately?"

"You could say so," said Sara, looking into his eyes.

"OK," he sighed. "Shoot."

"I could spare you all this crap," she said. "I could just leave and let you avoid the whole problem."

"Shoot," he repeated.

Sara Svenhagen looked up at the ceiling. She didn't quite know where to begin. She decided to make a long story short.

"The pseudonym of a paedophile, 'brambo', has been deliberately left out of our reports. It happened almost six months ago. When I looked into it, I discovered that all these incomplete reports had been filed by the same policeman."

394

Nyberg felt the same sense of foreboding as before. It ran through his veins instead of his blood, which had now coagulated completely.

"It was Ragnar Hellberg," she said.

"What?!" he exclaimed. "Party-Ragge?"

"I should've realised that it was absurd . . . Anyway, I kept on trying to identify this 'brambo'. It paid off eventually. It's a drug dealer called Rajko Nedic."

Gunnar Nyberg was motionless. Threads were worming around inside him, searching for one another. They were very close to forming a weave.

"I understand," he eventually lied.

"OK. Ragnar put me to work at home. It felt like he was trying to hide something. And suddenly, it seemed clear. He was letting me work unofficially so he could keep anything I might find away from the public eye. And that thing, it was that he was pressing Nedic for money. It couldn't have been anything else."

"The little beard," said Gunnar Nyberg, thinking of the Kvarnen bar on Tjärhovsgatan, at 21.42 on 23 June.

She looked at him sceptically, continuing. "That was it. I had to confront him. We met on Saturday. Unofficially. And he came out with a story that I've been fighting with for almost two days now. I haven't had a wink of sleep. He was insisting that he'd found out his name had been used on reports he hadn't written. That *someone else* had used Ragnar Hellberg's name — to frame him. This *other* person was one of two people. I've gone through it myself now. He's right so far. There are only two people in the group who could've done it. One of them was me. That's partly why he set me to work at home — to check whether it was me or not. If it had been me, I would hardly have contacted him about 'brambo's' existence. So it was the other candidate, instead."

Gunnar Nyberg could already feel himself weeping inside.

"Ludvig," was all he said.

"It's been a long weekend," said Sara Svenhagen. "Should I trust the idiotic party policeman or my own mentor, the colleague who was closest to me in the entire world? I've been turning myself inside out."

"And come to what . . .?"

"That I trust Party-Ragge. For the simple reason that he wouldn't have ever come up with the idea, much less pull it off. There's no doubt any more. Ludvig Johnsson has been blackmailing Rajko Nedic for money, and cast the shadow of blame onto the man who stole the paedophile group from him almost in passing. Its figurehead."

"Have you spoken to Ludvig?"

"He's on holiday. When he's on holiday, he makes himself uncontactable. No one knows where he is."

"What do you want to do? What does Hellberg want to do?"

"Say what you want about Hellberg, but he's no bureaucrat. He's ready to wait and see what happens. He knows I'm talking to you. So, what do you want to do?"

Gunnar Nyberg looked into her eyes.

"Leave Ludvig to me," he said.

She nodded. "I suspected you'd say that. I'll see whether I can confront Nedic somehow."

"Be careful, in that case. He's extremely dangerous."

"I know. I'll try to find a way."

"What've you got from the Web?"

"'Brambo's' pictures. I've got them here. Do you want to see?"

"No, I don't," said Gunnar Nyberg, holding out his mouse-arm to take the pictures. Colour printouts from the Internet. A whole cavalcade of degradation. He had got it into his head that it belonged to the past. He took his time; his thoughts were out of gear. Behind each picture, he saw Ludvig Johnsson's face.

"He can't have been planning to let Nedic go," he said. "He must've been planning some kind of double-dealing. Get the money from Nedic, leave the country *and* put him away. I can't imagine anything else."

Sara nodded. "I know how passionate he was about this. His own kids died, now he could save others. It was personal. Too personal, maybe. His passion burnt him out. But there's no way in hell he'd let a paedophile go for money."

Nyberg nodded and handed back the pictures. "There's a little girl there . . ." he said, pointing at them.

"Yeah," she said, casting a glance at the pile of pictures. "The poor thing appears more often than others. I'm going to try to track her down. And that gold cushioned room."

"Do it," he said, taking her hand. "We thought Nedic's operation was watertight, but we've found several leaks. There's a chance. If anyone in the organisation knows he's a paedophile, then it's not impossible that he or she doesn't like it. Try to find someone you can put pressure on."

Sara Svenhagen stood up. They were still holding hands.

"And you'll take care of Ludvig?" she asked. "Do it right, Gunnar. Promise me that."

He nodded, clasping her hand. "I promise, Sara," he said.

The journey to Grillby was no normal journey. It was an agonising journey. But also one of metamorphosis. Gunnar Nyberg was, to put it simply, doing a runner. Cutting the ties. Leaving the A-Unit. Maybe he would be dismissed, maybe even prosecuted, but he wasn't thinking about that. He was thinking: Now Ludvig can bloody well tidy up after himself.

Beside him on the passenger seat of the Renault were two laptops with mobile phone connections, two mobile phones and an adapter for the car's cigarette lighter. There was work to be done.

He stopped to buy food, beer and coffee at a petrol station. No Danish pastries, though.

He even checked to see whether he was being followed. He didn't quite trust Ragnar Hellberg.

The oilseed-rape fields were golden yellow, and when Gunnar Nyberg pulled up alongside the little cottage just outside Grillby, Ludvig Johnsson's car was there —

but not the man himself. He was probably out running. Nyberg tried the door. It was open. He stepped into the little cottage clutching the bag of food in his right hand, opened the gas-powered fridge and shoved the whole lot in. Then he opened a beer and sat down on the veranda. The sun shone kindly down on him.

Sure enough, Ludvig Johnsson came jogging back after an hour. He smiled faintly when he saw Nyberg on the veranda. Nyberg saw his smile. He saw what it held. The realisation.

It had all gone to hell.

"There's a barrel of rainwater round the back of the cottage," he said. "You pour the water over yourself."

"That can wait," said Nyberg.

"Yeah," said Ludvig Johnsson, sitting down on the steps. "It can wait. You got a beer for me?"

"I'm not planning on letting you go into the cottage alone," said Nyberg. "I'm not planning on leaving you alone, either. Not for a second."

Ludvig Johnsson looked up at the sky. His gaze seemed to disappear into the blueness.

"Who else knows?" he asked.

"It was Sara who found you. The 'policeman'. Through 'brambo', if that means anything to you."

"Sara," said Johnsson, smiling. "I should've guessed. And Hellberg?"

"Hellberg knows, too. But he's sitting on it for now. Waiting for me. So don't even think about killing me."

"Jesus!" exclaimed Ludvig Johnsson. "What is it you think of me?!"

"What I think is that your little operation has cost eight people their lives *so far*. Three ex-Yugoslav war criminals, a man called Lordan Vukotic, as well as Eskil Carlstedt, Sven Joakim Bergwall, Roger Sjöqvist and Dan Andersson. I could've lived with all of that. But the other day, two of my colleagues and closest friends were shot: Paul Hjelm and Kerstin Holm. You met them recently. Kerstin was talking about the marathon with you at that party for the World Police and Fire Games, if you remember."

Ludvig Johnsson met his eye. His gaze was completely broken. There was nothing left behind there.

"How are they?" he asked.

"They're alive. But only by a couple of centimetres."

"All I wanted was to go to a place where the winters are shorter . . ."

They sat a while in the shade. The sun's rays bore down stronger on the nearby field. It glowed yellow. The colour of betrayal.

"I wasn't planning on letting him go," said Ludvig Johnsson. "I wanted to get away. Then I was going to make sure that the material was sent to the police. I just wanted a little bonus."

"An expensive bonus."

"You know I put the entire paedophile unit together myself. It was me who made sure people started taking child pornography seriously in this *tolerant* country. Freedom of speech till the end. My own sons died. I saw all of these children suffering, I saw how the Internet meant an explosion of all kinds of sexual

400

assault on children. Each child I saved became my own, somehow. I trained Sara up, we were one hell of a team. Then Party-Ragge appeared and took all the credit. I didn't really care, that's how the world works, but I also didn't have anything against using him as my scapegoat."

"So you stuck a little beard on yourself when you met Nedic's gang in Kvarnen."

Johnsson chuckled. "Yeah. That was a bit stupid, but I needed a way out. He got to be the scapegoat. Those guys were tough negotiators; we sat in Kvarnen for a long time, going back and forth, just about the meeting place, and the thing being handed over wasn't even money or the material from the investigation. It was just two safe-deposit-box keys and a communication device. Eventually, we were going to let one another know which bank it was in. A pretty complicated way of doing things, but I let him pull the strings. All I did was get hold of the most modern police radio. Yeah, we were sitting arguing in Kvarnen, we'd just managed to agree on Sickla as the meeting place, at two the following morning, when that idiot smashed the beer glass over someone's head. I sent the Yugoslavs away pretty quickly and thanked God for that stupid little beard; I waited until they were out of sight and then the doormen turned up. I flashed them my ID to get out."

"You'd been bugged. Didn't you check the place out? A whole group of Nazis were listening to you from the corner."

Ludvig Johnsson nodded. "Was that how it happened? Yeah, it was lazy not to look around

401

properly, but I was damn scared. That simple. Those guys weren't to be messed with. Three real monsters from Bosnia. They could've just decided to torture me to get me to reveal my insurance."

"Insurance?"

"The standard. A copy of the entire investigation with an old childhood friend. In the event of my death, it would've been sent to the police and Rajko Nedic would be outed as a paedophile."

"You were photographed coming out, the whole group, by a paedophile up in Söder Torn. A bit ironic, don't you think?"

"So you've had me for a long time, then?"

"The picture was useless, unfortunately. You could see a bit of the beard, that was all."

Ludvig Johnsson laughed. "See," he said. "A blessing in disguise."

"Tell me everything now."

"OK. It was February, something like that. I found a whole load of hidden websites online and tracked down a whole group of pseudonyms. I put all of them away — all apart from one. The idea was born right away when I realised that 'brambo' was Nedic. Taking money from that bastard didn't feel so dangerous. My life was a complete mess. All I did was run. I was running for my life. Like the original marathon. I hated winter more and more. It was in winter that my family had been wiped out. Damn winter roads. I wanted to get away. Die in the warmth somewhere. I had the strange idea of just going to some Polynesian island and drinking myself to death. Me, someone who doesn't even like the strong stuff much. Anyway, I sent all the material to a friend in Säffle and got in touch with Nedic. He was completely dumbfounded. Had thought he was completely secure online. I put a sum that sounded good out there, ten million, and he went with it. I was speechless. *He went with it*. Ten mill. You have to wonder how much a man like that has . . . We agreed that I had to meet his men to decide on a handover. I suggested Kvarnen — as public as possible. Somehow, it must've got out."

"Nedic's closest man was called Lordan Vukotic. He knew the Kvarnen meeting was going to take place. He'd trained as a corporate laywer in the Kumla Bunker and was probably going to be the one looking after the empire's finances. Evidently, he told his friends inside about it, and one of them — a Croat called Risto Petrovic — told one of his old friends from the Foreign Legion, a right-wing extremist and former officer called Niklas Lindberg. He seems to have been the leader of some kind of 'Nazi clique' in Kumla. Sven Joakim Bergwall and Dan Andersson were involved in it, too. Andersson was released in February, so he was out when the information about the handover of ten million came up in . . ."

"It must've been May," said Johnsson.

"In May, the ideological motor Bergwall was released. By that point, Andersson might've already started to get a gang together to steal that ten million. Lindberg was inside until the twenty-fourth of June, the day after your meeting in Kvarnen. He knew that Bergwall and the men were going to listen to your meeting, but at roughly the same time he decided to torture Vukotic to find out what he knew about the meeting place. The next day, he was released. The men picked him up from Kumla in a van. Once he was safely outside the walls, he detonated a bomb, blowing the injured Vukotic to pieces. A farewell gesture to Kumla, a greeting for Nedic, and a way of erasing his tracks — all in one go.

"Then this gang of six right-wing extremists set off for the Sickla industrial estate. Lindberg blew up the car containing the three monsters from Bosnia. One of them died immediately. They took the briefcase containing the safe-deposit-box key and the radio, got a shock when there was no money in the briefcase, and that gave the battle-tested Bosnian monsters their chance: they whipped out their pistols using the mechanisms in their jacket sleeves and shot and killed two of them, Carlstedt and Bergwall, injuring another, Andersson. They died themselves, of course. But at the same time, *the briefcase disappeared*.

"A completely separate gang, calling itself Orpheus and Eurydice, some kind of Nedic defectors, also knew about your little delivery. In the middle of the firefight, they managed to steal the briefcase. They're not too thrilled about finding a key and a radio instead of money, either. They split up and set off into the countryside, looking for the bank. They must have some kind of idea about where it *should* be. That means they must be relatively close to Nedic. From the Nazi gang, Lindberg, Sjöqvist, Kullberg and an injured Andersson are left. Kullberg's a civil engineer, and made some kind of device for locating the police radio. They set off after Orpheus, Eurydice and the briefcase. Eurydice had the briefcase. After a couple of weeks of hunting, they found her. In Skövde. We were there. We killed Sjöqvist and Andersson and captured Kullberg. Lindberg managed to get away. Eurydice, too. Hjelm and Holm were shot."

Ludvig Johnsson stared at his formerly apathetic colleague, half amazed.

"Christ," he said. "You've been working hard. Who are this Orpheus and Eurydice?"

"That we don't know, and it's no longer of interest. We've got the key. Do you have any idea where the bank might be?"

"No, but it should be near town. Stockholm. My box, with the material from the investigation, is in town. The branch of Handelsbank on Odenplan. Why are you telling me all of this? The criminal? The 'policeman'?"

"So that you can tidy up after yourself. I've got computer equipment and mobile phones and connection devices in the car, enough for two men in a cottage without electricity or a telephone. I've filled your fridge with food. So now we're damn well going to stay here until we've cracked this!"

"But what's left?" Johnsson exclaimed.

"To hell with Nedic for the moment," Gunnar Nyberg said clearly. "I think Sara will deal with that. To hell with Orpheus and Eurydice, too. They're out of the game. What's left — properly left — is Niklas Lindberg. He wants your ten million for something particular. He

405

sets off advanced, extremely powerful microscopic bombs with pleasure, and he managed to steal almost a million kronor while he was hunting for Eurydice. He's hardly going to get hold of that ten million unless he goes directly for Nedic, but maybe that near-million he already has is enough."

"What do you think?" asked Johnsson.

"I think the first bombs were a test. He blew up Vukotic for fun, more or less, and the car in Sickla could've been stopped without using explosives. He's test-bombing. Like in Polynesia, that crazy bastard. They're *samples* he's setting off. That ten million is going towards a serious amount of the liquid explosive that apartheid South Africa's security services developed. It's connected to the same international, right-wing movement that Lindberg came into contact with in the Foreign Legion and which caused Nedic's colleague, the Croatian fascist Petrovic, to squeal to Lindberg. The explosive could've been smuggled into Kumla, and now it's going to be used for something bigger. You and I are going to find out what Niklas Lindberg is up to, and stop it. That's what we're going to do. You owe it to me, to Sara and the world, you stupid bastard."

Ludvig Johnsson looked at Gunnar Nyberg. What he saw was something remarkable. A kind of focused energy. An absolute determinedness that he never would have predicted. Though, on the other hand, he had never been part of the A-Unit.

"But what about you? Have you left the A-Unit?"

"If we can solve this, maybe we can save both our skins," said Gunnar Nyberg, heading towards his rusty old Renault.

CHAPTER
FORTY-ONE

Kerstin Holm had been moved to the Karolinska hospital. It was Tuesday, and her head hurt.

It wasn't so strange. She had seen the X-ray. It looked like there was a hole right into her head, but it was just that her skull was thin as an eggshell above her ear. Translucent. Dan Andersson had shot away a bit of her skull. Just one hit. A bit of her skull, gone with one hit. Part of her head had been trampled into a rain-soaked lawn in Skövde. Maybe a tiny Kerstin Holm would grow up out of it, to the surprise of the hotel guests.

Though that wasn't very likely.

She turned to Paul Hjelm, sitting on the edge of her bed with that expression of *compassion* that hospital visitors always have.

"Stop it," she said.

"Stop what?" he asked.

"That face."

"Sorry."

"It doesn't have to mean anything."

"What?"

"The thing with Ovid's *Metamorphoses*. It might be a coincidence."

"You're right."

"Don't say I'm right just because I'm in hospital and have awful hospital-breath. Tell me I'm wrong instead. Disagree with me."

"You're wrong."

"Thanks. Why am I wrong?"

"You don't have awful hospital-breath."

"*Why am I wrong?*"

"Because he's been in our thoughts for so long. Because he reacted so strangely to that mention of Orpheus. Because he was sitting reading Ovid's *Metamorphoses* in a packed pub. Because the others said he was *pretending* to read. Because, even though he was reading, he saw *everything* apart from the group sitting closest to him, speaking English right in his ear. Because he's one of the three witnesses who, in spite of everything, we can't get hold of. Because the young pair aren't using one but *two* of Ovid's metamorphoses when they contact one another. Orpheus and Eurydice *and* Philemon and Baucis."

"That's a lot."

"Per Karlsson. It can't shape the investigation, but we should keep him in mind."

"I agree. What happened, then? Unemployed, uneducated Per Karlsson, twenty years old, is sitting and listening to three ex-Yugoslavs and a 'policeman' coming to an agreement on a meeting place. Was he there by coincidence? Did he just happen to hear it? Or was he there *to listen?* In which case, how did he know those gangsters were going to be there? He and his girlfriend are using Internet-enabled mobile phones

belonging to Rajko Nedic's restaurant, the Thanatos —
the kingdom of the dead, of course. Something's
missing. Sure, Per Karlsson might've worked there
temporarily — illegally, that is, unregistered — as a
waiter or dishwasher, but it's not enough. Two
sophisticated mobile phones *and* knowledge that the
meeting in Kvarnen was going to take place. That
implies real closeness to Nedic, a man who doesn't let
anyone get close to him."

"Though it *could've* been a coincidence. He really
was in Kvarnen, trying to read. Then he hears the
conversation and gets hooked on it. He pretends to
read and doesn't say a word to us about the
neighbouring table. He sees it as a gift from above. X
number of millions as a gift to an unemployed slacker.
It's also very possible."

"But then they set off, each on their own, to look for
the safe-deposit box. Why did they go where they did?
Why to Dalarna and Västmanland, Halland and
Västergötland? I mean, they can't search the whole of
Sweden. Does that mean they've got some kind of close
knowledge of Nedic?"

"Maybe. But that has to fall in the shadow of Niklas
Lindberg. Per Karlsson didn't exactly seem like he was
a danger to society. Also, they seem to be out of the
game now."

"True. Bloody hell, everything's starting to spin
again."

Hjelm stood up and stared at her. She watched him
spin. He looked so *awkward*, like all hospital visitors.

"Stop it," said Kerstin Holm, spinning away.

CHAPTER
FORTY-TWO

Through the gates, you could catch a glimpse of paradise. But the walls were high and guarded by an armed cherub.

Which, in this case, was a surveillance camera, an entryphone and a metallic-sounding voice which said: "Name and business."

She cleared her throat and looked at the four thick-skinned police assistants she had in tow. All stared up into the camera. It was like an audition for a TV talent show.

"Detective Inspector Sara Svenhagen," she said. "Criminal Investigation Department. We're looking for Rajko Nedic."

"Mr Nedic is not available at the moment," said the metallic voice.

"Then we'd like to speak to someone else. Who is in charge?"

Silence. The gates of paradise slid open. The fantastic garden didn't seem to have allowed a single conceivable shade of colour to get away, and the brilliant sunshine only served to make them brighter. Sara Svenhagen felt almost blinded by the display of colours and drugged by the richness of scents. It really was fantastic. The Garden of Eden.

A well-dressed little man in his fifties came out to meet them in the garden. He held out his hand to Sara. She shook it.

"I'm Ljubomir Protic," he said in slightly broken Swedish. "I work for Mr Nedic. What can I help you with?"

"Isn't he home?" asked Sara Svenhagen.

"Unfortunately not," Ljubomir Protic said politely. "Is there anything I can do?"

"That depends who you are."

"I'm Mr Nedic's right-hand man, you could say."

"I thought that was Lordan Vukotic. Though he's dead, of course."

Protic maintained his polite smile, answering: "I don't recognise that name, unfortunately."

"Are you close to Rajko Nedic, Ljubomir?" asked Sara.

"Very close, Mrs Svenkragen."

"Svenhagen. And not Mrs Sara. You can call me Sara, Ljubomir. We're going to be talking a lot in the near future. And of course you're close to him. If I'm not mistaken, you left Yugoslavia together almost thirty years ago. Two youngsters, Rajko and Ljubomir, hitching their way through Europe on the way to a golden future in Sweden."

Ljubomir Protic looked at her, his smile beginning to falter.

"What are you getting at? I have nothing more to say. I think I'd like to ask you to leave now."

412

"I think I forgot to say where I've come from. The child pornography unit, CID. It has nothing to do with Nedic the drug dealer. This is about Nedic the *paedophile*."

His reaction was important.

Since her conversation with Gunnar, Sara had devoted her time to finding out as much as possible about Nedic's organisation. The drugs squad had a lot to offer when it came to its structure. The most important new addition was Ljubomir Protic, who had known Rajko Nedic for practically his entire life but had only recently entered the organisation as Nedic's right-hand man. From the outside, he seemed like the weakest link — but, on the other hand, there was an internal band of friendship that was even stronger.

His reaction was clear. He paled slightly. He tried to maintain his polite, obliging expression, but the colour of his face changed. It was the reaction she had been hoping for.

She turned to the other police officers.

"Take him with you," she said, wandering through the gates of paradise.

Ljubomir was in an interrogation room. It felt strange. Just him and the walls. The moment he blew on them, they would come tumbling down. He knew it. And so he tried to refrain from breathing. It felt as though life was being blown out with each breath.

Eventually, there was almost nothing left.

He had been there for two hours now. No one had been in to see him, but he knew that someone was

413

watching him. From somewhere within. And by this point, the great man would surely know where he was. He couldn't really see any kind of future.

He remembered what the great man had drilled into him. A rule book to use in the event of a confrontation with the police. Always be polite and obliging. Deny everything with an expression of regret. Be aware of yourself and the smallest of expressions. Don't say a single unnecessary word.

The great man had already made it clear to him that he was seen as a security risk. He knew roughly what he would be thinking by this point. Two hours with the police. He's already told them everything he knows. Good job he doesn't know anything.

But the great man didn't know *which* police unit he was with. The paedophile police. And he really did know *everything* about that.

The door opened and the short-haired policewoman came in. Finally. She seemed so unassuming. Young. Having your life shattered by a young woman wasn't so unusual after all, despite everything. And now she had been gathering her aces. Would he be able to keep calm — if *that place* was brought up?

She brought it up immediately.

Sara Svenhagen placed a pile of papers on the table and said: "By this point, he'll think you've told us everything, right? Which means your life isn't worth much. So you might as well tell us everything. About his paedophile den with the golden soundproofed walls, for example."

414

"Do you really think it's that easy to crack the organisation?" Ljubomir asked, sounding like he was reeling off a line he'd learned by heart. "Don't you think it's stronger than that?"

"Oh, sure," she said. "When it comes to the drugs. Then it's practically impossible to bring down. All the safety locks are still in place there. But this isn't about the drugs. It's about the *back route* into the organisation. Via Rajko Nedic's sexual escapades."

"I don't know what you're talking about, Sara," said Ljubomir. "I'm sorry."

"Of course not. What do you think about child pornography, Ljubomir? What do you think of small girls' vaginas, split to the navel by broken Coca-Cola bottles? What do you think of five-year-old boys whose anuses are so ruptured that the shit just runs straight out of them?"

"Jesus Christ," said Ljubomir, staring at her.

"I'm going to show you hundreds of pictures of your employer in such situations, and you're going to look at every single one of them, even it it means pinning your eyelids to your forehead. Do you understand?"

Ljubomir looked at the young woman with the cropped hair. He could see her determinedness and knew that it was over. He would fight it, but only because it was ingrained in him that he should fight. But it was over. He would start to cry. He would be forced to go to *that place* and see everything he'd been turning away from his entire life. It would all collapse in on him. He knew that when he looked into Sara Svenhagen's eyes. And he knew she could see it.

"Rajko Nedic, using the pseudonym 'brambo', has been particularly active in online paedophile circles. It's only now that we've managed to identify him. In practice, he's already out of the game. It would be good if you could tell us more, Ljubomir. What happened? Was he already a paedophile when you came to Sweden, two youths with the world at their fingertips? Was there something in his childhood that made him into what he is?"

"I want a lawyer," said Ljubomir.

"You wanted one two hours ago, too. The same applies now: you can't. The only thing you can do is look at these pictures. Your employer put them online. He's the most careful leader there is when it comes to the drugs trade, but he'll happily share pictures of his penis inside small children with the world. I've been working with paedophiles for a long time, much too long, but this strange, almost overpowering desire to share their perversions is something I'll never understand. It undoes all their caution."

She pushed the pile of pictures towards him. He looked at it, and closed his eyes.

"No," he said. "I don't want to."

"Well, you're going to."

She held up the first picture.

It was *her*.

Of course, it was *her* right away.

It went on and on and on, and though he was crying, it went on and on. All were of *her*.

He fell to pieces. He couldn't do it. He slumped forward onto the interrogation-room table, his tears spilling onto the printouts, causing the colours to run onto the table in one big mess, covering his face. When he looked up he was a clown, a sobbing, colourful clown.

"I could've stopped it," he wept. "She came to me each time. After every single time, she came to me, sat on my knee and called me 'Uncle Jubbe'; crying and crying, beyond tears, just staring at me without tears, unable to say a word because she had no words for it, and every time, I thought: this has to be the last time, otherwise I'll have to kill the bastard, but I didn't do it, I didn't do anything at all. I just looked away as she sat on my knee and said 'Uncle Jubbe' but really meant 'Help me, Uncle Jubbe, something's happening and I don't understand it and you're so kind and you can help me.' But I wasn't kind, I was the worst of the worst, because I turned a blind eye and saw nothing."

Sara Svenhagen closed her eyes for a moment, thinking wordlessly. She handed a tissue to Ljubomir Protic. He dried his eyes and looked down at the mix of colours on the paper. It looked like a paradise garden.

"Who is 'she'?" asked Sara Svenhagen.

Ljubomir looked at her through the haze, wronged.

"Sonja, of course," he said. "My little Sonja."

"And Sonja is . . .?"

"Rajko's daughter. His *daughter*, for Christ's sake."

"And that's her in these pictures?"

Ljubomir grimaced. Then he nodded.

"How old is Sonja Nedic now? Twenty?"

"Yes," said Ljubomir. "Exactly twenty."

"What kind of life does she live?"

"She's got her own car and her own flat. Studying maths at university. She tried to kill herself a year ago. Slashed her wrists. Lengthways. She almost died. But lately, whenever I've seen her in the house, she's seemed happier. I remember thinking: I hope she's found someone now, someone who can make her happy, who can give her a bit of the childhood she never had. I really hope so."

"Can you give us anything else?"

"Rajko had the same childhood. I know, because I sat with him in the same way. As a child. In the little mountain village in eastern Serbia. Failed to comfort him in the same way. That's why we left. To get away from it all. He thought he could leave his past behind and become someone else. But as soon as Sonja arrived, it returned. He started repeating his father's actions. And I just sat there. Again. Jesus. Uncle Jubbe."

"What about the rest of the family?"

"There are two children. He resisted temptation with the son. He's three years older and involved in the organisation now. But he couldn't resist Sonja. And the wife ignores it even more than I do. She shops her way out of reality, and Rajko cultivates his garden to create a paradise that he's never understood."

"Other children?"

"There have been others, too. I don't know where he gets them from. Now that Sonja's grown up, there are others. Maybe he buys them."

"Anything else?"

"It's too late now. I'll tell you everything I know, Sara. You seem to be a capable woman, but I should tell you that I don't actually know very much. I can start with his 'security consultants'. Two disgusting Swedes, former policemen. From the Security Service. They're called Gillis Döös and Max Grahn."

"You can tell the rest to the drugs squad. They're waiting outside. What I want to know is where his paedophile den is. The flat with the soundproofed walls, covered in golden cushions."

Ljubomir smiled slightly behind his smeared, coloured mask.

"He's there now," he said. "In *that place*."

"What do you mean?" Sara Svenhagen exclaimed. "And you didn't say anything?!"

"No, no," said Ljubomir. "It has another function now, that flat. Nothing to do with children."

Sara breathed out. She said: "And where is it?"

"By Hornstull. Hornsgatan 131. Four flights up. It has the name Ahlström on the door. But he has at least five men with him, so be careful, Sara. They've got lots of weapons."

She nodded, looking at the man in front of her. Something had lit up in his eyes. Things which had been shut off and sealed up for years had been let out. Maybe he had, in some small way, repaid a tiny, tiny part of the debt to Sonja Nedic. His little Sonja.

She leaned back and closed her eyes.

Now Ljubomir could die in peace.

He was Uncle Jubbe again.

And now he was — finally — doing something about it.

CHAPTER
FORTY-THREE

Paul Hjelm had killed.

He had been shot.

Seeming to be at death's door, Kerstin Holm had said that she loved him.

Each of these things had been enough to change his life. He was forced to repress the whole lot in order to be able to take up the role of interrogator.

Hultin had allocated the roles, after all.

"Bloody typical that Kerstin should go and get shot just now," he said gruffly. "You can take Jorge with you. The two of you can look after the interrogations of Kullberg and Petrovic."

And so it came to pass that the former heroes became authorised interrogators.

Jorge Chavez had panicked during the firefight.

He had been given a slap by Hultin.

He had built strange walls between him and the woman he had recently fallen in love with.

These were also enough for a couple of metamorphoses. And these, too, had to be repressed.

They entered the interrogation room in an isolated area of the police station. Inside, a short but broad man was sitting, a gap in his teeth, eyebrow taped up and bruises on his face. He smiled sardonically at them.

"Look who it is," said Agne 'Bullet' Kullberg. "The crybaby."

Chavez felt ill at ease. He sat down. Hjelm remained standing for a moment, looking at Kullberg. Trying to get a handle on him. Repressing the constant, nagging pain in his arm.

"You've got a tough old bastard as a boss, though," Bullet continued.

"Yup, Agne," said Hjelm. "We noticed that you were crying, that you were sick down the barrel of the gun. If we're talking about crybabies."

He sat down. The opening had been equalised. Now it was what followed that counted. Bullet seemed slightly deflated. He looked down at the table.

"We need to know what Niklas Lindberg is planning," said Hjelm calmly.

"You've been going on about that for a while now," Bullet said to the table. "But I don't bloody know. We were after the ten million kronor. That was the only plan I had in mind."

"So it was a normal robbery then, Agne? Without any ideological overtones?"

"Yeah, it was about the money. Nothing else."

"Tell us about that tracking device, Agne."

"Don't call me Agne all the time."

"I promise, Agne. Tell us now."

"Well, down in Sickla we got a quick look at the radio before the briefcase vanished. There was a piece of paper with the frequency on it. Using the type of radio and the frequency, I could put together a device to find the little tracking signal that kind of radio always puts out. We found a couple of signals early on and followed it along the E4. Then it disappeared. We kept driving down to Skåne anyway, 'til we realised that the briefcase must've disappeared somewhere on the way. Probably westwards. So we started making our way north. And in Trollhättan we found the signal again. And in Falköping. And then Skövde was logical. It was beeping the whole time there. We just had to follow it right into the hotel room."

"Shouldn't you use your talents for something more sensible?"

"I'm hoping to get the chance to do more training in Kumla. Then I'll be really honourable."

"Why did you steal so much on your way through western Sweden?"

"Why not? We stole everything we came across because it was there. No other reason. We're robbers and we were looking for money — and as long as the briefcase was missing, we had to make do with small change. A man's got to live, after all."

"Not necessarily. Lots of people died along the way, Agne. You don't seem to be missing your mates."

"They weren't my mates. They were colleagues."

"And Lindberg?"

"A good leader. Nothing more. A hell of a physique on that man."

"Practically all of your colleagues in the gang were organised right-wing extremists. Are you telling us there was no ideological motive behind it?"

422

"I'm not an organised right-wing extremist."

"But you're a member of a shooting club with other, known right-wing extremists, Agne. Among them a couple of shady colleagues of ours. People who've attracted attention in connection with the Palme murder."

"Only by conspiracy theorists on TV. No, I'm a member because I like shooting. Fine motor skills are fascinating. Precision. And stop calling me Agne."

"I promise, Agne. We need two things: the make, colour and registration number of the van, and Niklas Lindberg's current whereabouts."

"I've got no idea about any of that."

"You don't know what type of van you were driving in, Agne?"

"I've forgotten, unfortunately."

"Niklas Lindberg left just before we arrived at the hotel room. Why?"

Bullet fell quiet. That wasn't a common occurrence.

"Well, then," said Chavez. "The picture's quite clear. You're trying your damnedest to make us think that you're just a normal gang of robbers, interested only in money. Why's it so important to make us think that? And why can't you come up with any reasonable explanation as to why Niklas Lindberg wasn't there when we arrived? Couldn't he, I don't know . . . have just gone out to take care of the money you'd left behind in the van?"

"It was something like that," Bullet said apathetically. "The situation was under control. Danne and Rogge were going to have a bit of fun with the bird. That

423

wasn't Nicke's style. He went out for a while to check everything was all right."

"Nice work, Agne," said Chavez. "So now we've got a reasonable explanation for that, too."

"Was it your style, Agne?" asked Hjelm.

"What?" asked Bullet.

"Having 'a bit of fun with the bird'? A rape was actually taking place when we arrived."

"And you shot Danne in the back, yeah. Very brave. In the back. And then twice in the face while he was lying on the floor. He'd actually already been injured."

"I asked if it was your style, Agne."

"No, it wasn't my style. I wasn't planning on raping her. But someone has to be on guard."

"Do you know Risto Petrovic?"

"No."

"That was quick. Don't you think Agne answered really quickly, Jorge?"

"Yup, it was an *impressively* quick answer from Agne. You must know that he was the one who leaked information about the Nedic handover to Lindberg in Kumla."

"Nicke was looking after all of that. I didn't have anything to do with the Kumla part."

"Petrovic is a war criminal, organised fascist and Nicke's friend from the Foreign Legion."

"Is that so?"

"Yes, that's so, Agne. And it tells me that you weren't a normal robber gang at all, but rather a fascist cadre on a task for some kind of international right-wing

424

organisation, one which probably knows who murdered Olof Palme."

"You're kidding!"

"Yeah, I'm kidding, Agne. Danne Blood Pudding and apartheid South Africa's still-strong security services don't really go together."

"My name isn't Agne."

"No, Agne. The attack you're planning — and which Nicke surely hasn't put on ice — is your own idea. But to get hold of that highly volatile liquid explosive, you need contacts within international groups. The problem is that they want to be paid. Don't you get it, Agne, that you're just small fry? They want *money* from you. They've got no intention of paying for your stupid little attack."

Chavez fell silent. They paused and observed Bullet Kullberg. It was *here* his facial expression should change slightly. It should say: "Just wait and see, idiots."

Bullet stared down at the table with a gaze that said: "Just wait and see, idiots."

"Thanks," said Hjelm and Chavez in unison.

"For what?" asked Bullet, staring at them with suspicion.

"For the clue you just gave us, Agne," said Hjelm. "We're really most grateful for it."

"What're you up to, pea-brains?"

Worry spread over Bullet's face. His body began to tremble. Idiot, Chavez thought.

"Why did you say your name wasn't Agne, Agne?"

"Was it because *you* aren't called Agne, Agne?"

"Because the person who is called Agne, Agne, is a little runt who was forced down into the dirt in the playground at Östra Real."

"And you've left Agne long behind you, Agne."

"Nerdy little Agne, smallest in the class, is so far away."

"So long since Agne got a thrashing from the big boys, Agne."

"So long since the girls walked past, one after one, giggling at little Agne's hairless penis, Agne."

"So long since little Agne was throwing up down the barrel of a gun in Skövde, Agne."

"So long since Agne couldn't get it up when he was trying to rape a little foreign bird in a hotel room in Skövde, Agne."

"You're a bloody little shit, Agne."

"You're an absolute zero, Agne. Nobody likes you, everybody hates you, because you're just a worm."

"A devious little worm. Like your dick. A little worm with an even smaller worm. Agne Pagne."

Abrupt silence.

They didn't give a damn about Bullet now. Apathetic. Distant.

"Should we go for a coffee?" asked Chavez.

"I don't know. I've got to pick Lotta up from nursery."

"Should we just leave this? It's boring. *He's* boring. What was he called again? Arne?"

"Banarne."

They went to the door, talking among themselves.

426

"What do Stockholmers and sperm have in common?"

"Dunno."

"Not many of them ever become people."

"Gothenburg joke. Have you got one on Fulham — West Brom?"

"Like hell I have. But I've got to go by the bottle shop. What time is it?"

"Same as yesterday at the same time."

"Fuck off, you wog. Have you tried those new condoms with tees?"

"Tees? Golf condoms for dense rough."

"On the other hand, Dame Edna's running damn well at the minute. Sure bet in the seven at Valla."

"Benny Björn's a hell of a name for a horse."

They closed the door after them, and went over to look through the two-way mirror. Bullet looked completely out of balance. He was poking strangely at his forehead.

"Pick Lotta up from nursery?" asked Chavez, peeping through the window.

"Or Benny Björn," said Hjelm, peeping. "That's even."

They opened the door and went back into the room. Hjelm went straight up to Bullet and shouted, ten centimetres from his face: "World Police and Fire Games!"

Bullet went stiff. It was utterly obvious.

"I don't know anything about that," he said weakly.

"Thanks," said Hjelm and Chavez in unison.

★ ★ ★

"'Golf condoms for dense rough'?!" exclaimed Ludvig Johnsson, reading from his computer screen.

Gunnar Nyberg read his own. He laughed.

"Jorge never censors his reports," he said.

They read on. Once they were done, Johnsson said: "What a strange interrogation."

Nyberg bit into an ice-cold chicken leg, leaning back.

"They're damn reliable," he said. "A little unorthodox, but they know what they're doing. I normally just heave myself over them like a grizzly bear."

"What d'you think?"

"They seem to have got it right. First they threw him off balance, knocked down the wall, then they gave him the shove. And it makes sense. The opening of the World Police and Fire Games is being held in Stockholm Stadium at three on Saturday. That doesn't give us much time. I'll be damned if Niklas Lindberg is going to blow policemen up in Stockholm Stadium!"

They made their way to a little flat in the Stockholm suburb of Tumba, ringing Lars Viksjö from the car to let him know that they were coming. Viksjö, the stout policeman from Närke, had been abruptly transformed into Risto Petrovic's personal babysitter.

In the hall, three uniformed police assistants were sitting.

"Afternoon," Chavez said smoothly to the porn police. "Have you caught any Mediterranean shrimps lately?"

The porn police watched him sulkily.

428

They entered the living room. Lars Viksjö was smoking a badly rolled cigarette which was spitting glowing flakes of tobacco out over the room, and Risto Petrovic was wolfing down spaghetti in front of the TV. Hjelm thought to himself that it reminded him of a film, but he couldn't remember which. Several, probably.

They nodded briefly at Viksjö, pulled two chairs over to Petrovic's table, switched the TV off and sat down.

"For a possible Crown witness, you've said far too little," Hjelm said in English. "This is your last chance or you'll be going back to Kumla. And you know what'll happen then."

"Our colleague Gunnar Nyberg gave you a list of the information we need," said Chavez. "One: the link between you and Niklas Lindberg. Two: all imaginable and unimaginable information on Rajko Nedic's organisation. Three: the nature of the handover. Four: its recipient. Five: what Lindberg's going to use it for. Six: where Lindberg and his men are right now. Let's start from the end and modify number six: where is Niklas Lindberg right now?"

"I have no idea," said Risto Petrovic, a half-kilo of spaghetti twisted around his fork.

"No possible hideouts?"

"Sorry. No possible hideouts. I know very little about Sweden. I just came here for a job, but got locked up almost immediately."

"Let's go straight to number five, then. What was Lindberg going to use the money for?"

"Buying stuff. You buy stuff with money. That's why everyone wants it."

"Thanks for the foundation course in capitalist economics. He wasn't going to use the money for anything in particular, then?"

"Not as far as I know."

"Four: who was going to receive the money?"

"You're just asking the same questions as the others."

"Who?"

"A Swedish policeman. I don't know anything else. He was blackmailing Nedic for money. Ten million kronor."

"We've not heard about this sum before. It's a big one. The policeman must've found something valuable, then. Something which could sink the entire Nedic organisation."

"Yep," said Petrovic, his mouth full of spaghetti. "Must've done. But I don't know what."

"So that's three answered, too," said Hjelm. "And we were going to take half each. The second, then. Rajko Nedic's organisation."

Petrovic nodded, chewing away. When he was finished, he fished under the table and retrieved a pile of handwritten papers.

Hjelm took it from him, leafing through the pages. It looked solid. He must have really worked on it. On that, and nothing else. Sinking Nedic.

"Thanks," said Hjelm. "Impressive. Now it's starting to look like something."

"Thank you," said Risto Petrovic in English, starting to twist spaghetti again. Twist after twist after twist.

"Let's try number one, then. What's your relationship with Niklas Lindberg really like?"

"We met in the Foreign Legion. Neither of us really fitted in there. We became friends and survived a year together. Then we bumped into one another in the Kumla Bunker. It was a welcome reunion. I was working for Nedic and tipped Nicke off that he was going to hand over ten million kronor to a policeman. Later, Lordan mentioned that meeting would be taking place in Kvarnen. I told Nicke about that, too."

"And what did you get out of it?"

"Nothing. We're friends. If you'd been through what we went through in the Legion, you'd understand. Otherwise you can't."

Hjelm nodded and looked at Chavez. Chavez nodded and looked at Hjelm.

"Good," said Hjelm. "So now we know roughly where you stand, then. You want to sink Nedic whatever the cost, and you want to protect Lindberg whatever the cost. You're united by the tough experience you went through. You're friends in an almost Arab sense of the word. Friends for life. Thick as thieves."

It had taken him a moment to express himself in English.

"Sound familiar? he asked Chavez, still in English.

"I heard it just recently," Chavez answered in English. "We're *just* a normal group of robbers. We're *just* friends. Same pattern."

"Though I don't think we can talk about tees now."

"I don't think we'd get a bite, no. So let's do this."

Jorge Chavez ripped Petrovic's handwritten stack of papers into pieces.

Petrovic choked. Half-chewed spaghetti flew out into the room, uniting with the gaping Viksjö's glowing flakes of tobacco.

"You think that you're a Crown witness to squeal on Rajko Nedic, but that's not the case. We don't give a shit about Rajko Nedic. What we're interested in is the attack on Stockholm's Stadium in a few days' time. The World Police and Fire Games. Everything you know. Otherwise you're heading straight for Kumla, where you'll be back up close with Zoran Koco, Petar Klovic and the rest of Nedic's men."

Petrovic stopped coughing. The spaghetti was hanging like scraps of meat from his mouth. It looked like the final scenes of the *Jaws* films.

"What the hell does it say here?" asked Ludvig Johnsson. "In brackets?"

"*JC rips P's N mtrl*," Gunnar Nyberg read. "Apparently Jorge ripped up Petrovic's papers on Nedic."

"How can he justify that?"

"There's something fishy about it. He's bluffing. Presumably they'd already made a copy. But it's a nice twist. It'll be interesting to see what happened next."

"You were probably an organised right-wing extremist even before the war in Croatia broke out," said Hjelm. "The descendants of the old, ultra-nationalistic Ustaša. Serb-hate. Then during the war, you really went in for

432

your role as commander of a paramilitary unit. You probably widened your web of international contacts during that time. Got some false papers from them and fled to the Foreign Legion. Took the opportunity to recruit ideological kinsmen in the Legion to this contact web of international fascists. Among these was Niklas Lindberg, who then started to bomb and beat up Kurds, and went to prison. In turn, he scraped together friends to join to the web of contacts inside Kumla: the so-called 'Nazi clique', in which the known right-wing extremist Sven Joakim Bergwall, who died in the Sickla Slaughter, was active. Together, the three of you planned a bigger attack in Stockholm, and what could be more appropriate than this summer's World Police and Fire Games? Blow up policemen *and* prison guards. What a dream.

"You knew that there was a suitable kind of explosive available within your big international group of contacts. A highly volatile and reliably explosive liquid which uses a microscopic electronic detonator. The South Africans had developed it for the ANC's meetings, but apartheid ended before they had time to put it into use. So you smuggled a sample into Kumla and gave it to Lindberg, and you made sure that he would have enough money to get hold of a proper amount of this explosive. The money could be taken from your employer, Rajko Nedic — the Serbian bastard who'd managed to unite former enemies in his drugs organisation. A real peace organisation. Two birds with one stone. You could blow up policemen and Serbs in one go. Nice plan.

433

"Lindberg's still out there, and he's got money — if not ten million then at least almost one — and he'll be able to carry out the plan despite all the trouble. All while you, protected by four fine policemen, chew spaghetti, sink Nedic and are given a nice new identity by the Swedish state. Well planned, again. But you forgot the A-Unit."

"*What* did I forget?" Risto Petrovic exclaimed.

"Nothing," Hjelm continued. "Nothing at all. A parenthesis."

"What? When? How?" asked Chavez. "Otherwise, we're sending you back to Rajko Nedic. It's that simple. *Where* will the bomb be? Where will Lindberg be when he detonates it? *When* will the bomb be put in place? When will it be set off? And *how* is it all going to pan out?"

"You're wrong," said Risto Petrovic, wiping his mouth. "It's *not* so simple."

"Why not?"

"Because some things are bigger than any individual."

"What do you mean by that?"

"Send me back to Nedic if you want. This is bigger than me. I'm a dispensable cog in a big machine."

Hjelm and Chavez looked at one another. It had been going so well. And now, to be stopped in their tracks by something as unexpected as . . . idealism.

Sick, black idealism.

The most dangerous kind.

"Did they send him back?" asked Ludvig Johnsson.

Nyberg looked at him as he nibbled on yet another ice-cold chicken leg.

434

"Hardly," he said. "He might still be valuable."

"I don't think so," said Johnsson. "He's not going to talk. He's well versed in his warped idealism. He really believes in ethnic cleansing and ethnic purity. The weak link is Kullberg. There's still a chance there."

"If he knows enough. I'm wondering."

"I think he does. I think they're completely right, your colleagues. And I agree with you: they're damn reliable. I can't believe I missed them when I was gathering people for the paedophile unit. They're probably right that the planning took place in Kumla. Three intelligent fascists planning a clever attack: Petrovic, Lindberg, Bergwall. But there was another person to turn to: Kullberg. I don't think they left him out. The rest were foot soldiers, cannon fodder: Carlstedt, Andersson, Sjöqvist. But not Kullberg. He knows."

"Maybe. What do you think Niklas Lindberg is doing now?"

"The handover will take place soon. He's buying the explosive from the right-wing organisation. But he's still pissed off that the ten million got lost. That would've been an unforgettable bang. It'll be pretty good for a million too, don't get me wrong, but I'm damn sure he wants the ten million."

"You mean he's . . .?"

"Yes. I think he's going to go after Rajko Nedic directly."

CHAPTER
FORTY-FOUR

He is light, she is dark, and they are sitting in the sunshine, limbs entwined, on the steps of Högalid church. They aren't alone. Several young couples are sitting there, limbs entwined, enjoying the sunshine. They all look alike.

It's like a slice of nature thrown into the middle of the city. Greenery in all directions, but only for a short distance. Then the asphalt reappears. The concrete jungle.

They don't know whether it's an oasis or a mirage. They'll find out very soon.

Against the brilliant-blue sky above the waters of Riddar fjärden, small slivers of cloud dance. Constantly changing, they take on new, equally fleeting shapes.

A dance of metamorphosis.

He looks down at his four-year-old size 7 Reebok shoes; they're starting to feel mouldy. They've gone too far. She looks down at her new white sandals, size 7, and then up again, gazing at him until his eyes reach hers. Their mouths meet in a kiss. The light touch of tongues. The spark through their bodies.

They can't stop touching one another. They won't ever be alone again. Whatever happens now, they won't ever be alone again. They're planning to die together, to let "th' incroaching rinds their closing lips invade".

But they will be old by then.

They will follow the gods up to the top of the mountain.

They stand up and wander through the greenery of Högalids parken. On the church steps, a copy of *Expressen* has been left behind, from 24 June. The headline, ringed in felt pen shouts: THE SISTERS THAT VANISHED INTO THIN AIR.

But he pushes Ovid's *Metamorphoses* into his pocket. The paperback edition.

A large tree looms over them. It places a protective arm around their shoulders. It's still there as they come out onto Hornbruksgatan, turn down the short stretch of Lignagatan and out onto Hornsgatan. There they turn to the right, down towards Hornstull.

They stop outside the bank.

She casts a quick, furtive, shy glance over the street. Four floors up in the building opposite. She assumes that the black figure she catches sight of through the window is in her head.

They go into the bank.

The great man stands looking out of the window. It's unbearably warm. A shimmering green bluebottle has developed a liking for his sweat, and nosedives repeatedly towards his forehead. He doesn't bother swatting it away. Considerably bigger flies are nosediving towards his forehead. From within.

They can't be swatted away.

Leaks. Only a few weeks ago, the word had been unknown. It hadn't been in Rajko Nedic's Swedish vocabulary. Now it was popping up time after time after time.

First that difficult policeman Ludvig Johnsson, who had found the thing which absolutely couldn't be found. He would pay anything to deal with that problem. He knew all too well what happened to paedophiles in prison. Then came Risto Petrovic's betrayal. Crown witness. How would he deal with that? Maybe the damage could be limited. His workers didn't know enough to sink him, especially not those imported directly from the Balkans. Ljubomir's betrayal was worse. Though he didn't know a great deal about the business, either. Lordan was meant to shoulder that burden. But then he died. That was *his* only betrayal. And then those phones missing from the restaurant. He knew instinctively that it was no normal robbery.

It was a leak, too. Somehow.

And then he sees — he can't comprehend what it is he's seeing, the connections between his brain cells can't stretch to it. He sees his daughter. He sees Sonja outside the bank, together with a young man. It doesn't fit. It's an impossible equation. He's standing in the room with the soundproof walls, understanding nothing. He's utterly cold.

Two mobile phones stolen from the Thanatos restaurant.

He doesn't have time to react. He doesn't have time to give the sign to his men. Doesn't have time to give

438

them the order to storm the bank. The door flies open. A volley of silenced bullets spreads death through the flat. It's silent as they fall. Three of five. He looks at his body. No holes. No sneaky, belated gunshot wounds; the kind you notice only when it's too late.

His two surviving men raise their hands to the ceiling. Their expressionless faces haven't changed much. When he sees that, he understands what war damage is.

He can't see the man's face. It is covered by a golden balaclava. Smoke is rising from the sub-machine gun's silencer. He speaks crystal-clear English with a Swedish lilt.

"I know about those devices in your sleeves. Please don't use them. Then you'll live. Take the hidden pistols out. Carefully."

The two of them do as they're told. The man turns to Rajko Nedic. It's the first time in his life he's had a weapon pointed at him.

"Stay calm, Mr Nedic," the man says in well-mannered Swedish. A dialect, the great man thinks in confusion. Bohuslän or Västergötland. Uddevalla, Trollhättan.

There's a body sitting on the sofa. As though he had fallen asleep at his post — unthinkable. The others are lying on the floor. It's unbelievable. It can't have happened. He looks over his shoulder, out through the window. Sonja and the boy are going into the bank. He smiles. Awry. Suddenly, it's all so clear.

"Sit," the man says, pointing to the sofa. The two of them sit down beside the body, handing their pistols over to the man. He quickly and routinely wraps them in strong tape. The two men look like silver mummies.

Rajko Nedic can feel the time passing. He counts how much each second is costing. Sonja will still be waiting to get into the safe-deposit box. There's still time. Ten million kronor.

Ten million or a daughter.

The man turns to him. His eyes are icy blue behind the gold.

"How did you find us?" asks Rajko Nedic. He has to buy some time. He has to think while he talks; think about something else.

The man laughs. His gaze is steady.

"I followed you from Danderyd," he says with disgust, adding, more distinctly: "I need that ten million."

"So do I," says Rajko Nedic. "I can't get at it myself. But I don't understand — didn't you get hold of the key?"

"There's a lot you don't understand. Where's the money? In which bank? And what's the number of the box?"

The great man doesn't feel so great. He can imagine the scenario before him, can imagine him saying to the man: "The bank opposite. There are a boy and girl in there taking the money out *right now*." And he can imagine the man running over. The great man freeing his two men. They would follow after him. A firefight would break out in the bank. His war-damaged heroes would shoot the man. Rajko Nedic would get his ten million.

440

Then he would have to give up his daughter.

Then he would have to kill his daughter for a second time.

And in that moment, the screams break free from the walls. The clear, piercing screams which had been stored in the porous walls, clad with gold-coloured foam. They screech right into Rajko Nedic's ears, bursting his eardrums.

He says: "You'll never find out."

And for the first time in his life, the great man feels great.

The man looks over his shoulder. Out through the window. He doesn't like that gaze. He might catch sight of Sonja when she comes out of the bank. Maybe he'll recognise her.

But all the man sees is a fleeting glimpse of eight unmistakable figures, led by a young, short-haired woman. They're creeping along Hornsgatan, nearing the door.

The man sighs, binds Rajko Nedic's hands behind him using the silver tape, and takes a small metal box from his pocket. He pushes it into Nedic's mouth and tapes his jaws shut. He winds the tape around his jaws like a corpse. The great man can feel the little box on his tongue. It tastes of steel. He can't spit it out.

"An old promise," says the golden one, disappearing.

Sara Svenhagen is following her men. In the stairwell, they meet a well-built man with cropped hair and clear blue eyes. He nods to them. As though to colleagues, she thinks to herself. They wave him past and continue up the stairs.

On the fourth floor, they take out their service weapons. They find the door marked Ahlström. They gather around it.

Then they see that it has been kicked open. It isn't closed. It only looks like it's closed.

They press up against the wall. Pistols raised. Close to their bodies. They kick the door open.

They see blood. Lots of blood. Three bodies. And two silver mummies on a sofa.

And a man on his knees by the window. Sara recognises Rajko Nedic. As soon as the room has been secured, she goes over to him. He's deathly pale behind the silver tape. He's nodding his head strangely. A gesture. She reaches for the tape. He shakes his head frantically and continues to make the nodding gesture.

Then she understands.

The gesture is telling her: *get out, for Christ's sake.*

She reacts like lightning. Gets her men out into the stairwell.

Once they've gone, the great man feels great for the second time in his life. Then his head explodes.

Sara Svenhagen hears the blast from out in the stairwell. She both understands and doesn't understand it. They return. Cautiously.

Rajko Nedic is lying by the window. The silver tape has split over his mouth. Blood is trickling out. Sara forgets all her caution. She runs over and unwinds the tape.

His tongue falls out. A bloody lump.

442

Someone has blown the tongue out of Rajko Nedic's mouth.

She stands up. Takes several staggering steps over to the window. She has to get some fresh air. It doesn't work; she can't open the window. There isn't any fresh air to get.

A shimmering green bluebottle nosedives towards her forehead.

She throws up on the windowpane in the flat with the soundproofed walls.

They leave the bank, each clasping the other's hand. Hard, hard. A full-to-bursting bag dangles between them.

She casts a quick, furtive, shy glance over the street. Four floors up in the building opposite. She sees vomit running down the window.

She smiles. It's an appropriate farewell.

CHAPTER
FORTY-FIVE

Sara Svenhagen was pale and worn out. She was sitting at the front, on Hultin's desk, swinging her legs. He thought it was charming. But then, he was also an old chauvinist.

What she had just told them wasn't quite as charming. But it was illuminating. Horribly illuminating.

Aside from Gunnar Nyberg and Kerstin Holm, everyone was there. The World Police and Fire Games were getting off to a false start with a few events. At 3p.m. the following day, the opening ceremony would take place. Even if there wouldn't be as many competitors as planned, and even if the organisers had mismanaged it to the point of being put on trial, Stockholm Stadium would be full of policemen and women from all corners of the earth.

"So you met Niklas Lindberg on the stairs on the way up?" asked Arto Söderstedt.

"Yeah," said Sara Svenhagen. "Though we didn't know that there *was* a Niklas Lindberg. The walls between us have been much too high."

She cast a glance at Jorge Chavez. He was pale and worn out, but met her eyes. He looked deeply sorry.

"Has Rajko Nedic said anything?" asked Viggo Norlander.

Sara Svenhagen smiled grimly. It wasn't a smile, it just looked like one.

"No," she said. "He can't talk. He'll never be able to talk again."

"But he's alive?"

"Yes. He's in Söder hospital. They're trying to patch up his mouth, but his tongue couldn't be saved."

"A precisely calculated charge," said Hjelm. "Has Daddy said anything about the explosive?"

She gave him a dark look.

"Yes, Daddy said that it's the same explosive. And Rajko Nedic is under arrest for sexual assault of children, as well as distribution of child pornography. I'm sure you can add to the charges eventually."

"The thing with Gillis Döös and Max Grahn is interesting," said Söderstedt. "Former Security Service men, about to crack an earlier investigation for us, they were also supplying Nedic with information on the investigation?"

"They call themselves 'security consultants'. But they don't seem to have got hold of much."

"Overpaid consultants are a sign of our times," Söderstedt concluded.

"And the 'policeman' is Ludvig Johnsson," said Hultin. "He was blackmailing Nedic because he'd found out he was a paedophile. Now he's on holiday. And absolutely no one has any idea where?"

"No, someone does," said Sara Svenhagen. "He's there now."

"Gunnar, my Gunnar," Hultin nodded woefully. "Do you think he's in any danger? Do you think Johnsson might decide to bump Nyberg off to get away?"

"No," Sara said definitively. "No, there's no chance."

"Still, Gunnar Nyberg has cut himself off from the A-Unit again. This time he's hardly got the law on his side."

"Would you have done anything differently?" asked Sara, looking Hultin in the eye.

"Hardly," he said, gravely. "That's why I'm not planning on taking any action against him. For the moment. We'll see how it pans out, I suppose."

"I think they're busy working on a parallel investigation," said Hjelm. "Gunnar's pig-headedly set about getting Ludvig to tidy up after himself. And when Gunnar sets about doing something like that, he doesn't give up. Ever."

"That seems likely," said Hultin. "Anyway, these are all parentheses for the moment. We've got to focus on saving people's lives at the World Police and Fire Games now. We've got just over a day. We've got to start asking ourselves whether we should cancel the ceremony pretty soon. Bloody good advert for Stockholm and for the supremely competent Swedish police. We'll be the laughing stock of the world. We should try to avoid that. Can you summarise your interrogation, Paul?"

"Risto Petrovic is behind the whole mess. He's got links high up among the right-wing extremists. They're going to be supplying Niklas Lindberg with serious amounts of the liquid explosive sometime soon. Around

446

a million kronor's worth. It'll be a hell of a bang. Not a ten million-krona bang, that's true, but big enough. Stockholm Stadium'll probably become part of the townscape of the past.

"Worst-case scenario? He could kill thousands of people, mainly police. So how can we get to Lindberg? Four ways: through Kullberg, through Petrovic, through other acquaintances, through the right-wing umbrella organisation. The fourth is impossible in principle, we're talking about the most shadowy organisation imaginable, people who're probably at the top of societies all over the world, who want to see ethnic cleansing on a large scale. The second is difficult. It would only be possible if we could find a weak link in Petrovic, something which would get him to think like a person and not like a severely war-damaged sociopath. The first is probably our best bet. We loosened Agne up yesterday, we got the World Police and Fire Games out of him without him really knowing it. I think we can still get more out of him. The third is difficult, but we might have time to poke around in Lindberg's circle of acquaintances and find . . . some girlfriend or boyfriend or someone else he trusts."

Hultin looked cool. Cool under fire.

"You're hardly alone now," he said. "Mörner's released the entire thing to the press. Since he doesn't get more than about one per cent of any of this, he didn't give them much. But what he did give them were the four named incidents: 'the Kumla Bombing', one dead; 'the Sickla Slaughter', five dead, one injured; 'the Skövde Shooting', two dead, two injured; 'the

447

Hornstull Hit', three dead, one injured. It's starting to resemble a battlefield. We're up to eleven dead now and since we know that papers like *Svenska Dagbladet* are fond of counting bodies, we should try to pause.

"We've been lying low with Nedic, with the 'policeman', with Orpheus and Eurydice, and with the threat against the Police Games. The press is trying its best to put the pieces together, and the result is slowly becoming quite amusing, if you have that kind of gallows humour. Which we don't. Anyway, Niklas Lindberg's name and face are now on every front page in Sweden. That should limit his room for manoeuvre a bit. You've got access to every policeman or woman in the force. Put a baton in the hand of the National Commissioner and he'll wave it. The power's in your hands."

"Or maybe in yours," said Söderstedt.

Hultin ignored him completely.

"The power's in your hands," he repeated. "Use it well. The following work schedule applies. Paul and Jorge will work on the interrogation again. Press all the buttons you can find. Hit below the belt. Arto and Viggo, you'll take care of the international material on Petrovic. Look for possible areas for blackmail: parents, siblings, anything."

Hultin opened his mouth to continue. There was nothing left to say. There was no one left.

Though not quite.

"I can help with Lindberg's acquaintances," said Sara Svenhagen. "If we're tearing down the walls."

Another glance at Jorge.

"OK," said Hultin neutrally. "You and I will work on his acquaintances. We must be able to find something."

Jorge stood up. He looked profoundly serious. The weight of the seriousness of the moment.

"This thing with tearing down walls," he said, as though beginning a speech. "If Sara and I hadn't built those walls between us, the case could've been solved more quickly. We would've had the 'policeman' more quickly, we would've had Nedic more quickly and, not least, Sara would've been able to catch Lindberg in the stairwell at Hornsgatan 131. In a way, I'm glad she didn't. He wouldn't have given himself up willingly. And then my future wife would've been in mortal danger."

They looked at one another. A vacuum grew in the Supreme Command Centre. Time, working overtime, took a break. Burdens were lifted from shoulders. But only for a moment.

During that moment, Jorge Chavez said: "No more walls, Sara. Never again. I'm asking you in front of the people I'm closest to: will you marry me?"

Sara Svenhagen smiled faintly. "If we get Niklas Lindberg," she said.

They met in a kiss on Hultin's desk.

He didn't mind.

CHAPTER
FORTY-SIX

Night. A deserted garage somewhere in Stockholm. A waiting car. A shadow slipping into it.

A faint light fell onto the driver of the car. Stone-faced. He didn't turn round. Still, he saw.

"You can take that off," he said in English.

Niklas Lindberg took his gold-coloured balaclava off. He was holding a carrier bag in his hand.

"Is that the money?" the man asked with a certain disgust. "How could you lose millions? That's not a good sign."

"Sorry," said Lindberg. "There's nine hundred and twenty-six thousand, seven hundred and seventy kronor."

The man took the bag, weighing it in his hand.

"Hmmm," he said. "You'll have to do a better job than this in future. Otherwise we've got no use for you. And Petrovic is stuck."

"Stuck?"

"The police are interrogating him flat out. Detective Inspectors Hjelm and Chavez. Do you know them?"

"Wog? No."

"They've uncovered your entire plan. It doesn't look good. If they find a link to us, we won't be happy."

"Risto'll keep his mouth shut. There's nothing to worry about."

"What about Kullberg?"

"Him too. It's OK."

The man leaned his head back slightly. Six months seemed to pass before he said: "It's OK? You're leaving tracks behind you and saying it's OK? I'm telling you: it's *not* OK. Do you understand?"

"They won't talk, I promise. Isn't that enough?"

"Let's change the subject. Were you happy with the test samples?"

"Very. Has the explosive been put in place?"

"It's where it should be. The flag is in place."

"The flag? We talked about a corner post, didn't we?"

"Change of plan. The conditions are different now. The police are on high alert. We couldn't risk anything with the sniffer dogs. All our tests have shown that dogs don't react to the substance, but we've got to be one hundred per cent sure."

"Which flag?"

The man with the stony face laughed. Briefly. It passed. He said: "The substance is in the flag that's going to be carried in with the procession. *The Swedish flag*. It seemed appropriate, somehow."

"So we'll really be flying the flag, then," said Niklas Lindberg, laughing.

The man gave him an icy look, and he fell silent.

The man handed him an envelope. He opened it and took out a key, a scrap of paper and a flat little black box with a red button on it. It looked like a miniature calculator.

"The key for the door," said the man. "On the paper, you've got the new entrance code; they changed it yesterday. You know what to do with the detonator. Why did you blow Nedic's tongue out?"

"An old promise," said Niklas Lindberg, thrusting the three items into his pocket and opening the car door.

The man placed a hand on his arm.

"One more thing," he said. "There's a chance they'll cancel the opening ceremony. If that happens, we'll never see one another again. And I mean *never*. Is that clear?"

"That's fine," said Niklas Lindberg with emphasis. "I'm not planning on letting you down. I've been an admirer of yours since Palme, February '86."

"You can't have been very old then," said the man, releasing his grip.

Lindberg transformed into a shadow, becoming one with the darkness.

For a brief moment, the man with the stony face allowed himself to think about February 1986. It was worthy of a certain admiration. They had managed to change a country. An invisible coup.

A bomb had detonated under the Swedish flag.

It was time to do it again.

Enough nostalgia. The man with the stony face started the car and drove away.

Far away.

CHAPTER
FORTY-SEVEN

"It's not going to be cancelled," said Gunnar Nyberg, leaning back.

They were sitting under the glow of paraffin lamps and candles in the old nineteenth-century Uppland cottage. In front of them were the modern laptop computers, connected to the Internet and the central police computer via mobile phones.

"How do you know that?" asked Ludvig Johnsson, stroking his bald head.

"Internal message," said Nyberg, pointing at the screen. "The National Police Commissioner, the head of CID, the Minister for Justice, the Prime Minister, the head of the Secret Service and Mörner were in meetings late into the night. It can't happen. The loss of prestige would be too big. And there's international pressure. Police forces from across the world would be a laughing stock. If we can't even protect ourselves, how are we supposed to be able to protect others? There's a risk it'd be a deathblow to the police force as we know it."

"What kind of death blow will it be when it goes off, then?"

"Mmm . . . The reasoning goes like this: it *can't* go off. It's that simple, it *can't* go off. An argument rooted in practical reasoning."

Ludvig Johnsson sat motionless. He closed his eyes. He didn't know if he could really be held responsible for this, too. He didn't care. It was all his fault, he knew that, and now things were set to escalate dramatically.

He came to a decision.

"Another beer?" he asked, getting to his feet. His running clothes were plastered to his skin.

"Why not?" said Nyberg. "We're not getting anywhere. We're stuck. Hell, I thought we'd find an opening somewhere, but it's not working. Damn it, it's not working. Fuck."

Johnsson came back, placing a can of beer in front of him. It was open. Johnsson opened his with a hiss and took a couple of big gulps. Nyberg emptied half of his in one go.

"For God's sake, Ludvig," he said. "Lindberg broke Nedic. Nedic had his tongue blown out. Isn't there a clue in that, somewhere?"

Ludvig Johnsson stood motionless. He looked out into nothingness, shaking his head slowly.

"There's no solution," he said.

"What time is it?" asked Nyberg.

Johnsson took another gulp and looked at his watch.

"Almost six. Six in the morning, Saturday the seventeenth of July. Nine hours left until the opening."

Ludvig Johnsson was no longer motionless. Slowly but surely, he started to spin. Eventually, he was spinning through the room. And the room began to fold up like a book.

Nyberg slumped forward over the ill-placed plastic table. He was face down, and the room continued to fold in on itself, time and time again, until only a tiny square was left in the middle of all the blackness.

"I'm sorry, Gunnar," said Ludvig Johnsson's voice from somewhere far away. "I have to clean up on my own now. There's no other way."

And just like that, the little square disappeared.

Though Agne 'Bullet' Kullberg looked worn out, his gaze was crystal clear. He wouldn't let himself be duped a second time.

He had seen through their tricks now, and he had one single strategy: to keep his mouth shut. To not open his mouth even once.

It had worked for almost a day. It was eleven o'clock, and Paul Hjelm could feel the hopelessness rising.

There were four hours left until the opening of the World Police and Fire Games in Stockholm Stadium.

The past twenty-four hours had been strange. No one had slept. Söderstedt and Norlander had managed to find Petrovic's parents. They lived in Germany, and through them, they managed to find a brother in trouble with the law. They put together a fake deportation order to Serbia for the brother, and Hjelm and Chavez took it to Petrovic in Tumba. Lars Viksjö looked as though he had been sleeping in his clothes for the past six months.

"We've proved that your brother's Serbian and should be sent back to Belgrade," said Hjelm.

Petrovic stared at them, his eyes flitting from Hjelm to Chavez, Chavez to Hjelm.

Then he laughed. "My brother's an idiot," he said.

And so another attempt went down the drain. Petrovic didn't say another word. He was extremely steadfast. They went back to prison and the even more silent Bullet. It was starting to feel uncomfortable.

Sara Svenhagen sent a message from Trollhättan, saying that she had coaxed three previously unknown Stockholm addresses out of Lindberg's parents and ex-wife. Hultin and Norlander were talking to people who didn't understand a thing, who had never heard of Niklas Lindberg, and who were openly unpleasant. These were two men who didn't hesitate to get tough when they needed to, but that didn't get them very far. The unpleasant people really did know nothing.

Söderstedt came up with a vague new idea for Petrovic. He found a web page for an international fascist organisation which seemed unexpectedly official. What if they threatened to say that Petrovic had squealed to the police? Hjelm and Chavez took the threat to Petrovic. He did seem slightly worried. But not enough. They tried everything they could think of, but it didn't help. He remained silent.

Huge numbers of policemen were searching the stadium and the surrounding area. Lindberg wouldn't dare be inside the stadium when the bomb went off. Still, he had to be somewhere with a view of it. This meant going to every building with a view into the stadium in Östermalm. There were a few of them, and Operation Door Knocking was in full swing. So far, they had been given a few tips, but nothing hot. People didn't seem to like their neighbours.

The night passed. Hjelm and Chavez pressed Bullet again and again. It was hopeless. He wouldn't talk.

They began to seriously discuss more illegal methods. Torture was on the table for a while. It was a deeply uncomfortable moment, although they didn't realise this until afterwards. As though democracy had suddenly gone up in smoke. As though the Swedish flag had suddenly gone up with a bang.

Eventually, it was eleven o'clock. They were staring at one another. Bullet on the one side, Hjelm and Chavez on the other.

Deadlock.

"Four hours left," Hjelm said stubbornly. "If an attack on Stockholm Stadium takes place, you'll never see daylight again, other than through bars. It'll be a long training stretch."

Bullet peered at them.

"Are you ready to throw your whole life away for this stupid attack?" Chavez asked, equally stubbornly. "Is it really worth it, just to kill a few firemen from Venezuela?"

Bullet stared straight ahead.

"Fucking hell!" Chavez shouted, storming noisily out of Bullet's cell.

Hjelm remained. His mobile was ringing.

"One last chance," Hultin said in his ear. "One of those unpleasant people got in touch. She was talking about a possible girlfriend, Lindberg's, in Gnesta. Are you two coming?"

"Yes," said Hjelm without hesitation.

He called for the guard and made sure that the door was locked on Agne 'Bullet' Kullberg. The guard was a faithful old servant, shuffling off back to his desk out at the entrance to the station's cells. He watched Hjelm disappear. The whole night, he thought to himself, shaking his head. Don't you have a life, boys? Don't you have families? Friends? Look at me, I work nine to five and I'm doing fine. What's the use of wearing yourselves out like this? Does it make you happier?

After a few minutes, a man walked up to his desk, held up his police ID and said: "Agne Kullberg, please."

The guard shook his head and said: "You boys never give up, do you? Sign here, Detective Superintendent."

He followed the man along the corridors, letting him into Agne Kullberg's cell. A sought-after man.

The guard's eyes followed the man for a few seconds. He had just noticed the smell of old, ingrained sweat. Couldn't he at least have taken a shower first? And changed out of those old running clothes?

The guard shook his head and returned to the desk where he stood every weekday, nine to five. He had done what was expected of him.

Ludvig Johnsson moved towards Bullet and showed him his ID. Without a word, he stepped closer and pushed a needle into his arm.

458

Gunnar Nyberg came slowly back to life. A tiny square appeared somewhere and started to unfold, bit by bit, until his entire field of vision had returned. Though it didn't look the same. His head throbbed violently, and when he tried to get to his feet, all 146 kilos slumped back into the plastic chair with a thud.

The computers had run out of power, their screens jet black. He tried the first of the mobile phones. It had run out, too. There was a hint of life in the second.

As he keyed in Hultin's number, he tried to make sense of what had happened. He managed to raise his arm, looking at his watch. Christ, he thought. Twenty-five to four. It was all over.

Rather than growing desperate, he tried to think. There was one thing that Ludvig Johnsson had stressed during their attempt at a joint investigation, and one thing only. That Bullet Kullberg was the weak link.

"Hultin," said a voice in his ear.

"Where are you?" asked Nyberg, not recognising his own voice. It was a feeling he knew well.

"Gunnar? Where are *you*?"

"Grillby. But to hell with that. This is important."

"We're at the station. We just got back. We've been in Gnesta, talking to Lindberg's girlfriend. They split up six months ago, and had only ever seen one another in Kumla. Didn't give anything new."

"Ludvig's gone after Bullet. Check."

"Oh Jesus," said Hultin. "Are you coming?"

"As fast as I can," said Nyberg, hanging up.

He tried to get to his feet once again. It went better this time. Though God only knew if he could drive.

The only thing he knew was that he would never see Ludvig Johnsson again.

That was absolutely certain.

Sorrow coursed through him like hot lava.

Hultin, Hjelm and Chavez arrived at the desk by the cells in the police station in record time. The guard looked tired. Not again. Get a life, guys. Yes, Detective Superintendent Ludvig Johnsson had been there. In sweaty jogging clothes. Yes, he'd been in with Kullberg for almost an hour. No, no one had been there since.

They ran down the cell-lined corridor. The guard ran alongside them. It was a long time since his legs had done any running.

He let them in.

Bullet Kullberg was bound to the chair with four leather belts. His face was swollen and bruised, his nails sticking out at unnatural angles from his fingers. His trousers were around his ankles, his genitals black and blue. A strip of silver tape had been stuck over his mouth.

His eyes were closed.

Hultin tore the tape from his mouth. Bullet woke. He looked at them, alarmed.

"Don't kill me," he said faintly.

Hjelm looked into his eyes. His gaze had changed.

"He's been drugged," he said.

"Christ," said Chavez.

"Ludvig seems to have taken it personally," said Hultin. "OK, hello. Agne. We're not going to kill you. Take it easy. Just tell us what you told Johnsson. Then we'll save Lindberg."

"You were right," said Bullet, looking strangely at Hjelm and Chavez. "I was a nerd at school. Shitty Agne. I went by the name Shitty Agne the whole time I was at school. Always Shitty Agne. *My name isn't Agne, you bastards.*"

"What did you tell Ludvig Johnsson?" asked Hjelm. "Come on, Bullet."

"I said that there'd never been any parade of girls looking at my hairless dick. Never. But I remember when they tied my hands behind my back with a towel and hit my dick until it was blue. Look how blue it is."

"That was Ludvig Johnsson who did that, Bullet," said Chavez. "No one's calling you Agne any more."

"No," Bullet panted. "No. My name's Bullet. I'm the toughest guy you'll ever meet."

"Bullet!" Hjelm shouted. "Focus! Where's Nicke?"

"Valhallavägen 88, obviously. What do you think, you arseholes? That's it."

They left. Running through the police station.

"Time?" asked Hultin.

"Five past," said Chavez.

"The National Task Force?" asked Hjelm. "Where are they?"

"The stadium," said Hultin, keying in a number. "Hello? Task Force? We've got an address. Valhallavägen 88. Top floor, probably. It's vital that he doesn't get a chance to press the detonator. Everything else is irrelevant."

"Let's go," said Hjelm.

He was sitting on the balcony. In his hand lay the miniature calculator, one single red button. He ran his thumb gently down one side of it. All power gathered in a single point. That was how it should be. It was a simplification. People couldn't cope with democracy. The democratic era had been the bloodiest in the history of mankind. That spoke for itself. A simple, pure way of life. That was all he wanted. But it meant breaking a few eggs.

He looked down towards Stockholm Stadium. A perfect view. They really did have resources. He was impressed, and that didn't happen too often. Not since February '86.

The ceremony began. It was a fine summer's day, but rain clouds loomed in the distance. The weather would soon change.

It really would.

First the music — it was strangely distorted when it reached him. Then the procession. Presumably Sweden would be leading the other countries. The flag would explode. This had been in the works for so long. The flag would be torn to shreds. The proudest thing they had.

He felt a sharp pain in his hand. Like cramp. When he looked down, a wasp was hanging from his thumb. He put the detonator down on the table and squashed

462

the wasp with his middle finger. The pain spread through his hand.

Ironic, he thought, hearing the click.

The click of a gun being taken off safety.

He turned, looking back towards the flat. In the doorway stood a bald man dressed in running clothes. He was pointing a gun at him.

"I've been standing here for fifteen minutes, waiting for you to put that thing down," said Ludvig Johnsson.

"A wasp stung me," said Niklas Lindberg.

"The police force, saved by a wasp. So ironic."

"Isn't it?"

"Move towards it and I'll shoot. Come this way, slowly."

Niklas Lindberg was motionless. His pistol was jammed into the top of his trousers. He wouldn't have time to grab it. But the detonator? There would have to be a . . . victim. Posthumous recognition.

He tried. His hand moved quickly.

Ludvig Johnsson emptied the magazine into him. His hand reached the edge of the table but no further. It sank downwards.

Johnsson stood still, breathing heavily.

Hanna, Micke, Stefan — my gift to you.

He went out onto the balcony and carefully, carefully took hold of the little black device with the red button.

Just then, the door burst open. The National Task Force stormed in.

They saw the man on the balcony. In a flash, they saw the detonator in his hand. And they shot him.

They shot so many bullets into him that it would never be possible to count them. His body went limp, and they kept shooting. His body was thrown backwards towards the edge of the balcony, and they kept shooting. They kept shooting even as it floated down through the Stockholm air like a mediocre skydiver, hitting the pavement of Valhallavägen with a dull, inhuman thud.

On the table next to the dead Niklas Lindberg, the detonator lay.

It had fallen red side up.

Down in Stockholm Stadium, the opening ceremony was in full swing.

CHAPTER
FORTY-EIGHT

Gunnar Nyberg sang. He sang as though his life was at stake. He was standing at the edge of the choir in the beautiful Kungsholmen church, putting every ounce of his being into it. His bass tone risked overpowering the rest of the choir.

"The Time of Blossoming Now Arrives".

Simple as that.

At Ludvig Johnsson's funeral, he had sung solo. A short Verdi aria. One of many songs at the hero's funeral. Detective Superintendent Ragnar Hellberg had given a magnificent speech, and not a single irregularity was mentioned. On the contrary, the police corps had finally found its long-sought-after hero. The story was doctored to suit the tabloids, in firm control of the country's dramaturgy. Johnsson had tracked down Lindberg himself, rendered him harmless and been shot by him in the process. He had died a hero's death.

A hero who had tortured a suspect.

Two days after his death, the full material on Rajko Nedic's crimes arrived from Ludvig's childhood friend in Säffle.

As he sang, Nyberg imagined for a moment that he had caught sight of a family at the very back of the room. Two small boys, a mother and a father. The father had his arms around his family, laughing happily. At everything and at nothing.

On the other hand, he saw a lot while he sang.

As soon as this was all over, he would finally go on holiday. He would travel to Östhammar and descend upon his son's family. For a long, long while.

In the extensive material from the investigation, there were no irregularities when it came to Gunnar Nyberg.

He sang for his life, glancing over to the other side of the large police choir. Kerstin Holm was there, a bandage wrapped around her head. She smiled at him as she sang. He smiled back.

Kerstin Holm was the choir's second alto. She united the other voices even though what she was singing didn't remotely resemble "The Time of Blossoming Now Arrives".

She was singing for her life. Because several inexplicable millimetres had separated her from death. She sang and gave thanks, but she didn't know who to thank. Not even here, in this room, did she know for sure who to thank. Or why.

She thought of Orpheus and Eurydice. She and Paul had visited Per Karlsson's flat in Aspudden. No one had been there for quite some time. A layer of dust had started to gather on Ovid's *Metamorphoses*, which lay open on the table, and in the disorder, they had found an old yearbook from the school in Danderyd. After a few moments of searching, they found Per Karlsson's class photo. The seventh grade. He was small and pale, almost a head shorter than the second shortest in the

466

class. He looked *morose*. And in the background, there was a tall, dark girl. She looked *tough*. Her name was Sonja Nedic.

Eurydice had checked into the hotel in Skövde under the name Sonja Karlsson. Afterwards, she became Baucis.

Rajko Nedic's daughter must have taken the two mobile phones from her father's restaurant in Stockholm; she must have found out, somehow, that her father was planning to make a large financial transaction and that the meeting place would be decided in Kvarnen on the evening of 23 June. So she sent her beloved Per Karlsson, the Orpheus who had brought her back from the underworld, the Philemon with whom she would grow old and would die alongside, and he found out that the meeting would take place in the Sickla industrial estate. The pair made their way there, and if they had tried to steal from her father's ferocious gang of war criminals, then they would most likely have been slaughtered. But that didn't happen. Instead, they were more or less handed the briefcase — by a gang of Nazi robbers, paradoxically enough. They took it and fled. But there was no money inside, only a key. Sonja tried to think of possible safe-deposit boxes. She had no idea, but she knew where her father sold his drugs. They split up, each looking in a different place. Two meandering routes across the map of Sweden.

Paul and Kerstin wandered on through Per Karlsson's little flat. Strange wooden sculptures stood everywhere, shapes of all kinds, and a box room had been turned into a workshop. The floor was covered in iron filings, and in a rubbish bin there was a piece of sheet iron. From this, a key had been punched. A comparison with the safe-deposit-box key revealed identical teeth and notches.

And then, just over a week after the World Police and Fire Games began, a charity supporting the rights of children announced that a large sum of money had been deposited anonymously into their account. Five million kronor, to be precise. The money had been paid in from Paris.

Baucis and Philemon had found their safe-deposit box.

Kerstin Holm sang, thinking that for the first time in her life, justice had been done.

She looked down to Jan-Olov Hultin, sitting with his wife in the front row, in the middle of the rowdy Chavez family. Pappa Chavez, Carlos, glanced suspiciously from time to time at the man with the enormous nose and owl-like glasses. Hadn't someone very similar split his eyebrow during a veterans' football match once?

Hultin was longing for his lawn. He was longing, like Sisyphus, to push his manual lawnmower up and down the slope, avoiding all weeds in accordance with the sadly neglected principle of "Live and let live".

Then he would bathe in Ravalen, make a comeback in the Stockholm Police veterans' football team, travel to Greece, and never, ever shoot another person. Enough was enough.

Still, he wouldn't retire just yet.

And it was harder than ever to tell weeds from grass.

468

He glanced over the aisle to Viggo Norlander. He was sitting, dressed in a much-too-tight dress coat, next to Astrid. Little Charlotte, with her inward-backward-sloping mug, was hanging over his shoulder. From her mouth a chalk-white dribble of vomit ran like bird shit onto the shoulder of his jacket. Then she started to scream. Norlander patted her gently on the back, and didn't say "shut up" even once.

Norlander looked over the aisle towards a curious gathering of white heads. He had never seen the entire Söderstedt family gathered in one place before. Arto Söderstedt sat, hair slicked back like someone from the 1930s, following Norlander's eyes as they moved, step by step, over five white-haired children's heads, over a white-haired mother's head, and on to the slicked-back white hair of the father's. He saw these steps, laughed to himself, and pointed at his shoulder. Norlander prodded the mess with his finger and shook his head.

Söderstedt was thinking about the bank loan he had been forced to take out to pay for their brand-new family car, a Toyota Picnic. He knew that he should be thinking about lots of other things, but he didn't have the energy. Not yet. He thought about how fun it would be, driving again. It was finally time for a holiday — the family had a car, but no money to go anywhere. He thought that he was nearing a fundamental societal paradox. But he didn't have the energy to work it out. Not yet.

Not as the police choir's "The Time of Blossoming Now Arrives" died out in a distinctive, drawn-out bass tone which was replaced by the familiar opening notes of a wedding march.

The bridal couple passed slowly down the aisle. He was dark, she was light, and there were no walls between them.

Sara Svenhagen looked at her father as she walked down the aisle. Chief Forensic Technician Brynolf Svenhagen, cut from a traditional cloth, was already crying loudly. It's a bit premature, Sara thought to herself. Then she thought about the distorted images of loneliness, about how she had seen far too much for her age, and about the nightmares which had slowly begun to evaporate. The enormous stomach glowed on, undisturbed. She thought of Ludvig Johnsson, about the death of fathers, and about the way that their own steps ploughed a path which could never be followed. She thought about the virtual world, about the weightlessness of cybersphere compared to heavy reality. She thought about the connection between Eros and Thanatos, between love and death; she thought about the strange justice of fate, and about Rajko Nedic's tongue. And she thought about Jorge Chavez, about how unpredictable love is, about all of the prerequisites which make it possible, and she looked into his eyes and smiled, for the first time, it seemed to her, without any reservations.

Honeymoon in Chile, and then back to the new job. In the A-Unit.

It didn't sound too bad.

Jorge Chavez wasn't thinking about much. He was mostly worrying that the enormous Chavez clan

470

wouldn't be able to toe the line in the cool Protestant church. He thought to himself that the Chileans seemed to be in the majority. The black-headed mass seemed to be bubbling unpredictably. He surprised himself, looking out at the room through Niklas Lindberg's eyes. Why were they such a threat? What was it they were threatening? Nothing more than a warped self-image. A Swede looking in a mirror, seeing something completely different to what everyone else sees. Where everyone else saw a human being, Niklas Lindberg saw a superhuman. How had that metamorphosis taken place? Was it the same thing as when the geeky young Agne became Bullet, "the toughest guy you'll ever meet"? Or was that too simple?

Then it struck him that this was hardly what he should be thinking about as he walked down the aisle to marry his sweetheart. Certain bachelor tendencies still needed to be washed away. On both sides of the ruined walls. The previously mined areas needed to be rebuilt. Though carefully.

He turned round. Simply put, he was happy. Ecstatically happy. That was enough. For now.

He caught sight of Paul Hjelm, sitting alone, almost out of sight at the back of the church. Paul smiled to him, happily, as though you could actually share happiness. Jorge smiled back, believing for a moment that it was possible.

Hjelm had sat at the back of the room because he was alone. He was alone in being alone. Even Mörner up at the front had his missus with him. Or his mistress, at least. But Cilla and the children had stayed in Dalarö. He had spent a few weeks getting close to them again, returning as the Prodigal Son and slowly, slowly becoming part of the family again. They could stay behind if they wanted to — and why not? Why make a big deal of it?

After the Sickla Slaughter and all that had gone with it, it seemed difficult to make a big deal out of anything. Maybe this was maturity, or maybe it was tiredness. The line between the two is often as fine as a hair.

What he knew for certain was that he was a man who had killed.

He thought about mountain tops. Several different mountain tops. The A-Unit's, for example, the now-permanent A-Unit's. They had scaled their mountain, but the official story was partly doctored, partly missing a couple of figures — and with them, the very thing that the entire plot had hinged on. That which had claimed all those lives. Money.

It was always money.

And with that, he arrived at the next peak. Baucis and Philemon's:

The neighbourhood, said he,
Shall justly perish for impiety:
You stand alone exempted; but obey
With speed, and follow where we lead the way:
Leave these accurs'd; and to the mountain's
    height
Ascend; nor once look backward in your flight.

472

He smiled for a moment, and a Shakespeare quote popped into his head. From *A Midsummer Night's Dream*. "We will, fair queen, up to the mountain's top/And mark the musical confusion/Of hounds and echo in conjunction."

He climbed the next peak. An iceberg's. His thoughts turned to Conny Nilsson. The Kvarnen Killer. The tip of an iceberg. And now he had seen a lot of the iceberg.

Was it growing bigger, or about to melt?

Of the Nazi gang, only the humiliated Bullet Kullberg remained. How dangerous were men like that? How many were there? Were they a real threat to democracy? Were they in the process of — more subtly than with the Sickla Slaughter — infiltrating the whole of society? Were their values and judgements slowly gaining ground? Or were they just the modern equivalent of the inhumane undercurrent which had always flowed beneath society?

The only thing Paul Hjelm knew was that he didn't know.

Still, you could also twist the reasoning slightly. If Conny Nilsson hadn't cracked Anders Lundström's head in the Kvarnen bar at 21.42 on 23 June, then the Sickla Slaughter's complicated web would never have been revealed. It was a Gordian knot.

He tried to find a *sens moral* in that fact. It didn't work especially well. But he would keep looking.

The bridal pair had reached the front of the church. The marriage service began.

But Paul Hjelm didn't hear much. He was elsewhere. Trying to understand the *meaning*. He wondered if there was one. After all, it wasn't a work of literature he was living in.

But for a brief moment, he thought that he could make out the invisible pattern.

Maybe the meaning was the metamorphosis. The constant, necessary, lengthy, unavoidable, difficult-to-master transformation. Keeping your chin above the water, whatever the weather.

The marriage service ended. The bridal couple kissed. The police choir — led by a bellowing bass — broke into a paean. And Paul Hjelm thought to himself: a new millennium. He thought: Sweden. He thought: mankind.

And through him — the entire time, non-stop — a voice coursed; a voice which, with its last ounce of strength, said: "Paul, I love you."

His eyes drifted to Kerstin, to her chorister colleague Gunnar, to the bridal couple Sara and Jorge, to Jan-Olov, to Arto, to Viggo.

The song bounced off the church walls, blending with its own echo and becoming a confused tune. And suddenly, for a short, short moment, he imagined that he understood Rilke's *Duino Elegies*.

"For beauty is nothing but the beginning of terror, that we are still able to bear."

And Paul Hjelm sang.

He didn't really know what he was singing, but he sang.

Until the end.

474

CHAPTER
FORTY-NINE

He has lost his language. He sits, waiting, hunched over. He is a wordless little bundle. The footsteps come closer, and he waits wordlessly. He lies on the floor and pulls the sheet towards his face, as though it could protect him. He is lying on the floor because he can no longer sleep in a bed. Beds scare the life out of him. He hears the door swing open in that unmistakable way that should be soundless but isn't, it echoes through him, and he knows that it will echo through him for the rest of his life. However long that will be. The sheet is ripped away, a zip is opened, a crude laugh rings out and he cries and cries, beyond tears, and he cannot say a word, because he has no words for it.

His tongue is gone.

He is in the shadowy depths of Thanatos.

CHAPTER
FIFTY

The red light of dawn spills out over the pale, shining blue sea. The azure blue carving its way up out of the display of colours. A faint heat haze dances on the horizon, and above the treetops at the edge of the forest, a light, fleeting mist floats. Several small rain clouds gather above the little stone house — without blocking out the sun, still hesitating just above the curvature of the Earth.

The curvature of the Earth, so visible.

All weather conditions, all times of day seem to be gathered in one place.

On the porch of the little house, a man sits reading. It is warm but raining slightly. The rain patters gently on the roof of the porch, and when he looks up from his book, steam is rising between the falling raindrops.

A woman comes out of the house and stands beside him; she places a hand on his shoulders, and receives his arm around her hip.

She can see the foam along the edge of the pale blue water. And she hears a sound, a mysterious clicking sound. And she understands what it is.

It's the dolphins' song.